THE NEXT TO DIE

She was supposed to be the last.

Sharon.

But that was before, when it was all in a planning stage. And everyone knows that plans are subject to change.

Once the plans were under way, circumstances presented unexpected complications. Well, no matter. It will be even better this way. As it turns out, the pieces will fall perfectly into place with the addition of the last one.

Tasha.

Does she suspect what's coming?

Does she sense that peril is closing in on her even now, as she lies in her bed in the wee hours of this stormy Sunday morning?

Or is she peacefully asleep, unaware that before the day ahead has drawn to a close, her cozy little world will be shaken to its very core?

Sleep well, Tasha. This may be the last time you ever will. . . .

Books by Wendy Corsi Staub

DEARLY BELOVED

FADE TO BLACK

ALL THE WAY HOME

THE LAST TO KNOW

Published by Pinnacle Books

THE LAST TO KNOW

Wendy Corsi Staub

PINNACLE BOOKS
KENSINGTON PUBLISHING CORP.

www.pinnaclebooks.com

PINNACLE BOOKS are published by

Kensington Publishing Corp.
850 Third Avenue
New York, NY 10022

All Kensington Titles, Imprints, and Distributed Lines are available at special quantity discounts for bulk purchases for sales promotions, premiums, fund-raising, and educational or institutional use. Special book excerpts or customized printings can also be created to fit specific needs. For details, write or phone the office of the Kensington special sales manager: Kensington Publishing Corp., 850 Third Avenue, New York, NY 10022, attn: Special Sales Department, Phone: 1-800-221-2647.

Pinnacle and the P logo Reg. U.S. Pat. & TM Off.

First Printing: March 2001
10 9 8 7 6 5 4 3 2 1

Printed in the United States of America

ACKNOWLEDGMENTS

The author is grateful to the following professionals who so graciously assisted in the research for this book:

Rachel Paradise, Joseph Burger, and Marian Corsi

Tuesday, October 9

Prologue

"Come on, now, don't look so upset. You're lucky, you know, Janey."

Lucky . . .

Jane comprehends the word through the fog of mind-numbing dread.

Lucky?

Yes, she thinks, dazed, she has always been lucky. How many times has she heard that over the years, from wistful classmates and envious friends, even her own sister?

"You're so lucky, Jane, that you were born with those blond curls and big blue eyes . . . so lucky you can eat anything you want and look like that. . . ."

"You're so lucky, Jane, that your family is rolling in money and you'll never have to work. . . ."

"You're so lucky, Jane, to have Owen. He's crazy about you and your future is set. . . ."

Owen.

What will he do when he comes home from work and finds that she still hasn't returned from her afternoon run? Probably assume that she and Schuyler are at Starbucks with some of their Gymboree friends again, that she's lost track of time, as she often does these days. . . .

But not after dark. She never stays out past dark.

When Owen comes home, she's usually giving Schuyler her bath in the big marble tub in the master bathroom, which is more fun than the other tubs in the house, because Schuyler likes to see herself reflected in the mirrored walls. Or, if Owen misses the six forty-four out of Grand Central and takes a later train, he finds Jane in the nursery, singing softly and rocking the baby to sleep.

Oh, Christ.

Owen.

Schuyler.

"Please . . ." Jane begs.

Begs for her life.

"No, Janey," comes the firm reply. "Sorry, but this is the way it has to be."

"But . . . why?" she manages through hammering teeth.

Her body is trembling violently now. She doesn't dare turn her head, struggling to keep her balance on the narrow rock wall where she has been forced to sit, legs dangling over into space. Any movement can send her hurtling over the edge to her death on the distant jagged rocks edging the Hudson River below.

And she won't look behind her, anyway. Can't bear to see her precious baby, her little Schuyler, clutched in the arms of the familiar figure that suddenly loomed out of nowhere such a short time ago as she rounded a bend on the deserted jogging path that winds through the scenic park.

Though she was startled to see someone there, she wasn't afraid. Not when she saw who it was.

She wasn't afraid until she realized what was happening; understood that she'd somehow been naive, blind, never sensing the shocking truth.

Why didn't she suspect that the most sinister of souls inhabited her safe, suburban world? That lurking close by, cloaked in a convincingly harmless facade, was a monster who happened to look just like everyone else, act just like everyone else, never betraying the slightest hint of evil . . . until now.

Now, when it's too late.

"Look, you know why I have to do this, Janey."

The nickname is spoken with mocking familiarity.

She feels sick. Dizzy. Like she's going to faint.

No! Can't do that. If you faint, you fall. If you fall . . .

"You know what you did, Janey. And now it's time to pay."

If you fall, you die.

"No, please—"

"Jump, Janey. Just jump."

"No . . ."

"If you don't jump," the voice says, with chilling calm, "I will drop her. Just as I said before."

She feels movement behind her, sees from the corner of her eye the hands clutching her precious baby. They're outstretched now, reaching toward the wall as if to make a sacrificial offering.

Schuyler wails, makes a sound like "Mama."

Mahhh-mahhh.

The wail tears into Jane's gut. She struggles not to fall

apart, battles the overwhelming urge to turn around, to snatch her child from that deadly grasp.

It would be futile. She would lose her balance and go over the edge, maybe taking Schuyler with her.

"You promised you wouldn't hurt her," she says, finding her voice again, hearing the foreign infusion of hysteria in it. "You *promised.*"

"I did. And you know I won't hurt her. Not unless it's absolutely necessary. So. You'll jump. We'll even wave bye-bye to Mommy, right, Schuyler? Then I'll put her right back into the jogging stroller and tuck her in all cozy with her blankie, just the way she was before. I'll even push her back down to the path so that someone will find her more easily. I'll do that for you, Janey. Okay? Consider it my parting gift. Now go ahead."

"Oh, God . . ." Horror chokes Jane's throat, snatches her voice again.

Is this actually going to happen?

Is this it?

She's actually going to die?

Yes.

Here.

Now.

"You're lucky, Janey . . . not like the others. This isn't nearly as . . . messy."

She fights to stave back the panic as her thoughts whirl, struggling to find an escape, some shred of hope.

If another jogger happens to come along . . .

But she's too far from the path now. There's nothing back here but a tangle of trees and vines, and birds and squirrels, and the low rock wall that rims the western boundary of the park, with its sheer drop to the river below.

She won't survive the fall.

Suicides never do.

They'll find her water-bloated, broken body in the river, just as they've found others—mostly teenagers, dejected kids who left notes for broken-hearted families.

Will Owen believe that she jumped?

Will Schuyler grow up thinking that Mommy abandoned her?

"Just think. The others—they suffered, Janey."

The others?

She can't focus.

Can't comprehend.

Can think of nothing but Schuyler. And Owen.

They need me.

Her hands grip the rough, crumbling stone wall.

Don't look back.

Don't look down.

"You won't suffer like they did. A few seconds, and it'll be all over. You won't feel a thing."

She opens her mouth to beg again for her life.

"Jump!" the voice barks abruptly. "Let's go. I can't wait here all day. Jump!"

"No . . . please . . . I can't. . . ." She falters, her voice strangled with fear.

Silence.

Not a sound but the brisk breeze stirring the trees.

Then, behind her, an ominous sigh.

"All right, then, Janey. If you won't jump, I'll send your daughter down before you. That'll get you moving. You can try to land first and catch her, okay?"

She turns her head as a harsh chuckle assaults her ears and the meaning of those words filters through the haze to strike her full force.

Panic seizes her as she glimpses the hand again in her periphery, sees it clutching Schuyler's chubby arm.

The baby is dangling by one arm, dangling over the edge.

The warbling wails turn to screams.

Her baby is screaming.

Jane must save her.

Save Schuyler. Do whatever you have to do. Anything. Don't let anything happen to Schuyler. . . .

"I'm going to give you one last chance to jump, Janey, before I drop her." The words are matter-of-fact, spoken loudly above the baby's terrified howls.

"Maaaaahhhhh-maahhhh!"

OhmyGodohmyGodohmyGod . . .

Don't look back.

Don't look down.

"Schuyler," she sobs, and then, with an agonizing shriek and a prayer—for her child, for her own soul— Jane pushes off with her hands and hurls herself over the edge, into space.

Falling . . .

Falling.

Images swirl through her mind, a rapid-fire montage.

Her parents' big Tudor-style house in Scarsdale . . .

Her horses, her dollhouse, her canopy bed . . .

Daddy, alive, handsome, getting out of his Rolls on the circular drive, stretching out his arms to her, picking her up, spinning her around . . .

Owen, young, grinning at her in his morning coat as she makes her way down the aisle of the flower-bedecked Presbyterian church on Richmond Street . . .

Their eight-bedroom Victorian on Harding Place with its detached three-car garage, and the nursery whose walls she had sponge-painted herself—a soft yellow because they hadn't known if they were expecting a boy or a girl . . .

Schuyler, newborn, sticky with warm blood, squirming in her arms . . .

Jane Armstrong Kendall's last thought, before her body is shattered on the cruel, jutting rocks, is that her luck has finally run out . . .

Just as she's always known it would.

Wednesday, October 10

Chapter One

"Okay, guys, Mommy's going to get dressed. I'll be back in two seconds," Tasha Banks calls over her shoulder as she deftly unlocks the child-safety gate at the bottom of the staircase in the front hall.

She swiftly fastens the latch again from the other side, then takes the carpeted steps two at a time.

She's left them in the large family room at the back of the house.

Hunter, who is six, is cross-legged on the floor in front of the television, engrossed in a Pocket Dragons cartoon. He isn't the one she's worried about.

Victoria, who has just turned three, seems busy with her crayons at the table, but Tasha doesn't entirely trust her. Just the other day she caught her hitting Max over the head with a plastic hammer.

"But Mommy, we're playing workshop. I'm the tool guy and he's supposed to be a nail," Victoria had protested when Tasha snatched her helpless eleven-month-old from the floor and inspected his tender little head for damage.

I can leave them alone down there for three minutes, tops, Tasha thinks, pausing to scoop a stray dirty, kid-sized sock from the hall floor.

When she brought Max home from the hospital last November, Hunter took the new arrival in stride, which was no surprise. He had been laid-back about everything from the moment he arrived in the world, and big brotherhood was no exception.

Though Tasha had taken pains to read up on sibling rivalry before she and Joel presented Hunter with a little sister shortly after his second birthday, he had been gentle, patient, and remarkably understanding of the fact that he now had to share Mommy and Daddy with Victoria. He had reacted the same way to Max. If Tasha was busy with the baby and he had to wait for something, he would occupy himself with a book or some blocks until she was able to turn her attention to him.

Not Victoria.

When Max came along last year, she was clearly dismayed. She refused to speak to Tasha the whole first day she was home from the hospital. Even after she thawed out a bit over the next few weeks, whenever Tasha sat down to nurse the baby, Victoria would invariably declare that she needed something. *Now.*

If Tasha asked her to wait, she threw a tantrum.

Never, though, had she directed her anger toward Max. Only toward Tasha and Joel. The baby, she adored.

Or so we thought, Tasha tells herself, sticking her head into the kids' bathroom, tossing the sock into their overflowing hamper, and continuing on down the hall.

Last week, she barely caught Max before he struck his

head on the corner of the coffee table after Victoria shoved him as he crept around it in his new walking shoes. Of course, the toddler had feigned innocence, claiming she was trying to hug him, not hurt him.

"She lied to me, Joel," Tasha told her husband that night, still upset over the incident.

"Did you punish her?"

"I took away her Blues Clues videos for the rest of the week."

"Cruel and unusual." He grinned. "That'll teach her."

"But I don't think she's truly sorry. I don't think she understands that she could really have hurt Max."

"Sibling rivalry is a normal thing, Tasha. They'll get over it. Besides, Max has a hard head. Nothing fazes him. He crawls into walls head-first and laughs." Joel disappeared into his closet then, to hang up his suit, and Tasha sensed the conversation was over.

It's frustrating, the way Joel lately seems more wrapped up in what's going on at the office than in anything that happens at home.

Or maybe that's just Tasha's perception. Maybe she really is making a huge deal out of minor issues these days.

Joel accused her of that last night when she relayed to him, word for word, her confrontation with the cable company's customer service representative after discovering a two-dollar overcharge on their monthly bill. She was thinking of writing a letter to the supervisor to complain about how she'd been treated.

"Was it resolved?" Joel interrupted her to ask.

"Yes, but that's not the point. The woman acted as though I was asking her to go out of her way, when it was their mistake. Two dollars is two dollars."

"But they credited our account, right?"

"Right, but—"

"Then let it go."

That was when he mentioned that she might just be blowing things out of proportion these days—not just about the customer service representative, but with other issues as well.

Her defenses went up immediately. "What kinds of issues?" she demanded.

Joel told her in a maddeningly offhand tone that it seemed that every night when he came home, she was ready to report some crisis or other—something one of the kids had done, or something around the house that needed fixing.

"It's just that I don't get home until after eight o'clock most nights and I'm exhausted by then, Tash, from a long day at the office and then riding the train an hour from Grand Central—"

"I'm tired, too!" she snapped back. "You think a day here with the kids isn't exhausting?"

They didn't even finish the argument. Victoria had shown up in her nightgown in the doorway, claiming a big purple monster with sharp teeth was hiding in her closet. Joel went off to tuck her back in. Tasha finished helping Hunter with his homework while Joel reheated some of the chili she had made for dinner and gobbled it down. By the time she put Hunter to bed and returned to the living room, her husband was snoring in the recliner in front of a Yankees playoff game.

She hurries into the master bedroom now and makes a face when she spots the unmade oak four-poster bed and clutter piling up on every surface. She barely had a chance to take a shower this morning before the kids were awake, running all over the place, needing her.

You'd think Joel could make the bed once in a while.

But he never does. It doesn't seem to bother him if it doesn't get made.

Tasha flips on the television to see if she can catch a quick weather report. She's planning to take Victoria and Max over to the playground at High Ridge Park after she drops off Hunter at school this morning, but it's starting to look like rain.

She flips to channel four, tosses the remote on the bedside table, and begins hurriedly pulling the sheets and blankets up, smoothing them, then putting on the cream-and-rose-colored quilt with its double wedding-ring pattern. Joel bought it for her during a weekend trip to Pennsylvania Dutch Country the first year they were married. Every time she looks at it, she remembers how shocked she was when he picked it out.

"It's pink," she said, running her hands over the hand-stitched pattern.

"I know. You love pink."

"But you don't."

"It's okay. I love you," he said, brushing her hair with his lips.

On television, Matt Lauer and Katie Couric are discussing upcoming segments and Ann Curry is about to do the news. That means the weather report won't be on for a few more minutes. Tasha reaches over and presses the mute button on the remote so that she can hear what's going on downstairs.

So far, silence, except for the faint drone of Hunter's cartoon. She left Max sitting in his Exersaucer with several toys. Victoria seemed occupied with her Blue's Clues coloring book, seated at a small table on the other side of the room.

But what if the minute Tasha left the room, Victoria decided to stir up some trouble with Max? Hunter is usually pretty good at keeping an eye on things, but not when the television is on.

Tasha tosses the heart-shaped throw pillows into place on the bed and hurries out into the hallway, leaning over the bannister. "What's going on down there?"

Silence.

"Hunter?"

"What, Mommy?"

"Is everything all right down there?"

"Uh-huh."

"What's Max doing?"

"Eating his rattle."

"What's Victoria doing?"

"Coloring."

"Okay, I'll be down in a minute. Hold down the fort, okay, buddy?"

"What fort?" comes the reply.

She smiles. Hunter takes everything literally.

"Just keep an eye on things, okay, Hunter?"

She hurries back into the master bedroom, picking up Joel's pajama bottoms and T-shirt that are strewn on the floor by the closet. She puts them in the hamper in the blue-and-white-tiled master bathroom. It, too, is overflowing with laundry. She meant to get to it yesterday, but somehow the day flew by without completion of any of the tasks she hoped to accomplish. As usual.

Back in the bedroom, she opens the ivory pleated shade on the window opposite the bed and glances out. The sky is a milky, overcast shade of gray that looks more March than October.

The white-paned window overlooks the large, shady side yard bordered by a hedge of tall rhododendron bushes. They've been ravaged by the deer that frequently wander out of the woods that border the back of the property. Tasha's glance takes in the bright patches of chrysanthemums in full bloom in her flower garden, the expensive wooden swing set she and Joel bought for the kids after he got his last promotion, the new green Ford Expedition parked at the edge of the driveway.

And there, in the far corner of the yard, is the kids' vegetable garden. The deer have long since devoured the last of the tomatoes and beans, but the crowning glory remains: a giant pumpkin Hunter and Victoria grew from seed. After months of carefully tending their prize, which Tasha has kept protected with yards of deer-proof netting, the kids are planning to enter it in the pumpkin contest at the town's annual autumn festival this weekend.

The view from the master bedroom also includes two other houses visible through the trees, both of them center-hall colonials like this one. The one occupied by the Bankses' next-door neighbors, the Martins, is white with black shutters. So is the other, which belongs to the Leibermans across the street. The Banks home, however, is white with green shutters.

"Come on, Joel, let's live on the edge," Tasha had urged him in Home Depot on that Sunday afternoon two summers ago as he wondered, with characteristic caution, if they should go with green or stick with black when they repainted the house. "Let's dare to be different." She had picked up a paint brush and tickled his nose with the bristles. "Let's push the envelope and go with green."

"You're making fun of me, Tash," he accused.

"So? You made fun of me when I polished off the entire carton of Ben and Jerry's last night," she pointed out, poking him in the arm.

"Only because you looked so ridiculous, resting it on

your belly and shoveling it in like you hadn't eaten in months.''

"I'm pregnant," she said, adding her familiar "I'm eating for two.''

"Two *what?*" came his usual reply, and she laughed with him.

God, it seems like ages since we've teased each other that way, Tasha thinks now, turning away from the window. Joel is always so distant, wrapped up in work these days. And she's so . . .

What?

Busy?

Of course. Three kids keep a person busy. But that's not all she is. No, not just busy. More like . . . restless.

She sighs and glances at the television screen again. Al Roker is finally on, doing the weather. She turns up the volume and learns that the sun is going to shine later on and the high today is going to be in the mid-to-upper fifties. Not great, but not bad, either, for mid-October in the Northeast.

She opens a bureau drawer, notes that it's nearly empty, and reminds herself that she really has to do the laundry.

She takes out a pair of Levi's that she hasn't worn in a while and puts them on, frowning when the zipper doesn't glide up as easily as it should. It's been almost a year since she had Max. Another few weeks and this tummy won't officially be considered baby weight any-more—at least, not by her standards.

With Hunter, she gained thirty pounds and lost it all six months after he was born. With Victoria she gained forty pounds and it took her almost a year to lose it. But even then she got back into her favorite faded jeans and skimpy sun dresses, though nothing fit exactly as it used to.

This time, though, she gained fifty-five pounds, and she's still carrying ten of them. Not that she's been consciously trying to diet. And with three kids, who has time to exercise?

Of course, she didn't diet or exercise the other two times, either. The weight just seemed to come off.

They were living in the city when she had Hunter, and she used to walk the twenty-five blocks down Third Avenue every morning to the publishing house where she was an executive editor acquiring mass-market fiction. She was so busy with her workload that when she actually had time for lunch, she usually just grabbed a banana or a cup of low-fat yogurt from the deli on the corner.

By the time Victoria came along, they had moved up here to Townsend Heights. She hadn't gone back to work that time—it didn't make sense. Her salary would barely make up for the cost of putting two children into day care or hiring a nanny at Westchester County's sky-high rates. Joel was steadily climbing the ladder at his company and would soon make up for what they would lose financially if Tasha quit.

So she became a stay-at-home mom. Gladly.

She was so happy then, so incredibly busy and fulfilled with a newborn and a toddler, and with the house. The place seemed like a mansion after their cramped city apartment. Now that the passage of time has diminished the novelty, it certainly isn't anything spectacular—particularly not to Tasha, who grew up in a big Victorian in Centerbrook, Ohio. Her childhood home, where her widowed mother still lives, is filled with angular little nooks, pocket doors, ornate moldings, curved archways, and leaded stained-glass windows.

The layout of the Bankses' colonial is nearly identical

to the other homes on Orchard Lane. The rooms, windows, and doors are all simple rectangles. On the first floor, the front door opens onto a ceramic-tiled small center hall with a living room on the right and a dining room on the left. A staircase leads straight up to the second floor, and tucked beneath it is a small half bath. Along the back of the house is an open kitchen-family-room space with a fireplace at one end and sliding glass doors leading out to a deck. On the second floor, three small bedrooms, a linen closet, and a bathroom open off a short hallway running along one side of the house, with a master bedroom and connecting bath at the far end.

No, it's nothing like the home where Tasha grew up. It doesn't have inherent character. But she has done her best to give it a personality, to claim it as her own. She wallpapered and painted most of the rooms herself and sewed the cheerful curtains in the kids' bedrooms.

How she loved those days. How grateful she was to be bustling around her cozy little place in the suburbs, taking care of her children and feathering the nest instead of commuting to the city, dealing with office politics, a corporate wardrobe, business travel . . .

She willingly gave all of that up.

But now . . .

Well, now she can't help wondering if that was a mistake. If it would really be so bad to get dressed in real clothes in the morning, to put on makeup and fix her hair, to dash out the door and hop a train to the city. On the train, she could read the paper and sip a cup of coffee without constantly being interrupted to change the station on the television, refill a cereal bowl with more Cheerios, change a smelly diaper . . .

The grass is always greener, Tash.

That's what Joel told her not so long ago, when she made the mistake of wondering aloud what it would be like to go back to work.

"You don't want to go back to work, Tasha. Trust me. You're lucky you don't have to deal with a career anymore."

"I know, Joel, but—"

"Look, I'd love to be you. I'd give anything to spend my days here at home instead of chasing down to Manhattan and dealing with constant stress every day."

Stress.

Seems like it's all he ever talks about—the stress of working in the same high-powered advertising agency where he started his career. He was an account coordinator then and climbed steadily to account executive, then account supervisor. Then he was promoted to vice president last spring and took over a new snack-foods client in addition to the big cosmetics client he already handled. Ever since, he's been completely distracted by his work. He keeps saying he has to earn the big raise they've given him. Apparently that means working late almost every night, bringing home paperwork, even going in to the office some weekends.

And he's been traveling more on business, too. Next weekend he's flying to Chicago on Sunday for a Monday-morning meeting. Tasha is dreading that, as she always dreads his trips. She just doesn't like being in the house at night without Joel. He says it's because she's never lived alone. She went from her parents' house to a college dorm with a roommate to a Manhattan apartment with too many roommates—four women crammed into a small one-bedroom place. They were all in lowly entry-level publishing jobs, so it was either share a tight space in a terrific Village neighborhood or move to one of the boroughs—or worse, to Jersey. It wasn't so bad, really; there was always somebody home if you felt like hanging out or talking. And even if you didn't, well, there was always somebody home. So you were never alone at night.

Tasha met Joel at a pub, dispelling the platitude about nice girls not meeting worthwhile guys in bars. He was with a crowd of his friends—cute, available advertising men in suits—and she was with a crowd of hers: pretty, preppy publishing women, some in pearls, others with triple piercings. Publishing, after all, attracted an eclectic bunch.

It wasn't love at first sight—not even lust. She hadn't been looking for a corporate type back then. She'd been more drawn to unconventional men with shaggy hair and commitment issues: musicians, sculptors. But then there was Joel, appealing, with a great sense of humor. It was what she first noticed about him that first night, as her friends and his mingled and went from the pub to a club. It was why she said yes in surprise when he asked her out. She hadn't even known he was interested, but that's the thing about Joel. He's subtle.

Lately she's concluded that it's one of his more serious faults. Half the time she can't tell if he's detached because of work, or if their marriage has hit a rough spot.

And maybe she's afraid to come right out and ask.

In any case, there has been little hilarity in the Banks household these days. Joel's wit seems to have gone the way of her corporate wardrobe.

Tasha pulls a gray sweatshirt over her head, then shakes her still-damp shoulder-length dark hair and glances into the mirror above her wide oak bureau.

Her hair would look so much better if she could just blow it dry in the morning, but there's no way. Most days it's a miracle she manages to take a shower at all. That means getting up before Joel leaves so that he can keep an eye on the kids before he dashes off to the Metro North station. He's always pacing around, checking his watch, banging on the bathroom door to tell her to hurry up, he's going to miss his train.

As if she were in there taking a long, leisurely soak in the tub.

Ha.

She hasn't shaved her legs since last weekend. Hell, using conditioner in addition to regular shampoo is a luxury these days.

Take the time to dry her hair into an actual style? Not a chance.

At the sudden ringing of the telephone, she glances at the clock on the bedside table. It's too early for Joel to be calling from the office—he's still on the train. And though he has his cell phone with him, she can't imagine why he would use it to call home when he just left.

Who is it, then? Nobody ever calls until after nine, when she's back from dropping off Hunter at school.

Frowning, she grabs the receiver, poking her foot into a sneaker and bending to tie it as she says, "Hello?"

"Tasha?"

"Rach?"

"Yeah, it's me."

"What's the matter?" she asks, hearing the edge in her friend's voice. She straightens and glances out the window again at Rachel Leiberman's house across the street, half expecting some visual sign of whatever it is that's amiss.

"Did you see this morning's *Journal News* yet?"

"Are you kidding? It's probably still out on the driveway. I never have a chance to read the paper in the morning. I'm lucky if I get to—"

"So you haven't heard?"

"Heard what?"

"It was on *The Today Show*, too—"

"I'm watching *The Today Show*." She glances at the television screen, where Al Roker is interviewing some exuberant ruddy-cheeked woman who's waving a hand-lettered sign that reads

"HAPPY ANNIVERSARY BIG DADDY AND MAMA LULU IN SLIDELL, LOUISIANA."

"It was just on the newscast."

"I didn't see that part. What was on? What happened?"

"You know Jane Kendall?"

"Jane Kendall . . ." The name is familiar but it takes her a moment to place it. Then she remembers. "Jane from Gymboree?"

"Right."

"What about her?"

"She's missing."

"What do you mean, missing?"

"She never came back from jogging over at High Ridge Park last night. See, I told you she must work out to have that body, didn't I? Nobody who's got an eight-month-old just looks like that by accident."

"But what *happened*?" Tasha asks impatiently, putting on her other sneaker.

"Nobody knows. She went out for a jog with her daughter in one of those jogging stroller thingies and she never came home. Somebody found—hang on a second. *Noah! Get your fingers out of there before you get electrocuted!* Sorry. Somebody found the baby abandoned in a stroller in the park after dark."

"God."

"I know."

"What about the husband?"

"Owen? He's the one who reported her missing."

"You know his name?"

"Who doesn't? I've told you she was married to him, remember? He's one of the Kendall family that has the vacuum cleaners—you know. . . ."

No, Tasha doesn't know. She's new to the world of suburban blue bloods, unlike Rachel, who grew up in Westchester.

"Well anyway, the Kendalls have big, big bucks. I went to school with one of Owen's cousins. Dillard Kendall. He was a jackass. She's an Armstrong."

"Jane is?" Tasha is used to the dizzying pace of Rachel's aside-filled conversations.

"Yup. The Armstrongs practically founded Scarsdale. Blue blood, old money. Real Westchester money. Not like you or me."

"Speak for yourself, Rach," Tasha says wryly. "We pretty much have *no* money these days, real or not."

"I thought Joel got a big raise."

"Yeah, but we also have a new car payment, remember? The Honda died the month after his promotion. Plus, we needed to put a new roof on the house and replace the hot-water heater—"

"Okay, okay, so you guys are broke. The point is, we all are, compared to the Armstrongs and the Kendalls. Jane's family was wealthy. And her in-laws are loaded. That's why her disappearance is such huge news."

"Was she kidnapped, then, for a ransom or something?"

The idea seems bizarre. Does that type of thing really happen?

"Nobody knows. It's so 'Movie-of-the-Week,' isn't it?

They're offering a million-dollar reward for—hang on a second. *Mara! Let go of his nose right now! Can't you see he doesn't like that?*"

"Listen, Rachel, let me call you back later," Tasha says hurriedly, remembering that her own brood is still unattended in the family room. "I'm not on the cordless, and the kids are suspiciously quiet downstairs."

"Go," Rachel says with the instant understanding of a fellow mommy. "I'll talk to you later."

Tasha hangs up, turns off the television set, and heads for the stairs.

Tasha has known Jane Kendall since the week after Labor Day, which is when Tasha and Rachel started going to a Gymboree play group two mornings a week in nearby Mount Kisco. The purpose is supposedly for the kids to socialize with each other and to bond with their mothers, but it seems to Tasha that the mothers—most of them stay-at-home moms—are the ones who are desperate to socialize and bond with other adults. She and Rachel have met several women through the group, and a bunch of them have taken to having coffee together at Starbucks afterward.

Jane Kendall comes sometimes. She never says much, just kind of sits on the outskirts and smiles, cuddling her daughter on her lap as she sips her skim cappuccino.

So . . . God. What's happened to her?

Maybe she fell and hit her head or something while she was running, Tasha thinks hopefully. Maybe she came to this morning, and has already been found.

No, she realizes, a chill creeping down her spine, it can't be that simple. She's seen enough movies and read enough newspapers to know that women like Jane Kendall—beautiful, privileged, seemingly content women with husbands and children—don't just vanish temporarily. When they vanish, it's forever.

Something must have happened to Jane Kendall.

Something horrible.

But . . .

In Townsend Heights?

Nothing horrible ever happens here.

This small, old-fashioned, upscale town is *insulated*, somehow, from the harsh realities of the city where so many of its residents work.

Up here, as the real estate agent told Joel and Tasha, you can leave your doors unlocked—not that anyone ever *does*, but the point is that you *can*. This is the kind of place where shop owners know you by name, where high school kids hold doors open for you, where children play flashlight tag after dark in tree-lined neighborhoods filled with two-parent families living in one-family houses.

Tasha and Joel fell in love with this charming village the first time they laid eyes on it. Who could resist the quiet, shady streets in the heart of town, dotted with painted Victorians, picket fences, and well-tended gardens? She had her heart set on buying one of those picturesque homes, so similar to the one where she grew up—until she discovered that they were priced in the million-dollar range, thanks to Westchester's booming real estate market.

She and Joel concentrated their house hunting on a newer neighborhood that's still close enough to the broad main street lined with shops. Townsend Avenue has its share of pricey boutiques and cafés, all of them locally owned. In fact, the nice thing about Townsend Heights is that it really is an old-fashioned small town filled with family-run businesses, very much like the small Ohio town where Tasha grew up.

Only these days, Centerbrook's main drag is run-down and virtually deserted, with most of the mom-and-pop stores gone and the business district relocated to a series of chain-store-based strip malls out on the highway.

That's unlikely to happen here in Townsend Heights, where the wealthy residents cherish the local flavor and make sure that the small businesses thrive. Tasha figures she'll never be able to forget that this isn't quite Ohio. The little corner groceries offer exotic produce; the lunch counter and diner offer gourmet menus, but that's part of the charm. And she's found a place where her kids can grow up much as she did back in the seventies, which was her goal when she and Joel set out to find a place to settle down.

She'll never forget how they stumbled across Townsend Heights and immediately felt at home. They rented a car and drove the hour north from Manhattan for a day of house hunting, leaving Hunter with Joel's parents in Brooklyn. Tasha's in-laws, who never protested babysitting their beloved first grandchild, gave Tasha and Joel a terrible time on that particular occasion, wanting to know when they'd be back and why they were going in the first place.

"House hunting? In Westchester? Why would you move all the way up there? Why would you leave the city? How are you going to afford Westchester?"

Even after she and Joel found this house—this shuttered colonial on Orchard Way, a leafy, winding dead-end lane not far from the center of the village—the Bankses were pessimistic.

"They just don't want to see us move so far away," Joel told Tasha.

"They don't want to see you and Hunter move so far away," she corrected. "Me, they'd be happy to see move across the country. They'd probably help me load the van."

"Don't be ridiculous!" he said in that irritated tone he always uses when she claims his parents didn't like her.

But they *don't* like her.

They never have.

At first, she thought it was just because she wasn't Jewish. That, she could handle. In fact, that, she had pretty much expected.

But the knowledge that they don't like her because . . . well, because they just don't like her, that's hard to take, especially for someone who was once voted Miss Congeniality in a high school beauty pageant in Centerbrook.

"Okay, what makes you think they don't like you?" Joel asked her long ago, when he used to actually participate in the conversations she initiated about his parents.

"Your sister told me they don't."

He dismissed that with a wave of his hand. "Don't listen to Debbie. She likes to make trouble. She doesn't know what she's talking about."

"Of course she knows what she's talking about. She's their daughter. She lives with them. She says it's not because I'm not Jewish, either. She says your girlfriend in college, Heather Malloy, wasn't Jewish either, and your parents loved her."

"Heather Malloy?" Faint (or was it fond?) smile. "They didn't love her."

"Debbie says they did. It's me they don't love, Joel."

"That's your imagination."

She's long since given up on conversations like that. It's no use. Joel is either too blind to see the truth about his parents' feelings toward her, or he just can't deal with the situation and chooses to take the wimpy way out and ignore it.

At the bottom of the stairs, Tasha unlocks the safety gate, relocks it, and then pauses in the hall, glancing out the narrow window beside the front door. There's this morning's edition of the *Journal News,* still in its yellow plastic bag at the foot of the driveway. Does she dare risk leaving the kids for another few seconds and running out to get it now so she can read about Jane Kendall's disappearance? Or should she wait until she leaves to take Hunter to school in ten minutes?

She'd better wait, she decides reluctantly, heading toward the family room. She shouldn't have left Victoria and Max alone together for this long, even.

Guiltily she pokes her head into the big, carpeted room at the back of the house, prepared for the worst.

But there's still-bald Max in his Exersaucer in front of the brick fireplace, happily drooling as he chews on a yellow rubber Winnie the Pooh block. There's Victoria, her dark curls bent over the table in the opposite corner of the room, busily coloring. And there's Hunter, with his straight brown hair and huge, perpetually solemn brown eyes—eyes that are now transfixed on the television screen, where the "Pocket Dragons" credits are rolling.

"Hi, guys," Tasha says, about to go over and scoop up the baby, who is bouncing wildly with joy at the sight of her. She thinks better of it and heads toward Victoria first instead, bending to peek over her daughter's shoulder. "How beautiful, sweetheart. Did you color that whole picture all by yourself?"

"Uh-huh," Victoria says proudly, holding it up. "Even Mr. Salt and Mrs. Pepper. See what color I made them?"

"Blue."

"That's because blue's my favorite color. What's your favorite color, Mommy?"

"Green," Tasha tells her absently, patting her dark head and thinking about Jane Kendall.

"Green?" Victoria is clearly aghast. "But Mommy, you said it was red when I asked you yesterday!"

"Oh, you're right. It is red. I guess I just forgot," Tasha replies.

"You're silly, Mommy."

"I know, sweetie. Let's put the crayons away now. Hunter, it's time to get ready for school."

"No!" Victoria shouts.

Tasha sighs.

Hunter obediently turns off the television.

"Victoria, put the crayons away. Now. And Hunter, you go find your shoes."

"Can't I color for a few more minutes?"

"One more minute," Tasha relents, because it's easier, and because there's time.

Victoria happily picks up her blue crayon again.

Am I spoiling her to make up for the fact that she's the middle child now? Tasha wonders.

Those parenting manuals her friend Karen's always reading say that you should never change a *no* to a *yes* when you're dealing with toddlers. They're supposed to be learning that *no* means *no.*

But *no* is so hard, sometimes. When sticking firmly to a *no* means facing a just-turned-three-year-old's tantrum, and you're exhausted and a long day looms ahead, and a woman you know has inexplicably vanished . . .

Well, this is one of those times when *no* just isn't worth it.

Tasha goes over and picks up Max, trying to cuddle him against her. But he bounces excitedly in her arms, glad to see her. He always is. His little face lights up whenever she glances in his direction.

Babies need their mommies so much, Tasha thinks as she plants a kiss on his downy infant hair that is barely visible.

Poor little Schuyler Kendall. Where's her mommy? And is she ever coming back?

Jeremiah Gallagher slips his denim jacket over a hook in his locker and pauses to admire it for a moment. Uncle Fletch bought it for him yesterday.

"I thought you could use a new jean jacket, Jer'," he announced, whacking Jeremiah on the shoulders in that old-buddy-old-pal way of his.

"But I already have a jean jacket," Jeremiah said—not a protest exactly, because he likes the new jacket. He wants it.

It's faded and worn and expensive-looking, unlike the one he already has, which is all wrong. Too stiff, too dark, too cheap.

His stepmother bought that jacket for him just before she died. Ironically, the jacket he so disliked was one of his few belongings that survived the fire that killed Melissa; Jeremiah was wearing it that night because she insisted.

Too bad it didn't get burned up along with her, he thought later, a thought that was followed by instant, familiar guilt.

But he couldn't help the way he felt. He didn't like the jacket, and he didn't like Melissa.

Well, Melissa is gone.

Now, so is the stupid jacket. Thanks to Uncle Fletch, who has a way of noticing things like that, Jeremiah has a jacket that makes him look like all the other kids at Townsend Heights High.

Well, not really.

But Uncle Fletch is working on that, too. He's promised Jeremiah a trip to the eye doctor to see about getting fitted for contact lenses instead of glasses, which he has worn since he was three. And Uncle Fletch said Jeremiah can use his home gym equipment whenever he wants, probably hoping his nephew will build up some muscles and look more like him.

As if.

Jeremiah has never quite been able to believe that he and Fletch Gallagher are blood relatives. His father insists that Fletch is his brother and that Jeremiah wasn't adopted. But how is it that a hundred-pound, bespectacled, acne-scarred weakling like Jeremiah comes from the same gene pool as *the* Fletch Gallagher?

The handsome, muscular athlete, formerly a star pitcher for the Cleveland Indians, is now practically a celebrity, working during baseball season as a sportscaster for the New York Mets.

Jeremiah's father, Aidan, might not have Fletch's great looks or stud status, but he, too, has an aura of power and masculinity about him. Especially when he's dressed in his officer's uniform. Not that Jeremiah sees him in it often—or sees him much at all. He's been stationed in the Middle East since the last flare-up with Iraq, which happened right after Melissa was killed.

Before that, Dad was home more. Which was one of the few good things that had happened since he married Melissa. She didn't want to follow him around the way Mom had.

When his mother was alive, Jeremiah lived on army bases all over the world. She made every move seem like an adventure, transforming countless ugly, square military-base houses into homes for Jeremiah and his father.

Not Melissa.

She insisted on staying put right here on North Street in Townsend Heights while Dad was stationed overseas. She said she had no intention of dragging her daughters, Lily and Daisy, all over creation; they had already been through enough—a reference to the twins' father, who abandoned his family for another woman.

The better he got to know Melissa, who could be a real pain, the more Jeremiah didn't blame her ex-husband. She was spoiled, having grown up an only child in Connecticut. From what Jeremiah could tell, her parents—who both died around the same time her marriage ended—hadn't been rich, but clearly, her every wish had been their command. Which was exactly how his dad treated her. Why, Jeremiah couldn't figure out. Unless it was simply because Melissa was a beautiful blonde— so different from his mom—and Dad was psyched to have landed someone like her.

If you ask Jeremiah, Melissa was the lucky one. She'd been dumped, with two little girls to raise and no parents to help her. And his dad was a great catch.

After his father married Melissa, she, Jeremiah, and his twin stepsisters lived here, and Aidan came home a lot, sometimes for long periods of time. Jeremiah figured he could put up with Melissa most of the time if it meant seeing more of his father.

Then Melissa died, and the thing with Iraq happened, and Dad had to leave again. Which means Jeremiah, Lily, and Daisy have to stay with Uncle Fletch and Aunt Sharon for a while. But Dad's promised that pretty soon, he'll be home again—maybe even for good. Then maybe things will get back to normal.

Whatever normal is.

Jeremiah reaches up to the top shelf of his locker and looks for his chemistry notebook amid the clutter.

The locker door next to him bangs open and he glances up to see Lacey Birnbach taking off her leather jacket and chatting with a couple of her friends.

"Hi," Jeremiah says awkwardly. It comes out nearly silent. He clears his throat and tries again, managing to produce a faintly audible sound.

Lacey's really into whatever she's telling her friends, though, and doesn't bother to acknowledge Jeremiah. Not that he expects her to. She's one of those girls who doesn't seem to know he's alive—which pretty much sums up the entire female population of Townsend Heights High, he thinks wryly, returning to the hunt for his notebook.

"So is Peter, like, famous now?" one of Lacey's friends asks.

"Definitely. He told me he's going to be on the six o'clock news tonight. I'm going to call home and tell my mom to tape it because we have a late cheering practice today."

"I want a copy of the tape," another girl says. "He's so cute. Maybe he'll be discovered on TV and become a big star."

"Like, he's just being interviewed about finding that lady's screaming baby on the jogging path, Alyssa," says Lacey, tossing her shiny dark hair. "He's not going on some *Star Search* show. And he's not the actor type, you know? He's not into stuff like that."

"Yeah, but he's so cute. I love the way he looks in

those tight gray sweats he wears for football practice. You can see the outline of his—''

Alyssa has bent her head close to the other girls and Jeremiah can't hear anything until a burst of giggles erupts.

He shifts his weight uncomfortably and keeps looking for his notebook.

They're talking about Peter Frost. They must be. He's on the Townsend Heights High football team, and Jeremiah has seen him in those tight gray sweats they're talking about. If *he* ever wore something like that, he'd look ridiculous. But Peter Frost is a younger version of Uncle Fletch. He's muscular, handsome, charming, and the girls go crazy for him.

There's one major difference between Peter Frost and Uncle Fletch, though. Peter Frost would never try to help Jeremiah. In fact, he gets a kick out of doing exactly the opposite, tormenting Jeremiah every chance he gets, particularly in gym class, where he's always making snide comments under his breath.

His jaw clenched at the mere thought of his nemesis, Jeremiah finds his notebook, slams his locker door hard, and realizes that the abrupt sound has apparently startled Lacey and her friends.

"Oh, hi," Lacey says off-handedly, since she's looking right at him. "Geez, that was loud."

"S-s-sorry." Jeremiah feels his cheeks grow hot.

His stutter. It's back. Damn it, it always comes back when he's nervous. After all the money Dad spent on therapy years ago so that he could get over it, the stutter shadows him still, always lurking, always waiting to pounce.

"Hey . . ." Lacey pauses slightly in a way that indicates she can't remember his name, then goes on as if it doesn't matter, "did you hear about that woman who disappeared last night from the park?"

"Yeah, it w-was on the n-news this morning," Jeremiah mumbles, struggling to stay calm and will the stutter away, unable to fathom that Lacey Birnbach is actually talking to *him*, even if she has no idea what his name is.

"Well, guess who found her abandoned baby there?"

Jeremiah shrugs, not about to let on that he's already overheard the answer.

"Peter Frost. Can you believe it? He was, like, jogging and he came across the screaming little baby in her jogging stroller. Now he's this major hero."

"Wow." Apparently, Jeremiah's attempt to muster suitable awe is unsuccessful.

Lacey turns her attention back to her friends. Clearly he's been dismissed.

Jeremiah turns and drifts into the throng of students in the corridor, thinking it's too bad that it wasn't Peter Frost who vanished from High Ridge Park last night.

"Fancy meeting you here."

Paula Bailey turns to see a familiar face grinning at her from beneath the brim of a Yankees cap.

"Oh, hi, George." Her gaze flits back to the three-story red-brick Victorian mansion beyond the iron gate.

"Covering the crime beat these days?"

"What'd you think, that I'm just doing golden anniversary write-ups and reporting Brownie troop news?" Paula fights to keep her tone light.

It isn't easy. Not for someone like her. Not with someone like him.

Lord, I need a cigarette.

She's known George DeFand since they were both

freshmen in community college, where she took every communications course the meager department offered, and so did he. Of course, after two years, he went on to Columbia while she dropped out of the academic scene for good, knocked up by her boyfriend.

Now George is living down in Rye, married to a soap opera actress and reporting for the *New York Post,* and Paula is a single mom living in a one-bedroom apartment here in town and writing for the weekly *Townsend Gazette.*

Well, she thinks defensively, the *Post* is just a crummy tabloid—it's not like he's working at the *New York Times.* Still, she can't help noting George's khaki barn jacket that must have cost two hundred bucks. At least.

Well, she's wearing a designer suit. She bought it at a consignment shop down in Mount Kisco, but the boxy tweed jacket and matching slim skirt look practically new. The leather pumps *are* new, and appear far more expensive than they really were. Her reddish hair is pulled back in a businesslike but not unflattering ponytail, and she's fully made-up. She knows that she looks like a modern-day Lois Lane—far more professional than the other reporters milling around in their jeans, as George is.

She's run into him a few times these past few years. He never fails to remind her that he made a name for himself as an investigative reporter covering that fatal cop shooting in the Bronx a few years back—and the subsequent scandal that erupted when he broke the story that the cop's partner, and not the drug pusher they were chasing, had fired the fatal shots—deliberately.

She's not in the mood to hear about it again. Maybe she won't have to. An impossibly small, ringing digital Motorola cell phone materializes from his expensive jacket. He flips it open and says importantly, "DeFand here."

Paula gladly leaves him to his conversation and makes her way through the crowd of media people and law-enforcement officials congregated along the black iron fence surrounding the Kendall home.

The sprawling red-brick house sits on a corner lot that's entirely fenced in, allowing outsiders a view of the rear of the house and the sloping back yard that gives way to woods at the back of the property. Jane told Paula that the house was once part of a country estate built by Henry DeGolier, a millionaire merchant before the turn of the century. The rest of the land has long since been sold off in segments, and the crumbling, distant outbuildings have been swallowed up by woods or demolished to make room for other homes on the street.

Paula's been here since the husband filed a missing person report last night. She dropped Mitch at his friend Blake's house and rushed over here, hoping for an exclusive interview with one of the family members, attorneys, or household staff members who have been coming and going for the past twelve hours.

The other members of the press trickled in as the news spread, and by dawn the place was a circus: camera crews, satellite news vans, television reporters doing live feeds. The cops are doing their best to keep things under control. So far there's been no sign of Owen Kendall, who is apparently holed up inside with his infant daughter.

Being from Townsend Heights, and familiar with the faces of the locals, Paula has a definite edge over the other reporters. She alone recognized Minerva Fuentes, the Kendalls' longtime housekeeper, crossing the street and walking toward the gates an hour earlier. Naturally, she dashed right over to intercept the woman, whom she had encountered briefly when she interviewed Jane

Kendall about the charity ball last year. Jane was head of the committee.

Unfortunately, Minerva either didn't recognize her or didn't care that Paula had met her once before. She was clearly distraught by the crowd scene and waved Paula away just before a police officer intervened, abruptly escorting the weeping housekeeper inside as the rest of the media bellowed questions after her.

Shortly afterward, a sleek black limousine arrived and was promptly admitted through the gates, obviously expected and reportedly containing Owen Kendall's parents, Henry and Louisa.

Now Paula glances around, scanning the crowd and the street beyond again for familiar faces, hoping for an exclusive.

She sees a few people she recognizes—just locals who have come to gawk, though, none of whom appear to be the Kendalls' neighbors. You won't catch the other well-heeled residents of Harding Place out here with the commoners. No, but they're probably glued to their television sets inside the dozen or so stately multimillion-dollar mansions that line the short street, perhaps even occasionally allowing themselves furtive glimpses at the bedlam outside.

Paula sneaks a peek at her watch.

It's almost ten. She can't stay here much longer. She's not in a rush to file a story on a daily deadline like a lot of the press here; her paper's a weekly. But she's supposed to meet Mitch's fourth-grade teacher over at the elementary school at ten-thirty.

Since the academic year began last month she's had a couple of telephone conversations with Miss Bright about his behavior. Now, apparently, her son has been acting up in class again, and his grades are slipping. Miss

Bright has decided a face-to-face meeting can't wait until parent-teacher conferences next week.

I warned Mitch the last time this happened, she thinks, feeling a flash of renewed anger at her son.

Didn't she tell him that his obnoxious behavior reflects poorly on her parenting skills? If the other kids in his class, with their two-parent, well-off families, are behaving and pulling passing grades, and Mitch isn't, the school officials are likely to place the blame on the fact that his mother is too busy working to support the two of them.

And that he misses his father.

Paula knows her son talks about Frank every chance he gets, to anyone who will listen. Mitch, oblivious to his father's true slimeball status, thinks the man is God.

Damn Frank Ferrante!

Paula never should have tracked him down last year for child support payments.

You were desperate, she reminds herself. *They had shut off the phone, and the electricity was next. You couldn't possibly live under those circumstances. You had no choice but to find Frank.*

Frank.

The man who swept her off her feet with his dark good looks and smooth talk, knowing just what buttons to push with her.

The man who had shattered her dreams by knocking her up, then won her trust by marrying her.

The man who had abandoned her, first in the emotional sense when she miscarried the pregnancy; then in the literal sense, leaving her pregnant again, with a pile of bills and an overdrawn bank account. He just walked out one day and that was it.

She let him go, of course. She wasn't in love with him then, if she ever truly had been.

But she never had been one to forgive and forget. A typical Scorpio, her father used to call her—although he said it in admiration. Daddy admired pretty much everything about Paula.

Anyway, so what? Maybe her reasons for finding Frank and making him pay *were* more than purely monetary.

She hardly expected him to obey the court order to send her back child support for the years he had missed since he ran off with another woman, let alone keep up with the monthly payments from that point on. And she certainly hadn't anticipated his request for visitation with his son, who by then had stopped asking why he didn't have a daddy.

As it turns out, Frank—who when Paula knew him was an aimless dreamer and schemer—has managed to turn one of his countless half-baked ideas into a business. A really successful business. Money is no longer an issue with him, so he's made the payments. And he arranged for weekend visits with Mitch, time that seems to be spent mostly at the custom-built Long Island house where Frank lives with his wife, Shawna. A blonde, of course. Frank always was crazy about blondes.

Never in her wildest dreams did Paula ever imagine that Frank would not only win Mitch's affection and admiration, but would threaten her with a custody battle.

"It would be a lot easier on everyone involved if you'd just let the kid come live with me, Paula," he had the nerve to say when he first broached the subject with her six months ago.

"Not on everyone involved. Easier on you, Frank. Just you."

"And Mitch. It wouldn't be fair to him if we drag this out in court. And easier on you, too, Paula. Do you think I don't know how much you wanted a real career as a real reporter instead of settling for some small-town flunkie paper? If you hadn't gotten pregnant and married me, you would have gone to Syracuse to study journalism. You would have hit the big time by now. You were the most determined person I had ever met. Hell, maybe some of that ambition even rubbed off on me," he added—knowing, she was sure, full well how it would rankle.

She wanted to leap on him, to scream and scratch. She wanted to obliterate him, just as he was trying to obliterate her dreams.

But she kept her composure, saying only, "I don't regret dropping out of college and I don't regret having Mitch, Frank. All I regret is that I married you. But Mitch is the most important thing in my life, and there's no reason why I can't have him and my career."

"Yeah, well, at this rate, you're not going to turn into Woodward or Bernstein anytime soon, babe," he said with a smirk.

She doesn't know what got to her more: the reference to her once-idolized famed Watergate reporters, or the way he called her "babe." It was his pet name for her back in the days when she didn't know an imitation leather bomber jacket from the real thing, or cheap aftershave from designer cologne.

The irony is, now that she finally knows the difference, he's graduated to the good stuff.

Money can't change him, though. It might have given him a big house and a beautiful blond wife, but he has no class. No integrity. And no Mitch.

As far as she's concerned, that's how it will stay.

She doesn't give a damn that Frank can afford a lifestyle she's never even come close to providing for Mitch. And she sure as hell isn't swayed by Frank's sob story about how he and Shawna tried to conceive for a few years before finding out that even with fertility intervention she most likely will never be able to bear children of their own. That means Mitch is Frank's only child and always will be—at least, if he stays married to Shawna, which Paula figures isn't necessarily a given, considering his track record.

"He's my only child, too, Frank, and I'm going to raise him," Paula had said before throwing Frank out of her apartment that afternoon.

Now he's going ahead with the custody suit. And the thing that terrifies Paula most is that if the judge allows Mitch to choose which parent he wants to live with—as this judge has been rumored to do—Mitch might choose Frank.

Even if Mitch doesn't have a say, how will Paula stack up against her ex in court? She's a single parent, struggling to make ends meet. Mitch sleeps on a lumpy foldout couch in their cramped one-bedroom apartment— one of Townsend Heights's few rentals, located a block from the business district. She's never home. And he's getting into trouble in school, having to stay after class and bringing home notes from the teacher.

With Frank, Mitch would have his own room in a beautiful home in an exclusive neighborhood, private schools, a father who runs a thriving business, and a full-time stepmother who doesn't work.

But I'm his mother, Paula tells herself stoically. *Nothing is more important than that.*

Reluctantly she turns away from the Kendall house, knowing she'd better leave now if she's going to make it to the school for that meeting—and have time to smoke an entire cigarette in the car on the way over.

That's about the only place a smoker can indulge her

habit in Westchester County these days. In a car or at home. Anyplace else and you risk the wrath of nonsmokers.

Someday I'll quit, Paula thinks—not for the first time—as she hurries away.

She rounds the corner onto Grafton Avenue, where she parked her car the night before. She's almost reached the banged-up blue two-door Honda at the curb when she sees a taxi pass by and stop behind her at the corner of Harding.

Instinctively, she turns around.

A woman gets out of the cab.

In the fleeting moment her pale, plain face is turned in her direction, Paula realizes that she looks vaguely familiar.

But who is she?

The woman scurries around the corner onto Harding Place as the cab drives off in the opposite direction.

Paula slowly unlocks her car door and gets in, certain that she's seen her before.

But where?

Chapter Two

Balancing the baby on her hip and holding a cup of apple juice with one hand while clinging to a squirming Victoria's hand with the other, Tasha makes her way to the round corner table Rachel has staked out in the crowded Starbucks.

"There you are at last!" Rachel says, bouncing her thirteen-month-old, Noah, on her lap. He's holding his omnipresent blue plastic sippy cup. Rachel is in the process of weaning him from the bottle and complains that he refuses to take milk in anything other than this cup.

Tasha has told her to stop complaining. Sure, Hunter gave up his bottle, no questions asked, the week of his first birthday. But it was nearly impossible to wean Victoria, who had rejected all cups until she was nearly two.

Rachel looks great as usual. Her sleek, expertly dyed blond hair is cut stylishly short, and she's wearing makeup, earrings, and a crisply ironed ivory linen shirt tucked into jeans that hug her narrow hips. She used to work for Saks as a stylist, and looks like she still does.

The whole Leiberman family has that upscale, attractive thing going on, Tasha thinks wistfully. Aside from his darker coloring, Rachel's husband, Ben, is a masculine image of his wife: tall and attractive with a well-toned body. He's always impeccably dressed. So are the kids.

Tasha notices that Noah is wearing a plushy cotton tan-and-ivory-patterned romper that was recently in the window of Goody Gumdrops, the exclusive children's clothing boutique on Townsend Avenue. She thought when she first spotted it in the store that it would be great for Max—until she saw the label and price tag. Imported from France, and almost a hundred dollars.

"Look, Noah," Rachel says. "Your buddy Max is here!"

"Uh-oh, where's Mara?" Tasha asks, glancing down at Victoria and anticipating a tantrum when her daughter realizes Rachel's other child is nowhere in sight. Victoria adores Mara, who is four. "Don't tell me you left her home with the nanny again."

"I *wish*. There's no nanny today. Mrs. Tuccelli canceled again. This time it's her gallstones, or so she says. You wouldn't happen to know a reliable sitter, would you?"

"If I did, would I be dragging these two virtually everywhere I go?" Tasha asks, plopping into a chair at the table and reaching around Max to unbutton Victoria's pink rain slicker.

"I really need to find someone else. I'm going nuts." Rachel hands Noah a piece of bagel to chew on.

Tasha resists the urge to roll her eyes at the urgent tone in Rachel's voice. Her neighbor has become her closest friend in the past few years. But she can't help thinking sometimes that Rachel is more than a little spoiled. She's never had to work; the fashion stylist thing was mostly for kicks, since her parents paid the rent on her East Side apartment. She quit when she married Ben, who has a thriving pediatric practice in town. The Leibermans have a housekeeper and a full-time nanny, and Rachel spends most days shopping, golfing, lunching, and socializing *without* her kids.

Still, when she called from her car an hour ago and asked Tasha to meet her at Starbucks for coffee, she actually had both Mara and Noah with her.

"So where's Mara?" Tasha asks again, seeing Mara's favorite Barbie doll on the table. Rachel's always complaining that Mara never goes anywhere without the doll, whom she's cryptically named Clemmy, and who even Tasha admits is hideous-looking, with a dirty face, chewed-off feet, and most of her nylon hair missing.

"She's in the ladies' room with Karen. She offered to take her in—thank God—since I've got Noah. I swear, it was so much easier when she wasn't potty-trained."

"You can't convince me of that," Tasha says, hoisting a protesting Victoria into the chair beside hers, then running a hand through her rain-damp hair. She must look about as appealing as Clemmy does. Nothing new there, she thinks wryly.

"Well, did Victoria go when you put her on the potty yesterday?" Rachel asks.

"Nope," Tasha says with a sigh, not wanting to go there. Victoria's potty-training trials have been a bone of contention for months. Instead, she says, "So Karen's here too? I didn't know she was coming."

"We just bumped into her down the street at the dry cleaner's. She left the baby with Tom. He's working at home today. I figured that out when I saw his car there on my way into town."

Karen Wu lives at the opposite end of Orchard Way

with her accountant husband and their nine-month-old daughter, Taylor. The petite Chinese-American woman is on an extended maternity leave from her job teaching social studies at a public high school in lower Westchester. Sometimes she joins Tasha and Rachel at Gymboree.

"Did you tell her about Jane Kendall?" Tasha asks Rachel.

"Are you kidding me? She already knew. It's all anyone's talking about today. I don't think there's anyone who hasn't heard."

Yes, there is.

Joel.

Tasha tried calling him at the office a couple of times this morning but reached his voice mail every time. She left messages: "Joel, it's me. Call me, I have to tell you something."

She didn't bother to try his cell phone. He doesn't keep it turned on while he's in the office. In fact, he usually forgets to turn it on even when he's not.

She left deliberately vague messages, figuring he'll call her back more quickly. She knows he checks his voice mail constantly, even when he's out of the office, in case a client calls.

Of course, Joel *always* calls her back . . . eventually. But sometimes it takes a few hours.

"It's not that I don't want to talk to you, Tash, but I'm busy when I'm at work." That's his explanation whenever she gets on his case about not returning her calls promptly.

She resents his implication that she's bothering him while he tends to more important things. All right, so maybe there are times when she does call him just to check in and say hello. He used to do that, too, back before he reached this lofty rung on the corporate ladder.

When Hunter was a newborn and she was still on maternity leave, the phone would ring all day long, with Joel wanting to know how the baby was.

And okay, there were times back then when Tasha let the machine get it, or would even take it off the hook just so she could have some uninterrupted moments while the baby was napping.

But most of the time, she was happy to talk to her husband.

And these days, when she calls Joel at work it's for a reason. Maybe just to check and see if he wants her to drop his overcoat at the cleaners, or to find out where he put the checkbook, but those *are* reasons. It's frustrating to wait for hours to hear from him.

Besides, how does he know, when she leaves a message on his voice mail, that it isn't urgent?

"If it's an emergency, or if something is up with one of the kids, call my secretary directly and have her find me, Tash. And if it's not urgent, don't make me think that it is, okay? Just tell me what it is that you need, and I'll call back as soon as I can."

Today, she didn't want to tell him what it was that she needed from him, because she isn't really sure what it is. Just to tell him about Jane Kendall's disappearance, but more than that, maybe—to connect with him, to hear his voice reassure her, to feel safe. To know that she and Jane Kendall have less in common than it seems on the surface.

So she left the vague message, hoping he'd be curious enough to get back to her right away.

Apparently he wasn't, because he hasn't.

"Did he just say 'venti skim caramel machiato'?" Tasha zaps back to the present and peers at the kid behind the coffee bar, who has just set a foamy, steaming cup on the counter and called out something unintelligible.

Rachel shrugs. "I have no idea. I can never hear what they're saying in here. Go ahead and see if it's yours; I'll keep an eye on Victoria."

"Where's Mara?" Victoria is asking Rachel as Tasha walks up to the counter, carrying Max. She smiles to herself. Thank goodness Mara will be here as promised. It's the only way she got Victoria away from her Teletubbies video and into her car seat without a struggle.

"Is that a venti skim caramel machiato?" she asks the kid behind the coffee bar, who has a ponytail and a goatee and is now busily foaming milk in a whirring machine.

"It's a venti caramel machiato," he informs her above the noise.

"Not skim?"

"Nope."

"I ordered skim. Maybe that's for someone else."

He shrugs. "It's the only machiato order I've gotten. You want skim instead?" he offers reluctantly.

"Never mind." Tasha grabs the cup, fat-saturated milk and all, and carries it back to the table. She'll worry about her too-tight jeans another day. Today it seems frivolous, in light of the Jane Kendall thing.

It's all she's thought about all morning. In fact, she couldn't even bring herself to go to the park with the kids after all. No, not once she knew that Jane vanished from there only hours earlier.

Instead, she went to the supermarket to pick up a few things. She found herself pausing over the stacks of newspapers at the front of the store, disappointed that the tabloids, the *New York Post* and *Daily News,* had no coverage of the Kendall story. Coverage in the *Journal News* had been sketchy, and the local paper, the *Townsend Gazette,* isn't out yet; it's only a weekly.

She moved on when the baby started fussing because

she was standing motionless with the cart for too long, and she shifted her thoughts to selecting a new brand of cereal for a clamoring Victoria, and diapers for Max, who's on the brink of the next size.

But in the dairy aisle she overheard two women talking about the Kendall disappearance, and when she reached the register, the cashier—a chatty type Tasha knows by sight—actually brought it up.

"Did you hear about that lady who disappeared from the park?" she wanted to know as she bagged the purchases. When Tasha mentioned that she had actually been acquainted with her, the woman held up the line asking questions about Jane Kendall. Questions Tasha couldn't answer, because when you came right down to it, she hadn't known the missing woman well at all, despite the few times they sat together in the Gymboree group and at Starbucks.

Jane Kendall is the kind of person who can seem to be a part of things, yet maintain a distance, deliberate or not. Must come with money and breeding.

Tasha makes her way back over to the table with her brimming coffee drink.

"So did you hear anything new?" she asks Rachel when she is seated again and has settled Victoria with her apple juice and propped a bottle into Max's mouth as he leans against her.

Rachel doesn't have to ask what she's talking about. "No, but I heard that the police are investigating it as a possible suicide."

"A *suicide*?"

Somehow, she just can't connect that image to the perfectly nice, perfectly beautiful, perfectly . . . well, *perfect* woman from Gymboree. "Why would she kill herself?"

"Her father killed himself."

"Where did you hear that?'

"Ben told me when he called home this morning. One of his patients is a cop's kid."

"The kid told Ben Jane Kendall's father committed suicide?" Tasha asks doubtfully.

"I think the mother told him what her husband told her. I guess they think she might have jumped."

Tasha winces at the very idea of someone hurling herself over the rock-walled edge of the cliff that rises high above the Hudson River and forms the western boundary of High Ridge Park. It happens every once in a while, sure. Someone takes the deadly plunge. But usually you hear about a lovesick teenager doing it, or a distraught middle-aged man—not a suburban mom who has every reason to live, and who, by jumping, would be leaving her baby defenseless and alone in the park.

"Do you think she jumped?" Tasha asks Rachel.

"*I* don't think she did," Karen Wu says, materializing at the table with Mara.

Naturally, Victoria lights up at the sight of her toddler idol. Tasha allows her to pull up a chair next to the one Mara vacated earlier, and the two girls share a box of animal crackers Tasha pulls from her bag.

She turns her attention back to what Karen said. "So why don't you think she killed herself? I think I read someplace that children of parents who commit suicide are far more likely to kill themselves than the average person would be."

"That's true. But I just don't believe Jane Kendall did it."

"Why not?" Rachel persists.

Karen shakes her head. Her straight, shiny black hair swings back and forth at her shoulders, falling neatly back into place. "It's just a feeling I have. I barely knew the woman, after all. I'm not qualified to offer a professional opinion."

"I can't believe *anyone* would jump from that wall into the river," Tasha comments, and sips her coffee, savoring the dribble of caramel in the rich foam. She watches Noah drop the crust of bagel he was chewing.

"People do it all the time," Rachel points out, handing her son another piece of bagel without bothering to bend and pick up the chunk he dropped.

She's like that, Tasha has noticed. She tends to expect other people to clean up after her and her kids—probably because someone always has.

"People like Jane Kendall don't jump into the river all the time. Maybe she ran away," Tasha suggests, doubting it.

"Maybe. My housekeeper's cousin knows the Kendalls' housekeeper," Rachel says. "I can probably get some dirt out of her. You'd be surprised at what housekeepers know about the people they work for," Rachel says, and turns to Karen. "Speaking of household help, I need a stand-in sitter until I can get a new nanny. I think I'm going to have to let Mrs. Tuccelli go. Didn't you tell me last week that you might know of someone?"

Karen nods. "Sharon and Fletch Gallagher's nephew. He's living with them now."

Fletch Gallagher.

The name causes a startled little jump in Tasha's stomach. She busies herself plucking the bottle from Max's still-sucking mouth, putting him up on her shoulder to burp him even though it's no longer necessary at his age.

Rachel is hesitant, frowning. "A male sitter? I don't know. . . ."

"He's a good kid from what I can tell, Rachel," says

Karen, who lives next door to the Gallaghers and should know. "He seems like a real studious type—"

"I know who he is," Rachel cuts in. "His mother died in that awful house fire in July."

"August, actually, and that was his stepmother, Melissa Gallagher."

"No wonder," Rachel says.

"No wonder what?" Karen asks.

"No wonder the kid is so homely. Melissa Gallagher was an attractive woman. A blonde with a great figure, remember? No way could she produce a kid who looks like that."

Tasha rolls her eyes. "Rach, that's cruel. He's just a kid."

"I know, but . . . never mind. Go on, Karen."

"Anyway," Karen says, getting back to the point, "Sharon and Fletch have taken in Jeremiah and his two stepsisters until his father gets back to town. He's overseas on a military assignment."

Tasha toys with her coffee cup while Rachel and Karen discuss the Gallaghers' nephew. She's grateful when Victoria spills her apple juice all over herself, effectively curtailing the conversation.

Fletch Gallagher isn't someone she feels comfortable discussing, even now.

Even if not another living soul knows what happened.

"I've got to get her home and change her into dry clothes," Tasha tells Rachel and Karen, wiping the juice spatters from her daughter's pink overalls with napkins.

"She's not that wet," Rachel points out. "It'll dry fast."

"I know, but . . . I've got a lot to do at home," Tasha tells her, standing. "I was about to tackle a mountain of laundry when you called."

"Oh, laundry," Rachel says, wrinkling her nose. "Wouldn't you rather stay here and gossip with us?"

Not about Fletch Gallagher, Tasha thinks grimly as she reaches for her jacket.

Margaret Armstrong sets a steaming cup of tea on the desk in front of her brother-in-law, taking care to make sure the saucer is carefully positioned on the blotter so as not to mar the antique cherry finish.

Owen barely looks up at her and doesn't even glance at the tea, mumbling only, "Thanks."

His head rests heavily in his hand; his gaze is fixed bleakly on a framed photograph on the desk.

Margaret can see only its easel back but she knows the picture must be of Jane. Owen's large study is filled with photos of her sister, some formal studio shots, others candid snapshots, and a few of her with Schuyler.

On the wall over the fireplace behind the desk is an oil painting in an ornate gilt frame: Jane and Owen together on their wedding day. Jane, elegantly simple in Mother's silk gown that has faded to a mellow ivory. Owen, dashing in his morning coat, beaming at his bride. She's looking up at him, too, but, Margaret notices for the first time, she doesn't radiate bliss the way her new husband does.

That's Jane, she thinks to herself with a familiar flicker of anger, averting her eyes from the painting. *Oblivious to the fact that she's landed one of the most eligible men on the East Coast—and that he's wildly in love with her.*

Her sister has always taken Owen's devotion for granted, from the moment she first met him at the country club pool on that long ago Fourth of July weekend.

Jane was only thirteen then. Margaret, at eighteen, had been assigned to keep an eye on her younger sister while Mother was on the golf course and Daddy was in the bar.

Keeping an eye on Jane meant watching her frolic in a skimpy turquoise bikini that she filled out so remarkably that every teenaged boy—and most of the men—at the pool that day were in awe of her.

While her sister flirted—shyly at first, and then with maddening aplomb—Margaret sat in the shade at a pool-side umbrella table, her own modest black one-piece concealed under a terry cover-up that hid her pale skin and knobby, angular figure. She pretended to be engrossed in the novel she'd brought along: Dostoevsky.

But she was mostly watching Jane, wondering how it was that her kid sister was able to attain so effortlessly everything that had always eluded Margaret's grasp.

Then, as if to punctuate Margaret's covetous thoughts, *he* showed up, a gloriously masculine, broad-shouldered young blond man silhouetted against the bright blue summer sky as he bounced lightly on the edge of the high board.

Margaret found herself staring up at him, wondering why he was lingering, why it was taking him so long to leap over the edge. Was he leery? She didn't sense apprehension in his sanguine bouncing. No, she realized . . . he was waiting for something. He was gazing pointedly down into the water below, where Jane, surrounded by a crowd of male admirers, was treading water, her wet golden hair streaming back to reveal that flawless sun-kissed face.

He was waiting for Jane.

Finally, as though sensing the eyes intently focused on her from above, she glanced up at the man on the diving board.

And he, realizing he had her attention, executed a perfect somersault dive into the water below.

When he surfaced, he swam directly over to Jane.

Margaret watched as he chatted with her sister, who seemed coyly uninterested yet didn't seem to mind when her other admirers drifted away gradually, leaving her alone with him. Finally the two of them climbed out of the pool and headed over to the snack bar, passing Margaret on the way. Her sister waved casually, and the boy with her glanced in her direction. It was then that Margaret recognized him.

It was Owen Kendall, the eighteen-year-old heir to a vast Westchester fortune. Like her, he had graduated from high school weeks earlier. He had gone to Somerset Prep while she had attended its all-girls sister school, Dover Academy. All the Dover girls knew about handsome, affable, gentlemanly Owen Kendall, the consummate great catch.

It figured that he would land in Jane's lap before she even began her freshman year at Dover. Owen was patient, dating her the whole time he was away at Yale, proposing marriage on her eighteenth birthday.

Jane never had to work for anything in her life. She didn't know what it was like to yearn. To envy . . .

No, Margaret chastises herself. *Not now. Don't hate Jane now. Not when you should be focusing your energy on Owen. He needs you.*

That's why she's here, having so willingly left behind her life in Scarsdale—the idle days she struggles to fill with gardening, reading, television.

She has nothing to rush back to. She can stay here with Owen and Schuyler as long as she is needed.

And she *is* needed. Or so she has been struggling to convince herself.

She clears her throat.

He looks up. His light blue eyes are tormented.

"Do you . . . need anything?" Margaret asks, feeling herself flush under his gaze.

She is suddenly aware of the overwhelming silence in the study, broken only by the rhythmic ticking of the clock on the mantel.

He seems to ponder the question too long before shaking his head. "Nothing you can give me," he says with quiet bitterness.

Margaret knows he means no animosity toward her. That he can't possibly sense the secret, forbidden urges that torment her. Yet she can't help feeling a prickle of trepidation at his words.

Is he angry with her?

Is there the slightest chance that he somehow *knows?*

She forces her voice to remain level as she tells him, "I checked on Schuyler. She's asleep in the nursery."

"Are my parents still here?"

"Your mother is lying down upstairs. She has a headache. Your father is still on the phone in the library."

"With our lawyers, no doubt," Owen says dully.

Margaret doesn't have an answer for him. The Kendalls have pretty much ignored her since she arrived. Though they adore Jane—who doesn't?—they have never had much use for her family.

The Armstrongs were never quite as socially esteemed as the Kendalls, but they were certainly on par with the majority of Westchester's country club set—until Daddy blew his brains out one midnight on the golf course, later that same summer when Margaret was eighteen and Owen was following Jane around at the pool.

In the wake of that tragedy, the Armstrongs were tainted. But not Jane. Never Jane. She survived the scandal with her dignity intact, traded the tarnished Armstrong name for one that was pure gold. Jane became a

Kendall, welcomed into their ranks and thus protected from further unpleasant fallout from her father's scandalous suicide.

Mother, too, eventually remarried. Her second husband was Teddy Wright-Douglas, a British financier who was distantly related to the royal family.

Only Margaret still bears the Kendall name. Only Margaret has been left to slink in the shadows of her father's shameful legacy.

Yet perhaps now things will be different. Now that Jane is gone . . .

"Owen," Margaret says abruptly, to curtail the direction in which her thoughts are drifting, "won't you let me fix you some toast? Or maybe some soup. You should eat. You haven't eaten all day."

"I have absolutely no appetite," he tells her heavily, bowing his head and rubbing his temples with his fingers.

"But Owen, if you don't eat—"

"I'm fine," he cuts in sharply, silencing her.

As her thoughts race for something else to say, for something else to offer, he adds, "All I want right now, Margaret, is to be left alone."

Stung, yet willing herself not to show it, she nods and retreats from the study.

In the hallway outside she pulls the door quietly closed, then pauses with her hand still on the knob, uncertain where to go next.

Schuyler is asleep in her crib in the yellow-and-white second-floor nursery. Mother's flight from Heathrow doesn't get in until this evening, and Margaret has already arranged a car service for her rather than drive to the airport to meet the flight herself. She's not particularly anxious to see her mother under the best of circumstances. Today, she dreads it.

The house is large enough so that she doesn't have to share space with Owen's parents, the housekeeper, or the detectives working on the case. She, too, wants to be alone.

After a moment, she turns and heads to the kitchen and up the back staircase that leads to the second floor. From here she can go through a large walk-in dressing room and into the master bedroom.

She shouldn't be here. On some level, she knows that as she slips through the door into the sprawling room with its crown molding, fireplace, and cozy, gabled nooks.

She takes in the brocade wallpaper, the rich cranberry-colored draperies that frame floor-to-ceiling windows, the thick carpet with its floral Victorian pattern beneath her feet.

This is the private quarters her sister shares with Owen, a room Margaret has been in only once before, when Jane first gave her a grand tour of the entire house years ago. Back then this section was empty, awaiting not just delivery of the newly ordered furniture, but also the skills of the professional decorator who would transform it into the sumptuous suite it has become.

"Don't you love it?" Jane had asked. "This room— isn't it beautiful?"

Margaret nodded. "The whole house is beautiful, Jane."

"I'm glad you agree with me," Jane said in a tone that hinted to Margaret that Owen did not.

"What does Owen think?"

"He wanted a new house. He doesn't like old houses. He grew up in one. He calls it the mausoleum. But he gave in and bought this place for me because I fell in love with it. I adore all the quirks. Old houses are so interesting . . . and they have secrets."

She proceeded to show Margaret a few of them and described several others.

Now, remembering that day, Margaret stands in the middle of the master bedroom. Her gaze falls on the ornately carved king-size bed, the vast built-in armoire along one wall, and the sitting area with its period fainting couch and cheval mirror. She catches her reflection in it, and as always, it takes her by surprise.

Somehow, in her own mind, in her optimistic heart, she is younger, more attractive than the plain, nearly middle-aged woman in the glass. In her imagination, she belongs in a room like this.

In reality . . .

She takes in her own close-set, sparsely lashed black eyes, her lifeless dark hair parted in the middle and drawn severely back from her pale, angular face.

She has tried on occasion to do something with her appearance. To bring out her eyes with makeup, to give her hair a lift with a different style and some spray.

But the attempts have been futile. Nothing can transform her. . . .

Into Jane.

Isn't that what you want? she demands of the homely woman in the mirror. *You want to be Jane.*

You want to claim what belongs to Jane.

All of it.

Slowly she turns away from the mirror to gaze thoughtfully at the bed.

Fletch Gallagher opens the lid of the new red state-of-the-art blender he recently ordered from a Williams-Sonoma catalogue.

He peers inside, then taps on the glass container. Sturdy.

Outrageously expensive, too . . . but worth it. He'll use this thing every day, especially now that baseball season's over and he'll be hanging around the house more—Unless the Mets go into post-season play, which means his sportscasting duties can extend well into October. With any luck, he usually heads up to his cabin in the Catskills to unwind with a fishing pole, then south to spend some time golfing and lying in the sun. But this year, when the Mets narrowly missed getting into the playoffs and Fletch found himself free, Aidan begged him to stay put in Townsend Heights for a while. Keep an eye on his nephew and step-nieces. Make sure they're adjusting okay.

What could he do? The last thing he wants is to stick around here, but he can't refuse his brother. Not when the guy has just been widowed for the second time in his life.

He has to admit that Sharon's pitching in more than he expected her to, where the kids are concerned. After all, they're not her blood relations, and it's not like she's prone to bending over backward to do favors for Fletch these days. But she's spent more time at home lately, helping the twins with their homework and taking them shopping for new school clothes. Maybe it's because she misses Randi, their own daughter, who is away for her first semester at William and Mary. Sharon seems to enjoy having their two young nieces around the house.

She hasn't exactly bonded with Jeremiah, though. He's not the warmest, most lovable kid in town. Even Fletch hasn't made much progress getting him to come out of his shell on the few occasions he has tried. He has no idea whether it's because his nephew is still traumatized by the losses of his mother and stepmother, or because he's just a loner by nature.

Well, things seem to be settling down in the Middle

East. With any luck, Aidan will be back before the cold weather gets here. Then he can make other arrangements for the kids, and Fletch will be free to get the hell out of here. Maybe a weekend up at the cabin, just to clear his head before heading down to Boca for some relaxation and then flying back up to spend the holidays with Sharon and the kids. She always insists on that.

At least he got eighteen holes in today down at the country club, followed by a nice long nap on the couch in the family room. The house is silent, but he heard Sharon come in a while ago, slamming the back door and waking him from a sound sleep.

He tosses the banana he just peeled into the blender, then crosses the green ceramic-tile floor and opens the enormous stainless-steel fridge. After moving aside several bottles of fat-free salad dressing and the remains of last night's take-out Chinese, he pulls out a carton of skim milk. Way down on the bottom shelf behind a clear plastic container of mesclun greens, he finds a lone container of nonfat yogurt. Strawberry.

He makes a face.

He's told Sharon—how many times?—that he doesn't like strawberry. Raspberry yogurt is fine. Blueberry, too. Hell, even boysenberry. But not strawberry.

What does she buy?

Strawberry.

Fletch returns it to the fridge. As an afterthought, he puts the milk back in, too, then takes the yogurt out. He tosses the container into the trash compactor under the sink.

Nobody else will eat it. His brother's kids don't seem to like anything but junk food, and his son Derek has recently decided he's a vegan—whatever the hell that means. Something about not eating any animal products.

If it were up to Fletch, his son would eat thick steaks and ice cream like any other red-blooded American boy, but Sharon coddles him and his neo-hippie ideas. Tells Fletch to leave him alone. That Derek's twenty now, fully grown, and he can eat whatever he wants, even if he is still living under their roof.

Not that he's ever home. Where he spends his days— and nights—is a mystery to Fletch, and if Sharon knows, she's not telling. Leave it to her to keep Derek's secrets. After all, she's full of her own—or so she thinks. But Fletch knows more about what his wife's been up to lately than he does about their son. He knows Sharon's only biding her time with him, waiting for the right moment to leave him for her lover. Actually, for months he'd been expecting her to do it in August when Randi left for college, which would liberate Sharon from two decades of motherhood obligations. Then Melissa got killed and their nieces and nephew had moved in just as Randi moved out. How could Sharon walk out on Fletch at a time like that?

There's no doubt in his mind that she will, sooner or later. But far be it from him to force her hand.

Fletch pulls the banana out of the blender and takes a bite. A banana wasn't what he had in mind. He wanted a health shake, damn it.

He hears footsteps on the stairs.

Moments later, Sharon breezes into the kitchen. She has on one of those skimpy leotard things she wears to her kick-boxing class, and is jangling her car keys in her hand.

He glances over her toned body—small hips and high breasts—and at her thick blond hair pulled into a pony-tail. The remnants of her summer tan, helped along, no doubt, by regular visits to the tanning salon, cast a healthy glow over her face.

Two decades of marriage have all but obliterated not

just Fletch's appreciation for his wife's beauty, but his desire for her.

"Where are you going?" he asks, though it should be obvious. But some part of him wants to hear her say it.

"The gym." She unwraps a stick of gum and goes over to toss it into the garbage. "What's this?"

He shrugs.

She's staring down at the full container of yogurt he just threw in.

"Why'd you throw this away?" She pulls it out and inspects the date stamped on the cover, then turns accusing green eyes on him. "It still has two weeks left before it expires."

"Yeah, and it's strawberry. You know I don't like strawberry yogurt. I told you not to buy it."

"Well, somebody else will eat it."

"Who? You?"

"You know I'm lactose-intolerant."

Or so you say, he thinks but says nothing. As far as he's concerned, Sharon is a hypochondriac. Always has been. If she wants to believe she's lactose-intolerant, fine with him, as long as he doesn't have to listen to her go on and on about it.

"Maybe one of the kids will eat it," she says, putting it back into the fridge.

"I thought they only eat Little Debbies. And McDonald's. And Derek's—"

"I know. A vegan. Well, maybe someone'll eat it," she says again.

She takes a can of Diet Pepsi from the shelf in the door, closes the fridge, and pops the top.

He watches her as she takes a sip.

"You're going to drink that before you work out?" he asks.

For a moment their eyes meet. A look passes between them.

She says simply, "I'm thirsty," and heads toward the back door. She pauses halfway there to ask, "You didn't hear, did you?"

"Hear what?"

She seems to be studying his face, probing for something. Then she says, "Jane Kendall."

He tenses. "What about Jane Kendall?"

"She's missing."

"Missing?" he echoes, not meeting Sharon's eyes. "What do you mean, missing?"

She shrugs. "That's all I know. She disappeared from High Ridge Park."

"When?"

"Last night, I think."

"Huh." His hand trembles as he raises the banana to his mouth again, taking a bite and chewing mechanically. "Do they . . . do they think something happened to her?"

"Obviously." Sharon grabs her raincoat from a hook just inside the mudroom and pulls it on. "I've got to get to the gym. See you later."

"See you later."

Lies, he thinks, abruptly tossing the banana into the garbage can and heading upstairs to take a shower.

They both know she's not going to the gym, just as they both know they won't see each other later.

Fletch turns on the hot water tap full force. It runs into the tub, sending tendrils of steam skyward. Lost in thought, Fletch stares at his reflection in the wide mirror above the double sink until his features are swallowed up by the rising shroud of mist.

Chapter Three

"Mrs. Bailey?"

About to automatically correct the "Mrs.," Paula looks up to see Mitch's teacher standing in the doorway of the office waiting room and promptly changes her mind.

Sixtyish, with Barbara Bush white hair and pearls, an old-fashioned pastel wool dress, and a mouth that could be drawn as a thin, straight line if you tried to capture it on paper, Miss Bright is clearly disapproving as she looks Paula over. What's her problem?

"I'm sorry I'm late," Paula offers, aware of her own unapologetic tone, yet unable—unwilling—to change it as she rises from the bench where the school secretary directed her. "I've been covering a huge story and—"

"We won't have much time to talk," Miss Bright cuts in. "The children come back from gym class in five minutes. I had hoped to get more time than that with you."

Paula shrugs. "I'm working today. It isn't easy for me to get away."

The teacher bobs her head in a gesture that could be perceived as a sort of nod, but not an understanding one. She gestures for Paula to follow her and leads the way down the hall, past rows of lockers decorated with various construction-paper motifs: autumn leaves, pumpkins, ships . . .

"Why are there cutouts of ships on those lockers?" Paula asks Mitch's teacher because there is only the sound of their footsteps tapping down the hall and the silence is awkward.

"The Niña, the Pinta, and the Santa Maria," the teacher says simply.

"Oh, for Columbus Day."

"This is our room," the teacher announces, stopping at an open classroom door. She stands aside to let Paula through the door, then closes it behind her. She sits behind her desk. "Have a seat, Mrs. Bailey."

"Actually, it's Ms.," Paula says as she perches on the only available chair, a child-size wooden ladder-back that's beside the desk.

"Excuse me?"

"My name," Paula clarifies. "I'm a *Ms.*, not a *Mrs.* Mitch's father and I are divorced."

"I realize that." Miss Bailey—not *Ms.*—purses small lips that are encrusted with an unfashionably pale mauve lipstick.

Why couldn't Mitch have a different sort of teacher? Someone younger, more modern, less judgmental. His teacher last year, Ms. Richmond, had been right out of college. It didn't seem to faze her that Paula was a divorced working mother. In fact, Ms. Richmond was impressed by Paula's journalism career.

Not Miss Bright, though, who's treating Paula as though she's been caught turning tricks down in Yonkers. Well, if she thinks Paula's the least bit bothered by her attitude, she's wrong.

Paula looks away, glancing around the classroom. Typical—small blond-wood desks with smaller chairs; a green chalkboard running the length of two walls, and windows the length of another; a piano in one back corner and a library table in the other; and plenty of student artwork by way of decor.

"Your son's behavioral and academic problems seem to stem from the fact that he's not getting what he needs at home, Mrs.—*Ms.*—Bailey." Miss Bright folds her hands on the desk in front of her. The reporter in Paula notes that they're as white as her hair, with transparent skin and blue veins. Her unpolished nails are short, filed into perfect, boring ovals.

On her desk is a red wooden apple emblazoned with the phrase "Teachers give the best hugs." Paula tries, and fails, to imagine this woman hugging someone—anyone.

"What is it that you think he needs that I'm not giving him, Miss Bright?" Paula asks frostily.

"Time, Ms. Bailey," is the straightforward reply. "He needs more of your time."

"How do you know how much time I spend with my son?"

"I know that you didn't help him with his fractions the night before last. I sent home a worksheet that was specifically supposed to be done with the help of a parent, and Mitchell brought his back incomplete. His explanation was that you weren't home to help him. He tells me you were working."

It's Paula's turn to purse her lips.

"Mitchell was the only student in the class not to bring in a lightbulb for the arts and crafts project we worked on this morning—"

"I didn't know he needed one."

"It was in the note I sent home with all the students last week. We're making maracas as part of our lesson on Mexico."

"We have a pair of maracas at home. Maybe Mitch can bring—"

"The point is, Ms. Bailey, that you obviously need to be more attentive to Mitchell's needs."

"Just because I didn't know he needed a lightbulb for a project?" she asks in disbelief. This woman is too much.

"And the fractions worksheet. And many other small things this past week or two that add up to one thing, Ms. Bailey. Your son has needs that are being neglected. He's acting out as a way of getting attention in the classroom, and I suspect that it's because he isn't getting it at home. I didn't call you here to attack you—"

"You could've fooled me," Paula mutters. She grips the edges of the seat with her hands, seething.

"Please calm down, Ms. Bailey."

"I am calm," she snaps.

"I think that if we work together, we can come up with some solutions so that you can help to steer Mitchell back on track. Believe me, we want the same thing, you and I. We want Mitchell to thrive and to succeed. I'm sending home another worksheet that you can work on with him tonight. And perhaps we could meet again, with his father next time, so that—"

"His father is out of the picture," Paula interrupts.

The teacher raises her white eyebrows. "He is? But I thought—"

"He's out of the picture," she repeats.

"Mitchell talks about him as if—"

"As if what?" she cuts in, trying to quell the fury that rises in her gut.

"As if he sees his father often."

"Well, he doesn't. His father can't be bothered with him."

"In that case, Ms. Bailey, you have your work cut out for you."

"Believe me, Miss Bright, I've always had my work cut out for me. It isn't easy raising a child single-handedly and moving forward in a competitive career like mine."

"I'm sure it isn't."

"I've worked my butt off to get where I am."

There's a commotion in the hall—chattering voices, footsteps, locker doors slamming.

"The children are back from gym," Miss Bright says. "We haven't even begun to discuss the various ways in which Mitchell needs help. Perhaps you can come—"

"I've got it covered, Miss Bright," Paula says grimly, rising and walking to the door.

"But we need to talk about—"

"I'll take care of it, Miss Bright."

Knowing, and not caring, that it's rude not to say good-bye and thank the teacher for her concern, she steps out into the hall and glances at the throng of third-graders waiting to come back into their classroom.

Mitch isn't among them. Why not?

She grabs the arm of a freckle-faced blond kid who looks vaguely familiar. "Hey, you're a friend of Mitch's, aren't you?"

"Mitch S. or Mitch B.?"

"Mitch B."

"I used to be," the kid replies, "until he stole my Pokemon card."

"Until he stole . . ." Paula echoes, and shakes her head. What the hell is going on with Mitch? "Look, do you know where he is? Why isn't he here with everyone else?"

"He had to stay after in gym."

"Why?"

" 'Cause he tripped some kid during the relay."

Paula turns away, her heart pounding as she walks slowly down the hall, clutching her car keys in hands that are shaking in fury.

At Mitch . . .

At Miss Bright . . .

At Frank Ferrante . . .

Oh hell, at the entire world.

Tasha gingerly descends the steep basement stairs with a heaping laundry basket, thankful that Max is finally asleep. *He must be cutting a tooth,* she thinks, stepping around the double baby stroller with the broken wheel Joel has been planning to fix for months now.

Poor little Max. If it isn't a tooth, something's been making him cranky. Maybe he's picking up on Tasha's anxiety over Jane Kendall's disappearance.

He wept so pitifully when she put him into his crib that she couldn't bear to leave him there to fall asleep on his own. Joel would probably say she was spoiling him, but she had taken him out and sat in the rocker by the window, rocking him for almost an hour. Even then, he seemed a little fussy.

Finally, she gave him some Tylenol and put him back into the crib. He whimpered, but moments later he was silent, meaning either he finally wore himself out, or he really has been in pain from teething.

Now she has only Victoria to contend with for the next hour or so.

Victoria, and enough laundry to clothe an island nation.

She sorts it by color on the concrete basement floor, then stuffs all the towels she can fit into the washer. There are still half a dozen left over. When was the last time she did laundry? How does she manage to let household tasks like this get away from her these days?

There was a time when her every waking moment felt productive—when she sewed, wallpapered, and cooked dinners made from recipes in *The Joy of Cooking.* Now, she's lucky if she has a minute to run into the bathroom and pee.

She dumps a capful of detergent into the washing machine, closes the lid, and pulls the knob.

Nothing happens.

Frowning, she pushes in the knob, then pulls it out again.

No accompanying sound of water pouring into the machine.

She opens the lid. Peers inside. Closes it. Pushes and pulls the knob again.

Nothing.

She hears pattering footsteps overhead, and then a voice calls down from the kitchen.

"Mommy?"

"What's the matter, Victoria?"

"You said you would do my puzzle with me."

"I will. In a minute."

"What are you doing?" Victoria wants to know. Now she's on the basement steps.

"Get back up there, Victoria. You only have socks on, and it's dirty down here."

"Well, when are you coming up to do my puzzle with me?"

"As soon as I figure out why the washing machine won't start." Tasha jiggles the plug, making sure it's firmly inserted into the wall socket. It is.

Now what?

Why can't this have happened when Joel is home?

Well, she can't wait until he gets back tonight. Who knows when that will be?

She considers calling him at the office to ask, then quickly dismisses the idea. He still hasn't returned the message she left this morning. He doesn't even know that Jane Kendall is missing.

Well, when he calls back, she can tell him about that and about the broken washing machine.

But in the meantime, she'll have to check the booklet that came with the machine when they bought it. She keeps all that stuff in a drawer upstairs. With a sigh she goes up the steps, hoping the booklet will have one of those troubleshooting charts and an easily remedied explanation for why the washing machine refuses to work.

Victoria is standing on the second step from the top. Her face is smeared with something brown.

"What is that?" Tasha scoops her up and sets her on her feet in the kitchen. "What did you get into?"

"Nothing," Victoria says, swiping at her mouth with the sleeve of the white shirt she's wearing under the pink overalls that are still spattered with dried juice stains from this morning.

Great. More stuff to wash in the machine that doesn't work.

Tasha glances around, searching for the source of the mud-colored ooze her daughter is sporting. Her gaze falls on the fridge. The door is open. On the floor in front of it, a plastic bottle of Hershey's chocolate syrup lies on its side, the contents pooled across the pale yellow linoleum.

"Victoria! What did you do?"

"You weren't here, Mommy, and I was starving."

"I *was* here, Victoria. I was downstairs for all of two minutes. If you were hungry you should have waited until I got back up here. Look at that mess."

"I'm sorry."

"Uh-huh."

Victoria looks anything but sorry. Her lower lip is curled under in a "that'll teach you to leave me alone" expression.

Tasha grabs the sponge from the sink and bends to wipe up the mess. She puts the bottle of chocolate syrup back into the fridge and closes the door.

Victoria promptly whines, "I wanted that."

"Well, you can't have it," Tasha snaps.

Then, instantly feeling guilty, she softens her tone. "It's just that you can't eat that all by itself, Victoria."

After all, it's not her daughter's fault that the washing machine won't work or that Jane Kendall is missing or that somebody brought up Fletch Gallagher today.

"I'll tell you what," Tasha says, wetting a paper towel and gently wiping the chocolate smudges from her daughter's face, "after I figure out what's wrong with the washing machine, we'll have some ice cream with chocolate syrup on top. Okay?"

Victoria seems to mull that over. "With whipped cream?"

"I don't think we have whipped cream."

"I want whipped cream."

Tasha takes a deep breath. "Well, we don't have any whipped cream. But," she adds quickly when Victoria opens her mouth to protest, "we do have maraschino cherries."

"I don't like those."

Don't push me, kid, Tasha thinks grimly. *Not today.*

Through clenched teeth she says, "Then you can just have sprinkles. Okay? You like sprinkles. Everybody likes sprinkles."

"Okay," Victoria says, unexpectedly breaking into a smile. "I love you, Mommy."

"I love you, too, sweetie." Tasha breathes a sigh of relief and pushes a black curl away from her daughter's face.

Victoria looks so like her daddy, with the dark hair, intense features, and pale skin. But she doesn't have his chestnut eyes or his mellow nature.

Her blue eyes are courtesy of Tasha. As for her intense personality—well, Tasha might not be as laid-back as Joel, but she certainly isn't responsible for Victoria's high-maintenance character. She probably has her mother-in-law to thank for supplying that particular trait to the family gene pool.

Which reminds her: there was a message from Ruth on the answering machine when she got back from Starbucks earlier. She and Joel's father, Irv, want to come over on Saturday—*"if it's all right with you, Tasha."* She always makes a big point of asking permission, as though she assumes her son and grandchildren will welcome a visit anytime, and it's only her daughter-in-law potentially standing in the way of a happy get-together.

Yeah, right. As though Tasha has ever told them not to come.

In fact, in the early days of her marriage, she was the one who insisted to Joel that they see his parents every week. With her own family so far away, she had done her best to nurture the relationship with her husband's family. She used to go all out, cooking and cleaning for their visits, making sure that they had the Cel-ray tonic Irv drinks, and Sweet 'N Low for Ruth's tea. But after a while, when it became clear that her in-laws weren't going to like her no matter what she did, she stopped knocking herself out.

Now, when Ruth and Irv come over, they go out to eat, or get take-out.

Of course, that doesn't thrill the in-laws any more than Tasha's homemade latkes and rugelach ever did. Last time they came, Tasha went to the kosher deli over in Mount Kisco to get a cold-cut platter and some rice pudding.

"Oh, you have seeded rye," Joel's mother said when she picked up a piece of bread to make a sandwich.

"Don't you like seeded rye, Ruth?" Far be it from Tasha to call her "Mom." Ruth had never asked her to, and she had never dared offer.

"No, I buy the seedless. I always have. Joel only likes seedless," she said resolutely.

Naturally, Joel, who had one eye on the Yankees game, hadn't heard her. Or maybe he pretended not to so that he wouldn't have to tell his mother that he does, indeed, like seeded rye—and that he was, in fact, the one who bought it that day at the bakery. . . .

"Mommy?"

"Yes?" Tasha asks absently, looking down at her daughter.

"Why do you look so mad?"

"Do I look mad?" She tries to smile. "I'm not mad, Victoria. I'm just thinking about something."

"About what?"

"Never mind. You know what? Let's have that ice cream now. We can deal with everything later."

"What do we have to deal with?"

Tasha hesitates. "Just . . . oh, a bunch of yucky stuff, Victoria. Be glad you're only three."

"Why?"

"Because when you're three, you don't have to deal with yucky stuff."

"I do so. There's a lot of yucky stuff. Like when Max poops and—"

"That's not what I meant," Tasha says, grinning. "Come on, let's make a couple of big sundaes."

Satisfied that the kids are absorbed by the Winnie the Pooh video she just started for them, Rachel goes into the kitchen and picks up the phone.

She dials a familiar number, then, as it rings, pulls a pack of Salems from her purse. She puts it back just as quickly, realizing that if she lights one here in the house, Ben will sniff it out and realize she's smoking again. He'll eventually figure it out, of course, but she doesn't want him to realize it before the end of next week, when they leave for their long weekend in the Abaco Islands, just the two of them—her reward for kicking the habit.

Again the phone rings on the other end of the line. Rachel walks over to the counter and squirts some rose-scented lotion from a white porcelain dispenser into the palm of her hand.

There's a third ring as she starts rubbing it in, the receiver cradled between her ear and her shoulder. Her hands are starting to look chapped after a day of diaper changing and raw, rainy weather.

"Hello?" a masculine voice says, picking up on the other end.

"Hi." Rachel pauses. "Is this Jeremiah?"

"Yes, it is."

"Jeremiah, my name is Rachel Leiberman. I live down the street, in the white house with black shutters."

"Which one?"

Is the kid being a smart-ass, or is the question sincere? It's hard to tell.

Giving him the benefit of the doubt, she chuckles and says, "I know, they all kind of look alike, don't they?"

"Kind of. I mean, I know there are a couple of white houses with black shutters up that way—"

"We're number forty-eight. End of the block. The one with the basketball hoop and the three-car garage."

"Uh-huh," he says, and it isn't clear if he knows which house she means—not that it matters. He'll figure it out.

"I was wondering if you'd be interested in doing a little babysitting for me," Rachel says. "Our nanny just quit"—*well, actually, firing her will be the next phone call I make*—"and I'm kind of stuck for someone to watch my kids until I find a replacement."

"Well, uh, I have school—"

"I can work around your school schedule. I can pay you whatever the going rate is."

"I have no idea. I don't really babysit much. I mean, ever. But—"

"How about if I give you twelve bucks an hour, then."

"Twelve bucks an hour?" he echoes, stunned. "That would be *great.*"

"Good. Can you come tomorrow?"

"After school?"

"At around dinner time. If you're available."

"I'm available," he says quickly.

"And I would need you to stay until later in the evening. My husband is working."

"That's okay."

"Wonderful. Is there anything you want to know before I hang up?"

"I guess. I mean, uh, are your kids . . ."

He trails off, clearly not sure what to ask. Rachel helps him out. "Noah is thirteen months, and Mara is four. My husband is a pediatrician and he has office hours several evenings a week, to accommodate working parents."

"And you work evenings, too?"

"Me? No. I don't work. But I have an . . . appointment."

In the background, on Jeremiah's end, she hears another voice asking him who's on the phone.

"Just a second," Jeremiah says to her, and then there's a muffled sound as he apparently covers the receiver with his hand. His words are still clearly audible. "It's some lady from down the street, Uncle Fletch. She says she wants me to babysit tomorrow."

"Babysit?" Rachel hears Fletch Gallagher repeat.

"Uh, y-yeah," Jeremiah tells him. Rachel notes the stutter. She can practically see him squirming. She can just imagine the look on his uncle's face.

"What lady from down the street?" Rachel hears him ask.

"W-what did you s-say your n-name was?" Jeremiah asks, taking his hand off the receiver.

"Leiberman," Rachel says, squirting more lotion into her palm and swirling it in a circular motion into her skin. "Rachel Leiberman."

Jeremiah repeats her name for his uncle.

"No problem," Fletch Gallagher says.

"M-my uncle s-says it's fine with h-him," Jeremiah reports to Rachel.

"Good," she says, her mouth curving into a small smile. "Then we have a date."

"I'll make this as easy on you as possible, Ms. Armstrong," the burly detective says gruffly. He's a short, round man whose face is damp with perspiration even though it's drafty in the room. "Are you ready?"

Margaret nods, seated across from him in the small back parlor of her sister's house. They've all taken a turn in this chair: Owen, his parents, the housekeeper, and now her. The police want to question absolutely everyone who might be able to shed light on Jane's disappearance.

"First off, did your sister have any enemies that you are aware of?"

Margaret shakes her head. She gazes at the white-painted molding surrounding the brick fireplace, her eyes tracing the ornately carved swirling pattern.

"So you can't think of anyone who might want to hurt her?"

"No."

"How did she spend her time?"

"Taking care of Schuyler," she answers readily. "I mean, that's what I assume."

"Were you close to her?"

She considers the question. "I live about a half hour away from here."

"That isn't what I mean, Ms. Armstrong. I mean your relationship—were you close?"

"We saw each other every couple of weeks or so." She shifts her weight in the chair and it creaks beneath her. It's old—a Chippendale.

She remembers when Jane bought it—bought all the furniture for this room, in fact, on an antiquing trip to Vermont with Owen. She was so excited to show Margaret everything they purchased, spilling over with details about their trip. She went on and on about the shops, the inn where they stayed, and the restaurants where they ate. Then she confided that while they were away, they decided it was time to try and conceive a baby. "Maybe I'm pregnant now and don't even know it!" Jane exclaimed.

Even now, two years later, Margaret still can't shake the vivid images those words brought to her mind. Jane and Owen, snuggled in a four-poster bed in some quaint New England Inn, making love. . . .

"Ms. Armstrong?"

"Yes?" She drags her attention back to the present.

"Do you feel all right? You look pale. Upset."

"I'm fine." She sips from the glass of water the detective insisted be placed on the table near her before they started talking. As though he expected her to have a difficult time with the interview.

Determined to prove him wrong, she sets the glass back on the table and lifts her chin. "You can go on, Detective."

And he does. Asking question after question about Jane.

Then, unexpectedly, when she decides he must be finished, he says, "How would you describe your sister's relationship with her husband?"

Startled, Margaret is silent for a moment. Then, searching for the right words, she tells the detective, "Their marriage was successful."

"Happy?"

"Yes." Yes, damn it. Yes, Owen was happy with Jane. He was in love with Jane.

And Jane . . .

You never gave yourself completely to him, did you? Margaret silently asks her sister, bitterness seeping in. *You never loved him completely, the way he deserved to be loved. You always held some part of yourself back from him. I could see it. He had to see it, too.*

What had Jane done to deserve Owen? What had she done to deserve any of the blessings fate—and their parents—had bestowed upon her?

As for Margaret . . .

Where are her blessings?

When will her turn come?

Maybe sooner than she thinks.

And maybe never.

"Is there anything else you want to add, Ms. Armstrong?" the detective asks, zapping her back to the present again.

"Just that this is very difficult for our family. I hope you'll do all you can to find my sister," Margaret says stiffly before fleeing from the room.

Approaching the red-brick mansion for the second time that day, Paula sees that the crowd has swelled. There are news vans from all the networks, curious locals, police officers. It's a circus, and she's lost her prime spot at the fence, thanks to the infuriating Miss Bright and a quick detour to the local diner to gobble a bagel and see if the lunch crowd might yield anything or anyone interesting. Nothing but a bunch of regulars, mostly retirees and construction worker types speculating on what could have possibly happened to Jane Kendall.

Paula pushes past a reporter doing a live update on camera and a group of teenagers who have been confronted for truancy by a police officer. She peers around several heads and sees that there's no sign of life in the house beyond the iron fence.

"Has the family made any kind of statement yet?" she asks a nearby reporter who's scribbling furiously in a notebook.

The woman shakes her head, not lifting her eyes from the page of notes. "There are rumors about a police press conference tonight. Not confirmed, though."

Tonight. According to Miss Bright, Mitchell will be bringing home another fractions worksheet, to be done with Paula's help. *Tonight.*

Well, if there's a press conference, she'll have to drop him off at Blake's house again. Blake's mother can help him with the fractions.

That isn't exactly what Miss Bright had in mind.

But what can I do? This is my job, she tells herself, staring at the opulent home across the sweeping expanse of pure green lawn. When she called the managing editor at the office earlier to check in, he offered to send another reporter to take over if she couldn't handle it.

"Why wouldn't I be able to handle it?" she asked him shrilly.

"I know you have your son to worry about, Paula, and your other stories. This is huge, and time-consuming, and—"

"It's mine, Tim," she said firmly. "I was the first one to scoop it." Just as she was the first to scoop the Gallagher fire last summer on North Street. Her article landed on the front page with a byline, at last giving her a taste of something beyond the social and civic beat they'd had her covering for far too long.

"I've busted my butt here all day," she told Tim. "Don't worry. I'll make my other deadlines. But I'm not giving up on this. You're right. This is huge. And I'm on top of it."

He agreed, but she could hear the reluctance in his voice.

Covering this disappearance might be the most important thing I will ever do in my life, she thinks, clenching her hands into fists at the memory of that conversation. *It's my chance to make a name for myself, maybe break out of this small-time reporting and get the recognition I deserve, maybe make enough money to hire a lawyer who can get Frank the hell off my back. . . .*

She stares at the house, again thinking of the woman she glimpsed getting out of a cab earlier this afternoon. Where has she seen her before? The answer flutters at the edge of her consciousness, just out of reach.

"Paula!"

She turns to see an elderly man in a cream-colored windbreaker, a matching fishing hat planted squarely on his gray head. It takes her a moment to recognize him as one of her father's former local cronies, from the days when he was still going for coffee every morning down at the diner.

"Hello, Mr. Mieske." It's all she can do to sound friendly. The old man is a busybody.

"How's your dad?"

She studies his expression. His faded blue eyes are concerned—does that mean he knows? Or is he just wondering why Dad hasn't been coming around these past few years?

"He has his good days and his bad days," she answers. If Mr. Mieske doesn't know, she's not in the mood to tell him.

"Don't we all." He nods and gestures at the big house beyond the fence. "That's really something, isn't it?"

"Jane Kendall's disappearance?"

He waves his hand at her. "She's dead. No question about it. The only question is, did she kill herself, or did somebody kill her?"

"What's *your* guess?" She watches the old man's face.

"My guess is that somebody killed her. A woman like that, she has everything to live for. Why would she do herself in?"

Paula nods slowly.

Jane Kendall certainly had everything to live for.

And what about you, Paula? she asks herself thoughtfully, forgetting all about Mr. Mieske. *What do you have?*

She glances at her father's old friend. He's turned his attention toward a nearby network news reporter who's interviewing a police officer.

Your time is coming, Paula. You've always known that, haven't you? You've always believed in yourself. You've been patient. You've paid your dues.

Just wait. Just hang on, Paula. You'll see. Someday everything will be going your way.

"Hi, Stacey. Is Joel around?"

"Oh, hi, Tasha." There's a pause.

Tasha clutches the telephone receiver against her ear, picturing her husband's secretary on the other end of the line.

Stacey McCall is a pretty twenty-two-year-old brunette he hired right out of college last spring. Tasha has met her only once, when she stopped by Joel's office with the kids one afternoon in June on the way down to the

Central Park Zoo. Stacey fell all over Joel's "little angels," as she kept calling them, and was polite enough to Tasha.

Unwilling to allow herself to be one of those wives who feels threatened by her husband's young, attractive secretary, Tasha did her best not to notice Stacey's sun-kissed, unblemished skin, her thick, dark hair that was cut in a flattering layered look, or her willowy figure clad in a pale yellow Talbots summer suit without a blouse underneath, the jacket lapels cut so as not to reveal more than a hint of cleavage.

Tasha, feeling considerably older than her thirty-five years, her shoulders perpetually wet from the baby's drool, and everything in her wardrobe a throwback to seasons long past, told herself that even if Joel were ripe for an affair and did find Stacey attractive—okay, who wouldn't?—Stacey would have nothing to gain by getting involved with her middle-aged, married boss.

Joel has told Tasha that Stacey comes from a wealthy, Waspy Connecticut family; that she has moved into her parents' Sutton Place pied-à-terre and has a wallet full of their credit cards; that her entry-level salary is essentially spending money. Although she assured him during the interview that her goal is to work her way up the totem pole and become an account executive with the agency, it has since become obvious that she's merely killing time until her boyfriend gets his MBA from Harvard Business School and they get engaged.

And yet Joel found it necessary to point out to Tasha that Stacey certainly isn't stupid. In fact, he claims, she has a photographic memory. She knows his schedule, day in and day out, without having to glance at his calendar more than once.

"Actually, Tasha," Stacey says, after clearing her throat,

"he's in a meeting with a client and he asked not to be disturbed."

Tasha feels a surge of anger—perhaps irrational anger, aimed not just at Joel but at this perfect young woman planted squarely in the path of access to her husband.

"When do you expect him out of the meeting?" Tasha asks, trying not to allow a chill to creep into her voice.

Max whimpers suddenly in his Exersaucer nearby. Tasha glances sharply at Victoria, who is clutching a wooden block and looking guilty.

"It's hard to tell when the meeting will be over with. Can I have him call you back? I wrote down your other messages for him, and I know he picked them up when he broke for lunch a while ago."

Tasha's grip tightens on the receiver. She forgets to wonder whether Victoria has clocked Max with a block. "My other messages?"

"The ones you left on his voice mail," Stacey explains. "He has me check it for him lately, because he's been so busy. That way I can let him know if anyone important has called."

Apparently, his wife doesn't qualify as anybody important, Tasha thinks, knowing that if she allows herself to voice that realization to Stacey, she won't stop there. She's not exactly thrilled to learn that her husband allows his secretary to screen his voice mail. Her messages aren't intended for anybody's ears but Joel's. But she has no intention of embarrassing herself—or Joel—by launching into a tirade.

She glances at the clock on the microwave, then at Victoria, who is now moodily stacking blocks within reach of Max's flailing arms.

"Tell my husband when he gets out of his meeting to please call home," Tasha says succinctly.

"Is it an emergency, Tasha? Because I can—"

"Just have him call. I have to go pick up my son from school now, but I'll be right home afterward."

She hangs up, grabs the kids' jackets from the hooks by the back door, and walks toward them just in time to see Max's chubby fist topple Victoria's block tower.

"Look what you did!" Victoria shrieks, and turns on him swiftly. She slams a wooden block into his forehead.

Max erupts into a wail.

"Victoria!" Tasha yells, and, before she knows it, her hand has lashed out at her daughter, smacking her in the arm.

Now Victoria is crying as loudly as Max is.

Tasha pulls the baby from his Exersaucer and cradles him in her arms, kissing the splotch on his forehead that is already bright red.

"You hit me!" Victoria screams, her accusing blue eyes filled with tears. "You hit me!"

"I'm sorry, Victoria," Tasha says, her head throbbing. She rubs her temples with one hand, patting Max's back with the other. "I didn't mean to hit you. But I was angry—"

"You hit me!"

"You hit your brother!" Tasha shoots back, her patience completely dissolving. "He's just a baby. You hurt him!"

"You hurt me!"

"I didn't mean to," Tasha says again.

And she *didn't* mean to. She and Joel had agreed, when Hunter was born, that they would never hit their children in anger, though both of them had been spanked by their own parents. But that generation simply hadn't known any better. They hadn't read countless reports about children and violence and abuse. . . .

Never, until now, has Tasha ever come close to hitting one of her children.

Now her little girl is gazing at her with an expression of stark betrayal, and all she can think is that she needs to get away. She needs help; she needs a break; she needs to get out of this house and away from these children before she snaps.

But there is no escape.

This is her responsibility, her life.

There is nobody she can ask for help.

She certainly can't turn to Joel's parents. Her own widowed mother is five hundred miles away and working full time as a nurse. Her friends are busy with families of their own; she's long been out of touch with her former colleagues.

As for her husband, well, she might as well be a single mother for all the emotional support he provides these days.

Tasha takes a deep breath, counts to ten, and makes room in her arms for Victoria.

"I'm sorry, baby," she says as she strokes her daughter's hair. "Mommy will never hit you again. I don't know what got into me."

Chapter Four

Mitch's sneakered feet plod along the walk as he leaves the red brick school and heads toward the row of yellow buses parked at the curb.

His hands are jammed into the pockets of his worn jeans and his eyes are fastened on a worn spot in the toe of one of his sneakers. It figures these crummy shoes would wear out so fast. He's tried explaining to his mother that he needs good ones, like the kind with the soles you inflate with a built-in pump, but she says they're way too expensive.

She also said, "Don't you dare ask your father to buy you sneakers." Which was strange, because Mitch knew his father would be happy to buy them for him. Plus, he thought, back when Mom first told him he was going to meet his dad, that she wanted his dad to help them buy stuff they couldn't afford. But then that changed last spring for some reason, and lately his mother has been asking him not to go telling his dad that there's specific stuff he needs or wants that she can't afford—like the pump sneakers.

Instead she bought him these generic white shoes with some stupid bright blue stitching that he hates. All the other kids make fun of these shoes—especially Robbie Sussman. Which is why one of Mitch's cheap, ugly shoes found its way in front of one of Robbie's top-of-the-line Nikes as he was running the relay in gym class this morning.

Seeing the look of shock on Robbie's big, dumb oval face as he went flying forward was almost worth having to stay after class.

Almost.

Mitch's gut is killing him now from doing two hundred sit-ups for Mr. Atkins, the gym teacher.

"Why'd you trip Sussman, Bailey?" Mr. Atkins asked.

Then, when Mitch fumbled for answers, Mr. Atkins said the ones he gave— *"I don't know,"* and *" 'cause I felt like it"*—weren't good enough. He wanted a real reason before he would let Mitch go.

Finally, Mitch told Mr. Atkins the truth—well, part of it.

"I did it because he deserves it."

"Why does he deserve it?"

Because he has everything. Everything. And I have nothing. And he doesn't let me forget it. That's why.

But Mitch didn't say that. He would never say anything like that to a teacher—not that most teachers seem to give a you-know-what about anything Mitch has to say.

Mr. Atkins is okay, but Mrs. Chandler, who teaches art and music, hates him. So do the lunchroom monitors, but then, they're these grouchy old ladies who pretty much seem to hate everybody.

Then there's Miss Bright. Half the time she acts like she's mad at him, the other half like she feels sorry for him. Mitch doesn't know which is worse.

In his bookbag are a note she wrote to his mother—it's in a sealed envelope—and a fractions worksheet. He tucked that into the front zippered pocket beside the duplicate worksheet he brought home a few nights ago—the worksheet he was supposed to work on with Mom.

But as usual she didn't get home till after he fell asleep on the couch watching a World Wrestling Federation match, and when she woke him up and sent him to bed, he went. No way was he going to tell her about some dumb worksheet then.

Miss Bright gave him an *F* because it wasn't done.

Big deal. Big deal if he fails some stuff. Big deal if he flunks out of school. Then he can just stay home and play Super Nintendo instead.

Hey, maybe if he's not stuck going to Townsend Heights Elementary every day, his mother will let him spend more time out at his father's place.

Yeah, right.

And maybe Mom will be waiting for me at home today with fresh-baked cookies.

His mother hates his father more than . . .

Well, he can't even think of anything to compare it to. He just knows that anytime his father shows up to get Mitch—or even if Mitch just mentions his father's name—she gets this awful look on her face. Her mouth looks all sucked in and her eyes turn into little slits, and she either says something nasty about Dad or she changes the subject.

"Hey, Mitch!"

He doesn't even look up at the sound of his name. Whoever it is, he figures, is probably yelling to Mitch

Schmidt, a kid who shares his first name—though not much else.

Mitch S., who lives in one of those big old houses in the best part of town, has two parents who are still married, a bunch of brothers and sisters, and about a zillion friends. Everyone loves him, including the art teacher *and* the lunch room monitors.

"Mitchell!"

There's something familiar about the voice, though—something that makes Mitch look up.

"Dad!" He breaks into a run when he spots his father at the curb, waving.

"Hey, buddy." His dad claps him on the shoulder.

"Hi." Mitch claps him back.

Sometimes he wishes his father would just hug him, but he never does. Not since the first time Mitch ever saw him, when his dad put his arms around him and squeezed, but only for, like, a second.

Maybe he's just not the hugging type.

"What are you doing here?" he asks his father, seeing that he's wearing jeans and a sweatshirt instead of a suit and tie. A Mets cap sits on top of his dark, curly hair, and there's a dark shadow on his face, like he didn't shave today.

He should be at work out on Long Island at this time on a weekday, Mitch thinks. So what's up?

"I had the day off," his father tells him.

"Yeah? How come?"

"How come?" He shrugs. "Because I felt like taking it. You can do that when you're the boss, you know that, Mitch?"

His father says it like he wants Mitch to be a boss someday. Like that would make him really proud.

He's always talking about giving Mitch a job in his

business. Ferrante and Son, he wants to call it. Mitch figures that by the time he's old enough to go into the business, he'll know what his father actually does. Right now all he knows is that it has something to do with computers. Something boring. His father has tried to explain it a couple of times, but Mitch had trouble paying attention.

"Hey, Mitch, instead of riding the bus home today, why don't you come with me and we'll go get some pizza. Or ice cream. Would you like that? A banana split?"

"Well, I don't really like banana splits," Mitch says slowly as he thinks about what his mother would say about him going out for ice cream with his father. Then he wonders about the fact that his father's here on a weekday when he's not supposed to be.

Suddenly a terrible thought pops into his head. A thought so scary he gets a really bad pain in his chest, near his heart.

"Why are you really here, Dad? Did something happen to my mother?"

His father's black eyes get that even blacker look that always pops up when Mitch mentions something about his mom. It's pretty clear he can't stand her.

But if something happened to her, somebody like the police, or the school would probably call him to come and get Mitch, right? Is that the real reason he's here?

"Your mother is fine, as far as I know," his father says. "She's probably working, as usual. Right?"

Mitch lets out a big blast of breath, knowing Mom is okay. "Yeah, she's working. I mean, she works every day."

His father looks like he's about to say something other than what he does end up saying, which is, "Well, I thought that I'd take you out for ice cream and then drop you off at home. That way, you won't have to spend forty-five minutes riding around town on the bus. You'll get home at the same time you always do."

Mitch shrugs. "Okay, but . . ."

"What?"

"I don't have to have a banana split, right?"

His dad smiles. "No, you can have whatever you want. Just . . . Mitch . . . do me a favor."

Uh-oh.

"What?"

"Don't tell your mother I was here. Okay? We'll just keep it between us."

"Whatever."

Now it's his dad's turn to look relieved.

Mitch hopes he'll remember not to slip to Mom. There's a lot of stuff Mitch doesn't tell her these days.

So what's one more little secret?

Margaret rounds the corner from the shadowy back hall to the high-ceilinged kitchen and crashes into someone.

Owen's mother.

Louisa Kendall gasps and jumps back as Margaret reaches out, only intending to steady her. She's holding a cup and saucer, the contents now spreading in a dark stain across the front of her white silk blouse.

"Oh, Mrs. Kendall, I'm so sorry," Margaret says.

The woman says nothing, just puts the china aside with a clatter and grabs a dishtowel from the hook by the stainless-steel restaurant-type range. She starts blotting at her blouse, making sputtering noises of disgust.

"Was it coffee?" Margaret asks, running water over a wad of paper towels.

"Tea," she says curtly. She ignores the paper towels Margaret offers.

After a moment, Margaret tosses them into the garbage can. Looking around the spacious room, bent on avoiding eye contact with Owen's mother, her gaze falls on a large object in the far corner by the mudroom entrance.

"Is that Schuyler's stroller?"

"Yes."

"Where did it come from? I thought it was being held as evidence."

"The police have released it and somebody brought it back here." She continues to dab at her blouse.

Clenching her fists to keep her hands from trembling, Margaret crosses the room and peers into the carriage. It's a top-of-the-line model, a blue Peg Perego—not that Margaret ordinarily knows anything about such things. However, she happens to be the one who bought the carriage for Jane, presenting it to her sister at a baby shower shortly before her niece was born.

There's a large pouch underneath the stroller. In it Margaret sees several items.

"I'll empty this for Owen," she murmurs, not turning to look at his mother, now blotting her blouse by the sink, where she's running the water.

There is no reply.

She reaches into the carriage and takes out a purple Playtex sippy cup. Unscrewing the lid, she sees less than an inch of some yellowish liquid. Sniffing, she realizes it's apple juice. She sets it on the counter.

Next she pulls out a pink-and-white monogrammed wool carriage robe, and a small, stuffed fleece bunny. Beneath those items are a silver rattle from Tiffany's and a wooden Humpty Dumpty puzzle. At the very bottom of the pouch is a small bag containing a package of disposable wipes and a single Huggies diaper.

Her heart pounding, Margaret lines up everything on the counter and looks it over again.

"What are you doing?" Owen's mother asks sharply.

Margaret looks up to find Louisa Kendall's dark gaze probing her, as though . . . *as though she's suspicious of me,* Margaret realizes, and a sudden tide of panic washes over her.

"I told you," she says, keeping her voice steady, "I thought I'd empty the carriage so that Owen won't have to deal with it."

"What makes you think he won't want to deal with anything involving his own daughter?"

"I'm trying to help, Mrs. Kendall."

Margaret half-expects a perfunctory *Call me Louisa.* When it doesn't come, she realizes that of course it never will.

To Owen's mother, she is a nobody, because she is still—and most likely always will be—an Armstrong. Though Jane and Margaret share a gene pool, an upbringing, and yes, a life-altering tragedy, the Kendalls see Jane differently, simply by virtue of their son having saved her from a life in the shadow cast by their father's suicide.

None of them—not Mother nor Margaret nor Jane— ever suspected that Daddy, in the years leading up to his death, had lost a vast chunk of the Armstrong fortune through a series of poor investments. Faced with selling the enormous stone manor house that had been in his family for a century, and thus relinquishing the Armstrongs' long-held position amid Westchester's most elite families, he had chosen the only alternative.

Margaret will wonder for the rest of her life whether,

in his muddled last days, he was aware that he had let the larger of his two life insurance policies lapse. Had he realized that his death would leave his wife and daughters not just grief-stricken and ostracized, but also hopelessly in debt? Or did he kill himself so that they could cash in on insurance he thought he still had?

Margaret chooses to believe the latter: that her father was an unselfish soul making the supreme sacrifice for his family. She rarely allows herself to consider the alternative, to think that he simply didn't care what became of any of them in the certain turmoil after his death.

He was buried in the vast network of cemeteries in northern Westchester County, in a grave ironically only about a mile from Townsend Heights, where Jane settled with Owen so many years later.

Mother sold the house, the horses, the cars, and paid off the debts. Far from penniless, but no longer as wealthy as they had been all their lives, the three Armstrong women moved into a much smaller home in a respectable neighborhood. Soon after, Mother wed Teddy, whose wealth eclipsed even that of the Kendalls, and moved to his family's castlelike estate outside London. And of course, Jane married Owen.

Margaret continues to live in the two-story stucco house she has never liked; it has always felt cold and empty to her, even during the brief time she shared it with her mother and sister.

Lucky Jane, to have this sprawling, elegant yet comfortable home—and Owen to share it with.

"Where is Schuyler?" Louisa Kendall's voice intrudes on Margaret's thoughts, startling her.

"She's upstairs, with Minerva."

"Who's Minerva?"

"The housekeeper. She picked up Schuyler when she woke up from her nap."

"You left her with the housekeeper?"

"Schuyler sees her every day. She seemed comfortable with her," Margaret replies.

More comfortable than she is with me, she adds silently. Her niece, who had woken crying, buried her head in the other woman's shoulder when Margaret offered to take her.

"A housekeeper isn't a nanny," Louisa points out.

"Jane didn't ever want to hire a nanny," Margaret replies, though she has no idea what that has to do with anything. "She wanted to take care of Schuyler on her own, without help."

"Well, Jane isn't here," Owen's mother says. "And Schuyler needs comfort from someone other than a maid. I'll go to her."

Margaret knows little about the relationship between Owen's mother and Schuyler; Jane has never discussed it. Margaret doubts that Louisa Kendall is a hands-on grandmother, the type whose mere presence would bring comfort to a child missing its mother. She says nothing, though, just watches the woman leave the kitchen, heading down the hallway to the stairs.

After a moment, alone in the kitchen, Margaret turns her attention back to the things she has removed from Schuyler's carriage. After a moment, she picks up the baby's soft pink blanket, holds it to her cheek, and absently strokes it.

Karen Wu stands at her kitchen sink dumping a few ounces of unused soy formula from Taylor's bottle. She wrinkles her nose as the familiar smell of the stuff wafts up. No wonder Taylor made a face and pushed it away just now.

Then again, she usually gulps down the soy formula hungrily—as opposed to how she reacted when Karen tried nursing her during the first few weeks of her life. Armed with statistics showing that a mother's milk is far better than formula for newborns, Karen was determined to breast-feed her daughter at least through the first year. But when the baby grew increasingly fussy and constantly spit up, Ben Leiberman switched her to a soy formula despite Karen's reluctance.

Sure enough, that did the trick. Taylor's been on soy ever since, and she's thriving.

Today, however, she has had little appetite. When Karen returned from Starbucks this morning, Tom told her the baby wasn't interested in her bottle. She must be coming down with something.

Karen's nieces were sick with some sort of stomach bug late last week, and they dropped by on Sunday. Karen's younger sister, Lisa, mentioned their illness in passing. It would never occur to her to keep the girls home for fear of spreading germs to Taylor. Carefree Lisa never has been very responsible.

Unlike Karen, who seems to spend her days worrying. There are just so many dangers in the world—so many reasons to protect her tiny daughter. . . .

A door slams outside. Karen, running water into the empty bottle, looks up at the sound and notices a teenage boy emerge from the house next door. It's Jeremiah, Fletch Gallagher's nephew. He's a gangly sort of kid, she thinks, watching him make his way across the yard. At that awkward age, although even if he weren't, he wouldn't have his uncle's lady-killer looks.

She wonders if Rachel will call him to babysit. After she

made the recommendation this morning, she thought better of it. For one thing, she doesn't know the boy very well—has only met him a few times in passing. Not that Rachel is fussy about things like that. She's the total opposite of Karen, never seeming to fret about things like references even when it comes to her kids.

Karen watches Jeremiah Gallagher open the door to a wooden storage shed among the trees near the back of the property line next door. The boy disappears inside, closing the door behind him.

That seems odd. What can he possibly be doing in there? The space has to be only a few feet square, and probably houses a lawnmower, yard tools, that sort of thing. At least, that's what Tom keeps in their shed, Karen muses. But maybe the Gallaghers—

"Karen! Hey, Karen!" Tom shouts urgently from the next room.

"What's wrong?" She turns off the tap and tosses the bottle into the sink.

"Taylor just threw up all over me. Bring something to clean it up!"

Karen grabs a dish towel and hurries into the family room, silently cursing her sister. *Taylor's sick. I just knew it.*

"Mommy, can we have pizza for dinner?" Hunter asks, adding his lunchbox to the clutter on the kitchen counter and unzipping his jacket.

"We'll see." Tasha closes the door behind them, then locks it. There are days when she doesn't bother, but after the whole thing with Jane Kendall . . .

She had the car radio tuned to a local station on the way to the elementary school. The latest reports haven't revealed anything new. The woman is still missing, and her family is expected to give a statement later today. Anyone with any information about the case is asked to call a special toll-free hotline set up by the Townsend Heights police.

Tasha sets the baby on the worn blue-and-white-pinstriped family-room couch and takes off his little blue fleece coat. The fabric is pilling a bit—it's a hand-me-down from Hunter, like pretty much everything else in Max's wardrobe. He really deserves some new clothes, Tasha decides. Maybe she can go down to the mall in White Plains one of these days.

The thought of shopping brightens her spirits . . . but only a little. She'll have to lug Victoria and Max along with her in the double stroller, and they'll last maybe an hour, tops.

"Mommy, help me," Victoria says in a whiny voice, struggling with the buttons on her coat.

Tasha carefully counts to three before saying evenly, "Victoria, don't whine."

"But it's stuck," Victoria whines, and stomps her foot. "I can't do it!"

Patience, Tasha reminds herself as she puts Max on the floor. He crawls across the blue carpet toward a basket of foam blocks, and Tasha kneels to help her daughter take off her pink coat.

"Thank you, Mommy," Victoria says, throwing her arms around Tasha as though she's just been promised unlimited candy for dinner.

"You're welcome." Tasha smiles. All Victoria wants is attention. *This time.* Oh, who knows? Maybe all the time.

Maybe, Tasha thinks, as an oldest child with two younger brothers, she has a hard time relating to the needs of a middle child. She can't remember ever feeling like she needed more than her own parents could give.

In fact, Mom and Dad did a great job with Tasha and her brothers. The boys are both well-adjusted, successful adults with thriving careers. Gregg is a financial analyst in Cleveland with a bubbly, sweet blond wife, and their first child on the way around Christmas. Andrew, a tax accountant, is engaged to marry a hometown girl and lives a few blocks from their mother. He has looked out for her ever since Dad died almost two years ago from the lung cancer that ravaged him long before he drew his last breath.

Since then, Tasha hasn't gone home. She and Joel used to make the trip every Christmas. She used to tease him—back in the teasing days of their marriage—that she only married him because he was Jewish and they would never have to argue over where they would spend Christmas, the way so many of their friends seemed to do. They would simply celebrate Hanukkah whenever it fell in December and always go to Ohio at the end of the month.

Joel loved spending the holidays back in Centerbrook with her family. Her parents' sprawling Victorian would be decked out in garlands and lights, and it always seems to be snowing there. Tasha still remembers the first time she brought him home for Christmas, the year they got engaged. They drove that year, renting a car in Manhattan and playing corny carols on the tape deck the whole nine-hour trip. Every house on the block had a tree glowing in the front window, and her parents' porch roof was lined in colored lights, the old-fashioned kind with the big flame-shaped bulbs.

"It looks like something out of *It's a Wonderful Life,* Tash," Joel said, gazing at it in wonder.

She still remembers how she felt in that moment. As though she were going to spill over into laughter or tears from sheer joy.

How long has it been since she felt that way?

How long has it been since she and Joel went back to Ohio?

They haven't been back since Daddy's funeral. He had died in early December, so close to Christmas that it didn't make sense for them to return for the holiday a few weeks later. Joel had to use his vacation time for the funeral, anyway.

They were planning to go back for Christmas last year, even though Max was a newborn. They had even purchased plane tickets, but it turned out that Joel couldn't take the time away from the office. The agency was pitching new business, an important account that they ultimately won.

That didn't make Tasha feel much better about spending Christmas at home in Townsend Heights, just the five of them. Joel, overworked and exhausted, came down with a miserable cold that the kids promptly caught. Tasha spent Christmas Eve alone in the living room, watching some ridiculous cable movie starring Tim Allen as Santa Claus, drinking too much spiked eggnog, and crying and feeling sorry for herself as she put together the toys Santa would be leaving for the kids.

What a crummy Christmas.

They haven't even discussed what they'll be doing this year. She assumes they'll go to Ohio, but they had better make their airline reservations as soon as possible, come to think of it. It's only two months away. She'll have to talk to Joel about it tonight, along with everything else on her agenda.

Max is playing happily with his blocks. Hunter has

turned on the television set, and he and Victoria are already transfixed by a Disney cartoon. Tasha normally doesn't like them watching TV when Hunter comes home from school, but right now, if it keeps them occupied it's fine with her.

After hanging the coats in the hall closet, where there are somehow never enough empty hangers, Tasha goes into the kitchen. The red light on the answering machine is blinking.

She presses the "Play" button, the tape whirs, and Joel's hurried voice fills the room. "Tasha, Stacey said you called again. Is everything all right? It's been a crazy day. I'm leaving the office now. I have a meeting across town, and then I'm going to try and catch the six forty-four. I'll call if I don't make it."

The six forty-four? That means he'll be home by eight.

Suddenly, the day doesn't seem quite so grim.

Tasha opens the freezer and takes out a package of chicken breasts, putting it into the microwave to thaw. She'll give the kids a frozen pizza, put them down early, and make dinner for herself and Joel so that they can actually have a conversation.

"Can we have Spaghetti-Os?" Lily asks Jeremiah as he opens the wide stainless-steel refrigerator.

"You just had Spaghetti-Os last night," he tells the twins, who are sprawled on the two steps that lead from the kitchen to the adjoining family room. They're both wearing embroidered jeans with ragged hemlines, and short, tight tops that show their stomachs. Melissa would never have let them get away with looking like that, even though it's what all the kids are wearing, but Aunt Sharon and Uncle Fletch don't seem to mind. In fact, it was Aunt Sharon who bought them most of their new clothes.

"So what if we had Spaghetti-Os last night? We bring peanut butter sandwiches to school for lunch every day," Daisy points out. "Peanut butter's healthy, and so is spaghetti. What's the big deal if you eat a lot of something that's good for you?"

Jeremiah, who assumes it matters, but isn't sure exactly why, merely shrugs. He pushes past the cartons of Panda Palace takeout, the diet salad dressings, the imported beer, in search of something to give his stepsisters for supper. Finally, he closes the fridge and says, "Okay, whatever. You can have Spaghetti-Os."

They slap each other's hands in a high five.

As he opens the can, he tells them, "Tomorrow night, you guys are on your own. Tell Aunt Sharon or Uncle Fletch to get you something for dinner before they go out." He has no doubt that his aunt and uncle will have plans—they're rarely if ever home in the evenings. That's fine with him. In fact, he prefers it that way.

"Where will you be?" asks one of the twins—he doesn't bother to turn his head to see which one, and their voices are as identical as their faces.

But it's easy to tell them apart visually ever since Lily impulsively got her reddish curls lopped off a few weeks ago. To Jeremiah, she looks strangely shorn. He can only imagine what her mother would have said about the haircut. Melissa insisted on long hair for the twins and short hair for Jeremiah.

He's been growing his dark hair ever since her death. Now that it's getting shaggy, down past his ears and collar, he's been half-expecting Uncle Fletch and Aunt Sharon to ask him to cut it. But they haven't. At least, not yet.

Dad definitely will, when he gets back from overseas.

With his own military-short buzz, he's as conservative as Melissa was. But who knows when Dad will be back? Maybe by then, Jeremiah will be sick of the long hair and ready to cut it off anyway.

"Jer, I was talking to you! Where are you going tomorrow night?"

"I have to babysit," he tells Daisy.

"Babysit?" She and Lily exchange a glance.

Jeremiah knows what they're thinking. That babysitting is for girls. Well, they're wrong. He scowls and turns his back, dumping the Spaghetti-Os from the can into a small glass casserole dish.

After he hung up with Mrs. Leiberman earlier, Uncle Fletch said, "Babysitting, huh?" in a way that let Jeremiah know he thought it was for girls, too. Jeremiah felt his face grow hot.

Why is it that Uncle Fletch can make him feel so . . . wimpy? Just the way Peter Frost and his friends do. But Uncle Fletch doesn't mean to do it. He's been trying so hard to be a father figure to Jeremiah, who's sure his uncle isn't deliberately making him feel uncomfortable. But every time Uncle Fletch gives him that look—the sort of head-tilted, can't-relate look—Jeremiah feels angry.

"For who?"

Startled, he says, "Huh?"

Daisy repeats, "For who—I mean, you're babysitting for who tomorrow night?"

"For this lady down the street." He sticks the casserole dish into the microwave, sets it for three minutes, and glances at the twins. "When this beeps, serve yourselves."

"Aren't you gonna eat with us?"

"Nah."

"How come?"

"I've got stuff to do upstairs."

"Wait, Jer, we need to ask you something."

He pauses in the doorway. "What is it?"

"We need to get our pumpkin downtown for the judging on Saturday," Daisy says. "Will you help us?"

He hesitates. His sisters grew the giant pumpkin in the backyard of the house where they lived until the fire. They planted it last spring in hopes of winning the cash prize and getting their picture on the front page of the *Townsend Gazette*, a local tradition.

Ironically, before summer's end their mother's photo occupied that spot, above the caption

Melissa Gallagher of Townsend Heights lost her life in a blaze that destroyed her home yesterday.

As for the pumpkin, it got left behind in the small patch of garden behind their house. Jeremiah has walked the twins over every few weeks since they moved, so that they can weed around it. But they haven't mentioned it lately, leading him to think that maybe they've given up on entering it in the contest.

Guess not.

"I don't know," he says. "That pumpkin must weigh a ton. How are we supposed to get it there?"

"We can balance it in our wagon. It's still in the shed there," Lily says, like she's thought the whole thing through.

"Why don't you just ask Uncle Fletch or Aunt Sharon to help you?"

"Don't you want to do it?" Daisy asks, pouting. "You were the one who helped us plant it in the first place."

"Besides, Aunt Sharon always gets her nails done on Saturday mornings, and Uncle Fletch golfs," Lily adds.

"Okay," he says reluctantly. "I'll help you."

He leaves the kitchen, making his way through the big colonial-style house. It's one of the biggest on the block, and one of the oldest, too. Jeremiah wonders if his aunt and uncle will ever move from here. Melissa used to say that they can afford a much fancier place with all the money Uncle Fletch has made in baseball, and that they're just too lazy to go out and buy one.

Jeremiah passes through the big formal dining room, where nobody ever eats, and the sprawling living room with the kind of furniture you can't get comfortable on. Which doesn't matter, because nobody ever really sits in there. The giant-screen TV is in the family room, and there are televisions in all the bedrooms, too, but not in the living room. At the foot of the stairs in the foyer, Jeremiah glances into the adjoining den.

The French doors are closed, as always. Through the glass panels, Jeremiah can see the bookshelves lined with trophies and framed photographs of Uncle Fletch. There are more pictures of him on the wall, and some framed, matted newspaper articles and magazine interviews, too. The furniture is oversize, and upholstered in maroon leather. In one corner is a giant desk, and in another, a row of tall wooden filing cabinets. Jeremiah has never seen his uncle sit at the desk or open a filing cabinet. In fact, he spends very little time in the den. Jeremiah figures the room is pretty much just a shrine to his career as a pro player.

Jeremiah realizes that he has never set foot in the den—not on any of his occasional visits to the house with his dad, and not since he's been living here. Suddenly curious, he reaches out to turn the handle of one of the doors.

It's locked.

He tries the other door. It, too, refuses to budge.

Why would Uncle Fletch need to keep the den locked? None of the other doors in the house are ever locked when the rooms are empty. Not even the master bedroom.

Jeremiah abruptly releases the handle of the French door and turns toward the stairs again. No reason to hang around here wondering about the den now. He can hear his sisters' voices back in the kitchen, chattering.

Jeremiah takes the steps two at a time. He hurries past a row of closed bedroom and bathroom doors. At the end of the hall, he slips into the master bedroom.

Already a familiar guilt has overtaken him, yet he doesn't turn back.

Chapter Five

Dropping her cigarette in the street beside her Honda, Paula steps on it, grinding it out. Then, grabbing her cell phone—an outdated model, far bulkier than George DeFand's sleek state-of-the-art one—she tucks it into her pocket, closes the car door, and walks hurriedly up the sagging front steps of the small clapboard house that sorely needs a paint job. Built around the turn of the century, it must have once been a nice, decent home, conveniently located just a block from Townsend Avenue. Now the small porch is missing countless spindles from its rail, several shutters are hanging crookedly, and there's a huge crack in one of the panels in the round stained-glass window above the double front door.

Mr. Lomonaco, the elderly widower who owns the place, has been in a nursing home in Peekskill for the past two years. Paula has been sending her rent checks to his son in California, who has made it clear that he plans to sell the place as soon as his father dies.

Paula is hoping Mr. Lomonaco will hang on a while longer—not because she particularly likes the crotchety old guy, who has made it clear that he doesn't approve of divorced, working mothers—but because she won't be able to afford the rent once the house is sold.

Apparently Mr. Lomonaco and his son have no idea that with the current market value and scarcity of rental properties in Townsend Heights, they can probably get twice as much as she's paying for the one-bedroom second-floor apartment.

She has no idea where she and Mitch are going to go when they figure that out or sell the house, whichever comes first. She desperately wants to stay in town, but on her current salary she wouldn't be able to afford anything else in Townsend Heights even if there were abundant apartments available. She's been watching the classifieds for the past few months just to get an idea of what's out there, and there hasn't been a single local listing under rentals.

That means she's either going to have to make a lot more money by the time they have to move, or move away and find someplace she can afford—like one of those downscale urban apartment complexes in Yonkers or Mount Vernon. She doesn't think she can stand that; she really doesn't. Mitch would have to switch schools, and she would have to commute to work, and . . .

But maybe it won't happen, she tells herself now as she fishes in the jacket pocket of her suit for the sterling Tiffany keyring she treated herself to on her last birthday. *Maybe we won't have to move out of Townsend Heights.*

She lifts her chin.

Of course we won't. Sooner or later somebody's going to realize

I'm not just some small-town reporter. Somebody's going to finally pay me what I'm worth, and then Mitch and I will get Frank off our backs for good, and we'll live it up.

She checks the mailbox before unlocking the door. It's empty. Good. That means Mitch is home and safely upstairs.

Someday she'll be able to afford a sitter to stay with him after school until she gets home from work. For now she counts on him to take care of himself. If he ever needs anything, he's supposed to either call her on her cell phone or, if he can't reach her, knock on old Mrs. Ambrosini's door. She's in her eighties and lives in the first-floor apartment. She's *always* home, except on Sunday mornings, when her daughter picks her up and drives her the two blocks to Immaculate Conception, the local Catholic church, for mass.

So far, Mitch has never had to knock on Mrs. Ambrosini's door, for which Paula is grateful. The old lady isn't particularly neighborly and doesn't seem fond of children. But at least there's an adult in the house when Mitch is home alone.

Paula steps into the dim vestibule. She can hear the evening news blasting out of Mrs. Ambrosini's apartment. The old woman is practically deaf. There are times when her television is so loud it vibrates Paula's bed through the floor. She used to complain to Mr. Lomonaco about it, but he never did anything. Now there's nobody to complain to, except Mr. Lomonaco's son, and Paula figures he's not likely to care, either.

She walks past the old woman's closed door and starts up the creaky wooden staircase. The steps are treacherously steep, unbroken by landings, just a straight pitch from the first floor to the second. The bannisters are long gone, too. Mr. Lomonaco talked about replacing them, but he never has. She doubts he or his son will ever bother.

Perhaps the stairway was open once, but now that the house is chopped into two apartments, it's enclosed by a clumsily built wall. There's a circular mark on the ceiling where a real light fixture once must have hung; now there's only a naked bulb that does little from its lofty perch to dispel the shadows.

Paula used to fantasize about buying the house herself and restoring it. But much as she would love to own a home of her own in Townsend Heights, she doesn't want it to be this one. Not located here, on a short block dotted with commercial buildings and homes that are too close together and, though not quite shabby, not nearly up to par with the rest of the residences in town.

No, Paula doesn't want this small, scarred old house, situated on a tiny lot between a beauty shop and another old Victorian that provides office space for a dentist, a marriage counselor, and a Realtor.

She desperately wants to live in one of the newer, bigger homes on the outskirts of town—a house in one of the woodsy developments inhabited by seemingly perfect suburban families with their seemingly uncomplicated lives.

She wants that kind of house, that kind of life for herself and for Mitch. It's what he deserves. Hell, it's what *she* deserves.

She's never lived anyplace but an apartment. Not even when she was a little girl. Paula spent most of her childhood in a dingy three-family row house in the north Bronx, raised by an emotionally distant, self-absorbed mother and a seldom-there father who held down two jobs and went out whenever he wasn't working. Especially after Paula's baby sister died in her crib. Both Pop and Mom were heartbroken about that.

They talked for a while about having another baby, but Mom decided she couldn't bear to take a chance. Just in case SIDS really was hereditary, as the doctor had warned them it might be.

So it was just the three of them after that. Paula smiles remembering how excited Pop was when he realized a lifelong ambition and was finally able to move them to Westchester. Paula was a freshman in high school by then, already making plans for college and her journalism career. After she met Frank and moved out, her father stayed in the rent-controlled apartment in a downscale New Rochelle neighborhood until a few years ago, when he hurt his back and was unable to keep working. That was shortly after he was widowed.

He asked Paula to let him move in with her and Mitch. There wasn't much room, and it meant giving Pop the one bedroom while she shared the lumpy pullout couch with her son, but what else could she do? Pop had nowhere else to turn; she and Mitch were his only family after Mom died.

So Pop moved in, exhilarated by the fact that he was actually living in Townsend Heights. He spent his days and nights mingling with the locals, making friends more easily than Paula ever has. He really loved it here.

But in the end, Paula did what she had to do. Anyway, he's better off where he is now. She did the right thing.

She unlocks the apartment door and opens it, stepping into the small hall. "Mitch?"

"In here."

He's in the living room, as always, perched in front of the television watching one of those half-hour tabloid entertainment news programs.

"Hi," Paula says, dumping her bag on a worn chair and kicking off her shoes. She allows herself to wiggle her liberated nylon-clad toes, then reluctantly pushes them back into her black leather pumps. The heels are higher than she's used to, and the shoes might be a size too small, she realizes. But they were such a good bargain, and they looked so classy that she couldn't resist them.

"Hi, Mom." Mitch glances briefly away from the television screen.

"Did you eat dinner?"

"Yeah."

"What did you have?"

He shrugs, glued to the TV.

Paula frowns and walks into the kitchen. There's a sprinkling of crumbs on the ancient gas stove and cheap Formica countertops. An open package of American cheese and an almost-empty tub of margarine sit on the counter next to the fridge. A greasy frying pan soaks in the stained porcelain sink, and a plate—chipped, of course; they all are—sits on the already-cluttered table. On the plate are the crusts of a grilled cheese sandwich.

Paula closes her eyes briefly and yawns, exhausted.

She hasn't slept in . . . God, how long? How long since she had a good night's sleep? Has she ever?

She wearily picks up the plate and deposits it in the sink, then turns on the water to rinse it, careful not to splash on her suit. She has to wear it to the press conference, which is starting in—she glances at the clock on the stove, then automatically adds five minutes because it loses time—forty-five minutes.

She has to make arrangements for Mitch to stay with Blake, has to pack his things and get him over there. Still, forty-five minutes is plenty of time.

She lights a cigarette, then goes to the phone and dials

Blake's number again. She's been trying it for the past two hours, every time she can manage to get to a phone. Nobody's ever home.

"Who are you calling?" Mitch asks from the doorway. There's a commercial on the television in the living room now; she can hear Old Navy's latest theme song.

"I'm trying to reach Blake's house." She reaches for an ashtray. "You don't know if they had plans to do something tonight, do you?"

Mitch shrugs. "How come?"

"I need you to stay there again," Paula says, as the phone rings for the second time in her ear.

Come on, answer, she urges silently as she walks back to the sink, holding her cigarette in her left hand while she dumps the dirty water out of the frying pan with her right. "Mitch, you know, if you're old enough to make your own supper, you're old enough to clean up the mess."

He doesn't reply, just stands in the doorway glowering. He starts toward the table, and there's something furtive about the way he's walking that makes her look up sharply.

She spots an envelope and a sheet of paper amidst the clutter on the table, right before Mitch snatches them up and glances at her to see if she noticed.

"What is that?" she asks, as the phone rings again in her ear.

Where is Blake's family at this hour on a week night? They're always home . . .

"It's nothing. Just homework."

"Your fractions worksheet," Paula tells him. "I know all about it. I had a talk with Miss Bright today."

"Yeah, she told me."

"What's in the envelope?"

"Just some dumb note she wrote to you."

Great, Paula thinks. *You mean we didn't cover everything in this morning's conference?*

"Did you read it?" she asks Mitch, resting her cigarette in the ashtray and holding out her hand expectantly.

"Nope." He hesitates before placing the envelope in her palm.

"Then how do you know it's dumb?"

"Because everything about Miss Bright is dumb. I hate her."

Paula couldn't agree more.

Frustrated by the still-ringing telephone at her ear, she abruptly hangs up the receiver and turns her attention to the note.

It's written in teacher-perfect penmanship on lined, parchment-thin, old-lady-style lavender stationery.

> *Dear Ms. Bailey,*
>
> *In light of Mitchell's recent problems in school and the rushed quality of our meeting today, I would like to arrange another, more lengthy conference in the near future, preferably with the vice principal and school psychologist also in attendance. I sincerely hope that Mitchell's father will be able to join us as well, as I feel it is important for both parents to be involved in this matter. Please call the school to schedule the appointment through the secretary at your earliest convenience.*
>
> *Yours truly,*
> *Florence Bright*

Paula's hands shake with anger.

She snatches the cigarette from the ashtray and takes a deep drag.

She rereads the note.

"What's wrong, Mom?"

"Nothing," she says, tossing it aside—for now. "I have to work tonight, Mitch. There's a press conference I can't miss."

"Is it about that lady who jumped off the cliff?"

Startled, she glances at him. He wears a matter-of-fact expression. "How do you know about that?"

"Some kids at school were talking about it."

"They said she jumped off the cliff?"

"Yeah, either that or some crazy killer got her and dumped her body."

"Mitch! Don't talk like that!" Paula clenches her jaw so hard it hurts. "You're a nine-year-old boy. You shouldn't even be *thinking* about things like that."

He shrugs. "So I have to stay at Blake's house again?"

"If I can reach them. I don't know where they can possibly be."

"Maybe they're not answering the phone."

"Why wouldn't they answer the phone?"

"Maybe they know it's you. They've got that caller ID thing now, you know. They can tell who's calling when the phone rings. Last night Blake's mom didn't pick up for his dad's mother when she called. She said she wasn't in the mood to talk to her."

"Well, I'm not Blake's grandmother," Paula says, irritated.

"Maybe they don't want to talk to you, either. Maybe they know you're going to ask if I can spend the night there again, and they're sick of me doing that."

"That's ridiculous." Paula picks up the phone and dials again, rapidly punching out the numbers as she glances at the clock.

There's no answer.

Mitch mutters something as she hangs up the phone again.

"What did you say?" she asks him.

"Nothing."

But it wasn't nothing. She thought she heard the word *dad*. He said something about Frank.

"What did you say, Mitch?" she repeats icily.

"I *said*, I should've gone to Long Island with my dad if you weren't gonna be home tonight."

"That's ridiculous. You know you don't go to Long Island on weeknights." Paula tries to think of somebody else she can leave him with.

"I'm going to call Lianne," she tells Mitch.

"I thought you can't afford to pay her."

"I can't. But I'm desperate." She opens a drawer and pulls out the local phone book, looking up the number of the high school girl down the street. Lianne has sat for Mitch once or twice, but only in a pinch. The first time Paula went to pay her, she nearly gasped when Lianne said she charged ten dollars an hour. Paula had figured the rate at half of that.

Lianne answers the phone on the first ring, sounding breathless.

"Hi, this is Paula Bailey down the street. How are you, Lianne?"

"Oh, hi. I was actually just running out the door. I have play practice."

"Play practice?" *Damn, damn, damn.*

"For the junior class play. We're doing *Our Town*. I'm playing—"

"Can you skip it, Lianne? I'm desperate for a sitter for Mitch."

"Tonight? I can't. We only have practice every other

night because we have to share the auditorium with the debate club and—"

"Okay," Paula cuts her off. "Never mind. But listen, if you don't have play practice tomorrow night, can you sit for Mitch then?"

"Sure. I really need the money."

So do I, Paula thinks. But if Lianne is free tomorrow night, she'll use her. Which doesn't solve the problem of what to do with Mitch tonight.

She hangs up. That's it. She can't come up with anyone else who can possibly watch Mitch, especially on such short notice. For a moment, she's wistful about her father. Living with him wasn't easy, especially toward the end, but at least he was a built-in babysitter.

Well, the press conference won't last all night. What if . . .

Well, maybe she can leave Mitch home alone—

No.

Not at night. She can just imagine what would happen if anyone ever got wind of that. Especially Frank.

"Did you do your homework?" she asks Mitch abruptly.

"Not yet."

"Is that the fraction worksheet?" she gestures at the sheet of paper he's still holding.

He nods.

"Okay, pack that into your bookbag, along with the rest of your homework, and maybe a book to keep you occupied."

"A book?"

He doesn't read. She knows that.

"Okay, then a magazine. Or something. Just get some stuff ready to bring with you."

"Where am I going?"

"You're coming with me."

"Where to?"

"To a police press conference. You can sit down someplace and wait for me."

He groans. "I don't want to go out, Mom. I'm tired."

"You don't have a choice, Mitch. It isn't up to you. This is my job. Do you understand that? It's what I have to do. Go get your things together."

"But—"

"Go."

He shuffles out of the kitchen.

Paula stubs out the cigarette, realizing she's hungry. She can't wait till later. Her stomach is growling.

She opens the refrigerator and looks for something to grab on the run. There's nothing. Not even an apple. She really needs to get some groceries into the house . . . but when? And with what money?

She takes out a can of Diet Coke. *Some dinner,* she thinks as she opens it and takes a gulp.

"Hurry up, Mitch," she calls in a warning voice, sensing that he's parked himself in front of the TV once again.

"I should've gone to Long Island with my dad if you weren't gonna be home tonight."

His words echo in her mind, and she frowns. Why had that popped out? There's something about the way he said it—almost as if . . .

No. He couldn't have seen Frank today . . . could he?

Of course not.

But it almost sounded like he had.

You're just being paranoid, Paula tells herself. *Frank knows he'd better keep his distance unless he has a scheduled visit.*

He saw Mitch on Sunday. Mitch isn't supposed to go to his father's again until Friday evening.

Although, with this Kendall thing happening, it would

be convenient if Paula could ship Mitch out of here a day or two early. . . .

No way. The last thing she intends to do is send her son to his father's just because she has to work overtime. That would give Frank ammunition for his custody case when the time comes.

She drains the can of soda in one long gulp and crumples it in her fist with a satisfying crunch. *There's only one way he's going to take my son away,* she tells herself vehemently, *and that's over my dead body.*

"Excuse me . . . I have to go now," Minerva announces in her thick Hispanic accent.

Margaret, seated at the kitchen table with a cup of coffee, looks up to see the housekeeper standing in the doorway, Schuyler balanced on her hip.

The baby is wearing a fuzzy pink blanket sleeper and her hair looks damp, as though she's just been bathed.

"I need to go," Minerva says again, an expectant note in her voice.

Margaret nods, uncertain what the woman wants of her. Does she get paid by the day? Or does she need a ride home?

"You take her," Minerva says then. She crosses to the table and holds out the baby.

"Oh! All right . . . Come to Auntie Margaret, Schuyler," Margaret says awkwardly, reaching up.

The baby squirms and tries to pull away, clinging to Minerva's neck.

"It's all right," Margaret tells her, in a high-pitched voice that sounds fake even to her own ears.

"I can't find Mr. Owen." Minerva tries to wrestle herself from the little girl's grasp.

"He's gone downtown. There's going to be a press conference. His parents went with him."

When Owen stuck his head into the kitchen a short time ago to tell Margaret he was leaving, she almost offered to go with him. Not that she wanted to be a part of something like that, facing the glare of the cameras and the swarming reporters and the probing, painful questions.

She briefly considered going anyway, just . . . to give Owen support. To be there for him.

But then his mother popped up behind him and led him away quickly, telling Margaret, "We'll be back as soon as we can."

And when they do come back, her mother will be here. Margaret is expecting the car service to show up from the airport at any moment now.

She considered drinking something stronger than coffee, perhaps a stiff single-malt scotch, to help brace herself for the impending arrival of Bess Wright-Douglas. But she's never been a drinker, and now isn't a good time to start. Besides, she doesn't believe that any amount of alcohol can numb her sufficiently.

She takes Schuyler from Minerva. The baby is wailing pitifully, trying to escape Margaret's lap.

"She doesn't know me very well," she tells the housekeeper above Schuyler's anguished cries.

"She misses her mama." Minerva crosses herself and adds, her voice choked, "God bring her home safely."

Margaret averts her gaze, uncomfortable with the profound display of emotion—and religion. She doesn't know what to say.

But the housekeeper is leaving, pulling her coat from a closet by the back entrance and putting it on. "She already had her bath," she says in her accented English, gesturing toward the miserably sobbing Schuyler, whose arms are outstretched toward her.

"All right," Margaret says over the baby's wails.

"I can't stay," the woman says, although she seems to hesitate in front of the door, torn. "I have to catch my train back to the Bronx."

"It's all right," Margaret tells her. "Go. She'll be fine with me."

Minerva lingers another moment, looking worried, as though she wants to say something but is afraid to. Margaret tries her best to manage Schuyler, who is desperately trying to free herself from Margaret's grasp.

Finally, Minerva goes, promising to be back in the morning.

As the door closes behind her, Schuyler erupts in a shriek, attempting to hurl herself from Margaret's arms.

"Shhhh." Margaret pats Schuyler's silky blond hair strongly scented with baby shampoo. "Don't worry, little girl. You're going to be okay. No matter what."

Left alone in the huge house with the crying, squirming baby, Margaret rises from her chair, feeling anxious. She walks across the kitchen to a window that overlooks the large fenced back yard and peers out.

"Look, Schuyler, see? See outside?" she asks, though she can see nothing but blackness because of the glare on the glass. She wonders whether the crowd of media people is still congregated out front. Surely it must have thinned by now. Wouldn't most of the reporters have gone to the press conference?

Schuyler continues to weep, holding herself stiffly in Margaret's arms now as though in an effort to avoid contact.

Margaret fumbles, trying to cuddle her yet uncertain exactly how to do it.

"Don't cry, Schuyler," she murmurs. "Be happy, sweetie. Be happy. You're going to be just fine."

Isn't that the truth. She thinks about the life ahead for her niece, certain of her destiny. She'll grow up in the privileged Westchester world her mother had before her—and her aunt, too. But Schuyler, unlike Margaret, will fit in. She'll be beautiful and confident, like Jane. She'll grow up to marry a handsome, wealthy man who will adore her and take care of her, and she'll have sweet, beautiful children. She'll have it all.

Just like Jane.

Just like so many of the women Margaret sees every single day—perfect, all of them, with perfect lives, taking it all for granted . . .

Schuyler, oblivious to her gilded future, won't stop screaming.

She pats her niece's head again and looks around the kitchen for a way to distract her. Her gaze falls on the carriage still parked in the corner, and the pile of things she removed from it earlier and set on the counter.

She walks over and picks up the wooden puzzle. "Schuyler, this is Humpty Dumpty. See Humpty Dumpty? Humpty Dumpty sat on a wall; Humpty Dumpty had a great fall; all the king's horses and all the king's men couldn't put Humpty together again."

The baby doesn't seem the least bit comforted by the nursery rhyme. But she does reach out a chubby little hand toward the puzzle, seizing one of the pieces in her fist.

"You want to play with that? Okay. You can hold it if you—"

The ringing of the doorbell reverberates through the silent house.

"Oh. That's Mother." Margaret's voice is flat. She sighs

and, balancing Schuyler on one hip the way she had seen Minerva do, heads toward the front hall.

She opens the door.

"Mother."

"Oh, Margaret. Is there any word?" Bess Wright-Douglas asks, launching herself over the threshold.

She's wearing a smart black suit and perfume, both Chanel, and a string of perfect pearls. But her face, usually impeccably made up, is unexpectedly haggard, her eyes swollen. She's a blue-eyed blonde like Jane, although Margaret has suspected her of dying her hair in recent years, something Bess vehemently denied on the one occasion when Margaret dared bring up the subject. It was probably in response to some subtle dig her mother had directed at her, of course. After all, Margaret never goes on the offensive unless forced to.

"We haven't heard anything yet—"

"I'm just beside myself," her mother wails as the uniformed car service driver deposits her bags just inside the door, tips his hat, and walks off into the night. "And all those people out by the gate—"

"They're still there?" Margaret looks out the open door. In the yellow glow of the streetlight, she can see shadowy figures still congregated beyond the fence.

"They're vultures." She embraces Margaret in a hug that is little more than perfunctory, then wipes tears from her eyes.

"Schuyler, oh, my poor, dear grandchild." Sobbing, Bess holds out her arms toward the baby. "Come to Mere."

Mere. The French word for Mother. Bess announced, shortly after Schuyler's birth, that it was what she would like to be called by her grandchildren. " 'Grandmother'

just sounds elderly,'' she told Jane, who agreed, of course.
Jane has always been willing to please Mother.

"Come to Mere, Schuyler,'' Bess urges again.

Margaret half-expects her to cling to Margaret, the
way she did to Minerva. But Schuyler, still sniffling and
whimpering, goes to the grandmother she's only seen a
handful of times in her life.

"What is this?'' Bess asks, as the baby settles into her
arms, clutching her hand to her mouth. "What is she
chewing on?''

"It's a piece of one of her puzzles,'' Margaret tells her.

"Where did she get it?'' Bess seizes the baby's tight
fist and pries it open. "Surely you didn't give it to her?''

Margaret falters. "She picked it up. I let her have it.
It's hers.''

"It can't be. Look at the size of it.''

Margaret looks at the puzzle piece, and then, blankly,
at her mother. Her heart is pounding and it's all she can
do not to flee. She can't deal with this. She can't. Not
now.

"What was I thinking? Of course you wouldn't know.
You've never had children.'' Her mother smiles faintly,
as though her words are meant to exonerate Margaret,
but Margaret hears the accusation in her tone.

You've never had children.

Never been married.

Never done most of the things that Jane has done, the
things that have made their mother so proud.

"What wouldn't I know, Mother?'' Margaret manages
to keep her voice even, watching her mother struggle to
remove the puzzle piece from the baby's clenched fingers
despite Schuyler's angry shouts of protest.

"You wouldn't know that she can't have a puzzle with
pieces this size,'' she says above the baby's howls. "See?

It's much too small. A choking hazard. The puzzle belongs to an older child."

"It was hers," Margaret says succinctly. "It was with her things. Otherwise I wouldn't have given it to her." She raises her voice almost to a shout on the last part, partly in anger, and partly to be heard above Schuyler's renewed screams over having been deprived of her prize.

"Please take this, Margaret," her mother says, pressing the saliva-soaked wooden piece into her hand. "I'll calm the poor baby. Where is Owen?"

"He's with the police. Holding a press conference."

"Oh, my God." Her mother chokes up again. "If anything has happened to Jane, I'll . . ." She trails off.

"You'll what, Mother?" Margaret asks icily, somehow unable to help herself.

You'll kill yourself, like Daddy did? she wants to ask but can't quite bring herself to utter the harsh phrase.

She doesn't have to. Unrestrained resentment mingles with the suffering in the flooded blue gaze her mother levels at Margaret. She says nothing, only walks away down the hall, cooing to Jane's sobbing baby.

Seated in the living room in front of the television, Tasha nearly bolts from the couch when she hears a noise outside. She grabs the remote control and mutes the volume on the television, then cocks her head, listening.

It must be Joel, she tells herself, glancing at the clock on the mantel. About a quarter after nine. It has to be him. She heard a train whistle a short time ago and wondered if he was on it. He sure as hell wasn't on the six-forty-four. Or the seven twenty-one. Nor has he called to tell her he'll be late, as he promised to do.

Meanwhile, here she is, jumping at every little sound,

glancing constantly out the window at the empty, silent street, wondering if whatever happened to Jane Kendall could possibly happen to somebody else. Somebody like Tasha, alone in the house at night.

Well, not alone. The kids are here. She put them to bed early, giving Max some Tylenol to make sure he would sleep well, poor baby. That tooth is giving him such a hard time. . . .

There's another thump outside.

Tasha puts the remote on the coffee table and walks toward the back door. It swings open just as she reaches it.

She screams.

"What the hell?" Joel sticks his head in. "Tash, it's me."

"Oh, my God." She clutches her collar. "You scared me!"

"Obviously. But who else would it possibly be?" He locks the door behind him and shrugs out of his black Burberry trench coat. Darkly handsome in his charcoal Paul Stuart suit and tie—another post-promotion splurge—a still crisply starched white shirt, and polished black wing tips, he looks as though he belongs someplace else. To someone else. Not in this sticky, crumb-laden suburban kitchen that smells of dried-out chicken casserole, with a wife who's wearing decade-old men's flannel pajamas and hasn't combed her hair since this morning.

"Sorry I'm late," he says, depositing his briefcase on the kitchen table next to Hunter's finished homework and packed vinyl lunch bag for tomorrow morning.

Tasha doesn't want to be living a horrible cliche. She desperately doesn't want to be the wife stuck at home in the suburbs, clock-watching and wondering about her husband and his pretty secretary.

The wife is always the last to know.

Or so the saying goes. But it doesn't apply to her. Not her. Not Joel.

"Tash?"

"Mmm?"

"I said I'm sorry I'm late."

"It's okay," she says, biting back, *I thought you were going to call if you didn't make the early train.*

"I tried to call and let you know," he says, as if he's reading her mind. "But my phone battery is dead." As if to punctuate the remark, he pulls his cell phone out of his suit coat pocket and fishes in the utensil drawer for the charger he insists on keeping there, adding to the clutter. He plugs one end into the phone and the other into the wall next to the toaster oven.

Tasha watches him, wanting to ask why he didn't just do the old-fashioned thing and call her from a pay phone in Grand Central, the way he used to before he was promoted to account supervisor and got the cell phone. But maybe she doesn't want to know the answer.

He brushes by her, taking off his jacket and loosening his tie. "I smell chicken."

She sniffs the air. "Really? I smell cologne." An irritating voice in her head wants to know why he would come home smelling of cologne at this hour, after a long day at work.

"Yeah, me too. And the chicken smells better. This stuff is giving me a headache, to tell you the truth. But I had to wear it. It's one of the products for the new account, and I had to go over to the client for that meeting. . . ." He sits on a chair and bends over to untie his shoes.

Cologne. One of the products on the new packaged-goods account he helped to win. That's right. He did mention something like that a while back. Relieved, Tasha turns away before he can glimpse her face and realize what she was thinking.

She doesn't have to worry. She can see in the reflection of the oven door that he isn't even looking at her. Now that his shoes are off, he's rubbing his temples, his eyes closed, as though he's had an exhausting day.

She turns back to him. "Did you hear about Jane Kendall?"

"Jane Kendall?" He frowns. "Who's Jane Kendall?"

"That woman I told you about? From Gymboree?"

He looks vacant, and she realizes that she might not have ever mentioned Jane Kendall to him after all. For some reason, though, she's still irritated when he shakes his head and says, "Never heard of her."

"I definitely told you about her, Joel."

Her insinuation hangs in the air between them. He never listens anymore when she talks to him. He doesn't think anything she has to say is important.

"Maybe you did," he says with a shrug. "What about her?"

"Where are you going?"

"Upstairs to change, as soon as you tell me about this Jane Kendall person."

"You're going to leave your shoes there in the middle of the kitchen floor?"

"No, I'm going to take them with me," he snaps, grabbing them. He heads for the doorway to the hall.

"Joel!"

"What?"

"What are you doing?"

"Taking my shoes with me, like you said."

Seething, she says, "You don't even care what I was about to tell you."

His back to her, he just stands there. Like he's waiting. Or maybe counting to ten before he speaks.

But he doesn't speak.

She strides over to him and grabs his arm. "Joel, I'm trying to tell you that this woman, this friend of mine, just vanished into thin air today from High Ridge Park!"

He looks down at her with an expression she can't read. "What do you mean, she vanished? What happened?"

"Nobody knows. People are saying she might have jumped. Or maybe she was kidnapped. She's from a wealthy family—the Armstrongs—and her husband is one of the Kendalls. The vacuum cleaner family. Rachel told me they're like the Rockefellers or something."

"Rachel would say that."

Joel doesn't like Rachel much. He thinks she's spoiled and a gossip. Which she is, for the most part, but Tasha isn't about to let him deride her friend now. Not when he's behaving in such a frustratingly cold way, as though he couldn't care less that one of his wife's friends has disappeared.

Maybe Jane Kendall isn't exactly a friend, Tasha concedes, but that doesn't mean this hasn't totally upset her. She knows the woman, for Christ's sake. Sees her every week. Watches her playing with her daughter. And now she's—

"Is this why you kept calling me at work today?" Joel asks.

"*Kept* calling you? I didn't *keep* calling you! Is that what Stacey told you?"

"She said you called a few times, yes."

"I needed to talk to you. You could have called back."

"I did."

"At three-thirty this afternoon."

"That was the first chance I had. I was in meetings—"

"You're always in meetings, Joel. Whatever." She waves her hand in dismissal and stalks over to the oven, yanking the door open.

"You have no idea what kind of day I've had, Tasha," he says angrily. "You have no idea what kind of pressure I'm under."

"You have no idea what kind of day I've had, either," she shoots back. "You want to know about pressure?"

"What else happened?"

"You mean aside from Jane Kendall vanishing from the park? Isn't that enough?"

He pauses. "Look, I'm sorry about your friend. I know you're upset. But—"

"The washing machine is broken, Joel." She turns away from the open oven to glare at him.

He stares back at her, almost . . . incredulous.

"I know, it's not even a year old," she says. "I couldn't believe it either."

"What I can't believe is that you're bringing up a broken washing machine as evidence of how stressful your day is. Try managing a thirty-million-dollar advertising account for a bunch of stuffy guys in designer suits."

"Gladly!" Tasha shot back. "And you try staying here for a day, keeping the kids and the laundry and everything else under control without losing it."

Joel just looks at her, then shakes his head and continues into the hall with his shoes dangling from his hand.

Tasha bangs the oven door shut and starts to follow him, then thinks better of it. She's furious, yes, but utterly and completely drained. Too drained to get into an argument with him now.

She stands in the kitchen staring at her clenched fists, hearing his footsteps go steadily up the stairs.

* * *

The phone rings just as Karen takes the last tiny pink Onesie out of the drier. She tosses it into the laundry basket with the rest of the clothes Taylor wore—and vomited on—earlier today. Balancing the basket on her hip, she hurries into the kitchen to answer it.

"It's me," Rachel's voice says.

"Hi, Rach." She sets the laundry on the table and reaches for something to fold. "What's up?"

"I called your neighbor to babysit. He's coming tomorrow night. I just wanted to say thanks. I never thought of him before."

Karen remembers how Jeremiah Gallagher disappeared into the storage shed this afternoon. Should she mention it to Rachel? Nah. After all, he wasn't doing anything wrong as far as she knows. It's just a feeling she had.

And maybe Tom is right. He just told her, over a late dinner of takeout sandwiches, that she worries too much.

No, she isn't overly anxious. Just conscientious, she thinks stubbornly. There's a big difference.

She tells Rachel, "I hope it works out," as she matches a pair of tiny socks.

"I'm sure it'll be fine," Rachel says breezily. "I need someone full time, though. I just fired Mrs. Tuccelli. I don't supposed you've run into anyone Mary Poppinsish and unemployed since I saw you this morning?"

"No, but if I do, you'll be the first person I call," Karen says, examining the collar of the pink turtleneck Taylor has been wearing. It's faintly stained, but not too bad. She folds it.

"Okay, thanks. Well, see you."

Karen hangs up and returns to the laundry. Rachel

didn't even ask what's going on with Karen. That's typical, though. Karen used to think Rachel was merely self-absorbed, but lately she wonders if her friend is bordering on a case of narcissistic personality disorder. Karen had a troubled student a few years back who was diagnosed by the school psychologist as having NPD. She shared certain personality traits with Rachel, Karen has noticed lately. Her friend isn't the most empathetic person in the world, and she takes advantage of her household help—and yes, sometimes her friends. Most of the time, she's wrapped up in her own self-importance. And she certainly doesn't react well to criticism.

Karen remembers an incident a while back in Starbucks, when Rachel had spread honey on a piece of bagel she was going to give to Noah. She told Rachel that honey could be toxic to small children, and Rachel snapped at her, saying she knew far more about what to feed children than Karen did. At the time, Taylor was only a few weeks old, as Rachel pointed out. And besides, Rachel was married to a pediatrician.

"You're right about that, Rachel, and you probably know more than I do about a lot of parenting issues, but it could be dangerous to give Noah honey," Karen insisted.

At that, Rachel stormed out in a huff, leaving Karen and Tasha to look at each other and shrug.

"She'll get over it," Tasha said. "She doesn't like to be criticized."

Tasha was right. Rachel got over it. And Karen has never seen her give Noah honey again. She'd be willing to bet that Rachel checked with Ben and discovered Karen was right—not that Rachel would ever be likely to admit it.

In any case, she still considers Rachel a friend. She has her good points, and besides, she lives right down the street. These days, Karen's social calender centers on convenience and on her daughter's schedule. The women she spends time with now tend to be other moms from the neighborhood, which is fine most of the time. But on occasion, Karen longs for the people she has left behind. Since moving to Orchard Lane almost two years ago, Karen has drifted from her circle of city friends, many of whom juggle marriage and babies and careers as she does.

Did, she corrects herself. She's been on maternity leave since last Christmas. She had intended to go back to work two months ago when school started again, but she realized she couldn't leave Taylor behind. Not yet.

Luckily, she's been teaching there long enough for her job to remain secure during the unpaid leave for at least a while longer. And Tom's CPA business has been doing phenomenally well here in the suburbs, so they haven't missed her income. Well enough, he keeps saying, that Karen might not have to go back to work if she doesn't want to.

Does she want to?

Maybe. But not yet.

She folds the last tiny undershirt and picks up the basket, heading up the stairs, suddenly missing her daughter.

The door to Tom's office—a spare bedroom, really— is closed. She can hear his calculator whirring on the other side and knows he won't be coming to bed anytime soon.

She tiptoes down the hall and peeks into the baby's room. Taylor is in her crib asleep. She's lying on her side.

Karen strokes the soft, black fuzz covering her head. "Are you feeling better now, sweetheart?" she whispers. "Is your tummy settling down? Don't you worry. You'll be fine. And Mommy's here to make sure of that. I'll always be here, baby."

A press conference, Mitchell learns, is even more boring than listening to Miss Bright drone on and on about some stupid dead president.

All that happens at a press conference is that a bunch of sad-looking people and some cops and guys in suits stand in front of a microphone in a big room, and they talk, and then they answer questions. Everyone's talking about some lady who's missing from the park, and her husband, the good-looking guy standing with the cops, keeps wiping tears from his eyes. Mitch wonders if he's embarrassed to be crying in front of everyone this way. Grown-ups aren't supposed to cry—especially men. Mom never even does.

Mitch thinks she looks nicer than the rest of the reporters here, and she asks a lot of questions. He knows she's good at this job. She's even won awards for being a reporter.

He mentioned that to his dad this afternoon—partly because his dad said his mother should quit being a reporter and try some other job so she could make more money. Mitch pointed out that she was really good at it, that she had won all these awards.

"Oh, yeah?" his father said. "How do you know that?"

"Because she told me," Mitch said.

His father made this sound that Mitch didn't understand, and he was shaking his head for some reason. So Mitch asked him why.

"You believe everything your mother tells you, Mitch?" his father asked.

Mitch nodded.

"Well, don't."

"What's that supposed to mean?" Mitch asked.

His father shook his head. "Forget it. Just don't bring up your mother to me anymore, okay?"

The press conference is over. Mitch tucks his math work sheet into his notebook and stands up. His mother found him a chair in the back of the room but said she had to sit down in front with the other reporters. Now he's lost sight of her; she's been swallowed up in the crowd that's milling around.

"Hey, kid, be careful," someone barks when Mitch accidentally bumps into him.

"Sorry," Mitch mutters. Where's Mom? He can't wait to get out of here.

He spots her. She's standing talking to two cops, one of them a skinny guy with a blond crewcut, the other a stocky African-American. They're all laughing about something. Mitch taps his mom on the arm.

"Mitch! There you are, sweetie. Guys, this is my son," his mother says. "Mitch, this is Officer Mulvaney and Officer Wilson."

"Hey, buddy," the black cop says. The other one just grins at him. They look a lot different than they did a few minutes ago, when they were answering questions up there. Everyone was in such a gloomy mood then.

"Mom, can we go now?" Mitch asks.

"In a minute. So listen, you'll tip me off if anything happens?"

"Anything for you, Paula," the blond-haired cop, Officer Mulvaney, tells her.

"I'm serious, Brian. I'm local. These guys aren't." She

gestures at the rest of the reporters. "Plus, I'm good at what I do. You never know. I just might stumble across something that can help you with the case."

"Knowing you, Paula, you just might," Officer Wilson says.

"Mom," Mitch says again, tugging at her sleeve. "Come on. It's a school night."

"Go ahead, Paula," Officer Mulvaney says. "Get your boy home. He looks beat."

"So am I," Mom tells him. "It's been a long day. Okay, Mitch, come on, let's go."

Outside, they walk along the street toward home. It's only two blocks away.

It's windy and dark. Leaves make dry, rustling sounds on the sidewalk. Mitch thinks about Halloween, only a few weeks away. Maybe he won't have to make his own costume again this year. Maybe Mom can actually buy him one.

Then again, she'll probably say she doesn't have the money.

Maybe he should just ask Dad for it.

Maybe he should just go live with Dad, he thinks, and then guilt seeps in.

He can't leave his mother. She would be all alone. She needs him.

"Mom?" he asks.

"Hmm?" She sounds like she's busy thinking about something else.

"Can I have a real Halloween costume this year?"

"Maybe."

"Really?" He's shocked. He expected her to say flat-out no.

"I said maybe, Mitch. We'll see, okay?"

She sounds like she's in a good mood. That must be because she's doing so well at her job. He knows work makes her happy.

They walk in silence a while longer. It's a little spooky out here. He shivers.

"Cold?" his mother asks.

"No ... it's just scary," he admits. "You know ... at night. Are you scared?"

"Nope," she says with a shrug.

"Aren't you scared of anything?"

She hesitates. Then shakes her head.

But he can tell she's lying. She's afraid of stuff. She just doesn't want to admit it. She goes around acting brave all the time.

Mitch wishes he could be more like her. Maybe when he's older.

"Is there anything to eat at home?" he asks, suddenly realizing his stomach feels empty.

"Hmm?"

"I'm hungry."

"Me, too," his mother says. "Let's stop and buy a couple of ice-cream bars at the deli, okay?"

An ice-cream bar isn't exactly what he had in mind. At Blake's house there's hot food every night. Like meat loaf and roast chicken.

Mom never makes stuff like that. But Blake's mother doesn't work. She has time to cook. Mom doesn't. Mom doesn't have time for anything—sometimes, not even for Mitch.

"Ice cream would be great," he says, pushing away another stab of guilt.

* * *

"Another beer, Fletch?"

He nods at Jimmy, the bartender, then takes a last gulp from the nearly empty glass in front of him.

The eleven o'clock newscast will be starting in a few minutes. He's tempted to ask Jimmy to raise the volume on the television above the bar, but he thinks better of it. Not that it would arouse suspicion, but you never know. Especially in a town this size.

Fletch leans against the stool's backrest and glances into the mirror on the far wall. He notes that he could use a haircut. He likes a young, longish style, but this is bordering on unkempt. He makes a mental note to call his stylist, Heather, tomorrow. She'll probably be booked, but she'll find a way to fit him in. She always does.

He looks around. Not much of a crowd here at the Station House Inn, so named because it's located in the old brick building that had once housed the Townsend Heights train station.

Well, it's never busy on a weeknight. Fletch scans the few occupied tables—mostly couples sharing deep-fried appetizers and bottles of wine. Perched on the other seats at the bar are a handful of businessmen—probably commuters who walked over for a nightcap after getting off a train at the Metro North station on the opposite side of Townsend Avenue. The hardcore locals still call that the "new" station even though it was built almost two decades ago.

His gaze falls on the only two women at the bar. He doesn't recognize either of them, but that's not unusual. He usually doesn't spend much time here in town from Pitchers and Catchers until late September—or the rest of the year, really.

Hmm. A blonde and a brunette, sitting together, sipping gin and tonic. Both are in their forties, well-dressed, and attractive. He's caught them both sneaking glances in his direction. Now the brunette is at it again.

Fletch smiles slightly at her but turns his attention back to the television set above the bar. He's not encouraging anything. Not here. Not tonight. Especially not with them. No wedding rings on either of them.

"Here you go, Fletch," Jimmy says, setting the foam-brimming glass on the bar.

"Thanks, Jimmy."

The bartender gestures up at the television set, where the newscast is beginning. "You hear about that Kendall woman?"

"Yeah, I heard," Fletch says, reaching for his beer. He glances up at the screen, trying not to wince at the sight of Jane's photograph plastered across it, above a shadowy black graphic that says "Missing."

"Too bad, huh?" Jimmy shakes his head. "What a waste."

"Yeah," Fletch agrees, taking a sip. "What a waste."

He wishes now that he hadn't ordered another beer. All he wants is to be safely back at home, in bed. Preferably alone.

Letterman is over. Tasha stands and turns off the television set, yawning.

This is the first time she's seen *The Late Show* since the baby started sleeping through the night. It came on following the news, and after seeing the extensive coverage of the Kendall disappearance, sleep was the last thing on her mind. So she stayed here in the family room and watched David Letterman, his dry sarcasm a welcome distraction from her fear—and her anger at Joel.

Now she can't delay going up to bed any longer. If she doesn't get some rest, she'll be sorry when the alarm goes off at dawn.

She hasn't seen Joel since he stormed up the stairs earlier. She had been sure he would come back down to get something to eat. Joel never goes to bed hungry. And they rarely go to bed angry at each other.

Maybe, she tells herself as she turns off the light and makes her way to the stairs, *he's up there lying awake. Waiting for me. Ready to apologize.*

She quietly starts up the steps, thinking that if he does apologize, she'll accept it. Life is too short to stay mad. Look at what happened to Jane Kendall.

Then again . . . what *did* happen to Jane Kendall?

Did she jump?

Was she kidnapped?

Murdered?

What if it's none of the above? What if she only made it look like she was dead? What if she had simply had it with her life, so she staged a disappearance as a way of escaping?

That's not likely, Tasha tells herself.

No woman could willingly leave her child, her husband, her home—not when all of it was so perfect.

Or seemed that way.

Maybe that's how my life seems from the outside looking in, too, Tasha thinks. *Maybe the other mothers at Gymboree think I'm perfectly happy. That I've got it all together.*

Don't I?

Not anymore.

Not if the idea of escaping her life can bring even a momentary prickle of interest.

And it does, damn it.

She wonders what it would feel like to get away, just leave it all behind—the broken washing machine and the mountain of laundry and the in-laws and . . .

And Joel?

And the kids?

No.

No!

She cherishes Joel and the kids. They're her life. She would never want to leave them. *Never.*

She'd never do anything to jeopardize what she has.

Or would she?

Fletch.

It always comes back to haunt her. She shoves the thought of him, the image of him, from her mind.

Reaching the second floor, she stops in the shadowy hallway and cracks open the door to the small nursery. Little Max is sound asleep on his back in the crib, his tiny fists clenched at either side of his fat cheeks. She crosses the room and peers at him in the dim light from the night light, pulling the blanket over his chubby belly.

He's precious. So are Hunter and Victoria.

Tasha closes her eyes against a surge of remorse. How could she have even imagined leaving her babies?

And Joel . . .

She loves Joel. Still. After so many years of marriage, and three babies, she loves him. She does.

But he's acting like a stranger lately. He's rarely home. When he is, his mind is someplace else.

Where?

Maybe she doesn't want to know.

She sighs and backs out of the baby's room, her sock-clad feet making not a sound on the pale blue wall-to-wall carpeting.

If Joel is awake, she thinks, heading down the hall to the master bedroom, she'll have a heart-to-heart talk with him. She'll tell him how much she misses him, how much she needs him. Maybe they can talk things through. Maybe he'll be willing to change.

She opens the door.

Joel is in bed, his back to her.

"Joel?"

He doesn't answer.

She stands listening to his breathing. Notices that his soft breaths aren't quite keeping a steady rhythm.

Is he only pretending to be asleep?

"Joel?" she asks again, still quietly.

Nothing.

She turns away and goes into the bathroom, closing the door behind her.

The wind has picked up outside, rattling the windowpanes and gusting through the slightest cracks around the edges of the windows, creating a draft in the dark, silent room.

There's nothing worse than lying in bed, staring at the ceiling, unable to drift into slumber. Most nights, after a while, sleep gradually seeps in. But it won't tonight, that's for certain. Not with the wind howling out there. Not after a day like today . . . and a night like last night. Not with tomorrow looming.

Well, there's no turning back now.

Everything is in motion.

And after mentally living it so many times, actually killing Jane wasn't so hard after all. Not once you got past that look in her eyes. Who would have thought that taking a life could be so easy? So uncomplicated? So different from the first time? That hadn't been planned. That had been an accident. But it was the spark that triggered the flame. . . .

And now it's time for the next one. After all, that's the only way this is going to work. It has to be done right, from start to finish. No loose ends. Keep the momentum.

What if somebody figures out that it was me? What if I give myself away somehow?

No. You won't. That can't happen. It didn't before. It won't now. You can't let it.

Take a deep breath.

You can do this.

You will do this.

You have no choice.

Thursday, October 11

Chapter Six

With the kids settled in front of *Sesame Street*, Rachel drifts out the front door, pulling her silk robe more tightly around her just in case anyone's watching. Just last month she caught Mr. Martin staring intently at her from across the street when she sneaked out to get the paper in her short summer nightie. He caught her noticing him leering and quickly pretended to be watering those god-awful orange marigolds that he insists keep the deer away.

Not surprising. Rachel's always had him pegged for a dirty old man. But even after she told Tasha about the spying incident, Tasha is still convinced it's Rachel imagination.

That's Tasha, though. She always believes the best about people. Must be that Ohio thing she has going on. Midwesterners are so naive.

Orchard Lane is deserted this morning, and so is the

Martins' yard. Good. Rachel shivers in her robe as she makes her way down the sidewalk toward the curb in her thick-soled, fleece-lined L.L. Bean slippers. It's chilly and windy, but the sun is peeking through a billowy pile of fast-moving clouds high in the blue-gray sky.

As she bends to pick up the newspaper, she has the sudden sensation that she's being watched.

Looking up sharply, she surveys the Martins' impeccably kept yard. No sign of Mr. Martin. Too late in the year for him to do any watering. All that's in bloom now are the chrysanthemums along the foundation. Those are a garish orange, too.

Somebody should really talk to the man about his horticultural color scheme, Rachel thinks. As long as it's not Mrs. Martin, an aging redhead who tends to wear a lot of blue eye shadow and hot pink sweaters.

Rachel's gaze shifts to the Bankses' house next door to the Martins'. It looks quiet. The shades are drawn upstairs and down. Joel's car is still in the driveway.

Frowning, Rachel scans the street. Not a soul in sight. So why the creepy feeling that she's being watched?

Must be her imagination, she thinks, bending over to retrieve the newspaper in its yellow plastic bag. She opens it and examines the front page, knowing what she'll see there.

Sure enough, Jane Kendall's photo stares back at her, beneath a bold headline.

SEARCH CONTINUES FOR MISSING TOWNSEND HEIGHTS HEIRESS.

"Oh, God," Rachel mutters, unfolding the paper and skimming the story. As she reads, goose bumps form on her arms. Well, it's freezing out here in just this thin robe, she tells herself when she notices.

But that's not why she has goose bumps. It's the growing sensation of being watched. She can't shake it.

Abruptly, she tucks the paper under her arm and strides back toward the house, fighting the urge to turn around and give Mr. Martin's house the finger, certain the old pervert's watching her silently from one of the windows.

After all . . . who else can it be?

She shudders as she reaches the front door, which has been left ajar.

Jane Kendall. Did she really kill herself? Or was somebody else responsible for what happened? And if it was somebody else, was Jane Kendall stalked before she was killed? Did she, too, feel as though somebody was watching her?

Oh, come on. You're scaring yourself, you idiot!

Rachel throws open the front door and slips back into the warm house, closing and locking it behind her.

"Rachel?"

She cries out at the sound of the voice right behind her, spinning around in alarm.

Ben stands there, looking surprised. "What's wrong?"

"You scared the shit out of me!" She holds her palm against her pounding heart and shakes her head at her husband. He's dressed for work in camel-colored corduroys and a yellow button-down shirt beneath a brown sweater vest.

The yellow's too bright, she notices absently, vaguely irritated. It would work better with a butter-colored shirt.

Ben opens the closet beside the door and takes out his khaki trench coat. "Don't forget, I'll be later tonight than usual. Tonight's the staff meeting with expectant parents.''

"Lucky you.''

Ben is always complaining about the monthly get-togethers at the hospital, when he and his nurses answer questions from pregnant women who are considering bringing their future newborns to his practice.

"Yeah. I get sick of answering the same questions over and over,'' Ben says, tucking his beeper into his pocket.

"Really? You should try spending a day with your daughter,'' Rachel says with a grin. "By the way, I won't be home till late tonight either.''

"No? What's up?''

"I'm having dinner with Allen,'' she tells him easily.

She can't use Tasha or Karen as the excuse—too easy for Ben to run into one of them. Allen is one of her gay friends who lives in the city. He's a leftover from her pre-Ben days as a fashion stylist for Saks—and he happens to be in Tuscany for a few weeks on a shoot.

Ben raises an eyebrow. "What about Mrs. Tuccelli?''

"What about her?''

"I thought you fired her last night. Who's going to watch the kids?''

"That boy from down the street,'' Rachel tells him.

"What boy from down the street?''

"The one who's staying with the Gallaghers. Their nephew.''

"Oh. You know him?''

"He's a nice kid,'' she says with a shrug. "And if he needs anything, his aunt and uncle are right down the street.'' *Well, his aunt will be.*

"Have you seen my keys?'' Ben asks, distracted, patting the pocket of his trench coat.

"Nope.''

"Must be in my other coat." He opens the closet again and reaches for his black trenchcoat.

Rachel tiptoes up and gives him a kiss on the cheek. "Have a good day, Ben. I'm going to go have some coffee and read the paper."

"Did they find that Kendall woman yet?"

She shakes her head. "Not according to the headline. What do you think happened to her?"

"Nothing good. Here they are." Waving his keys, he closes the closet door and picks up his bag. "I'll call you later. Give the kids a kiss for me."

"Aren't you going to do it yourself?"

"I did. They didn't notice. They're all wrapped up in *Sesame Street*. I think they're watching too much TV, Rach."

She shrugs. "There are worse things that could happen to them, Ben. See you tonight."

"You'll probably beat me home. I've got some HMO paperwork to catch up on after the meeting. Have fun."

"I will," she tells him, smiling to herself as he walks out the door.

Mitch stands at the bottom of a tree with a big gun aimed at Robbie Sussman, who is whimpering and clinging to a branch overhead. Mitch is just centering Robbie's dumb, tear-stained face in the sight when a shrill siren shatters everything.

Run! It's the police, he thinks in the split second before he realizes that it's not a siren after all, but the bleating of the alarm clock, and that the whole thing with Robbie was just a dream.

Oh.

Mitch fumbles for it on the end table beside the couch, his fingers finally making contact with the snooze button. There. Silence.

After a moment, he realizes that the place is too silent. Where's Mom?

He opens his eyes. The first thing he sees is a folded note on the coffee table, which has been pushed away to make room for the pullout bed.

He knows what it says before he sits up and reads it. Sure enough . . .

Mitch, I had to leave early again to cover this story. Eat breakfast. Don't be late for school! Love, Mom

Good. When she's here in the morning, she nags him to hurry. Today he can have a few extra minutes to lie in bed. He sinks back against the pillow and thinks about his father. If he lived with Dad, he would never have the house to himself. Shawna would always be hovering around, trying to take care of him.

Sometimes he likes the way she tries to act like a mother. She makes him cookies from one of those Pillsbury mixes—not from scratch the way Blake's mother does, but they're still pretty good. She buys him little presents—mostly stuff to wear, though.

And she tries to hug him. That, he doesn't like. Maybe because the person he wishes would hug him is his dad. And his dad never has.

Plus, he knows how much it would upset his mom if she thought Shawna was going around hugging him, acting like she's his mother. She's not supposed to hug him, or tell him to eat his vegetables, or make sure he washes behind his ears. That's the kind of stuff only a mom is allowed to do.

If Mitch lived with Dad and Shawna right now, Shawna would probably be standing over him, telling him to hurry up and get out of bed so he won't be late for school.

Yeah, so . . .

Thank God he doesn't live with Dad and Shawna.

Mitch rolls over and closes his eyes again.

Fletch steps from the steamy master bathroom back to the bedroom, a towel wrapped low around his lean waist. He catches sight of his reflection in a cheval mirror across the room and admires his bulging biceps and washboard stomach. Later he'll hit the gym. He was hoping to play golf this morning, but it's too late now. He slept past his usual tee time at the country club.

Yawning, he crosses the room to the built-in bureau, glancing at the rumpled bed as he passes. Sharon is there, asleep, her mouth slightly open. She's been sleeping in that position since he came home last night, and he wasn't thrilled to find her already in their bed. He likes to have it all to himself these days, and often does.

He stares at his wife, noting the weighty tousle of blond hair on the pillowcase, the unnaturally tanned skin against the white bed linen, the skinny black strap of her silk teddy that has slipped down over her exposed shoulder. She has drawers full of lingerie like that, he knows. He used to be impressed by her sexy sleepwear. But that wore off years ago.

She's so motionless. . . .

She looks like she's dead, he notes without the humor that accompanied that particular observation in the past.

When they first met, she informed him that nothing could rouse her from a deep sleep, and Fletch soon discovered she was right. He could talk to her, turn on lights, raise the volume on the television, even shake her, and still she slept as soundly as a corpse. Always had. Still does, unless she's faking.

But why would she do that?

To avoid talking to me?

Maybe. After all, he's done his share of playing dead in bed for that same reason.

Well, he couldn't care less whether she's actually asleep at the moment or is faking it. He rubs his tense shoulders and reaches for a pair of sweats, anxious to get to the gym and pound out some of this aching tension in a kick-boxing class.

Margaret emerges from the third-floor guest room dressed in gray slacks, a white silk blouse, and a navy blazer. Her hair is pulled back neatly and tied at her neck. She's wearing the perfect string of pearls her father bought her for her fifteenth birthday.

"You're my beautiful girl," he said that morning, fastening them around her neck.

Beautiful. In her whole life, only Daddy ever called her that. Only Daddy ever complimented her and seemed to mean it.

She never heard him call Jane beautiful. He probably did; she has no doubt that her father adored her sister. Who didn't? But he was the only person who was ever sensitive to Margaret's plight as Jane's sister. He didn't compare them; didn't make Margaret feel inferior—something that had been second nature to Mother.

Mother.

Having descended the stairway to the second floor, Margaret passes the closed door of the other guest room, the bigger one with the adjoining bathroom. Naturally, her mother is staying there, having requested, after her arrival last night, that Margaret move her things to the third floor. She blamed it on her arthritis, saying it's too difficult to climb all those stairs, but Margaret knows that's merely an excuse. Her mother simply isn't willing to settle for second-best. She wants the better guest room.

The better daughter.

Mother wants Jane. She hasn't come right out and admitted it, but Margaret knows what she's thinking. That the wrong daughter has disappeared. That Margaret should have been the one to go missing.

Not Jane.

Margaret clenches her hands into fists at her sides as she walks down the second-floor corridor, heading for the next flight of steps.

Not perfect Jane with her perfect house and perfect daughter and perfect husband.

The thought of Owen calms Margaret enough so that she relaxes her hands, realizing that her fingernails have been digging painfully into her palms.

She passes the nursery and pauses in the open doorway, looking in at Schuyler's cheerful yellow-and-white room. The curtains are still drawn, but the crib is vacant. Margaret thought that if she stayed in the second-floor guest room, she would be able to hear Schuyler when she woke.

Way upstairs, she hasn't been in earshot of the baby's cries. Did Mother tend to Jane's daughter, or was it Owen? Or perhaps Minerva, who said she would be back early this morning?

Margaret simmers with frustration. She had planned to be the one who came to calm the little girl in the night. She had intended to be the one who picked her up when she cried out this morning, to cuddle her and dress her and feed her.

She turns away from the nursery and continues along the silent hallway.

The door to the master bedroom is ajar. She wonders, did Owen even make it to bed last night?

When he returned from the press conference, he went straight to his study and closed the door. Mother had already been in bed by then, exhausted from her trip. But Margaret waited up, wanting to be there for Owen if he needed her. He didn't even see her sitting in the living room when he passed, nor did he hear her calling to him as he went to his study.

Now, back on the ground floor, Margaret walks slowly to the study and finds the door closed, just as it was last night.

She does what she hadn't found the courage to do then, knocking softly.

No reply.

Tapping a bit harder, she calls, "Owen? Are you in here?"

Still no reply.

After a moment's hesitation, she reaches out and gingerly turns the knob, half-expecting to find the door locked. It isn't.

She opens it halfway and pokes her head inside.

The desk lamp is on.

Owen is seated there, his head buried in his arms. For an instant, Margaret thinks he's asleep.

Then she sees his shoulders heave and hears a slight sound: his muffled sobbing.

She urgently wants to go to him, to gather him into her arms and cradle his head against her breast. She longs to comfort him; to be the one who takes his pain away.

Poised in the doorway, she watches him. Then, gathering her courage, she puts one sensible navy blue flat over the threshold.

There's a sound behind her, a footstep, and then a soft gasp.

"Owen! You poor thing! Are you crying?"

Bess swoops past Margaret into the room. She hurries over to the desk and puts her arms around her son-in-law. "I know just how you feel, Owen," she sobs. "Oh, God, I know, I know. . . ."

Owen lifts his head, his face a mask of anguish. "This is a nightmare, Bess," he chokes out, his voice raw. "What am I going to do?"

For a moment, Margaret watches, incredulous, as her brother-in-law cries in her mother's arms.

Then she spins on her heel and storms away, fury churning with the pain in her gut.

Tasha raises the shade on the bedroom window facing the street just in time to see Ben Leiberman pulling out of the driveway in his black BMW. That reminds her—she should call his office today and schedule Max for his first-year checkup next month.

As if he's aware she's thinking of him, Max babbles loudly on the floor behind her. She turns, sees that he's chewing on one of Joel's loafers, and scoops him up.

"Ba-ba-ba-ba-ba? Is that what you said, Maxie? What does that mean? Oh, wait, I know. It means, how about some real breakfast instead of this yucky leather?" She pries the shoe out of his hands. He screams in protest when she tosses it in the general direction of the closet. "No, Max, that's disgusting."

She struggles to hang on to his squirming little body as she raises the shades on the other windows. Then she eyes the rumpled bed. If she puts Max down now so that she can make it, he'll get into something else. She sighs. She'll leave the bed for later.

Right now she has to go down and find the washing machine booklet so that she can check out the trouble-shooting chart. She can't go another day without doing the laundry.

"Bye, guys," Joel's voice calls up from the front hall downstairs, over the distant strains of the closing music to *Sesame Street*, which Hunter is watching down in the family room.

Tasha hasn't spoken to Joel all morning. After a restless night, she got up and took a shower before the alarm. When she came out, Max was crying in his crib. She was changing him while Joel showered and feeding him downstairs while Joel got dressed. By the time he was heading downstairs to make coffee, Tasha was trying to drag a sleepy Hunter out of bed. Meanwhile, of course, Victoria had bounded awake and instantly into action, causing one disruption after another as Tasha tried to help Hunter get dressed and find something to bring for show-and-tell.

Tasha decides to ignore his casual "Bye, guys," irritated that he's apparently going to act as though nothing happened between them last night. How typical of Joel. Anything to avoid an argument.

"Wait, Daddy!"

Uh-oh. Tasha hears running footsteps in the hall. It's Victoria, who has been ordered to play with her Kelly

Doll in her room while Tasha combs her still-damp hair and throws on the same pair of jeans she wore yesterday.

"Daddy! Wait! Don't go! I want a kiss!"

"Careful on the stairs, Victoria!" Tasha rushes out of the bedroom just in time to see Victoria almost pitch forward on the top step. Her chubby little hand grabs the banister just in time and she steadies herself.

Tasha's eyes meet Joel's. He's at the bottom of the steps, looking up.

For a split second, they exchange a glance of mutual parental relief that Victoria wasn't hurt. Then Joel's gaze flits away.

"Come on down, Tori," he says, arms outstretched.

"Joel, come up and get her. She's not supposed to go down the steps herself."

"She's fine. Come on, Tori, Daddy's going to miss his train."

"No, Victoria, don't rush," Tasha says, juggling the baby to her other hip and catching up with her daughter midway down the flight. She reaches down to take Victoria's hand. "Hold on to Mommy, sweetheart. Careful. Slow down."

Joel looks at his watch.

The gesture says it all.

Renewed anger sparks in Tasha.

"Just go, Joel," she snaps.

He looks up in surprise.

"I know you're in a hurry, so go."

"Mommy, no! I want to kiss Daddy!" Victoria protests, wrenching her hand out of Tasha's grasp. She launches herself forward and her foot misses a step.

Joel reaches out and catches her.

For a minute, there is silence.

"Don't ever do that again, Tori," Joel says, holding

her close in his arms. "Mommy's right. You can get hurt on the stairs."

"I wanted to hug you, Daddy. I never get to see you anymore."

Tasha waits to see a flicker of guilt in his face. It's there, but not for long.

"I know, Tori," Joel says. "But Daddy's very busy at work lately. I'd be here if I could. You know that."

Would you? Tasha wonders, watching him plant a kiss on his daughter's cheek.

"Bye, Max," he says, reaching up to pat the baby's head.

Again his gaze meets Tasha's. She thinks fleetingly of the old days, when he used to kiss her every time he walked out of—or into—the house.

"I already told Hunter good-bye. He's watching *Sesame Street.*"

She nods.

"I'll see you tonight."

"Okay."

He turns to go.

"Joel," Tasha says, remembering something.

"Yeah?" He doesn't turn to face her again.

"Your mother called yesterday. Your parents are coming over on Saturday," she tells his back.

"Okay," is all he says before he walks out the front door, closing it firmly behind him.

Tasha glares after him.

"Mommy!" Hunter's voice calls from the next room. Hearing him, Victoria takes off in that direction.

Tasha follows, with Max balanced on her hip. "What's wrong, Hunter?"

"This stupid lady has been talking for hours!"

He gestures at the television set, where a smiling PBS

woman is soliciting pledges for their fund-raising drive. Tasha hates when they do this. Instead of a minute or two in between programs, there's a big break—long enough for the kids to lose interest and drift away.

What kind of mother are you? she asks herself, realizing what she's thinking. She never wanted to be one of those people who rely on their TV to keep their kids occupied. But today she just doesn't have the patience to deal with them. All she wants is for them to be distracted so she can sort through her thoughts.

"Mommy! I don't want to watch this lady," Victoria says shrilly. "I want to watch *The Big Comfy Couch*! Put it on!"

"I can't put it on, Victoria. It's not a video. I can't just make it appear. You'll have to wait."

"I want *The Big Comfy Couch* to be on now!"

"Believe me, so do I," Tasha tells her.

The phone rings.

Ignoring Victoria's whining, Tasha plunks Max into his Exersaucer and grabs the receiver.

"What are you doing?" Rachel asks.

"Cursing PBS," Tasha replies, going into the kitchen.

"Oh, I know. They're doing that fund-raising thing again. Mara's all pissed off that *The Big Comfy Couch* isn't on yet."

"So is Victoria." Tasha wedges the receiver between her shoulder and ear and pours herself a cup of coffee from the pot Joel made. It splashes on her sleeve.

That reminds her. The washing machine. She needs to do something about it today.

"Did you see the paper?"

"No, why?"

"Jane Kendall's still missing."

Tasha bites her lip. Jane Kendall. Somehow, she'd almost forgotten.

"Do the police have any idea what could have happened to her?" she asks Rachel.

"Nothing new. But I got all creeped out when I was outside getting the paper this morning. I felt like whoever got Jane Kendall was hiding in the bushes, watching me."

"Yeah, or maybe it was just Mr. Martin again," Tasha says, rolling her eyes. She knows Rachel's convinced that the kindly old retiree is some sort of pervert. That's the thing about Rachel—she's a typical New Yorker, skeptical of everything and everyone.

"If it was, then he was lurking in the junipers this time, because I didn't see any sign of him."

The image of Mr. Martin as a Peeping Tom is just too ludicrous. Tasha laughs.

"What's so funny?" Rachel asks.

"Never mind. So what are you doing today?"

"I was supposed to have a facial and manicure, but now I don't have anyone to watch the kids while I go. I was wondering if you wouldn't mind keeping an eye on them for about an hour this afternoon."

Vaguely irked by Rachel's life of leisure, Tasha hesitates, then decides she might as well say yes. Mara can keep Victoria company, and Max always loves to see Noah. If she can get them all busy with toys in the family room, maybe she can even wash the kitchen floor. "What time do you want to drop them off?" she asks Rachel.

"Actually, I thought maybe you could come over here. I have to be there at one, which is Noah's nap time. You'd only have to watch Mara, really. Noah will sleep through."

"All right," Tasha says reluctantly. There goes her clean kitchen floor. She glances down and sees dried spatters of spilled milk on the linoleum where she's standing. She's definitely got to wash the floor before her in-laws come on Saturday.

"Great," Rachel says. "You're such a great friend, Tasha. Anytime I can return the favor, just ask."

"I definitely will," Tasha tells her. She really could use an hour or two to herself sometime. Like . . . now.

"Ouch—Mommy!" Victoria screams suddenly from the next room.

"Hey, cut it out! . . . Mommy! She's hitting me!" Hunter yells.

"Uh-oh, gotta run," Tasha wearily tells Rachel. "I'll see you this afternoon."

"Karen?"

"Ben!" Karen says, relieved to hear his voice on the other end of the line. "Thanks for calling back."

"No problem. What's wrong with Taylor?"

"Vomiting and diarrhea."

Ben asks her a series of questions about how much formula the baby's had since last night, whether her diapers are wet, and how she's been acting.

"She's sleeping right now," Karen tells him. "She's exhausted. She was up all night."

"Which means you were, too," Ben says sympathetically.

"Right." He's such a sweet guy. Not for the first time, Karen wonders what ever drew him to Rachel. Beyond her looks, that is.

The more she thinks about her friend today, the more irritated she becomes with the way Rachel thinks the world revolves around herself and her problems.

"Listen, Karen, keep her hydrated with Pedialyte and

don't force her to eat. If she's not better by the end of the day, bring her in and I'll take a look at her."

"How late are you there?"

"Late. I have office hours tonight, and I'm meeting with expectant parents after that. So call if you need me. I'll be here."

"Thanks, Ben." Karen hangs up and goes back to the living room, where Taylor is asleep in her playpen. The television drones in the background. Karen had turned on *Sesame Street* for her daughter. Taylor always smiles when she sees Elmo. She didn't today.

Karen turns off the television, abruptly curtailing the announcer's cheerful description of gifts that can be yours if you pledge a donation to PBS.

She stands by the playpen, staring down at her tiny daughter, noticing that she looks pale. Worried, she pulls a white knit blanket up around the baby's shoulders.

"Was that the doctor?"

Karen looks up to see Tom standing in the doorway behind her. He's wearing his work-at-home uniform: faded jeans and a big Rutgers sweatshirt.

That was where they met, in college. He was a sophomore and she was a senior. She had surprisingly much in common with him from the start, despite the two-year age gap and the fact that he was a mild-mannered WASP from Connecticut. They were engaged two years later, while she was in the midst of getting her master's in education, and married two years after that.

They waited to start a family, though, until both their careers were well established. To her dismay, when they finally decided they were ready, it took longer for her to conceive than she had expected. So long that she was about to consult a fertility expert when she finally found herself pregnant.

"What did he say?" Tom asks, coming to stand beside her and staring down at their daughter.

Karen recaps the conversation with Ben.

"Pedialyte? Do we have that in the house?"

Karen shakes her head. This is the first time Taylor has been really sick, aside from her trouble with breast milk months ago.

"Want me to go to the store?" Tom asks, eyeing her flannel pajamas.

She can tell he's reluctant to break away from his work for that long. He told her earlier he's buried in paperwork today.

"No, it's okay," she tells him. "I'll go later, after I've taken a shower and gotten dressed."

"What if she wakes up in the meantime? Shouldn't we have some of that stuff on hand to give her as soon as she does?"

"I'll call Tasha," Karen decides, crossing to the phone. With three kids, Tasha is often her source of borrowed baby items. "She probably has some. Maybe she can drop it off when she drives Hunter to school. She should be leaving any minute."

"Let's go that way," Lily says, pausing on the corner of Townsend Avenue and North Street. With her enormous navy book bag seeming to weigh down her slender shoulders, her stylishly oversize jeans brushing the sidewalk at her heels, and her short red hair fashionably rumpled, she looks even younger than she is.

"Again?" Jeremiah asks reluctantly, knowing he'll give in. "I thought we were going to start taking the short way again."

"Not yet," Daisy tells him, glancing from her twin to

her older stepbrother. "We don't want to do that yet, Jer'."

"Besides," Lily says, "we need to check our pumpkin. The contest is on Saturday."

He sighs. They begin walking up North Street. The girls' school is a block and a half in the other direction, but the girls like to walk by the house—or rather, what's left of it.

He promised Uncle Fletch before they left home that he would walk them all the way to the door of the middle school this time, instead of just leaving them at the corner. Uncle Fletch had said that he should be extra careful because of that lady disappearing and nobody knowing what happened to her.

Jeremiah shoves his hands in the pockets of his jean jacket as they walk down the street, their shoes making scuffling noises in the piles of leaves that litter the sidewalk.

It's a nice neighborhood. He likes it better than the one where they live now. Here, the houses are older—maybe more than a hundred years old, he would guess, judging by their old-fashioned front porches with gingerbread trim, scallop-type shingles, and gabled roof lines. Enormous trees in the front yards cast the sidewalk and most of the houses in dappled shadows. A tangle of woods borders the backyards of the properties.

Most of the homes on the block are decorated for Halloween. Thick skeins of cotton, meant to look like cobwebs, are strewn across bushes. Miniature white ghosts dangle from trees. Curbs are dotted with leaf-filled plastic garbage bags meant to look like fat orange pumpkins. One house even has a make-believe cemetery on the front lawn, with realistic-looking headstones of papier-mâché. Last year while trick-or-treating, Jeremiah tapped one and figured it out.

He thinks back over the months to that strange holiday, remembering how reluctant he had been to go trick-or-treating with the twins, yet just as reluctant to give it up quite yet. There's a certain thrill in taking on somebody else's identity, in hiding behind a mask or makeup and clothing that doesn't belong to you. It's sort of an escape.

An escape from being Jeremiah Gallagher.

He remembers that night last year: how he dressed in a costume he designed himself after being struck by inspiration one day walking past an antique shop in town. It was the Victorian dress on a mannequin in the window that had triggered the idea.

It was a perfect costume. Perfect, except that nobody recognized who he was trying to impersonate.

"Who are you supposed to be?" he heard time and again, from his sisters, passersby, and puzzled neighbors poised on doorsteps with baskets full of miniature candy bars.

How could they not know? The dress, with its Gay Nineties–style high collar and puffy sleeves, was just right. So was the wig, a woman's prim bun in a reddish hue. He smuggled both out of the drama club's storage room at school; they had been used in a production of *Our Town* years ago, and nobody missed them.

What made the costume, of course, had been the axe. He borrowed it from the woodpile behind the shed. With his father away so much, nobody noticed that missing, either. Melissa never went out into the yard unless she was on her way to the car.

He smeared the blade with fake blood, cutting his hand in the process, tainting the ketchup-corn syrup mixture with the real thing.

"Who are you supposed to be?"

How could they not have figured it out?

Lizzie Borden was only the most notorious female murderer who had ever lived—if you believed she was guilty.

"She killed her father and mother, didn't she?" Melissa asked him when he explained his costume, more irritated with her than with the others who asked. Everything she did got on his nerves. *Everything.*

"Stepmother," he'd corrected her icily, pleased to see her squirm and look away.

He remembered that now. Remembered the twins' shrieks of disgust when they saw the fake blood. Remembered how reluctantly they wore the costumes that Melissa had made them.

"You're adorable," she exclaimed as they glowered in their outfits. One was a salt shaker. One was a pepper shaker. Melissa came up with that idea herself and thought it was brilliant.

Jeremiah thought it was ridiculous. So did Uncle Fletch, who stopped by right before he left to take his sisters trick-or-treating. He came over a lot those days. Almost every day. Said he was checking on everyone, making sure they were all okay with Jeremiah's father overseas.

"Salt and pepper shakers?" he asked when he saw the twins, shaking his head and turning to his brother's wife. "Mel, don't they ever get to dress as individuals?"

She shushed him, of course, but good-naturedly. She was never moody when Uncle Fletch was around.

He didn't get the Lizzie Borden thing, either.

Jeremiah and the twins trekked around the neighborhood that windy, moonless night, ringing doorbells and collecting candy in their plastic pumpkins. The girls admired the decorations on house after house and chattered about what they would do if their mother let them decorate their own house next year.

Well, now their house is by far the eeriest place on the block, Jeremiah realizes as it comes into view between the tall trees shielding it from the sidewalk.

The three of them stop and stare in silence at what little there is to see within the grim perimeter of yellow police tape encircling the property.

It'll be gone soon, he knows, staring at the pile of charred rubble punctuated by a brick chimney and a few standing beams. His stepmother's body was found in there someplace, burned beyond recognition.

Beyond the house, the shed stands unscathed, its contents untouched. He'll have to go in there to get the wagon on Saturday morning.

"Do you want to go check your pumpkin?" Jeremiah asks the twins, glancing at the garden just in front of the shed, well beyond the wreck where the house used to be. Even from here he can see the plump orange pumpkins amid the low foliage, with the biggest—the one the girls are entering in the contest this weekend—rising above the rest like a mountain.

"Will you come with us?" Lily asks quietly.

But he doesn't want to go any closer. Not now. He shakes his head. "Just leave it for today," he tells them. "It's fine. I can see it from here."

"Okay," Daisy agrees. "We'll come back and get it Saturday morning, right?"

He nods.

They stand there for a long moment. Then Jeremiah puts one hand on each stepsister's shoulder and wordlessly ushers them away.

* * *

Tasha pulls up at the curb in front of Karen's house, parking beside the curbside mailbox marked Wu/Simmons. She's struck, as always, by the blatant reminder that Karen has kept her maiden name.

When she married Joel, Tasha toyed with the idea of keeping her maiden name. She might have, if she had liked it. But Tasha Banks sounds so much better than Tasha Shaughnessy, which she always thought had one too many *sha* sounds. Besides, it's easier to spell.

She puts the car into park and grabs the plastic grocery bag containing the Pedialyte from the seat beside her.

"What are you doing, Mommy?" Hunter asks from the back seat, where he's strapped in between Victoria's booster and Max's car seat.

"I'm just dropping this off for Taylor's mommy," Tasha tells him, getting out of the car. She grabs her keys from the ignition as an afterthought. You never know when a car-jacker might be lurking, although the prospect seems laughable in this neighborhood, at this hour of the day.

A sudden bang shatters the stillness, making her jump.

Just a car door slamming nearby, she realizes, her heart racing.

Glancing up, she sees Fletch Gallagher behind the wheel of his Mercedes in the driveway of the house next door to Karen's.

Tasha freezes.

Has he seen her?

He waves at her through the windshield.

She waves back. Clutching the shopping bag, she starts toward Karen's front door.

Drive away, Fletch, she bids silently. Just go.

He's getting out of the car.

"How's it going, Tasha?" he asks, walking toward her. His keychain jangles casually in his hand.

She forces herself to stop, to face him, when what she really wants to do is take off running. "I'm fine," she says stiffly. Defensively, almost. As if daring him to speculate that she might not be coping well after—

"Haven't seen you around lately."

That's because I avoid this end of the street. When I have to pass your house I put my head down and step on the accelerator just in case you're around. . . .

But he rarely is.

At least, he wasn't until lately. Not with baseball season in full swing and a busy travel schedule.

Now, the Mets are out of the playoffs and he's out of a job until next spring.

"Why aren't you in Florida?" she hears herself ask.

He smiles faintly. "How'd you know I go to Florida in October?"

She shrugs, trying not to squirm. The last thing she wants to do is admit she remembers anything he ever told her. But then, the fact that he likes to winter in Florida is mild compared to the other things that still echo through her head.

"Visiting Karen?" he asks.

She nods.

"Leaving the kids in the car?" He peers over her shoulder, at the small heads bobbing in the back seat of the Expedition.

"I'm just dropping something off, actually."

"Did you lock them in?" he asks, motioning at the car.

She shakes her head.

"I wouldn't take any chances," Fletch tells her. "Did you hear about Jane Kendall?"

"That she disappeared?"

He nods.

In his clouded golden-hazel eyes, she glimpses an unexpected expression, something other than casual concern. It's gone before she can read it. She pushes away a flicker of suspicion, relieved when he says abruptly with a shrug, "Well, just make sure you're careful, Tasha. And I'd keep a close eye on my kids if I were you."

"I always keep a close eye on my kids, Fletch."

He smiles. "I know you do. Well, I'll see you later, Tasha."

A chill skids through her as he walks back to his car, jangling his keys. She can't help but wonder whether it's just her imagination or if there's something forced about his nonchalance.

Paula drives up in front of the train station just as the northbound eight twenty-two pulls into the station. The train is coming from Manhattan, having made stops in Harlem and the Bronx as well as lower Westchester.

The vast majority of disembarking passengers are nannies and maids and day laborers, all of them heading off to another day's work for the wealthy local families. They chatter cheerfully to each other as they move toward the steps leading up from the tracks, some speaking in accented English, others in different languages.

Those already waiting on the platform for the eight thirty-three southbound to Manhattan—the well-heeled residents of Townsend Heights—are quiet by contrast. Some are jean-clad, headphone-wearing private school or college students with knapsacks, but most are business commuters in suits and trench coats, clutching briefcases, newspapers, and steaming paper cups of coffee from the small bakery café opposite the train parking lot.

Paula leaves the engine running and the windows open to let the smoke out, then gets out of her car, dropping the remains of her lit cigarette beside the curb and grinding it out with her shoe. She hurries toward the foot of the steps leading down from the pedestrian overpass. She scans the crowd of passengers, looking for a familiar face, praying she hasn't missed her.

"Minerva!" she calls, spotting her target at last. "Minerva Fuentes?"

Startled, the woman darts a glance in her direction. Paula smiles encouragingly and beckons to her.

The Kendalls' housekeeper pauses on the steps, her hand grasping the railing, looking like she doesn't know whether or not she should acknowledge Paula.

"Can I please talk to you for a moment?" Paula calls out, still smiling.

Minerva continues down the stairway, her eyes averted. She arrives at Paula's side and seems inclined to keep walking past her. Paula reaches out and touches her arm.

The woman looks up at her, startled.

"I'm Paula Bailey. We met last year."

"We . . . we did?" Minerva asks uncertainly.

"At the Kendalls' house," Paula says, glad Minerva doesn't remember the occasion. No need to tell her she's a reporter . . . yet. "I was there talking to Jane. You brought us tea and cookies—delicious lemon cookies that Jane said you had made yourself."

Minerva lights up at that, but her smile is quickly shadowed with sorrow. "Mrs. Jane loves my lemon cookies."

"They were wonderful," Paula tells her. "Where did you get the recipe?"

Minerva taps her forehead proudly. "I like to bake. I made it up."

"You're kidding!" Paula shakes her head. "I'm impressed. I can't even make up a recipe for a peanut butter sandwich."

Minerva laughs.

Paula does, too. Then she says gently, "I know you must be upset about what's happened to Jane."

Tears spring to the woman's big dark eyes, and she nods. "God bring her home safely," she says, crossing herself.

"I've been praying for the same thing," Paula tells her. "Listen, are you headed over to the Kendalls' now?"

Minerva nods again.

"Why don't I give you a ride? I know it isn't far to walk, but I'm headed in that direction anyway."

"All right," Minerva says after only a moment's pause.

"I'm parked right over there," Paula tells her, leading the way.

Once they're settled inside the car, she takes her time pulling away from the curb. Even if she takes a round-about route and drives as slowly as she possibly can, she'll have only three or four minutes, tops, before she reaches their destination.

"How are things at the Kendalls' house, Minerva?" she asks as she heads away from the main street. "I know Owen must be taking this very badly."

"He is. Everybody is upset. Even little Schuyler, she cries for her Mama."

"Are you the one who's taking care of her?"

"Not just me. Her grandparents are there—Mr. Owen's mother and father." It's clear from her tone that Minerva doesn't think much of the Kendalls. "And her aunt is there, too. Jane's sister."

Jane's sister.

The words immediately trigger a memory, an image, in Paula's mind. She remembers the gilt picture frame she saw in the living room of the Kendalls' home last year when she interviewed Jane. It was a photo that had been taken on Jane and Owen's wedding day, showing a beaming bride with a painfully plain woman at her side.

"Who's that?" she asked Jane.

"My maid of honor—my older sister, Margaret," Jane replied.

And Paula, staring at the picture, was struck by the stark physical contrast between the two women. She almost forgot the incident until now . . .

Now, as last year's recollection rushes back at her, another, far more recent memory comes with it.

Yesterday—the woman she saw hurrying toward the Kendall home—the one who looked so familiar . . .

She was Jane's sister.

Filing away that information, Paula asks Minerva, "So Schuyler is cared for by her aunt right now?"

The housekeeper shrugs, distaste apparent on her face. "She doesn't know much about taking care of babies."

"What do you think happened to Jane, Minerva?" Paula asks softly, turning onto the street leading to Harding Place, knowing there isn't time to beat around the bush.

"I don't know!" Minerva exclaims. Rather than hedging, which Paula expected, it's as though she's eager to talk. Her voice spills over, trembling with emotion. "I keep trying to imagine what could have happened. I heard them saying on the news that she could have killed herself, but I know Mrs. Jane. She loved that baby. She would never kill herself."

"That's what I thought. But who would have wanted to hurt her, Minerva? Did she have any enemies that you knew of?"

For a split second, Minerva is silent. Then she says, "No."

But the fractional pause is telling. Paula pulls up to a stop sign, and turns to look at the housekeeper as she brakes the car. "What is it, Minerva? What are you thinking?"

"Nothing . . ."

"You can tell me, Minerva. Whatever it is. I don't believe that Jane jumped from the cliff, either. I want to know what happened. Maybe she's still alive. Maybe we can save her if she is."

"I don't want to talk to the police again," Minerva says nervously. "I'm not supposed to be working here. If they—"

"If you know something, then maybe I can go to them with it. I don't have to tell them where I found out."

"I told them I don't know what happened." Minerva's hands are clenched in her lap as she looks out the window. "And that was the truth. I don't know what happened."

"But you have an idea," Paula tells her. A block from the Kendalls' house, she pulls up along the curb, hoping the housekeeper won't notice. "You know something that you didn't mention to the police."

"I just wanted to get away from them." Minerva turns back to Paula. "I was afraid that if they kept talking to me, they would start asking me about my visa. I don't want to go back."

"Back where?"

"To the Dominican Republic, where I'm from. I need to work here."

"I understand. I would never do anything to jeopardize your job or get you deported, Minerva. I never reveal a source." Paula leans closer to her. "What is it that you know about Jane, Minerva? Did she have an enemy? Who was it?"

"I don't know if she had an enemy, but . . ."

"But?" Paula prods, gently touching her arm.

"Mrs. Jane had a secret. A bad secret," Minerva tells Paula fearfully. "And I'm afraid it got her into trouble."

Tasha lugs Victoria and Max across the street at ten till one. Rachel is waiting, waving from the front door with her coat on. She rushes past them as they come up the front steps, calling over her shoulder, "Mara's in the kitchen with a peanut butter sandwich. Ramira's upstairs cleaning the bathroom. She said she was going to vacuum, but I told her not to because it'll wake Noah. If she makes noise, you have my permission to fire her."

Tasha smiles. Ramira is the Leibermans' latest housekeeper, poor thing. She wonders how long this one will last.

"What's 'fire,' Mommy?" Victoria asks as Tasha closes the door after Rachel.

"It's when someone takes your job away."

"Oh." Clearly, she was expecting something more exciting.

"Run into the kitchen and see Mara, Victoria. I'm just going to find some things for Max to play with."

For a change, her daughter obeys her. That's just because she idolizes Mara. She's been obstinate all morning, trying Tasha's patience and frazzling her nerves, keeping her from everything else she has to do, including troubleshooting the broken washer. Poor Max has been all but abandoned in his Exersaucer until now, thanks to his sister's antics.

"Come on, Maxie, you want some of Noah's blocks or something?" Tasha goes into the small playroom next to the dining room. It's crammed full of toys, all of them organized neatly in bins and on shelves. Ramira's job, Tasha knows, but Rachel does her share of straightening. She's one of those compulsively neat people who likes everything in its place.

She and Max browse for a few minutes. Upstairs, she can hear Ramira's footsteps as she goes about her work. She knows the woman refuses to let Rachel give her child-care responsibilities in addition to her household chores, probably because she figures—correctly, in all likelihood—that Rachel would take advantage.

Max picks up a tub of Duplo building blocks.

"You like those, Max? Okay. Let's bring them into the kitchen and go check on the girls."

Tasha brings him and the Duplo into the spotless kitchen, with its state-of-the-art stainless-steel appliances, sleek black-and-white countertops, and vase of budded stargazer lilies in the center of the table. What a contrast to her own crumb-strewn, sticky-floored kitchen.

Tasha plops Max down on the sparkling white tile floor.

"How's your sandwich, Mara?" she asks Rachel's daughter, who's doing her best to eat with Victoria wedged onto her chair beside her.

Mara shrugs.

"Victoria, why don't you sit over here and give Mara some room?"

"I want to sit with Mara," is the stubborn reply.

Tasha sighs. "Victoria, Mara can't eat when you're on top of her like that. Give her some space. Sit over here."

"I don't want to."

Tasha glances from the dangerous gleam in Victoria's eyes to Mara's faintly amused expression. Since she doesn't seem particularly bothered, Tasha decides to let Victoria win this battle. It's so much easier than dealing with another tantrum.

She goes over to the fridge and looks inside for something to eat. She never had a chance to grab lunch amid the hassle of feeding the kids before they left home. Looks like she's out of luck here, though. There are plenty of condiments and beverages, but no real food. She knows the Leibermans eat a lot of takeout, since Rachel doesn't cook.

Tasha grabs a can of Diet Pepsi and considers making herself a sandwich. Mara's looks good. But peanut butter is so fattening. . . .

She remembers running into Fletch this morning. He was clearly on his way to the gym. She wonders if he noticed that she's not as fit as she used to be before Max came along. Knowing Fletch, he probably did.

Okay, so skipping lunch won't kill her. She closes the fridge just as the phone rings.

"Telephone, Mommy!" Victoria shrieks.

"I know, I know." She hurries toward it, wondering if it's Joel in the split second before she remembers that she's not at home; she's at Rachel's. She waited for her own phone to ring all morning at home, and it didn't. And for a change, she didn't call his office, either.

"Hello?"

Silence.

"Hello?"

There's a pause, then a click.

Tasha frowns, holding the receiver for a moment.

"Who is it, Mommy?" Victoria wants to know.

"Nobody." She hangs up slowly. Probably somebody

who was confused by hearing a strange voice at the Leiber-mans', she tells herself.

But her heart is pounding. A vague sense of uneasiness creeps over her once again.

Now she's imagining all sorts of things—but it's just that, she reminds herself. Just her imagination. She's always had an active one. Making up preposterous stories as a child, fearing bogeymen and monsters, scaring herself to death. Her mother always told her that her worst enemy was her own mind, that she needed to be careful not to let it carry her too far from reality. That she could think herself *out* of being afraid the same way she had thought herself *in*.

"How can it be nobody if the phone rang?" Mara is asking.

Tasha shrugs, suddenly wondering whether she locked the door when she came in. So much for talking herself out of fear.

"Where are you going, Mommy?" Victoria asks.

"I just need to check something. Be right back," she says, scurrying into the hall. She goes to the door and locks it, then slides the bolt firmly into place.

There.

Safe and sound.

Make sure you're careful, Tasha.

She turns back toward the kitchen, Fletch Gallagher's words echoing through her mind.

Margaret lifts the lace panel on the foyer window and peers at the throng that has engulfed the once-quiet street. Reporters and dozens of onlookers line the blue wooden barricades the police have set up. Even from here, the hubbub is audible. The neighbors must be furious.

Dropping the curtain, Margaret realizes that this is what it must feel like to be in prison. Helpless. Trapped. Desperate to escape.

Except that she isn't really—

"Margaret?"

She jumps at the sound of her name.

Mother.

She sighs, turning to see Bess standing behind her, Schuyler in her arms.

"Have you seen Owen?"

Margaret shakes her head. She hasn't seen him since she left him in the study this morning, sobbing in Mother's arms.

"He must have left with the detectives again," Bess says, a catch in her voice. "This is too much to bear, Margaret. If it weren't for this precious child . . ."

Margaret looks at Schuyler. Her niece's eyes meet hers. The little girl whimpers and buries her face in Bess's neck.

"What's the matter, sweetheart?" Bess asks, patting her back. "Don't cry now. *Mere* is here. *Mere* will take good care of you. Margaret, I'm going to put her down for a nap and take one myself. Please listen for the phone and doorbell. Call me if you hear anything at all."

Margaret watches her mother climb the stairs with Schuyler.

After a few moments, the nursery door closes quietly above. Footsteps move down the hall, and then a second door closes.

Margaret can't stand this gilded cage another moment. Minerva is here somewhere. She can answer the phone and the door.

Thanks to the press, Owen's parents are not here and have said they have no intention of coming back. Not until this is over.

And good riddance to you, Margaret thought at the time, marveling at their cold-hearted selfishness. So they would rather avoid the media circus than be here for their son. She isn't surprised.

Having made her decision, Margaret goes up to her room to change her clothes, neatly replacing the blouse, slacks, and blazer on hangers in the small gabled closet.

Then, clad in a black cotton pullover and a pair of rarely worn jeans that are still indigo-colored and stiff, Margaret descends once again from the third floor, dark glasses in her hand.

This time she goes straight to the kitchen. There's no sign of Minerva. She must be dusting somewhere.

Good.

Opening the door that leads to the basement, Margaret slowly descends a steep flight of stairs, glad that old houses—like people—have their secrets.

Chapter Seven

The doorbell rings downstairs just as Rachel is standing before her bureau, fastening her gold necklace around her neck. She takes one last look at her reflection, admiring the way her black V-necked sweater and short skirt hug her curves. She turns away from the mirror and catches sight of her discarded black-lace bra and panties on the bed. She changed her mind about wearing them after all; a thong is all she has on under this outfit. She smiles, thinking of his reaction when he sees it.

After spritzing Chanel No. 5 behind her ears, she swiftly descends the staircase to the front hall and opens the door just as the bell rings again.

"Jeremiah, right?" she tosses over her shoulder, briefly glancing at the teenager on the step before she hurries away, toward the back of the house. "Come with me. I need to check the kids. I hope they didn't get into anything."

They haven't. They're right where she left them ten minutes ago when she dashed upstairs to get dressed. The kitchen is spotless, just as Ramira left it earlier.

Mara sits at the table, intently turning the knobs on her Etch-A-Sketch. Noah is on the floor, happily stacking Tupperware containers.

"This is Jeremiah, guys," Rachel announces. "That's Mara, and that's Noah."

She turns to Fletch Gallagher's nephew, noticing that he has a prominent case of acne. Poor kid. Everything about him is awkward, including the way he meets her gaze, then, blushing bright red, looks down at his scuffed white sneakers.

"The kids are fed and bathed," she tells him. She slipped her housekeeper an extra twenty bucks to accomplish those chores for her while she was soaking in a bubble bath. Ramira, who is always reminding Rachel that she isn't a nanny, accepted it willingly enough, but cautioned Rachel not to make it a habit.

She definitely has to find a new nanny. But for tonight, she has Jeremiah.

She bends over to hug Mara and plants a kiss on Noah's head. He babbles contentedly.

"D-do . . . do they cry when you leave?"Jeremiah asks, speaking for the first time. His voice cracks in that awkward teenage-boy way. Again, she feels sorry for him.

"Cry? Nope, they don't ever cry when I leave. They're probably glad to see me go." Rachel grins, tousling Mara's hair. Her daughter glances blankly up at her, then back down at her geometric Etch-A-Sketch masterpiece, absorbed in that.

"I'll see you when I get home, guys," Rachel tells her children, picking up her black pocketbook from the uncluttered counter. "I'll come in and give you kisses in your beds."

"Where are y-you going?" Jeremiah asks as she heads for the door, pulling on her black coat as she goes.

Startled by the question, she wonders for a moment if he's suspicious. Then she reminds herself that he's just a kid—and new at babysitting, at that. He's being cautious. Probably wants to know where he can reach her in case of an emergency.

She side-steps his question. "My cell phone number is on the pad by the phone," she tells him. "So is the number for my husband's office, and his beeper. So you're all set. And so am I. Bye—"

"W-wait," he calls.

Frustrated, she looks back.

"I mean, I d-don't know what time you'll b-be home or when they g-go to b-bed or anything," he stutters.

He's so nervous. Why? For a split second, she reconsiders leaving him here with the kids. After all, what does he know about babysitting? And what does she really know about him? He's a stranger, really.

No. He's a neighbor. And she knows his family.

Besides, what could possibly happen?

She recalls the strange feeling she had as she was picking up the paper this morning. She was certain she was being watched. But she quickly got over it.

Still . . .

Jane Kendall.

"Make sure you lock the door behind me, Jeremiah," she tells him, looking back at her children.

He nods, following her into the hall. "When will you be home?"

"Geez, I don't know. Most likely not until around

eleven or midnight. My husband will probably beat me here. He should be back by eleven."

"Okay." Jeremiah seems edgy.

Suddenly, she realizes why.

Opening her bag, she grabs some bills and shoves them into his hand. "There you go, Jeremiah. In case my husband gets here first. He won't know how much we agreed on."

"Th-thanks. And . . . b-bedtime? For the k-kids?"

"Whenever they're tired," she says. "I need to go now. Don't worry. Everything will be fine."

With that, she breezes out into the chilly October night, determined to ignore a sudden, inexplicable sense of foreboding.

"Want to watch the millionaire show later?" Mitch asks Lianne, who is sitting beside him on the couch.

"Sure," she says, turning a page of her magazine. She doesn't talk much. At least, not to him. But he's noticed that when she gets on the phone with one of her friends or her boyfriend, she goes on and on, like she's forgotten all about him.

When that happens, he sometimes wonders if it wouldn't be better if his mother just left him alone. Not that he likes that, either.

He guesses it's good to have someone to talk to. Even if it's just Lianne.

"Hey, did you hear about that lady who disappeared from the park?" he asks, wanting to get her to do something other than stare at that dumb article she's reading. It's about losing weight.

If you ask him, Lianne doesn't need to lose any weight.

She's super-skinny. Pretty, too, with really white skin and long black hair that almost reaches her butt.

She looks up at him. "You mean Jane Kendall?"

"Yeah." Pleased that he got her attention, Mitch says, "My mom is doing a story about that case."

"She is? Cool. I know the kid who found the baby carriage in the park. Peter Frost."

"Yeah? What'd he say about it?"

"I guess the baby was screaming and he had to rescue her from some kind of wild animal. He was totally brave."

"Huh." Mitch thinks about that, wondering what kind of wild animals live in High Ridge Park. He would've thought just squirrels and deer and maybe skunks, but none of those animals would attack a baby. There must be bears. Or wildcats, even.

"What do you think happened to her?" Lianne asks him. She looks kind of worried.

"The baby? I thought you said your friend rescued her." Alarmed, he pictures a baby being eaten by a bear.

"No, he did. I meant the mother," Lianne says. "Do you think she jumped into the river?"

"Probably." Mitch thinks about the press conference his mother took him to last night, trying to remember what was said. Most of it was pretty boring. He doesn't think there was anything about anybody jumping into a river. Then again, he can't be sure. He hadn't really been paying much attention. All he really remembers is that guy, the lady's husband, crying in front of everyone.

Mitch wonders if he was embarrassed later. *He* would never cry in front of anyone. He hardly ever even cries when he's alone. Crying's for babies. And girls.

Except Mom. She doesn't cry, either. She's always brave.

Shawna isn't, Mitch thinks in disgust. His stepmother's

always bawling about something. Like, when she watches a movie on TV and she knows it's going to be sad, she'll get a box of tissues and put it by the couch. Mitch's dad teases her about it. Shawna doesn't seem to mind.

Mitch doesn't really mind when his dad teases him, either. Even though sometimes it makes him feel kind of bad. Like the time at the beach last summer, when Mitch told his father he was afraid to go into the water and that he wished he was a girl.

"Why?" his father had asked.

"Because man-eating sharks don't eat girls. They eat men. Probably boys, too."

His father had thought that was hilarious. Well, how was Mitch supposed to know that "man-eating" didn't really mean the sharks only ate men?

"Hey, Mitch, does your mom know any inside stuff about the case?" Lianne asks.

"I don't know. Probably."

"Like what?"

He shrugs. "You should ask her."

"You know what I think happened? I think there's a serial killer on the loose. Like in those *Scream* movies. I think he killed Jane Kendall, and he's going to strike again."

Horror bubbles up inside of Mitch. He watched the first *Scream* on cable one night when his mom was working late. It scared him so much that he almost ran downstairs and knocked on Mrs. Ambrosini's door.

"You mean you think some guy in a creepy mask and robe is going around killing people here in Townsend Heights?" he asks Lianne.

"Maybe."

How come she doesn't look freaked out by that?

Mitch looks over his shoulder at the door, making sure

it's locked. Yup. The latch is turned. But suddenly he's feeling panicky. What if the killer already got into the apartment and is hiding in the bathroom or something?

Suddenly, Mitch wants his mother. Or his father. Shawna, even.

"Who do you think the killer is?" he asks Lianne, trying not to let his voice shake.

"I don't know. That's what's so scary. Maybe your mom has some idea, since she's the reporter working on the case."

Mitch thinks about the *Scream* movie. There was a reporter in that, too. And she was one of the few people who didn't die in the end.

"You don't think my mom is in danger, do you?" he asks Lianne.

"God, I don't know," she says.

It isn't the answer Mitch expects. If Lianne were an adult, she'd probably say, "Of course not!" Adults never want kids to worry.

Lianne doesn't seem to care if he worries or not.

What if something happens to his mother?

Mitch remembers how yesterday, when his father showed up at school, he thought for a second that his mother had been hurt or even killed.

If something like that did ever happen, he supposes he would go live with Dad and Shawna. Shawna would probably like it if that happened. She wants a kid really bad. He heard her crying on the phone one day about that. She was talking to one of her friends.

But Mitch figures she probably wasn't thinking she wanted a ten-year-old kid who already has a mother. She meant a baby of her own.

From what Mitch could figure out from the conversation, Shawna can't have babies of her own.

So maybe she'd be really happy if something happened to his mother—like if she died of lung cancer from smoking so much, and Mitch had to come and live with her and Dad. Then Shawna could be his new mother. . . .

And Dad could be his dad all the time, not just on weekends.

For a second, Mitch is so psyched about the latter thought that he forgets what made him think of it.

Something happening to Mom.

Afraid again, he says to Lianne, "Can we talk about something else? Something that's not scary?"

"Sure," she says, standing up. "Right after I call my friend. I'll only be on for a second."

Yeah, right, Mitch thinks gloomily, slumping on the couch and hugging a pillow against his suddenly churning stomach.

Margaret's gaze darts nervously from side to side as she picks her way along the paved, sloping path bordered by woods on both sides. She rounds a bend and sees that there's a small clearing ahead.

One might expect this particular section of the sprawling park to have drawn its share of onlookers tonight, assuming that the curiosity seekers who are so compelled to stare at the house would want to see this, too: the site where Jane's daughter was discovered abandoned in her stroller. The actual site was pinpointed on a map in today's newspaper, with a circled *X* marking the spot that Margaret is nearing now.

But the path is deserted, with not a jogger or even a stray dog in sight. Maybe it's because of the hour. Dusk has descended over the woodland park high above the Hudson River.

Or maybe it's because of what happened to Jane here.

Maybe people are frightened.

Maybe they think that what happened to her could happen to them.

Her jaw set grimly, Margaret quickens her pace until she's standing at the edge of a waist-high, narrow rock wall. She reaches into her pocket and takes out a neatly folded tissue.

You never know, she thinks, feeling numb.

Clutching it, she looks straight out. She can see the steep boulders and trees on the Rockland County shore across the river.

Looking down, she notes that there is only dark water, jagged rocks . . . and several boats moored directly below. Their lights cast an eerie glow across the choppy surface. Several figures in wetsuits are clustered on the deck of one boat.

Divers, she realizes, watching the scene for a few moments.

She knows what they're looking for.

Margaret turns and makes her way back to the path, the fingers on one hand shredding the tissue she holds in the other.

She didn't need it after all.

Tasha hasn't heard from Joel all day.

As she puts the kids' plastic supper plates into the dishwasher, she attempts to convince herself that he might have tried to call earlier when she wasn't here, and decided not to leave a message.

But she knows that's not likely. Joel would want credit for a phone call if he made one, since she's always ragging on him about never calling home.

So. Is he making a deliberate statement, still angry about last night, or is he simply caught up in his work once again? There's no way to tell. Not until he gets home. Who knows when that will be?

And what if it isn't his work that's keeping him so busy?

Tasha closes the dishwasher and stands in the middle of the kitchen floor, listening for movement overhead. She put the kids to bed almost a half hour ago, but she doubts they're asleep. It was almost an hour before their bedtime, but she couldn't wait to put them down. She just couldn't handle them anymore.

Her headstrong daughter had thrown one tantrum after another ever since they came home from Rachel's this afternoon. Hunter came home from school with a big science project that needed to be done for tomorrow morning. Tasha ended up doing most of it herself, just to get it over with. And little Max was fussy again, either teething or coming down with something.

Tasha thinks about Karen's daughter, Taylor, who has some kind of stomach bug. *Please, God, don't let it be that.* If Max has it, they'll all get it. The very thought of a houseful of sick kids is enough to send Tasha out the front door shrieking.

She goes over to the phone, thinking she should call Karen to see how Taylor is. Karen looked so worried and exhausted when Tasha dropped off the Pedialyte this morning. It's a first-time-mom thing. Tasha remembers rushing Hunter to Ben's office every time he so much as sneezed.

She peels a banana as she dials Karen's number, realizing she's hungry. She never did get a chance to eat today.

"Hello?"

"Karen, hi. It's me, Tasha."

"Hi!"

"How's Taylor? Still sick?"

"She seems a little better, actually," Karen tells her. "She had diarrhea and vomiting all morning, then that stopped this afternoon, and she actually took some Pedialyte and kept it down."

"Must be a twenty-four-hour thing." Good. Even if the kids get it, it won't drag on for days. "So what are you up to?"

"Just more laundry. The baby's sleeping again. I think she's wiped out by this. Tom had to go out for a while to go over some paperwork with a client of his, so I'm on my own."

"So am I," Tasha says around a bite of banana.

"Joel's working late again?"

"Mm-hmm." Tasha hesitates, then blurts, "Or so he says."

There's a moment of silence. Karen asks, "Is something going on with him, Tasha?"

"I don't know," she admits, half wishing she hadn't brought it up, half relieved that she did. She tells Karen about their argument, and then about how busy Joel is at work lately.

"But he just got a promotion, didn't he? More responsibility?"

"Yes . . ." She sighs. "I guess I'm just suspicious all of a sudden, for some reason."

"If it's any comfort, I can't imagine Joel cheating."

It is a comfort. Not that Karen knows him all that well. But still . . .

"Yeah," Tasha says, "I can't imagine him cheating, either."

The thing is . . .

Even a person who wouldn't ordinarily cheat can get caught up in unexpected passion.

Tasha tries to swallow the banana in her suddenly dry mouth.

One minute, you can be the most committed spouse in the world. The next, you can find yourself in a stranger's arms and contemplating—

"Oh, I hear the baby," Karen says abruptly. "I'm going to try and get her up and feed her before I put her upstairs in her crib for the night. I've got to run."

"Okay."

"Listen, Tasha, any time you want to talk, I'm here. Okay? But I wouldn't worry about Joel. It's probably just work. It's so easy to forget what it's like when you haven't been working for a while. Whenever Tom gets busy with a client, I find myself getting irritated that he's taking so much time away from the family. But I used to do the same thing when I was working. I probably will again. But hopefully not until Taylor's old enough not to need me so much. Anyway . . ."

"I'll let you go," Tasha says reluctantly, hanging up.

She stands in the kitchen, listening for footsteps. For a key in the lock.

Missing Joel.

Maybe he'll be home soon. She might as well watch television in the meantime. *Saving Private Ryan* is supposed to be on again. She's already seen it—once in the movies with Joel—and once on cable—but she's suddenly in the mood for a long, depressing war movie.

"Something that will make my problems look like a piece of cake," she says aloud, breaking the silence she longed for only an hour ago—silence that suddenly seems more ominous than peaceful.

She realizes she's still holding the limp banana peel and tosses it into the garbage, then goes into the unlit living room. She crosses toward the lamp on the end table.

Outside, the wind gusts. Dry leaves scrape against the concrete.

Tasha pauses at the window and looks out.

The Leibermans' house is unusually dark. She realizes the porch light and lamppost haven't been turned on as they always are at this hour. Then she remembers that Rachel isn't home. She said something about meeting friends for dinner, and that she had hired Fletch's nephew, Jeremiah, to babysit. Tasha told her to leave the Bankses' number with him in case he needed anything.

Rachel waved her off, saying thanks but she was sure he'd be fine.

When Tasha and Joel go out, they always leave several phone numbers, including the Leibermans'. Well, that's mostly because Ben is their pediatrician, Tasha tells herself, feeling suddenly overprotective.

And anyway, she doesn't like to take chances.

Unlike Rachel.

Sometimes Tasha thinks that in a decade, when her kids are older, Rachel is going to run off someplace in search of adventure. Or maybe she won't even wait that long.

The funny thing is, Tasha figures Ben and the kids would ultimately be okay without Rachel. After all, she's not the warmest or most devoted wife and mother in the world. In fact, she's pretty self-centered.

But that doesn't mean she wants to leave her family, Tasha reminds herself, wondering why she even thought of such a ridiculous thing.

But she knows. It's the Jane Kendall situation. She can't shake the thought of perfect Jane running away from her life.

Or the thought of doing the same thing herself.

But of course it's only a fantasy. And she has plenty of fantasies. That doesn't mean she's going to act on any of them.

Guilt surges through Tasha again.

Damn it.

Damn Fletch Gallagher.

She turns away from the window and flicks the switch on a nearby lamp, abruptly chasing the shadows from the room.

If the silver Mercedes doesn't slow down, Paula's going to lose sight of it. Her junky little blue Honda can't negotiate the sharp curves of the Sawmill River Parkway at this speed. Any faster, and she's going to lose control and wind up in a ditch or wrapped around a tree. Preferably alive, but on this road you never—

"Damn you!" she curses the driver as he swerves into the left lane to pass a slow-moving car.

Paula, too, goes into the left lane, careering at an unsafe speed alongside the concrete Jersey barriers that separate her from the oncoming traffic. She sees the Mercedes's taillights go back into the right lane and then unexpectedly shoot off to the right even farther.

She realizes he's taken an exit ramp.

Terrific.

Gunning the motor, she sharply moves to the right lane, cutting off a Jeep. The driver sits on his horn.

"Sorry," Paula yells unapologetically as she takes the exit, her eyes peeled for the Mercedes, praying she hasn't lost him.

No. He's right up ahead, stopped at a light.

She watches the car intently through narrowed eyes as

the driver's head turns toward the passenger's. They're having a conversation. Then they kiss, their silhouettes clearly outlined in Paula's headlights.

"Bet you think he's all yours," she murmurs to the unsuspecting woman in Gallagher's arms.

No, Jane Kendall isn't the only one in Townsend Heights who has a bad secret, Paula thinks, shaking her head and pushing in the cigarette lighter on the dashboard.

The traffic signal changes to green.

For a moment the Mercedes stays where it is, the driver otherwise occupied.

Paula doesn't dare blast the horn.

Finally, Gallagher sees the light and pulls forward through the intersection.

So does Paula, placing a cigarette between her lips. She maneuvers the wheel with her left hand. With her right, she removes the lighter from its slot and holds the glowing red coil to the end of her cigarette until it catches.

She follows the Mercedes through an unfamiliar, winding residential neighborhood and then into a commercial district. McDonald's and Burger King. Car dealers and supermarkets. Strip malls and restaurants. Gas stations, too.

Paula glances at her gauge. It's dangerously low. The red "Check Fuel" light has been on for a few miles. If she stops now to fill the tank, she'll lose the Mercedes. If she doesn't, she'll wind up stranded and out of gas.

It's a no-win situation.

Damn, damn, damn . . .

Then she sees the car ahead put on its right turn signal.

"You dog, Fletch Gallagher," she murmurs, realizing he's pulling into a Holiday Inn parking lot.

And there's a Mobil station right next door.

"This just might turn out to be your lucky day after all," Paula tells herself, breaking into a broad grin as she flicks her right turn signal.

Bathed in the glow of the night-light, Karen puts the baby into her crib, covers her with a velvety pink blanket, and whispers, "Good night, sweetheart."

She kisses her own fingertips, then touches them gently to her daughter's downy head, not wanting to leave the room just yet. Not when Taylor's been so sick, poor thing.

Well, she's getting over it now. She drank a few ounces of formula just now, and she started taking the Pedialyte late this afternoon after rejecting it all morning. Karen had thought she was going to have to call Ben again and bring the baby to the office to be examined, but then, luckily, her condition improved.

Only when Taylor was past the worst of it did Tom decide to leave the house to meet with his client. The guy, a local business owner, had been calling all day, frantic about some tax crisis. Once Karen answered the phone and found herself tempted to tell the guy to leave her husband alone. That Tom had a sick baby and more on his mind than somebody else's screwed-up taxes.

Luckily, she held her tongue.

Now that the crisis with Taylor is over, Karen realizes she was just high-strung and over-tired. All she wants now is to rest. She should probably be glad she has the house to herself for a while.

She takes a last look at the baby sleeping soundly in her crib.

"Don't worry, angel," she says softly. "Mommy's watching over you."

She turns on the baby monitor and leaves the room, cracking the door slightly.

Back downstairs, she plops on the couch and reaches for the remote control. She's not very big on television, aside from The Learning Channel and PBS documentaries, but tonight she's in the mood for something mindless. Something reassuring.

Like the *Who Wants to be a Millionaire* game show.

Finding it, she leaves it on and loses herself in it for a few minutes. If she were a contestant, she would have won $125,000.

She's about to try and double the money when she hears a car door slamming outside.

Tom's home, she thinks, relieved. She didn't realize how uneasy she has felt about being alone until now.

She presses the "Mute" button on the television set and waits for the sound of his footsteps coming in the back door.

Only silence.

Getting up, Karen goes over to the window that looks out on the driveway. Only her Volvo station wagon is parked there. No sign of Tom's little black Saab.

So he's not home yet after all.

Disappointment mingles with anxiety in her gut.

She glances at the Gallaghers' house next door. Their driveway is separated from Karen's by a narrow strip of grass. Fletch's car is missing, but Sharon's Lexus SUV is there. Karen must have heard her coming home.

She returns to the couch and picks up the remote again.

But this time she can't concentrate on the question Regis Philbin is asking.

She realizes that she wants Tom here with her. And it isn't just because the baby's been sick.

Karen pulls her knees up to her chest, wrapping her arms around them, filled with inexplicable apprehension as she wonders again what happened to Jane Kendall.

Jeremiah slowly opens the door to the little boy's room, praying that it won't creak. It doesn't.

He spots Noah in his crib. He can hear his gentle snoring from here. He's sound asleep.

Mara is, too. He just checked.

Jeremiah pulls the door closed again, holding his breath until it makes a quiet click, then pausing with his hand on the knob in case the baby stirs on the other side.

He hears nothing.

Good.

Turning away from the door, he walks slowly back down the long hallway. Strange, being alone in somebody else's house at night.

Of course, this is how he used to feel at Aunt Sharon and Uncle Fletch's, too. Until he got used to it.

But they're family.

Rachel Leiberman is different.

Jeremiah stands at the head of the stairs, his head cocked, listening for the slightest sound. Nothing. It's as if the whole house is holding its breath, waiting to see what he's going to do next.

Trembling slightly, he checks his watch. He's got time. Plenty of time.

His heart pounding, he steps forward.

He pauses one more moment, uncertain whether he wants to go through with this.

Then, reaching a decision, he opens the master-bedroom door, and slips over the threshold.

* * *

It's past midnight when Rachel arrives home. Humming to herself, she steps into the silent house, tossing her keys into a basket on the low table by the door. She can hear the television in the family room.

Stepping out of her shoes, she carries them as she pads barefoot toward the back of the house. Jeremiah is there, sitting on the couch. Not dozing the way you might expect to find a teenager at this hour on a school night. Not even lounging.

He's perched on the very edge of the seat, hands at his sides, both feet neatly placed in front of him on the floor. There's something odd about that, Rachel thinks uneasily. He seems almost guilty, sitting there in that tense, deliberate position.

"I guess I beat my husband home after all," she says, trying to sound casual. "How were the kids?"

"P-perfect. They're b-both asleep," he says quickly, despite the stutter.

Too quickly?

"They'd better be, at this time of night," she tells him, trying to sound more upbeat than she feels.

He looks at her—a fleeting, intense glance—before turning his gaze to the television. It's tuned to MTV, yet something tells her he hasn't been absorbed in the video. She senses that he turned it on to give the appearance of normalcy—just a regular babysitter, hanging out watching MTV.

She wants him out of here. Now.

She opens her purse. "I'll just pay you and you can—"

"You already d-did," he cuts in.

Right. She paid him earlier, before she left.

"Okay, then," she says, and clears her throat. What if he doesn't leave? Oh, God, what if he tries something?

But he takes her cue and stands.

He walks toward her.

Her breath catches in her throat.

He's not looking at her, but down at his feet. There's something about his behavior that tells her he's up to something. What the hell can it be? Did he eat the carton of ice cream that's in the freezer? Did one of the kids break something while she was gone?

"I'll s-see you again s-sometime," he says, walking toward the hall.

"Sure."

Not on your life, she thinks, sighing in relief, locking the door after him and turning on the outside light for Ben.

When the front light goes on outside the Leibermans' front door, it illuminates most of the front lawn and a good portion of the side yard. Thankfully, the clump of evergreen shrubs remains in the shadows. No neighbor glancing out a window will see the dark-clad figure hidden among the low-hanging boughs, and neither will Rachel, should trepidation steal over her, causing her to peer out into the night.

She's left the light on for her husband.

That's clear.

What if Ben Leiberman comes home before the goal is accomplished?

You'll just have to slip out before anybody sees you, then wait for another chance.

But that could take days. This can't go on forever.

The longer it drags on, the greater the chance of being caught.

The key!

Relax. There it is, still in your pocket.

Getting it was surprisingly easy, thanks to Mrs. Tuccelli. It wasn't hard to find out that Rachel's former nanny goes to daily morning mass at Immaculate Conception. Nor was it hard to slip into the pew behind her . . . or sneak her keys out of her purse while she was kneeling after communion. Thankfully, the organ music had concealed the slight jangling noise, and by the time Mrs. Tuccelli finished her prayer and settled on the seat again, the pew behind her was empty.

When had the old lady realized her keys were missing? Would the police question her after they found Rachel tomorrow? What would she tell them about her missing keys? That she had lost them? Probably. She would never suspect that they had been stolen during mass.

Just as Rachel most likely doesn't suspect, right now, that the curtain is about to come down on her charmed life.

Or does she?

If she does, there's nothing she can do about it. No way for her to know for sure—or to stop it even if she suspects what's about to happen.

The sense of power is intoxicating. It's tempting to stay here a bit longer, basking in the sensation.

But that wouldn't be wise.

A light has gone on in the master bedroom upstairs.

It's time to move.

No need to risk detection under the glare of the front porch light. A trial run earlier indicated that the deadbolts on the front and rear doors can be opened with the same key.

The back yard is dark. Deserted. Gusting wind smothers the sound of footsteps crunching in fallen leaves. Ten seconds from the bushes to the door. Five seconds to insert the key and turn the lock, opening and closing the door in near silence.

There are footsteps above.

Rachel in her room.

Her faint humming is audible from the stairway.

You sound so content, Rachel. Like a woman who has just come from a rendezvous with her secret lover. Like a woman who doesn't know she's about to die.

The upstairs hallway is dark, but a pool of light spills from the master bedroom. The door is ajar.

Something is visible through the crack in the door.

It's a barbell.

So that's how you keep your figure, Rachel. You work out at home, too. Not just at your fancy gym. You lift weights in the privacy of your lovely bedroom.

The rage is building again. Just like the last time.

Let it in. Embrace it. It will help.

You're going to wish you didn't do that, Rachel.

You'll wish you didn't spend so much time making yourself perfect.

Familiar rage, white-hot, toxic.

Because I can lift weights, too, you know.

I can lift them up, and I can bring them down. Hard. Hard enough to destroy a beautiful face like yours forever.

"Tash?"

"Mmm?" She rolls over in bed, burrowing under the down comforter, slipping easily back toward sleep. . . .

"Tasha . . ."

Back toward the nightmare that had her in its grip.

And then, once again, she's in a bombed-out town in the French countryside, battling the Nazis as air-raid sirens blast.

"Tasha!"

Her eyes snap open.

The room is dark, but she can see Joel standing over the bed, backlit by the light from the hall. He's wearing a suit beneath his unbuttoned trenchcoat. Is he coming in or going out? What time is it?

She glances toward the clock. Two-thirty in the morning.

That shrill whining isn't part of her dream, and it isn't an air-raid siren. It's a police car or a fire truck.

"What are you doing?" she asks Joel, confused, rubbing her eyes and propping herself on her elbows.

"I just got home."

Then why is he waking her up? Why isn't he taking off his coat, his suit? Why isn't he using the bathroom and climbing into bed?

He sits beside her. Surprised, she looks at him. His face is cast in shadows. He reaches for her hand, takes it, squeezes it.

He's going to say he's sorry for the stupid argument, she realizes in relief.

Her next thought: *He's going to tell me he's in love with another woman and he's leaving me.*

Oh, God. She's not ready for this. For all her suspicions and insecurities, she never thought it was actually going to happen. Not really.

"Tasha . . ." He pauses. Is silent again. There's not a sound but the siren in the distance, drawing closer.

"Just say it, Joel."

"Say it?" he echoes, sounding incredulous. "Then . . . you know?"

It's true. He's leaving.

The knowledge slams into her like a commuter train and it's all she can do to keep from hurling herself on him, pounding him with her fists.

She opens her mouth to ask him who it is—whether it's his secretary or someone else—but before she can speak, he says, "When did you find out?"

Suddenly too weary for anger, she says only, "I just figured it out."

Just silence.

And the siren.

Again.

Say something else, you bastard! a voice shrieks in her head. *Tell me who it is! Tell me how you can justify throwing away everything we have!*

"Tasha, I don't think we're talking about the same thing," Joel says at last.

She stares numbly at his face. It's still shrouded in darkness. But he's still holding her hand. Still squeezing her hand. He wouldn't be doing that if he were trying to tell her that he didn't love her anymore.

"What's going on, Joel?" she asks, suddenly more afraid than she was when she thought he was leaving.

Something is wrong. She can sense it, even as she realizes that the siren is coming much too close. It sounds like it's right down the street. . . .

"There's no easy way to tell you this, Tasha. It's Rachel. She's been killed."

Sirens.

They're shrill even through the closed window, shrill enough to jar the sleeping town into awareness. Are people waking in their beds, wondering whether there's been some kind of accident or tragedy? Do they stir at all?

Or are they deep in slumber, oblivious, having trained themselves to ignore early-morning police emergencies, certain that whatever has gone wrong has nothing to do with them?

After all, Townsend Heights is the kind of town where nothing truly terrible ever happens. At least, it was.

Well, not anymore.

The people of Townsend Heights are going to wake up to reality. They're going to realize that there's a cold-blooded killer in their midst. And when they do . . .

Nobody will feel safe. Except, of course, for me.

Friday, October 12

Chapter Eight

"Margaret? Are you in here?"

Startled, Margaret looks up from the television screen to see her mother hovering behind her in the doorway of the Kendalls' family room.

"Margaret, something awful has—oh. You know," Mother says, her gaze shifting from Margaret's face to the TV.

It's tuned to Channel 12, the local Westchester station, where a grim-faced reporter is standing live at the scene outside a cordoned-off two-story white colonial home with black shutters. The blue-black sky in the background shows the first streaks of pink.

Absorbed in the television news coverage, Margaret hadn't realized that it's dawn already. She glances out the floor-to-ceiling window nearest the couch. Sure enough, the trees just beyond are bathed in a gauzy light.

She checks the clock on the mantel. It's already past six A.M.

"Margaret? You know, don't you?" Mother persists.

"About the Leiberman woman? Yes, I know." Margaret turns her attention back to the television.

Her mother crosses the room and sinks heavily into the couch beside her. "What are you doing up so early?"

"I couldn't sleep—"

"I haven't either." Leave it to Mother to turn the conversation back to herself. And Jane. "I've had terrible insomnia ever since Jane—"

"—and I heard the sirens," Margaret continues as though her mother hadn't interrupted her original explanation.

"I can't bear this," Bess wails. "This other woman is dead. If this has anything to do with your sister's disappearance . . ."

"Nobody has said that it does, Mother," Margaret tells her.

"But she's so like Jane. Beautiful—not in the same way, but very striking. Did you see her picture?"

Margaret nods. Yes, Rachel Leiberman *was* beautiful. And she, like Jane, had it all. Everything money could buy, and the precious things it could not: an adoring, successful husband, cherubic children . . .

The perfect life.

Now someone has taken it away.

Margaret eyes her mother's trembling hands, wondering if she should reach over and hold them.

She rarely touches her mother these days. Never has, really. Not like affectionate Jane, who was always patting Mother's arm or casually slinging an arm around her shoulder. If Jane were here and Mother were this upset, she would be hugging her, comforting her.

But Jane's not here. Which, of course, is why Mother is upset.

And God help her, Margaret can't quite bring herself to comfort Bess, even now. At least, not physically.

"This woman was found bludgeoned in her bed, Mother. In her own home. Jane hasn't turned up dead. She's only missing. One might have nothing to do with the other."

"This is Townsend Heights, Margaret. For God's sake, are you telling me that there are *two* homicidal maniacs on the loose in this town?"

"Jane hasn't been murdered, Mother." Margaret grips the remote control in her lap, tension aching in her fingers, her jaw, her shoulders. "She's just gone. Nobody is telling us that she's been murdered."

Bess just stares stiffly at the television, her eyes brimming with tears.

Margaret looks at her for a long moment, then looks away, out the window.

On television the reporter is interviewing a woman who says she works in Benjamin Leiberman's office. She's sobbing, talking about how wonderful the doctor is and how tragic it is that something has happened to his wife. How his poor children have been left motherless . . .

Schuyler.

"I'll go listen for the baby, Mother," Margaret says, remembering her niece. "She should be up soon."

"She's already awake. Owen has her upstairs, in his room."

"I'll go see if he wants me to take her." Margaret stands, putting the television remote onto the polished cherry-wood coffee table.

She hasn't seen Owen yet this morning. Her hands flutter to her hair, making sure it's neatly combed back.

She was tempted to leave it loose this morning for a change. But then she lost her nerve, pulling it into a bun as usual.

Suddenly aware of her mother's shrewd gaze on her, she quickly lowers her hands, thrusting them into the pockets of her black wool slacks.

"Leave Owen and Schuyler alone, Margaret." Bess's voice is stern. Knowing.

"But I'm not trying to—Mother, he must be exhausted. I heard him walking around the house at all hours. I'll just go take the baby off his hands."

"No. If he needs help with her, I'll do it. Schuyler is more comfortable with me."

Margaret spins on her heel and leaves the room, stung, yet knowing it's the truth.

"Let's go over this one more time," the gray-haired police detective says, folding his thick arms across his broad chest. "Exactly when did you put the children to bed?"

"I already t-told you. . . ." Jeremiah's voice cracks. "It was around eight."

"And then you watched television in the Leibermans' family room. But you can't remember what you watched."

Fletch looks at his nephew. The kid squirms on the couch.

"I w-wasn't really w-watching it," he says. "I was studying, t-too. So I wasn't p-paying much attention t-to the TV."

"I see."

The detective turns to Sharon, who's seated in a chair across the room. "Your nephew says Mrs. Leiberman sent him home at around midnight, Mrs. Gallagher. Did you hear him come in?"

"No. I was in bed, asleep. I sleep very soundly." She looks toward Fletch, seated on the couch beside Jeremiah. Her expression clearly says, *Back me up here.*

He intends to say nothing until he realizes that the detective, too, is looking questioningly at him.

Fletch admits, "Yes, she sleeps soundly."

"And did you hear your nephew come in, Mr. Gallagher?"

He shifts his weight on the cushion, forcing himself to say evenly, "No, I didn't. I was asleep then, too."

"And you sleep as soundly as your wife does."

He shrugs. It isn't a question. Is the detective suspicious of him? No, Fletch reminds himself. Jeremiah's the suspect here. Not him, or Sharon. They're just witnesses. Or not.

"And when you came home, Jeremiah, what did you do?" the detective asks.

"I w-went to b-bed."

"And what time was that?"

"I t-told you already, I th-th-think it was around m-midnight. I d-didn't look at the c-clock." Jeremiah looks at Fletch, his eyes pleading.

All right. It's time to put an end to this. The police have been questioning the boy for hours, ever since the doorbell rang in the middle of the night and Fletch opened it to find two dour-looking cops on the step.

He rises from the couch. "Yes, you did tell him. Over and over again. Don't say anything else, Jeremiah," Fletch orders his nephew.

"Mr. Gallagher—"

"Yes?" He glares at the detective. Summers, he said his name was. Moved up here after spending almost two decades working in the South Bronx. He probably figured he would have an uneventful cruise toward retirement.

"If you'd let us finish questioning your nephew, we'd—"

"Not without a lawyer," Fletch says firmly. "I should have called him in the first place. I would have, but—" He breaks off, clears his throat. Makes himself look directly at the detective, unwilling to appear as anything other than a concerned uncle. And neighbor. After all, Rachel Leiberman lived right down the street. . . .

"So you want to hold off on further questioning until your lawyer is present?" the detective prods.

"Absolutely." Fletch realizes he's been biting his lip. Hard. He tastes tangy, salty blood on his tongue.

"Fletch . . . are you sure?" Sharon speaks up from her chair across the room, beside the fireplace.

"I'm positive," he tells her. He follows her gaze back to Jeremiah.

His nephew is the picture of pathetic, shivering in his short-sleeved T-shirt and boxer shorts, his scrawny white arms wrapped around his thin chest in an effort to keep warm. The big, seldom-used living room is chilly at this hour. Fletch absently reminds himself to turn up the heat after the detective leaves.

What more does he want from the kid now? Jeremiah has painstakingly given him the rundown of last night, several times. His story never varied. He said he had put the Leiberman kids to bed, then watched television in their family room for a few hours. Then Rachel had come home at around midnight and sent him on his way. He came straight home, let himself into the house, and went to bed.

Finally the detective does go—reluctantly, and only after telling the Gallaghers he'll be in touch again later.

The moment he closes the door behind him, Fletch lets out an enormous, shaky sigh. He bows his head and rubs his burning eyes.

"You don't think he did it, do you?"

He jumps at the whispered voice behind him; sees that Sharon has followed him into the front hall. She stands there, bundled in her white silk robe, staring up at him.

Is that an accusing look in her eyes? Is she suspicious of *him*?

Suddenly overwhelmed, Fletch abruptly strides away, first to the thermostat on the wall, which he adjusts to sixty-eight degrees, then back toward the living room and Jeremiah.

"Fletch? You don't think he's actually guilty, do you?" Sharon asks in a low voice, hurrying after him, touching his arm.

He stops, turns to her. "I don't know, Sharon. I honestly don't know."

"My God, Fletch. Are you saying you think Jeremiah—"

"I'm saying I don't know what I think. Just don't say a word about him to anyone. Including the cops."

He crosses the threshold into the living room. His nephew is still sitting on the couch. Tears are streaming down his pock-marked face.

"Jeremiah . . ." Fletch goes to him, sits next to him. He doesn't know what to say. Finally, he settles on, "I'll call my lawyer."

The boy nods. "What ab-bout my d-dad?"

"I'll call him, too. Unless you want to."

Jeremiah shakes his head mutely.

Struggling to conceal his inner turmoil, Fletch pats

the boy's bony arm. Across the room, he sees Sharon in the doorway, watching him, an inscrutable expression on her face.

"Are you sure you're okay, Tash?" Joel asks, watching her as she yanks a navy turtleneck over her head. They're both in the master bathroom with the door closed, the air swirling with mist from their showers.

Yet somehow it's freezing in here, she thinks vaguely. *Or maybe it's just me.* Her entire body is covered in goose bumps. The cotton fabric of the shirt seems to irritate her skin everywhere it touches.

"Tash?"

She pulls her damp hair free of the neckline, then looks at him. He's watching her, one hand on the knob of the closed door. He's put on a dress shirt and has a tie dangling around his neck.

"So you really are going to the office today?" she asks him.

When he first said that he was, she reacted in disbelief. After all they've been through in these past few hours . . .

Joel rushed back over to Ben's right after he told Tasha what had happened. She had been torn between wanting to go and needing to stay here, with her children. The whole time Joel was gone, she prowled the house, going from window to window, from door to door, making sure the house was secure, never quite believing that it was, no matter how many locks she checked and rechecked.

Finally, Joel came back across the street, carrying one of the sleeping Leiberman kids. Mara. Tasha tucked the little girl into bed in the master bedroom, then swiftly set up their portable crib alongside the bed. A minute later, Joel came back with Noah, and Tasha gently laid the sleeping baby in the crib.

She and Joel tiptoed back downstairs to collapse into each other's arms, Tasha weeping, Joel comforting.

Later, they drank coffee and took turns peeking out the window at the commotion in front of the house across the street. Police officers came and went. So did the coroner. The media came and stayed, their number growing steadily through the wee hours. By daybreak, the street was clogged with vans and reporters and camera crews.

The Leiberman children slept through all of it. So did the Banks children.

Joel told Tasha that Ben was a mess. Hysterical. In shock.

"One of us should go be with him," Tasha kept saying. But Joel insisted that they should remain here at home, out of the way. Ben's sister was on her way over from her home in Bedford. She would stay with him.

And Joel would stay with Tasha.

Or so she thought.

"Can't you cancel your client meeting?" Tasha asks her husband now, not looking at him as she pulls on the same pair of jeans she wore yesterday. And the day before.

The washing machine, she remembers, distracted. She still hasn't touched it. Well, it doesn't seem nearly as pressing now. She can wear these jeans every day if she has to. It doesn't matter.

"I told you," Joel says wearily, with forced patience, wiping at the fogged mirror with a towel, "it's not a meeting. It's a shoot. I'm already late as it is. The CEOs of both the client and the agency are going to be there, and I need to be there, too. Like I said, I'll come straight home as soon as it's over."

She knows.

He *did* say it all before. Went into detail, telling her that the shoot can't be delayed because the talent is a supermodel who has a busy schedule, and they're shooting on location in midtown, which means applying for permits galore. The bottom line is that Joel can't cancel the shoot merely because of a murder.

While he swiftly knots his tie, standing in front of the mirror, Tasha jams her feet into her sneakers, not bothering to tie them.

"All set?" he asks.

She nods.

"Okay, I'm opening the door now," Joel whispers.

She flips off the bathroom light and follows him through their darkened bedroom, glancing at the small figures huddled in the bed and crib. Rachel's children are still sound asleep, unaware that they no longer have a mommy.

Will I have to be the one to tell them when they wake up? Tasha wonders in dread.

Damn Joel for leaving her alone with them at a time like this.

He holds open the door from the bedroom to the hall for her. She steps across the threshold. He pulls the door closed behind her with a quiet click.

"Are you going to be okay while I'm gone?" he asks her.

What will he say if she tells him that she won't?

"Yeah," she replies, walking toward the stairs.

He follows.

"Don't open the door for anyone while I'm gone," he tells her as they descend to the first floor. "Keep Hunter home from school."

She nods. They already agreed to do that.

"I told Ben to call over here when he's ready to see the kids."

She nods again. He's said this before, too.

At the foot of the stairs, he opens the hall closet and removes his trench coat. "The police are going to want to talk to you at some point, Tash."

She looks at him in surprise. "To *me*?"

"You were over there yesterday—"

"They don't think I had something to do with it, do they?" Her heart is pounding.

"I doubt it. But they'll be talking to anyone who might know something."

"I don't know anything."

"Are you sure?" Joel looks carefully at her, seeming to probe her face. "Can you think of anything that might help? Anything at all?"

"I . . . I don't know, Joel," she says slowly, looking into his brown eyes.

A thin wail erupts overhead.

"There's Max," she says. "I'll get him before he wakes everyone else."

"I'll be home as soon as I possibly can, Tasha," Joel calls after her, picking up his briefcase and heading for the door.

"Okay," she says, wishing she believed him.

Jeremiah hears a door slam downstairs. Going to the window of his room, he sees his uncle in the driveway below with Lily and Daisy. Uncle Fletch is no longer wearing the sweatpants and T-shirt he had on earlier. Now he's in black corduroys and a plaid button-down shirt under his black leather jacket. The girls, whom Jeremiah hasn't yet seen today, are dressed in jeans and sweaters, carrying bookbags. They climb into the silver Mercedes. Uncle Fletch starts the engine and backs out quickly.

Obviously, he's driving them to Townsend Heights Elementary. He didn't even suggest that Jeremiah get ready for school after the detective left, and Jeremiah didn't ask him about it. They both assumed he wouldn't be going. Not after what happened. Not considering the fact that he's the last person who saw Rachel Leiberman alive, and the police said they want to talk to him again.

Thank God Uncle Fletch finally interrupted Detective Summers. Jeremiah didn't think he could take much more at that point. The detective kept grilling him about his actions the night before, wanting to know every single move he had made while he was at the Leibermans' house.

When Uncle Fletch cut in and said he was going to call a lawyer, Jeremiah was actually on the verge of breaking down, perilously close to admitting everything.

Well, that didn't happen, thanks to Uncle Fletch.

He turns away from the window. His gaze falls on his desk. It's littered with piles of papers and books. On top of the pile is a newspaper clipping from a mid-August edition of the *Townsend Gazette*. He's read it dozens of times, but he does so again now, after looking at the photo of his stepmother.

It was taken when Melissa was younger—maybe even before she had the twins. She's smiling and tanned in the photo, her blond hair loose and falling past her shoulders. When Jeremiah met her it was shorter than that. And she hadn't smiled much—at least, not at him. Not unless his father was around.

NORTH STREET HOUSE FIRE LEAVES ONE DEAD
By Paula Bailey

A deadly inferno on Friday night left a Townsend Heights family homeless—and three children without a mother. Melissa Gallagher, 40, of 27 North Street in the village, died in the blaze, which started in the kitchen in the early evening hours. The cause is still under investigation.

The woman's teenage son, Jeremiah, and young daughters, Lily and Daisy, were not home at the time. Her husband, Aidan Gallagher, has been overseas on military duty since mid-June. He could not be reached for comment.

According to his brother, Fletcher Gallagher—also a Townsend Heights resident, and a former Cleveland Indians pitcher who is now a sportscaster for the New York Mets—the family had owned the North Street home for several years. "My wife and I are just devastated by this loss," Fletcher Gallagher said on Saturday. "We will be keeping the children until their father returns home. My brother has already been widowed once before. This has just overwhelmed him."

Townsend Heights Fire Chief Ray Wisnewski stated that the fast-moving fire engulfed the wood-frame house. The victim was found in the kitchen, so badly burned that the body could not be positively identified at the scene. "We are engaged in an ongoing investigation," Chief Wisnewski told the Gazette.

Melissa Gallagher was born in Fairfield County, Connecticut, graduated with a teaching degree from Vassar, and taught at several private elementary schools in Westchester County more than a decade ago. Funeral services will be held on Monday morning at Holy Father Church in Townsend Heights, followed by private burial in Fairfield County.

A creaking, groaning noise suddenly disturbs the silent household.

Jeremiah recognizes it: water in the pipes. He hears the sound every time somebody takes a shower.

He tosses the newspaper clipping back on the desk, walks over to the door of his room, and opens it cautiously. Aunt Sharon is the only one home. Sure enough, it sounds like she's in the shower of the master bedroom.

Jeremiah goes back into his room and hurriedly pulls on jeans and a fleece pullover Uncle Fletch bought him. He starts to put on sneakers, then changes his mind and finds his thick-soled boots. His warm parka, too.

Moments later he slips out into the hall and down the stairs, knowing that this is his chance. His aunt lingers in the shower sometimes, but it won't take his uncle very long to drop the girls at school. Five minutes, tops, if he comes straight home.

In the front hall on the first floor, Jeremiah peers out the window facing the wide, tree-lined street. There are cars parked everywhere, and even from here he can see the crowd gathered at the far end, where the Leibermans' house is. He half-expects to see an officer stationed in front of the Gallagher house, keeping an eye on things, but there isn't one. Jeremiah pauses to consider this, rethinking his plan.

Maybe they don't suspect him of killing Rachel Leiberman after all.

But that Detective Summers sure acted like he did.

Jeremiah can't take any chances.

What if Detective Summers comes back? What if he searches the house and the shed? What if he arrests Jeremiah?

He has to act now.

But what are you going to do? You don't have enough time

to get rid of everything, a voice in his head reminds him as he heads to the kitchen.

He surveys the manicured yard, making sure it's empty.

Then, brimming with uncertainty, he ventures outside and crosses the grass, knowing only that he has to do everything he can to protect himself—before it's too late.

Paula hesitates only a moment before ringing the Bankses' doorbell. It's still early, not even eight o'clock yet.

But she has a job to do, she reminds herself as she presses the button. Besides, how likely is it that anyone on this block is asleep? The commotion in front of the Leibermans' house is even greater than the hubbub of the past few days on Harding Place.

"Who is it?" a female voice calls through the door.

"It's Paula Bailey."

A pause.

"Who?"

"Paula Bailey. I live here in town. I need to talk to you, Mrs. Banks."

"About what?" comes the suspicious reply.

"Can I please come in?" Paula asks. "Look, I'm a mom. Just like you are. I know how you must feel, but you can trust me. Really."

To her shock, the door opens. Just a crack, but still . . .

A tired-looking female face framed by lank dark hair peers out at Paula. She recognizes Tasha Banks and sees by her expression that the woman finds her familiar, too. Well, it's a small town. They've probably passed each other on the street dozens of times.

"I'd like to talk to you just for a minute," Paula says. "Please?"

"You're a reporter, aren't you?"

"For the *Townsend Gazette*," Paula tells her in a tone meant to convince Tasha Banks that she's different from the other news hounds clogging the once-quiet cul-de-sac. She's not bloodthirsty like they are. She's a concerned citizen of this town.

Tasha just looks at her.

"Listen, I know I'm not the first reporter to show up at your door this morning," Paula says.

"No, you're not."

"Have you spoken to anyone else?" Paula asks cautiously.

"No. And I shouldn't speak to you, either. . . ."

"But you will?" Paula prods, just as she hears a child's cry coming from somewhere over Tasha's shoulder.

"That's my son. I've got to go see—"

"It's okay. I'll wait." Paula catches the door as it starts to swing closed. She steps into the house and pulls the door closed behind her. It's a bold move, but she doesn't have a choice. This is her job.

Tasha glances back at her, clearly dismayed. Then, stepping over several toys on the floor, she hurries into the kitchen at the back of the house. She's back moments later, a sobbing baby on her hip.

"Hey, what happened to you, little guy?" Paula asks, reaching out to gently pat the baby's head. She looks at Tasha. "Did he get hurt?"

"No. He was just upset that I left the room. He's been fussy all morning. I think he's coming down with something. He wants me to hold him constantly."

"I remember when my son went through that. He's probably teething," Paula offers in a mother-to-mother tone. "At least, that's what it always was with Mitch. Whenever he was cutting a tooth, he wanted me to carry him around for hours on end."

"That's probably it," Tasha agrees. She seems to have relaxed a little. "My other kids never did this when they were cutting teeth, though. Hunter, my oldest son, was always pretty independent and laid-back. He never really fussed or acted clingy. And my daughter, Victoria . . . well, she fussed constantly, so it was hard to tell when she was out of sorts. She hasn't changed much. Although she behaves a lot better for my husband."

"That's good."

"It would be if he were around," Tasha mutters.

"So he's away a lot?" Paula asks, surprised by her candor.

Tasha shrugs. "He might as well be. He works in the city. You know—the commute, the long hours, and sometimes he travels on business."

"That's hard. Then you're alone with the kids," Paula says.

"Yeah, and it's not even that I'd mind so much if it were only on weekdays, but now it's starting to cut into our weekends. Like this Sunday, he has to fly out of here in the afternoon so that he can be in Chicago for an early meeting on Monday—but look, I don't know why I'm unloading on you."

"Because it stinks. Look, I know what it's like to be on your own as a mom." *Do I ever*, Paula thinks wryly. "After a while, you could really use another pair of hands, right?"

"Exactly."

Paula grins and is rewarded when Tasha flashes her a brief smile. It dims quickly, though, and Tasha looks down at the still-whimpering baby in her arms.

Paula can practically read her mind. She's thinking about Rachel Leiberman. Paula's done her homework.

The two were close friends. "You must be so upset today, Tasha," she says. "I'm so sorry about Rachel."

"I can't believe it," Tasha says, turning tear-filled eyes toward Paula. "It's like a nightmare. And the worst part is . . . her daughter's upstairs, playing with mine. And her son is sleeping. They have no idea what's going on."

"Nobody's told them?"

"No. And I don't think I should. They wanted to know why they were here when they woke up, and I told them their parents had some things they had to take care of. They're so little. They didn't even question it." Tasha's voice breaks.

Paula reaches into her pocket and pulls out a neatly folded tissue. She hands it to Tasha.

"Thank you," Tasha says, sniffling. She wipes her red-rimmed eyes.

"Look, I know this is a terrible time, and the last thing I want to do is make things harder for you. But if I could just ask you a few questions about your friend—"

"What kind of questions?"

"I'm an investigative reporter."

Okay, that isn't technically the truth—at least, not according to her boss, Tim. But he has no idea what Paula is capable of doing, if only given the chance. And now, tired of waiting for the chance to be handed to her, she's simply taking the initiative to go for it. To prove herself.

She tells Tasha, "I'm hoping to uncover a lead that will help me to figure out who murdered your friend."

"Isn't that the cops' job?"

"Definitely. But I'm going to do anything I can to help. If there's a murderer on the loose in Townsend Heights, I want him caught before he strikes again."

"So do I," Tasha says in a small voice. "I'm scared

to—What do you mean '*if* there's a murderer on the loose'?"

Paula shrugs. "It isn't clear why your friend was killed."

"You don't think it was random? That it could have happened to anyone?"

"Do you?"

"I have no idea," Tasha says slowly.

The baby fusses.

Absently, Tasha bends and retrieves a small plastic car from the floor by her feet, handing it to him. Then she says, "I keep thinking about Jane Kendall, wondering whether this has anything to do with that."

"Well, what do you think? Did you know Jane, too?"

"Only slightly."

"Is there anything you can think of that Jane and Rachel might have had in common? Anything at all?"

"Just Gymboree," Tasha says. "That's it. We all go to the class once a week with our kids. Other than that, Rachel and Jane travel in completely different circles."

"And you can't think of anyone who'd have a reason to want either of them dead?"

Tasha flinches. "No."

That's it. She's done talking to me, Paula realizes, watching a veil descend over Tasha's face.

It was the word *dead.* Too strong. Paula shouldn't have used it. But she momentarily forgot to tread carefully. Maybe she can still—

"You know what? I've got to go up and check on the kids," Tasha says abruptly. "Right now."

"I'll wait here . . ."

"No. I'd rather have you leave . . . if you don't mind."

She's trying to be firm, Paula realizes, but it isn't really her nature. Good. She might get something out of Tasha Banks yet. But not today.

"Can we get together again and talk about this?" Paula asks. "Maybe meet for coffee in a day or two, when things die down? How about while your husband's away? Maybe you'll feel like getting out of the house."

"I'd have my kids with me. . . ."

"Then we can make it pizza. Look, I'll call you," Paula says hurriedly. She fishes in her purse and hands over a card. "In the meantime, here's my number. Office, home, cell phone. If you think of anything at all that might help, call me. Please."

"I will," Tasha says, glancing at the card, then at Paula.

"I really am sorry about your friend," Paula tells her, pressing her hand gently, holding it more than shaking it. "Look, if there's anything I can do for you—even just taking your kids off your hands—let me know. Okay?"

Tasha looks surprised. "Thank you."

Paula smiles. "Like I said, I'm a mom, too. I know how draining it is when they're so young. Just take it easy, okay?"

"I'll try. And maybe we can have coffee or pizza or something."

"I'd like that. See you, Tasha."

Paula walks out the front door and glances at the house across the street. The throng has swelled. There'll be no getting near Ben Leiberman today.

She glances down the block.

The Gallaghers' house is barely visible from here, but she can clearly see a silver Mercedes parked in the driveway. For a moment she considers a confrontation with Fletch.

No.

Not yet.

It's too soon.

She has to wait until the time is right.

* * *

"Mitchell?"

He looks up from the masked, robed figure he's doodling on the inside of his notebook cover with a black ballpoint pen.

Uh-oh. Miss Bright is watching him. He was supposed to be working on the questions at the end of section three in his science textbook.

"Yeah?" Mitch asks cautiously.

"I've just received a note." She waves a piece of paper in her hand.

Mitch frowns. He hadn't even seen a messenger from the office.

Well, that's because he was so caught up in what he was drawing—and in worrying about the killer on the loose in Townsend Heights.

Looks like Lianne was right about that. His mother woke him up early this morning and sent him to Blake's, saying there had been a murder and she had to go cover it.

It turned out something happened to another lady from Townsend Heights. Mitch did his best not to show how scared he was as he watched the Channel 12 news with Blake's family before school, scanning the crowd outside the dead lady's house for his mom's face. He thought he'd seen her once, but he wasn't sure.

"You're wanted in the principal's office immediately," Miss Bright tells Mitch. "Bring your books with you."

There's a quiet snicker behind him.

"What'd you do this time, Bailey?" Robbie Sussman whispers.

He frowns. He hasn't done anything. Why would he be wanted in the principal's office? Unless . . .

There's a sickening thud in his stomach.

Mom.

Has something happened to her?

He grabs his notebook and textbook and forces his rubbery legs to carry him toward the door.

Standing at her kitchen sink, Karen pours the last of the coffee in the pot down the drain. It's grown dark and bitter after sitting on the hot burner for several hours. She made it around three this morning, when she and Tom had realized they wouldn't be able to get any more sleep and might as well get up for good.

She replays the events of the past six hours again, forcing herself to remember every detail—to confront the realization that what happened to Rachel could have happened to her. Or so it seems.

She, too, was alone in the house around midnight. She, too, turned out the lights and went up to bed, deciding not to wait up for her husband.

Tom came home soon afterward, crawling into bed beside her, finding her still awake. She snuggled against his reassuring warmth, telling him that the baby was sleeping soundly, apparently over the worst of her illness. Tom, in turn, told her about his ordeal with the client and that the man wanted to meet with him again the next day.

They made love, then—quietly, quickly—before Karen drifted off to sleep in her husband's arms.

Sirens awakened them both. Only when they realized the police cars were rushing up their quiet dead-end street did they climb out of bed to see what had happened. It was Tom who walked down the block, then returned with the shocking news of Rachel's murder.

Even now, hours later, Karen still can't quite absorb what has happened.

She can't grasp the fact that her friend is dead.

Not just dead. *Murdered.* Violently. In her own bed.

At least, that's what Tom told her. But he was fuzzy on the details, saying that the cops had tried to shoo him away, and that he couldn't even talk to Ben Leiberman, who was distraught.

Now Tom is dozing on the couch.

Taylor is in her swing, having greedily sucked down her morning bottle, which means she's back to normal.

Earlier, Karen spoke to Tasha. She hadn't known anything more than what Tom had told Karen. She had Rachel's children at her house and was doing her best to shield them from the scene across the street. Karen knows she should offer to go down there and help. She can always leave Taylor with Tom. Yet some part of her is reluctant to confront what has happened. As long as she stays here at home, in her safe little cocoon, she can avoid the horror of the truth for a while longer.

But not forever . . .

Out of the corner of her eye, Karen spots a sudden movement through the window above the sink. She glances up.

Jeremiah Gallagher, clad in a heavy parka, jeans, and boots, is walking across the yard next door.

No, not walking.

Slinking, Karen thinks. There's something decidedly furtive about the way he's moving. As though he's up to something and he's worried somebody might catch him.

She sets the coffee pot in the sink and instinctively steps back away from the window. Just in case he glances in her direction and sees her watching.

She can still see him from here, through the space between the white ruffled curtains. But he won't see her.

What in the world is he doing? He's going into the storage shed again and closing the door behind him.

Why?

What's in there?

Karen toys with a strand of her long, dark hair, wondering what to do. Should she wake Tom and tell him?

Why would she? Just because the boy next door has gone into the storage shed?

No, she reminds herself. Because the boy next door is the last person who saw Rachel alive. And now he's acting suspiciously. As though there's something in the shed that he doesn't want anyone to know about.

Karen's eyes narrow as the door to the shed abruptly opens again.

Jeremiah emerges, carrying something. Karen glimpses it: a dark bundle of some sort.

He pauses in the yard.

For a moment she expects him to turn toward the house again with his bundle, giving her a better view.

Instead he hurries toward the dense woods at the back of the property, looking over his shoulder as though expecting to be followed.

Karen waits until he disappears between the trees. Then she turns away from the window, wondering what to do.

Chapter Nine

"Are you sure Mom's okay?" Mitch asks his father as Frank Ferrante switches lanes, following a green highway sign that reads WHITESTONE BRIDGE. This is the road they take every weekend to Long Island, but it's usually Friday night when they go, and it takes a lot longer because of the rush-hour traffic.

Right now, at eleven-something on a Friday morning, there isn't much traffic. They left Mitch's house only half an hour ago, after stopping there so that he could grab some clothes for the weekend.

"I'm sure your mother's fine," Mitch's father tells him.

"And she said it was okay if I got out of school early to go with you?" Mitch asks doubtfully.

"It's fine, Mitch. I'm your father. It's not like I'm kidnapping you. I can get you out of school and bring you home with me early if I have to. Like I said, I was in town on business this morning and I don't see any reason to hang around waiting until after school to pick you up."

Mitch nods. That makes sense. But it's hard to believe that his mother said it would be okay for his father to spend extra time with him. She doesn't agree with much of anything his dad says or does, especially when Mitch is involved.

"Dad?"

"Yeah?"

"What will we do when we get to Long Island?"

"I figure we'll stop and have some lunch," his father tells him. "There's a great new place not far from my house. You like spaghetti, right?"

"It's my favorite food."

"That's because you're Italian," his father says, looking pleased.

"Mom's not Italian."

"But I am. And you're half mine. So you're half Italian."

"Really? I never thought of that before."

"That's because your mother changed your name," his father growls. "It should be the same as mine. Ferrante. She has you going by Bailey."

"Yeah." Uncomfortable, Mitch looks out the window at the green-and-pink signs designating the express lanes at the toll bridge. There's no backup here, either. They'll probably be at the restaurant in half an hour, or even less. "What will we do after lunch, Dad?"

"I'll drop you off at home. Shawna will be there. I have some business I have to take care of this afternoon."

"Oh." Mitch is disappointed. He'd been hoping that he and his father might be able to spend the day together, just the two of them.

Now he'll have to hang around with Shawna until his dad gets back.

Oh, well. He figures it's still better than staying in school. Maybe he can tune her out and fool around with the Sony PlayStation his father bought him.

He grins and turns to look out his window at the distant New York City skyline as they cruise over the bridge. The sky is a brilliant blue, and the bright October sunlight glints on a plane that is just coming in for a landing at La Guardia airport, directly to the west.

"It sure is nice," he comments.

"What is?"

"The view," Mitch tells his father.

"It is pretty nice," his dad agrees, glancing in that direction and smiling.

For a brief moment, Mitch feels like he's absolutely bursting with happiness.

Then he remembers his mother. She's all alone back home. What if the killer goes after her next? There'll be no one to protect her. Maybe Mitch shouldn't leave right now. Maybe he should skip this weekend on Long Island.

"Dad?" Mitch asks, his heart beating really fast.

"Hmm?"

He pauses. Looks at his father.

"Never mind," Mitch says, and turns back to the view of the skyline.

"Tasha?"

"Ben!" She clutches the telephone receiver tightly against her ear. "Are you okay? Oh, Ben . . ." She breaks off on a choking sob and presses her hand to her quavering lips. This is the first time she's spoken to him today.

"How are the kids?" he asks hoarsely. "Are they okay?"

"They don't know. . . ." She sinks into a kitchen chair.

"I have to tell them. I need to see them."

"Do you want me to bring them over?"

"I'm not at home, Tasha."

"Where are you?"

"At the police station."

For some reason, this catches her off guard. All morning, she's assumed he's in seclusion across the street. But if he's at the police station . . . "Ben, they don't think you—"

"I don't know what they think! They've been questioning me all night, all morning. I keep saying I don't know what happened. All I know is that I came home late—I got buried in paperwork at the office. When I got here, I found her. In bed. And I . . . I didn't even know it was her, her head was so . . . If she hadn't been wearing that black lacy thing of hers I wouldn't have even believed it was really her. . . ."

"Ben." Tasha bites back a sob. "Oh, God . . ."

"Listen," he says, getting hold of himself. "My sister is picking up the kids in about an hour. Okay? Just tell them that Aunt Carol is coming, and that I'll see them at her house. If they ask about Rachel . . ."

"They have been," Tasha tells him, her insides roiling with grief.

"Tell them that—no." He changes his mind. His voice is tight. "No, don't tell them anything. I'll tell them."

"Okay, Ben. Okay. And if you need anything . . ."

"Thanks, Tasha."

She barely manages to murmur some inane reply before hanging up and bursting into tears all over again.

"Oh, Rachel," she says softly, wiping her nose with a soggy tissue from her pocket. "What happened to you? Who did this to you?"

She sits in her silent kitchen, listening to the muffled sound of the children's voices upstairs. Noah and Max are napping, but Hunter is playing ring-around-a-rosy with the girls. The three of them are giggling.

They're so innocent, Tasha thinks. *They have no idea that their world is falling apart around them.*

She desperately wants to call Joel, needing to bare her sorrow, needing comfort. But she knows there's no way to reach him. He's not at the office; he's at the shoot, and she's already tried his cell phone twice. There was no answer.

You'd think he would call her to make sure she and the kids are okay. Well, maybe he will. Or maybe he's already on his way home. He said he would get back here as soon as he could.

The doorbell rings.

Tasha sighs. It's been doing that all morning. It's the press every time. She'll have to ignore it . . . again.

She thinks about that reporter from the local paper. She was different from the others who have turned up on the Bankses' doorstep. Not as pushy or brusque, and she didn't have a camera crew—or even a notebook. She really seemed to care about Rachel. Jane Kendall, too. Like she can relate to them, just as Tasha can. Tasha wonders if Paula, like Tasha, is wondering, with a sick feeling in the pit of her stomach, who might be next.

The doorbell rings again.

Remembering that Ben said his sister would be coming to pick up the kids, Tasha reluctantly goes to answer it. Ben said she wouldn't be here for an hour, but maybe he was wrong.

"Who is it?" she calls through the door, wishing it had a window so that she could just look out and glimpse whoever's standing on the other side. The door is solid wood, and the narrow foyer windows on either side are positioned so that from inside the house there's no way to see who is ringing the bell.

For the first time, it occurs to Tasha that this isn't very safe. In the city, they had a peephole. Four or five locks, too.

Here there's only one latch. It has never occurred to Tasha that they might need something more. She has always felt safe in Townsend Heights.

"My name is George DeFand, Mrs. Banks," a masculine voice says. "I'm with the *New York Post.* I was wondering if—"

"Leave me alone!" she calls through the door, suddenly as angry as she is weary. "Just go. I don't have anything to say."

He persists until she threatens to call the police. Even then, she isn't sure he's really gone until she looks out the window and sees a male figure retreating toward the street.

The circus in front of the Leibermans' house looks like the scene in front of the Kendalls' home these past few days. How many times has she turned on the television and seen a view of their stately brick mansion surrounded by police and reporters?

It has obviously received full coverage on the national news. Her mother called from Centerbrook earlier, worried, having recognized Rachel's name and the images of Orchard Lane. Tasha assured her that she and Joel and the children are safe. That they'll keep in touch, and yes, they're coming for Christmas. They just haven't had time to make arrangements, but they will. As soon as things die down . . .

Tasha wonders again whether what happened to Rachel has anything to do with Jane Kendall's disappear-

ance. She's been mulling it over all morning, ever since
Paula Bailey asked her about it. Half the time Tasha
concludes that the two cases must be linked. The other
half, she tells herself that this could just be a coincidence.

After all, Rachel has turned up dead. Jane hasn't . . .

Yet, a voice whispers ominously in her head.

"Jeremiah?" Fletch knocks on his nephew's door
again, then calls more loudly. "Jeremiah?"

No reply.

He pauses only a moment before turning the knob. If it
were Derek or Randi sullenly barricaded inside, ignoring
him, he'd have done it without hesitation. But then,
Derek and Randi are his own kids. Jeremiah belongs to
his brother.

Fletch has consciously tried to avoid invading his nephew's privacy ever since the boy moved in here, giving him
as much space as he seems to need. After all, he's been
through a lot. And he seems to need a lot of space. Derek
and Randi did too at that age.

Still do, in fact.

And they sure have their faults, especially Derek.

But Jeremiah's different. He's a quirky kid. A real odd-
ball. It isn't as if Fletch hasn't tried to help him, but
there's not much you can do with a kid like that. It would
take a lot more than buying him new clothes and teaching
him how to hit a baseball. Or even taking him up to the
cabin in the Catskills for a weekend to teach him how
to hunt and fish.

Fletch pushes the door open, bracing himself for whatever he's going to find on the other side. He imagines
the boy lying on his bed sulking, or even smoking ciga-

rettes or dope. What he doesn't expect to find is an empty room.

"Jeremiah?"

Puzzled, Fletch looks around. He hasn't really been inside the former guest room since his nephew moved in. It certainly is lived-in. Clothes and books are strewn over the unmade bed, the bureau, the chair. The computer is turned on; a dragon screen saver glowing formidably. There are empty soda cans and food wrappers on the desk and floor. Sharon's going to have a fit when she sees this, Fletch thinks. The housekeeper doesn't come until Monday. This kid's an even bigger slob than Derek ever was.

And he's not here.

Where the hell did he go?

He steps back out into the hall.

The door to the master bedroom opens. Sharon peers out. Her head is wrapped in a towel, turban-style, and she's wearing a terry cloth robe.

"What's going on? More reporters banging on the door downstairs?" she asks.

He shakes his head.

It's been happening all morning. Fletch has answered the door and given every one of them a terse "No comment." Thank God their phone number is unlisted. So far, no reporters have managed to track down the number, but he figures it's only a matter of time before they do.

"Have you seen Jeremiah?" Fletch asks her.

"He was in his room a few minutes ago when I went in to take a shower. Why?"

"Well, he's not there now."

Fletch exchanges a long glance with his wife.

Then he says, "He wouldn't run away, Sharon."

"Of course he would," she shoots back. "That detective scared the shit out of him."

"Well, he'll be back."

"Don't be so sure, Fletch."

"Oh, come on, Sharon. Where's he going to go?"

"As far away from Townsend Heights as he can get— *if* he's guilty. And if he's not . . ."

Fletch waits for her to finish.

She merely shrugs and goes back into the master bedroom, closing the door behind her.

"But what if he had something to do with Rachel's murder?" Karen asks Tom, pacing across the living room. She steps around the gently rocking baby swing, where Taylor is snoozing, her little head tilted sideways in what looks like an uncomfortable position. Karen decides against trying to straighten her head, not wanting to wake her.

"If you really think he did, then go ahead. Tell the cops," Tom says with a shrug. "I just don't think it's a good idea to involve yourself in this by making a big deal out of something that was innocent in all likelihood. So the kid next door was in the storage shed with the door closed. So what?"

"He went off into the woods carrying something, Tom," Karen reminds him, going back to sit beside him on the couch. Maybe she shouldn't have woken him up to ask what he thought. She should have known that a level-headed accountant would think she is reading too much into what she has seen.

Besides, Tom has such a *thing* about them keeping to themselves as much as possible. She figures it stems from his New England background—the old Yankee privacy ethic. The last thing he would want to do is have his wife admit to spying on the neighbors, even if that wasn't exactly what Karen had been doing.

Well, what were you doing? she demands of herself. *You stepped back from the window so he wouldn't see you watching him.*

Yes, but, *she* isn't exactly the type to go around poking her nose into things that don't concern her, either. After all, she grew up in the city, where people mind their own business with a vengeance. Live and let live, right?

Right.

So why does she suddenly feel compelled to keep track of the neighbors' nephew's comings and goings—to report him to the authorities, even. Is she just paranoid?

Maybe.

Or maybe she should have just trusted her instincts and gone ahead and called the cops without consulting Tom.

He hates this, all of it. He's been on edge all day, what with the doorbell constantly ringing and reporters asking for their comments on the case. He's turned them all away and lowered all the shades at the front of the house to block out the hubbub at the other end of the block— and perhaps the prying eyes of the press, as well.

"He's a kid, Karen," her husband is saying. "Kids like to play in the woods. And unless he was carrying a dead body or a bloody weapon—"

"Oh, come on, Tom. . . ."

"Well, was he?"

"Of course not. But I don't know what he was carrying. He looked suspicious."

"Are you sure?" Tom asks. "Maybe you're reading

too much into it. You're upset about what happened to Rachel. She was your friend."

"I don't know," she says slowly. "Maybe you're right. Maybe I just thought he was sneaking around. Maybe he's not up to anything after all."

"Or maybe you were right and he *was* up to something, Karen. Like smoking. Or reading *Penthouse*. That could be what was in the bundle. He's a kid," he says again, to her irritation. Christ. She wishes she'd never started this. "That's what kids do," Tom goes on. "They sneak around and they use poor judgment. But the vast majority of them don't slaughter innocent women in their beds."

"But somebody did, Tom. Somebody walked into Rachel's bedroom and—" She breaks off, emotion clogging her throat.

"I know." He puts an arm around her, pulls her close. "Take it easy, Karen. Trust the police to do their job. You saw that detective going into the Gallaghers' house this morning. He stayed a long time. He had to be questioning the kid thoroughly. He's on top of the situation. If he thought he had a serious suspect, he'd have arrested him or something."

"I guess."

"Look, if you're that concerned, at least tell Fletch or Sharon what you saw first. Let them take care of it. If they think they should go to the police, they will."

She considers that option.

The baby stirs in her swing, waking up.

Karen goes over to unstrap her.

"So what are you going to do?" Tom asks.

"Right now, I'm going to feed Taylor," she answers, lifting her daughter and snuggling her warm skin against her neck. "I'll figure out the rest later."

* * *

Joel shows up right after Tasha puts Max down for his nap. Hearing the front door open and close, Tasha has a moment of panic, thinking she might have forgotten to lock it and that another reporter has crept in. But when she rushes to the top of the stairs, she sees her husband there in the foyer, locking the door behind him.

"What are you doing here?" she asks, going down the steps toward him.

"I told you I'd be home as soon as I could." He takes off his trench coat and opens the hall closet. Sliding hangers around, he mutters, "There's no place to put this."

"We never have enough hangers," Tasha says, coming to a halt at the foot of the stairs. "You can hang it on a hook in the kitchen. . . ."

"Never mind." He drapes his coat over a hanger that already holds one of Hunter's jackets, and closes the door. "Are Rachel's kids still here?"

Rachel's kids. Just the way he puts it brings a lump to Tasha's throat. Mara and Noah are not Rachel's kids anymore. Only Ben's. Rachel's gone, and she isn't coming back.

Funny how Tasha speculated just the other night about their friend leaving them, running off in search of adventure. Her notoriously over-active imagination getting carried away again . . .

Unless it was a premonition. Had some part of her actually sensed that Rachel really would be gone only hours later? Had it ever crossed her mind that Rachel might die?

No.

No, it was just a coincidence.

Thinking back, she realizes that she was afraid for herself, wasn't she, in those tense days after Jane Kendall's disappearance? It's hard to recall now. Everything is such a blur. Lack of sleep will do that. So will traumatic shock.

"Ben's sister came and got the kids a while ago," she tells Joel.

"Do they know?"

Tasha shakes her head. "I didn't tell them. Ben is going to."

"He's still home, isn't he? I saw his car in their driveway."

"He's not there. He's down at the police station. They're questioning him."

Joel doesn't look surprised. "Have the police come here to talk to you yet?"

Tasha shakes her head.

"Well, it's only a matter of time before they do."

It's maddening, the matter-of-fact way he says it. But she knows he's probably right. Of course the police will want to question her. She was there, yesterday, in the Leibermans' house. She was one of Rachel's friends.

A lump rises painfully in her throat at the thought of Rachel. How can she be gone? She was just here, breezy, irreverent, beautiful. Now she's lying in a morgue someplace, cold and dead. Unrecognizable, Ben had said.

She doesn't want to think about what he saw when he walked into the bedroom and found her. And she doesn't want to think about—or see—Rachel dead.

Tasha knows that they've taken her body out of the house. She sneaked a peek at the latest television newscast upstairs in the bedroom just now while she was rocking a cranky Max to sleep. She found herself sobbing at the prerecorded image that mercifully she hadn't happened to glimpse when it happened live outside her own window—a bulky, covered stretcher being borne out the Leibermans' front door. Caught off guard by the macabre image, she tried to muffle her sobs and kept the volume on the television turned low so that Hunter and Victoria wouldn't hear.

She hasn't told them yet. Oh, God, how is she ever going to tell them? They'll be so upset. Worried. Afraid.

Maybe Joel will do it.

"I'm so glad you're home," Tasha tells him, peering out the window beside the door for the hundredth time that day. The street is still crawling with media. "Did the reporters attack you on the way in?"

He nods. "I just said no comment and ordered them off our property. It's a mob scene out there. Have they tried to talk to you?"

"All day. Every once in a while one of them rings the doorbell."

"You didn't say anything to anyone, did you?"

She thinks about Paula Bailey, the local reporter. Should she mention to Joel that she spoke to her? No. He won't like that. He said not to talk to the press, and he wouldn't understand that Paula is different. That Tasha found herself wanting to help her, if only because she's local, and a fellow mom, and she knows what it's like to have a fussy child permanently attached to your hip.

"No, I didn't say anything to anyone," Tasha tells Joel.

"So how's Ben holding up?"

She shrugs. "He's having a hard time. Who wouldn't?"

"What did his sister say when she came?"

"That she'll call and let us know when the funeral will be."

"Tomorrow, won't it? That's the custom," says Joel, who, like the Leibermans, is Jewish.

When his grandfather died suddenly of a heart attack the year they were married, Tasha marveled at the way the death ritual is handled in Judaism as opposed to Catholicism. The morning after Grandpa Jake died, they found themselves shoveling dirt on his casket after the long trek to the cemetery on Long Island.

By contrast, Tasha's father's funeral happened three days after he died. Thank goodness for that, because they had to travel to Ohio with the kids, which took almost a whole day in itself. Joel was frustrated by the two days and nights of wake before the funeral. He said it only dragged things out. Tasha, on the other hand, found it comforting.

"Rachel's funeral won't be tomorrow, Joel. The police haven't released—" she hesitates, then manages, "the *body* for burial yet. It's a murder investigation. I don't know how long it'll take."

He nods. "I hadn't thought of that. Well, I hope I'll be here for it."

"What do you mean?"

"I've got a business trip this week, remember? I have to fly out to Chicago on Sunday night. I'll be gone until Monday night."

She had momentarily forgotten about that.

For a while, they're both silent.

"So how'd it go today?" she asks, now that the specter of his job has reared its head.

"Hmm?"

"Your shoot," she reminds him. "In the city. With the supermodel."

"Oh, that. It was fine," he says, and heads for the stairs. "I'm going to go change my clothes."

"Good luck finding something to wear," she calls after him.

He pauses. "What do you mean?"

"I still haven't been able to do the laundry. The washing machine is broken, remember?"

He tilts his head back, as though he's exasperated. "It hasn't been fixed yet?"

"Nope."

He sighs. "Okay, I'll go down and take a look at it. Where's the manual?"

"In the drawer in the kitchen." She still hasn't had the chance to take it out and check out the troubleshooting chart. It seems like years ago that she went down to the basement and found out the machine wasn't working. Has it really only been a few days?

Back then she was preoccupied with the Jane Kendall disappearance.

Now there's Rachel.

The fleeting television reports Tasha has managed to see today seem to assume that one has something to do with the other, although the police haven't actually come out and confirmed a link between the two cases.

Tasha doesn't know what to think anymore.

Well, Joel's home now, she reminds herself. *You should feel safe—at least for the moment.*

So why don't you?

Opening the door to the apartment, Paula expects to hear the television. Instead, there's a pronounced silence, marred only by the refrigerator's hum.

"Mitch?" she calls, surprised.

No reply.

She steps into the living room and looks around. No

sign of her son. She doesn't have to check the bedroom, kitchen, or bathroom to know that the place is deserted. The first thing Mitch does any time he walks in the door is turn on the TV. If it's off, he's not here. It's that simple.

She frowns, glancing at her watch. It's a little past three. Though she's seldom around when Frank picks him up on Friday afternoons, she knows Mitch doesn't usually leave until after four. In fact, that's been a bone of contention between Paula and her ex-husband, because it means Mitch needs to be at home by himself for more than an hour after school on Fridays while Paula's working.

Granted, he's alone other times. But Paula can't understand why Frank can't just get here an hour earlier on Fridays, especially after making such a big deal about getting full weekend visitation rights, rather than the single day Paula offered. He had some excuse about not being able to leave work that early. But Paula's no fool. Frank's self-employed, right? She doesn't doubt that he could get here by three if he really wanted to, or even pick up Mitch at school at two forty-five, as she had originally requested.

He's just pushing her buttons at their son's expense, knowing the visitation situation infuriates her in the first place.

So if Mitch isn't here, and it's too early for Frank to pick him up, where is he?

Miss Bright probably made him stay after again, Paula realizes, striding to the phone. Too anxious to waste time looking up the telephone number in the Townsend Heights directory, she dials information for it, then accepts the extra charge to be directly connected rather than dialing the number herself.

Come on, come on. . . .

She only stopped home to change her clothes before going back over to Orchard Lane. She found out her friend Brian Mulvaney is on duty guarding the Leiberman house, and she's going to request a little favor from him. She wonders what it will take for him to let her inside the house—just for a quick walk-through of the murder scene. She knows it's off-limits to the press, but she's local. And Brian's her buddy.

Besides, he owes her a favor.

Didn't she keep his name out of the paper last year when he came close to being arrested in a bar brawl in the next county?

As she listens to the phone ring in her ear, she kicks off her pumps and wiggles her toes. Those shoes pinch. She really needs a new pair—

"Townsend Heights Elementary School. May I help you?"

"This is Paula Bailey. My son, Mitch, is a student there. He hasn't come home from school yet. May I please speak to his teacher, Miss Bright?"

"Just a moment, and I'll see if she's still here, Mrs. Bailey."

"It's *Ms.,*" she says through clenched teeth.

She lights a cigarette, then goes into the bedroom, tucking the receiver between her shoulder and her ear while she picks out another outfit. Something warmer and more comfortable than the skirt and blouse she put on this morning. There's no telling when she'll get back here tonight, and the temperature is supposed to drop into the thirties.

The phone clicks. "This is Miss Bright."

"Is Mitch there with you?" Paula asks without preamble.

A slight pause. "No, he's—"

"You didn't keep him after school again?"

"No, *Ms.* Bailey, I didn't," the teacher says crisply. "His father picked him up this morning. He said there was a family emergency."

"And you let him take Mitch?" Paula shrieks in disbelief.

"He's the parent, Ms. Bailey. He's authorized to pick up your son at school. You signed the form yourself."

"That's because I had originally thought he'd be picking him up after school on visitation days. Not because I wanted him to have permission to just pull Mitch out of class whenever he feels like it!"

"Well, you'll have to resolve that with your ex-husband."

"Believe me, I will." Steaming, Paula hangs up without even saying good-bye.

She takes a deep drag on the cigarette, striding across the bedroom, cursing Frank under her breath as she exhales the smoke. Who the hell does he think he is?

Worry flits into her mind, and then right out again. Of course Mitch is fine—and of course, there's no family emergency. And even if there were, what does she care about Frank or his idiot wife? All that matters to her is Mitch—and keeping him away from her ex-husband's influence. Frank is going to do everything in his power to turn Mitch against her and convince him to come live on Long Island.

It isn't fair. How is she supposed to compete with everything Frank has to offer? And he knows it, damn it. He knows she doesn't have the means to provide for Mitch what Frank can. Here there's no stay-at-home stepparent, no pool, no separate bedroom for Mitch with an entertainment center and his own bathroom.

But there's a mother who is determined to fight to

keep her son, Paula thinks grimly as she dials information again and asks for Frank's number.

"I have it as unlisted at the customer's request, ma'am," the operator informs her.

"Damn!" She slams the phone down and looks around quickly for her address book. Finding it in a desk drawer, she opens it to the *F* page and scans for Frank's number.

Moments later, she's clutching the receiver as the line rings in her ear.

Finally, a click. "You have reached the Ferrante residence," Frank's voice says with uncharacteristic enunciation. "Sorry we can't come to the phone right now, but if you'll leave your name, number, and the time you called, we'll get right back to you."

"You bastard!" Paula snarls into the receiver. "How dare you take my son out of school without my permission? I want Mitch to call me on my cell phone the minute you get this message. I mean it."

She slams the phone down, shaking.

Takes another deep drag, needing to steady her frayed nerves.

She has Frank's address. Should she drive out to Long Island and get Mitch herself?

Would her car even be able to make the trip? When was the last time she got it serviced?

And what about her job, damn it? She's involved in the biggest story of her career. Her entire future is riding on this one—and so is custody of Mitch.

Is she supposed to just drop everything just because her ex has pushed the envelope with his visitation rights?

She doesn't like what Frank has done. In fact, she hates it. Hates *him*. Nor does she trust him.

However, he *was* supposed to have Mitch for the weekend. If she drives out to Long Island, she'll have to bring

Mitch home with her—not to mention threaten Frank with legal action that will require attorney consultation that she can't afford. Then she'll have to leave Mitch at home alone all weekend while she covers the Leiberman murder and the Kendall disappearance—providing Frank with all the more ammunition to use against her.

She has no choice but to proceed with her plans.

"But I'll make you pay someday, Frank Ferrante," she promises aloud, stubbing out the cigarette in a bedside ashtray. She goes to her closet and jerks the door open. "You're not going to win this one in the end. I guarantee you that."

"Margaret?"

She glances up at the sound of Owen's voice, feeling a twinge of pleasure at the sound of her name on his lips. It's not something she's heard often. In fact, in all the years she's known him, he's rarely addressed her directly. Nor have the two ever spent any amount of time together without Jane. Before Jane disappeared, there had been only one instance when Margaret had been alone with Owen.

It was the morning after Schuyler was born. Margaret arrived at the hospital to visit her sister and niece, bearing a large bouquet of pastel flowers for her sister and an expensive porcelain doll for the newborn baby. The first person she saw upon walking into the private room was Owen, proudly beaming and seated in the chair where he had spent the night.

Jane was in bed, wearing a white peignoir and looking wan and exhausted. Mother hovered beside her, cautioning Margaret not to bother her sister, who was worn out after the ordeal of giving birth.

Feeling like an intruder and wondering why Mother did not, Margaret said awkwardly that she would take a quick peek at the baby in the nursery and then be on her way. Owen leapt to his feet, offering to escort her.

Margaret reminds herself now, as she did then, that he had merely been eager to show off his new offspring. Yet she still feels warmed by the memory of walking alongside him down the hushed hospital corridors that morning. Conversation came easily between them even before they reached the baby, with Owen describing the dramatic miracle of the night before in great detail. He was so clearly awestruck by the birth—and even more so by Jane's role in it, telling Margaret at length how brave her sister had been, making it seem like some heroic feat rather than something billions of other women had done since the beginning of time.

Now, as Margaret gazes at her brother-in-law standing in the doorway of the kitchen while she sits at the table with a cup of coffee, she realizes that he looks a decade older than he did that morning last year. His eyes are underscored by lines and shadows, his skin is sallow, and she's shocked to spot graying hair at his temples; it literally must have appeared there overnight.

She is engulfed by a fierce rush of yearning.

I've loved him from the first moment I ever saw him.

No, that isn't true. She was attracted to him then, but she didn't truly love him, because she didn't know him. Not as she does now, having shared a part of his life for so many years.

Yes, she shared it through Jane. Yet in a strange way, that doesn't matter. She has seen what Owen is like when he's in love—has witnessed his steadfast devotion, his playful affection. He has grown into the kind of man any woman would desire—the kind of man for whom a woman would do *anything*.

Anything at all.

Now Owen needs help. He needs someone to hold him and tell him everything's going to be okay.

Margaret so wants to be that person that it's all she can do not to reach out and touch him. To be safe, she clasps her hands around her warm mug of tea on the table.

"Do you know whether Jane has always kept a journal?" Owen asks her.

"She did, growing up. I wouldn't be surprised if she still does," Margaret tells him, her insides quaking simply because she's alone with him and has his undivided attention. For once there's no Jane, or Mother, or even Schuyler.

"She does," Owen says, and Margaret, looking into his eyes, is momentarily confused, unable to recall what they're even talking about. "At least, she did when we were first married. She used to write in it first thing in the morning."

Oh, yes. Jane's journal.

"That's what she did as a child," Margaret tells Owen. "Every day, before breakfast. Does she still?"

"I don't know," Owen says. "I leave for the office so early. And there's Schuyler for her to take care of now. Still, I can't imagine that she'd ever just give up something that was such a habit all her life. Can you?"

"No. Jane found comfort in rituals," Margaret remembers. "She liked to stick to a routine, even when she was a little girl."

"That's what I thought."

Something about that is troubling Owen. Margaret senses it in the faraway expression in his eyes, sees it in the way he bends and straightens his fingers as his arms hang stiffly at his sides. She doesn't ask, doesn't want to prod him, hoping that if she's patient, he'll tell her whatever it is that's on his mind.

She doesn't have to wait long.

He pulls out the chair beside hers and sits at the table, clasping his hands in front of him.

"Her journals are all on the built-in bookshelf in our bedroom, Margaret. They're in chronological order, and every time she's finished with one, she takes it to the engraver and has the start and finish dates stamped on the spine. The one she's writing in now is there. I looked at it. She writes almost every day. Mostly just short entries about what Schuyler's doing, and where they've been, and who they've seen. Sometimes there are just abbreviated notes."

"Really? She used to write long pages when she was younger," Margaret tells him, then hastily adds, "I never snooped. She used to show me sometimes."

So many of those entries were about Owen. How many times had Margaret cringed inside, reading page after page of Jane's girlish outpourings of longing for Owen, wondering how her sister would react if she discovered that her words mirrored Margaret's own secret yearnings. . . .

"She did write lengthy passages earlier in our marriage," Owen tells Margaret, admitting uncomfortably, "I checked them out. Not with her permission. But not until yesterday. I never violated her privacy before, and I did it now only because I thought I might find something in the journals that would help the police in their investigation."

"And did you?"

He shakes his head. "No. But I did discover something

strange, Margaret." He leans closer, so close that she can smell his scent. Soap and cologne.

Her heart quickens its pace. It's all she can do not to lean toward him, too, when all she wants is to bury her nose in his skin, breathing his essence. Her voice trembles as she asks him, "What is it?"

He takes a deep breath. "There's a gap in the dates. Unless she took almost a year off from writing—and you seem to think that that's as unlikely as I do—one of Jane's journals is missing, Margaret. And I've turned the house upside down trying to find it."

Saturday, October 13

Chapter Ten

On Saturday morning, Tasha awakens to the sound of the ringing telephone.

Joel fumbles for it on the bedside table and mutters a groggy "Hello?"

Her heart racing as she comes awake and remembers everything that happened yesterday, Tasha sits up and wraps her arms around her knees, under the quilt. Last night, utterly fatigued yet suffering from insomnia, she resorted to taking several Tylenol PM tablets after tossing and turning until midnight. That was Joel's suggestion. He seemed concerned that she get some rest, yet she found herself wondering whether his real motivation was to knock her out because her thrashing about in bed was keeping him awake.

Now she looks at the clock and sees that it's past seven already. She's slept through the night and feels as though she could go on sleeping all day, her head fuzzy from the drug or exhaustion or a combination of the two.

"Hang on, she's right here." Joel turns to her.

"Who is it?" Tasha asks him.

"It's Ben," he whispers.

She gives him a questioning look.

"He wants to talk to you."

"I know, but . . ."

"Here," Joel said, passing her the phone.

Reluctantly she takes it. She doesn't want to talk to Ben right now. Her thoughts are too scattered; she isn't yet ready to face the stark reality of what has happened.

"Hi, Ben," she says, steeling herself against the emotions that, sure enough, are trickling in already.

"Hi, Tasha." His voice is raspy. He hasn't slept, she thinks vaguely. Or he's been crying. Or both.

"How are the kids?" she asks helplessly when he doesn't say anything else right away.

"As well as you'd expect. I don't think they really understand."

"When did you tell them?"

"When I got back to Carol's last night after I finished at the police station—which took hours."

"Have they . . ." How can she put it delicately? Realizing she can't, she asks gingerly, "Have they cleared you?"

He laughs, a brittle sound. "If you can call it that. They let me go. But I get the feeling they aren't through with me yet. My lawyer said that in cases like this one, the husband is often guilty."

Uncomfortable, Tasha glances at Joel, who is lying back against the pillows again. But he's watching her, a concerned expression on his face. She shrugs at him, saying into the phone, "But Ben, you and Rachel weren't—I mean, why would they suspect you of something so horrible? There's no reason—"

"They asked me if I knew that Rachel was having an affair," Ben cuts in.

Stunned, Tasha just grips the phone.

"What?" Joel whispers, reaching out and touching her arm.

Her mind is racing. Rachel was having an affair?

Of course she was, a voice tells her. *You were blind not to notice.*

Rachel was having an affair.

Why is that so startling?

Because she has never really considered the possibility before. She was so caught up in her own whirlwind days, and in resenting Rachel's life of relative leisure, that it never occurred to her to wonder what, specifically, Rachel was doing with her spare time. She just assumed she was playing golf and getting her nails done.

And she really *was.* Tasha doesn't doubt that. But . . .

"Tasha?" Ben asks. "Do you think it's true? Did she ever say anything to you?"

"About having an affair?"

She feels Joel's body stiffen beside her. She turns to look at him as she says, "My God, Ben, no. I never knew. She never said anything."

Joel is rubbing his cheek, listening. She tries to catch his eye but he's looking in the opposite direction. Why? Because her mentioning the word "affair" brought on his own guilt?

In the aftermath of Rachel's shocking death, she almost lost track of her suspicions about Joel. Almost. Now she finds herself wondering again whether it's work, or another woman, that's distracting him lately.

"You never saw her with another man?" Ben asks in her ear.

She forces her attention back to him, and Rachel. *One thing at a time,* she tells herself, saying aloud, "No, Ben, I swear I never did. Do you know who it was?"

"I have no idea."

"How can the police know about this?"

"They've been questioning people. I guess somebody told them. So." He gives that brittle laugh again. "I guess I'm the last to know."

"Maybe it isn't true," Tasha says, mostly because she feels like she has to.

"Maybe it isn't." He clears his throat. "Listen, the reason I called you is that we're going to stay here at my sister's for a few days. My kids need stuff. . . . Mara wants some toy called a Clemmy—"

"It's her doll."

"Do you know which one?"

"Yes."

"Thank God. Tasha, would you mind going over to our house and getting some of their stuff together? And can you or Joel drop it off here later? I know it's an imposition—"

"It's okay, Ben, we want to help you."

"It's just . . . I really can't go back there right now. I've been watching TV, and I know the press is still camped out front. I just can't face all that on top of . . . everything."

"I'll do it," Tasha tells him, uncertain whether she can face it, either. But what choice does she have? Ben needs her. He has nowhere else to turn. Poor Ben, alone now, with the kids—having to live the rest of his life with the horror of what happened to Rachel. How will he bear it?

"I really appreciate it," he says. "The police are at the house. They'll let you in. They'll want to keep an eye on you the whole time you're there—it's a crime scene and they don't want anybody touching anything."

"What do you need besides Clemmy?"

He gives her a short list. She memorizes it: a couple of the kids' toys and certain items of clothing, along with his address book, which he says is in the drawer of his desk in the den.

"There are people I have to call, to tell them about Rachel, and the funeral arrangements," he says, his voice hollow.

"Do you want me to make any calls for you, Ben?" Tasha offers.

"No. No, Carol can help. And Rachel's parents. They flew in from Florida last night."

"They must be devastated." As far as she can tell, Rachel, an only child, was thoroughly spoiled by her doting parents, who had her late in life. Rachel laughingly told Tasha, on more than one occasion, that her parents' world revolved around her.

"They are devastated," Ben says, his voice strained.

"I'll let you go, Ben. Joel or I will drop off the stuff at your sister's later. What's the address?"

Ben tells her. She repeats it aloud for Joel's benefit, knowing he'll remember. She promises Ben that she'll get dressed and go over as soon as she can, so that Mara won't have long to wait for her Clemmy.

Hanging up, she looks at Joel.

"Well?" he asks.

"You pretty much heard the conversation. Ben needs me to go get some things out of the house," she tells him, getting up. "I'll go now, while the kids are still sleeping. I have to go take a shower."

"I'll start another load of laundry when you're out," Joel says, standing on the opposite side of the bed. He fixed the washing machine yesterday—at least temporarily. He doesn't think it'll hold. It's under warranty to Sears and he wants Tasha to call for a repairman to come next week.

"What about your parents? And the pumpkin contest?" Tasha asks him.

He pauses, looking at her. "What do you want to do?"

"I don't know." But she does know. What she *wants* to do, right now, is put her head on Joel's shoulder and feel his arms around her. But the bed lies between them like a vast divide.

"I can call my parents back and tell them not to come today."

She contemplates that. Her in-laws called yesterday—several times, in fact. They had heard the news about Rachel's murder on television and suggested that Joel, Tasha, and the kids come stay with them until the killer is caught. Tasha was momentarily tempted, if only out of fear—rational or not. But Joel vetoed the idea, saying they would be safe right here at home.

Naturally, his parents then insisted on coming up here today as planned. Tasha figures they'll try again to talk her and Joel into coming back to Brooklyn with them. Still . . .

"No. Let them come," she tells Joel. "It'll be a good distraction for the kids."

Joel's parents might not make a secret of the fact that they dislike her, but they blatantly adore their grandchildren, and the feeling is mutual. The Bankses always show up bearing treats and goodies.

"Should we still go down to the harvest festival in town?" Joel asks.

"If it's still on, with everything that's happened," Tasha decides, heading toward the bathroom. As an afterthought, she tosses over her shoulder, "Thanks for doing all the laundry, Joel."

"It's okay."

She smiles at him. He smiles back. For a moment, they're the old Joel and Tasha, minus the kids and the house and the promotion to vice president. He's no longer the stranger he has been lately, and she's no longer resentful, suspicious. If only it always could be like it is right this second, she thinks.

Then she remembers. This moment is hardly idyllic. She's about to face, head-on, the horror of what happened across the street.

Her smile dims. She turns away from her husband, goes into the bathroom, and shuts the door.

As she takes off her clothes, she finds herself wondering why Joel has suddenly decided to help her around the house. She hadn't asked him to start the laundry yesterday after he finished fixing the washing machine—he just did it, while she was giving the kids their baths. And after their dinner of takeout pizza, he put the dishes into the dishwasher while she read bedtime stories. Usually, courtesy of the mother who spoiled him, he gets up and leaves the table unless she asks him to help clear it.

Is he feeling bad because he knows Tasha's been devastated by her friend's death?

Or just . . . guilty?

Ben hadn't suspected Rachel was having an affair. Nor had Tasha.

But just these past few days, she has almost convinced herself that Joel has been cheating on her. Based on what? The fact that he's been busier than ever before at work and seems detached from her when he's at home.

There haven't been classic signs of philandering: no lipstick on his collar or stray earrings in his car, no credit card bills with hotel rooms and jewelry shop purchases, no mysterious-hang-up telephone calls.

Struck by this last thought, she remembers how she answered the phone that day at Rachel's to hear nothing but breathing, then a click. Was it her lover, trying to reach her? Had Rachel been with him that last night of her life while Jeremiah Gallagher babysat her children?

Who was he?

Tasha runs through the men she's heard Rachel mention recently. Just the other day she was raving about Claude, her hairdresser—but Tasha assumed he's gay. Rachel often talks about Michael, her personal trainer from the gym, describing his muscular body and, in awe, how much weight he can bench-press. And there's Jason, the golf pro who gave her lessons all summer and who, according to Rachel, has eyes bluer than Rockefeller blood.

But nothing Rachel said about any of them led Tasha to believe she was romantically involved with them. She would have sensed it . . . wouldn't she?

Her mind whirling with other possible identities for Rachel's shadowy lover, Tasha pushes one particularly nagging idea out of her head.

No, she tells herself firmly as she turns on the water in the tub. *It couldn't be him. That would be too coincidental. It has to be somebody else. But who? And what, if anything, did he have to do with Rachel's death?*

Paula is awakened by a ringing telephone. Feeling for the receiver on her nightstand, she picks it up, looking at the clock as she does, and groaning. She's only been in bed three hours. After interviewing every possible source for the Leiberman case, and sitting through an endless press briefing during which nothing more was revealed, she went back to her office at the newspaper to file her story for this week's edition.

"Hello?" she mumbles into the phone.

It has to be Mitch. He never called her cell phone, and there were no messages on her machine from him or from Frank when she got home earlier.

"Ms. Bailey?"

"Yes?" She frowns at the sound of an unfamiliar female voice, propping herself on one elbow. "Who is this?"

"My name is Glenda Kline. I'm a nurse at Haven Meadows."

Haven Meadows. Where Pop is.

"Is something wrong?" Paula asks, her pulse accelerating.

"Your father has been asking for you. He seems rather . . . desperate. We thought it best that we get in touch and let you know."

"He's been asking for me?" Paula echoes. Her father doesn't speak. Not since the breakdown that forced her to put him into a home with round-the-clock medical care.

"Just saying your name," the nurse tells her. "But he's agitated. Maybe he's worried about you, since he hasn't seen you in some time. . . ."

Is that an accusing note in Glenda Kline's voice? Paula rubs her eyes. They're burning from lack of sleep. If Glenda Kline only knew about the pressure she's under right now . . .

"If you came to visit, just to show him that you're all right, I think it might help, Ms. Bailey."

She contemplates that. Thinks about the interviews she

has scheduled for today, and the leads she has to follow, and then there's Mitch . . .

But she hasn't been out to Haven Meadows in a few weeks now. On that last visit, Pop's condition was the same as always. He sat staring at his hands in his lap, not listening to her or looking at the picture Mitch had drawn for him—a seascape drawn in markers. The nurse on duty that day had taped it to the wall by his bed, saying that it would really help to cheer up Mr. Bailey.

At the time, Paula privately thought that cheering up is hardly what her father needs. No, he isn't sad or depressed. He's just . . . gone. And as far as she's been able to tell, he's never coming back.

Or is he?

Maybe something has changed. If so, she needs to be there.

"All right," she tells the nurse, her mind whirling through her obligations for the day ahead. "Tell him I'll be there this afternoon."

"I'm sure he'll be pleased," the nurse says.

Are you? Paula wonders, hanging up. Her father has shown no emotion for several years now. Even seeing Mitch hasn't brought a flicker of recognition, let alone pleasure, to his aging face. In fact, Mitch can't stand visiting his grandfather anymore. He says it's too disturbing, seeing him like that. Paula rarely insists that he go these days, although he does continue to send handmade artwork and little notes addressed to "Grandpop."

Mitch.

Paula rises, lights a cigarette, and goes into the next room to find Frank's telephone number again. She swiftly dials it.

"Hello?" a groggy female voice answers on the third ring.

"This is Paula. I need to speak with Frank."

"Just a second."

There's a muffled sound, then an unintelligible murmuring. Paula realizes Frank's second wife has her hand over the mouthpiece for some reason. Why? What are the two of them scheming?

"What is it?" Frank asks, coming on the line.

"I left a message for you to have Mitch call me yesterday, damn it. I never heard from him."

"Well, we drove out east for dinner and got home late. He was tired. He went right up to bed. He's fine, so don't—"

"Don't tell me what to do," she cuts in. "You went to school yesterday morning and stole my son—"

"He's *our* son, and I didn't steal him. I just picked him up early. I was supposed to have him for the weekend anyway. I didn't even think you'd notice he was gone."

"What is that supposed to mean?" Paula keeps her voice level. He won't get to her this time. She won't let him.

"I thought you were working, that's all. Mitch said you're busy covering some story over there."

He must have heard what's been going on in Townsend Heights, even if Mitch didn't tell him. It's been all over the wire services these past few days. You'd have to be living on an island without television or the Internet to escape hearing about the small-town murder of one young wife and mother and the disappearance of another.

Choosing to ignore Frank's dig about her work, Paula says evenly, "He can't afford to miss school. Don't you dare take it upon yourself to pull him out without my permission ever again, or I'll do everything I can to cut off your visitation rights.''

"As if you already aren't doing just that," Frank mutters.

"Put Mitch on the phone," she snaps. "I want to talk to him."

"He's asleep."

"Wake him up."

"No. He needs to rest. He'll call you when he gets up."

She won't be here then, damn it.

"Make sure he does. On my cell phone," she tells Frank, not about to go into any detail about her plans for the day.

She hangs up without saying anything else. She imagines Frank turning to his blond wife in their bed, probably calling Paula a bitch. Maybe the two of them are laughing at her. Maybe they're making plans for the day that they get full custody of Mitch.

"But you won't," Paula murmurs, striding to the kitchen to make coffee, hoping the caffeine and the tobacco will jump-start her sluggish body. She feels sore and weary from head to toe, wanting only to sink back into bed and drift back into numbing sleep.

But she has a full day ahead, including a visit to Haven Meadows—and paying a visit to Fletch Gallagher.

Fletch waits until a respectable hour—eight o'clock—to call his lawyer again. He makes the call from behind the closed French doors of his den, not wanting his nieces to overhear. Naturally they know what's going on—that the woman down the street has been murdered, and that their brother is a suspect and has disappeared. They cried themselves to sleep last night, Sharon said.

"Has Jeremiah turned up yet?" David asks.

"Still missing," Fletch reports. "I spent most of last night out looking for him. I drove through every neighborhood in town more than once, and Sharon stayed here by the phone in case he called. Of course, he didn't."

"Any idea where he could possibly be?"

"None." That's not true. He has an idea, but it's so far-fetched it's not worth mentioning to the lawyer.

The cabin in the Catskills. It's the one place Fletch hasn't checked. For one thing, although Jeremiah knows it exists, he's never been there, and it isn't exactly easy to find even if you have the address. For another, it's almost a two-hour drive from here, so how would Jeremiah even get there? And even if he had the means, Fletch checked both his keychain and Sharon's, and the keys for the cabin are still on both of them.

"This doesn't look good for him, Fletch," his lawyer is saying.

Gee, yuh think, Dave? he wants to say, but he holds the sarcasm in check.

The last thing he needs right now is to alienate his lawyer. He might need David himself, if that detective decides to read anything into Fletch's response to yesterday's questioning. His stomach turns over at the very idea, and he forces it from his mind.

One thing at a time, he cautions himself.

Aloud, he asks David, "How much longer are we going to be able to stall the cops?"

"Until they show up at your door with a warrant," David replies. "Which could be any second now. . . ."

"Or it could be never," Fletch says hopefully. "Maybe they believed the kid."

"Maybe they did," David tells him. Fletch can hear the doubt in his voice; it's echoed in Fletch's gut. "Listen, I've got a racquetball game in twenty minutes, Fletch. If you need me, dial my beeper. Otherwise, I'll catch up with you a little later on. Okay?"

"No problem," Fletch says, hanging up.

He sits there at his desk, gazing absently at the trophies on his shelf, wondering where the kid is—and when his father's going to call.

He left two messages for his brother yesterday but was told he couldn't be reached. Some kind of military mission, presumably.

He resents Aidan, not for the first time, for dumping his son and stepdaughters on Fletch's doorstep and then heading back overseas in the wake of his second wife's death. But then, whenever the going got tough, Aidan got going—in the opposite direction. Escape always was his style. Just like their old man.

But Fletch doesn't want to think about their father now. He's spent a lifetime dissecting what happened— how their father walked out on Mom, leaving her in a small Queens apartment with two preschool boys and a mountain of debt. She managed to survive, working as a secretary in Manhattan to support the three of them. She's been gone for years now, a victim of a virulent cancer that took her within weeks of her diagnosis.

As for Dad, the bastard never looked back. Nor has Fletch sought him out—or, for years now, even wondered why he left. After all, he knew his parents weren't happy. It wasn't that they argued often, or anything that obvious. They were just distant from each other. Cold. There was clearly no love between them.

It wasn't until Fletch was in high school that he and Aidan stumbled upon the ugly, shocking truth about

their father. The teenage brothers vowed to carry it to
their graves, so profoundly affected by the revelation that
it influenced the career and relationship paths they took
from that day forward.

And even now, as the memory of his father flits through
his mind, Fletch clenches his fists, a familiar hatred bub-
bling forth in his soul.

In her third-floor bedroom, Margaret finally hears the
sound she's been listening for all morning. A door
creaking open and then shutting on the second floor,
then the unmistakable tread of Owen's footsteps in the
hall and on the stairs.

He's slept later than usual this morning. She wonders
whether he finally gave in and took the prescription drug
his doctor gave him a few days ago, after Jane disappeared. It was supposed to calm his nerves and help him
to sleep.

And what about me? Margaret wonders, reaching up to
rub the burning ache of fatigue between her shoulder
blades. For several nights now, she hasn't slept more than
an hour at a stretch, waking from frequent nightmares
to find herself in the strange bed in the third-floor bedroom of her sister's house. Sometimes she drifts back to
sleep after a while. Other times, she lies awake, waiting
for daybreak and sounds of life below.

This time, she rose upon awakening at around three
and washed and dressed. She took extra time with her
hair and put on a bit of makeup, knowing she would see
him. It's driving her mad, spending night after night
under his roof like this, her imagination frequently dragging her to places she'd be wise to avoid. At least, for
the time being.

Now, hearing Owen's footsteps, she stands poised by the door. She cracked it open earlier, knowing that if she didn't, the thick, old wood might muffle sounds from below. But she clearly heard Schuyler's first whimpering in her crib, as well as Mother's hurried footsteps down the hall, and her baby-talk murmuring to her granddaughter. She brought the baby downstairs over an hour ago, and Margaret is certain they won't be coming back up to the second floor until Schuyler's naptime, which isn't for another hour. Minerva doesn't work on weekends. Owen's descent means the second floor is now finally deserted, including the master bedroom.

Creeping down the stairs, Margaret holds her breath. It's daring, what she's about to do.

Yet she has no choice.

Owen asked her about Jane's journal.

But he didn't invite you to snoop through his bedroom, she reminds herself. *He only wanted to know whether you thought a volume was missing.*

Well, she does think so. Like Owen, Margaret knew her sister well enough to realize that she wouldn't just take a year off from her daily ritual.

And unlike Owen, Margaret is almost certain that she knows where her sister stashed the missing volume.

Feeling as though she's betraying her brother-in-law, she stops in front of the closed door to the master bedroom.

Why must you do it this way? she asks herself. *Why didn't you just tell him your suspicion last night?*

Ignoring the voice in her head, she reaches out and opens the door, stepping into the big, elaborate room her sister shared with Owen. A room that, like the rest of the house—and perhaps its mistress as well—has its share of secrets.

* * *

After settling Taylor in her swing for a catnap, Karen turns on the television. She really shouldn't. After all, she still hasn't cleaned up the breakfast dishes in the kitchen, and she still has to take a shower, which she can only do while the baby is asleep.

But she can't get Rachel Leiberman off her mind. She needs to know if there have been any new developments since she fell asleep in front of the television last night, not budging from it until Tom woke her and made her go to bed.

Now she flips to Channel 12, the local news station, and sits on the edge of the couch. It's almost the top of the hour, which means the newscast will be starting in a minute or two. Right now there's a commercial for a kids' clothing boutique in White Plains. Ironic. Just a few days ago, Rachel mentioned shopping in that particular store.

Now she's gone.

Karen slept fitfully last night, haunted by nightmares in which she was being chased by some nameless, faceless creature. More than once she woke with a gasp, only to curl up against Tom's warm back and try to reassure herself that there's nothing to be afraid of. That whoever had killed Rachel isn't, even now, stalking another victim.

She wishes Tom were home.

But he's with that demanding client again, and he said he most likely won't be back until early evening. Which leaves Karen alone with the baby and a long, lonely Saturday stretching ahead.

There's a harvest festival in town. Maybe she'll call Tasha later and see if she wants to go.

A throbbing musical interlude from the TV alerts her

to the fact that the newscast is starting. She turns up the volume.

"Good morning," the pretty anchorwoman says, seated behind her nondescript desk in the studio. "At the top of our news this morning, more than twenty-four hours after the murder of a Townsend Heights woman, her killer roams free and there are seemingly few clues to his or her identity. Police have yet to name a suspect in the slaying of Rachel Leiberman, who was found dead yesterday morning in her two-story home on a quiet suburban lane. We take you now to the scene, where our reporter Ted Jackson is standing by."

So the Leibermans' house is still surrounded by the press, Karen notices as the scene shifts. Maybe even more of a crowd than yesterday. So far nobody's rung their bell yet today, but she's been poised for the deluge of reporters to begin. Now Tom isn't here to deflect the questions and slam the door in their faces.

The reporter mentions that there are still no leads in the Kendall disappearance and that the Kendall family has no comment on whether it might be tied into the Leiberman murder.

"However," the reporter concludes, "it hasn't escaped anyone's attention that both Rachel Leiberman and Jane Kendall were young stay-at-home mothers, unlikely targets for random violence in this tony Westchester suburb. Until Jane Kendall is found, the questions will remain—and very likely, many young mothers of Townsend Heights will be

locking their doors and looking over their shoulders."

On that ominous note, the camera shifts to coverage
of police divers on boats beneath the spot where Jane
Kendall's baby was found. The water is particularly deep
at that point, and the winds have made it choppy. Now
a storm is forecast, which will further hinder the divers'
efforts.

"But," says the reporter, "if Jane Kendall's body
is trapped in the murky depths, these divers are
determined to find her."

Shuddering, Karen turns off the television, not wanting
to hear any more.

His stomach coiled with intense hunger, his body
racked with cold, Jeremiah huddles on the damp, musty
bed of leaves, his back against a large boulder. Wisps of
mist hang eerily low among the trees.

It's morning now. He has watched the sky go from
black to charcoal to ashen and overcast as the night
sounds of the forest give way to chirping birds and the
air turns from frigid to just chilly.

Thankful for the insulating, cushioning layer of fleece
beneath his parka, he ponders his next move. When he
left home he was so consumed by the urgent need to
take the evidence and escape that he hadn't known where
he was going. If he had anticipated spending the night
in the woods, he would have brought food, water, a blanket . . .

Well, it's too late for that now.

Wishing he had stuck out Boy Scouting, as his father urged him to do, he looks around. Nothing but a tangle of trees, vines, and rocks. The ground is rugged, sloping, marshy from streams in some spots, rocky in others. He's seen snakes and big spiders with thick, jointed legs—none of them poisonous, or so he tried to convince himself. He has also encountered plenty of deer, raccoons, possums, squirrels, and even a skunk that luckily hadn't sprayed him. And every so often, he hears movement: rustling, thrashing, or branches snapping beneath the weight of some concealed beast.

He heard at school that Peter Frost had fought off a wild animal when he was rescuing Jane Kendall's little girl the other night. He didn't believe it at the time, mostly because he heard two different versions within fifteen minutes of each other. One had Peter beating off a bear with a tree branch. The other had a bobcat attacking and Peter swinging to safety on a vine with the baby in his arms.

Are there actually bears—and *bobcats*—in these woods? Jeremiah isn't sure.

How far did he hike yesterday?

He has no idea about that, either.

It was slow going, though. He stopped frequently to rest, and finally, long before twilight set in, he gave up and settled in for the night, his bundle beside him. He was weary enough to sleep, and he did, but mostly he had needed to stop to collect his scrambled thoughts. To plan his next move.

All he came up with is that he needs to stay lost in the woods for as long as possible. Maybe forever.

But this is Westchester County—or perhaps Putnam, depending on how far he's come. It's not the northern wilderness. There's only so much forest around here, and it's bordered by parks and estates and suburban development. It's not as though he has a clear escape route, say, north to the Canadian border. If he had some kind of map, or even a more thorough knowledge of the geography of the area, maybe he could chart a course. Instead he's forced to travel blindly, feeling his way.

Still, he spent enough time in scouting to know that his first priority should be to provide the necessities: shelter, water, and food.

There's plenty of water, though he squeamishly hesitated to drink from the streams yesterday. Today he definitely will.

And maybe he can find a cave or something.

As for food, well . . .

It's October, damn it. The woods aren't exactly laden with wild berry brambles. The vegetation that's been spared by the deer is dying, shriveling away. What is he supposed to eat? Bugs? Worms? His stomach churns at the thought.

Well, maybe he can catch fish. Or a rabbit, or something. Regular people eat fish. Rabbit, too.

Cooked.

Jeremiah doesn't have matches, nor can he risk starting a fire and alerting anyone to his whereabouts.

They're probably looking for him by now. Maybe they even have dogs on his trail. Maybe he should just turn himself in. He can always bury the evidence here, deep in the woods, cover any earth he's disturbed with piles of leaves. What are the odds that anyone will ever find it?

Still, if he shows up back home again now, they'll assume his guilt, evidence or no. After all, no innocent person would take off the way he did.

I have to keep going, Jeremiah tells himself firmly. *No matter what. I won't turn myself in. Let them come and get me.*

He gets stiffly to his feet and brushes away the wet leaves—snails, too—that cling to the back of his jeans. Shuddering, he attempts to wipe his filthy hands on a crumpled tissue he finds in the pocket of his parka.

Then, miserably, he picks up the bundle and begins moving forward again.

The policeman at the Leibermans' front door, who introduces himself as Officer Mulvaney, tells Tasha that he's been expecting her. Ben let them know she would be coming over.

Thus, she's admitted to the house without question.

She steps past the door, festooned with the dried-flower wreath Rachel bought not long ago, and into the familiar front hall. She's escorted by a young police officer whose ears stick out boyishly from his blond crewcut.

As the door closes behind her, she realizes that she might have been hoping they would detain her outside. That they would say that nobody is allowed on the premises, under any circumstances, even Ben Leiberman's request.

But here she is, inside.

She takes a deep breath.

She's always been aware that every house has a unique aroma. Her in-laws' city apartment smells of disinfectant, mothballs, and ripening fruit. Her mother's home back in Centerbook smells like homemade bread, old wood, and the cinnamon-apple potpourri she keeps in bowls everywhere. And the Liebermans' house smells like the lemon furniture polish Ramira uses, and fresh flowers, and Rachel's perfume.

Inhaling the scent, realizing that today it's slightly tinged with a foreign odor, Tasha sways, suddenly dizzy.

It's death. The smell of death.

"Are you all right?" the police officer asks.

She nods mutely, steeling herself against the flood of emotions.

Rachel was murdered upstairs.

Somebody walked into this house and killed her while her children were asleep down the hall . . .

No, Tasha. Don't go there.

She wants to bolt.

She half-turns back toward the door.

Stop. You need to do this for Ben.

Then she has to get this over with. The sooner she gathers the things he asked her to retrieve, the sooner she can escape this house.

She numbly moves forward, down the hall, into the small playroom. It's still impeccably organized. The Duplo blocks she removed for Max to play with the other day are back on their shelf, and so are the Barbie dolls and clothes that Mara and Victoria took out later.

"I just need to remind you that this is a crime scene, ma'am," Officer Mulvaney says behind her. "Everything is exactly as it was left on Thursday night. Please touch only the items you need to get for Mr. Leiberman, and I'll need you to show me what you're taking before you remove anything."

"All right." Tasha locates Noah's yellow dump truck and Mara's Etch-A-Sketch in their familiar spots on the shelf, shows them to the cop, and hastily retreats from the room.

The sippy cup is next. Noah's blue one. Tasha can hear Rachel's voice complaining, *He refuses to take milk from anything else. It has to be that cup.*

Tasha swallows hard.

Oh, Rach. You'll never see him weaned. You'll never see him go to kindergarten, or play soccer . . .

Pushing back the lump in her throat, she turns abruptly to the police officer. "I need to go into the kitchen."

He nods his permission.

As always, she's struck by the polished stainless-steel appliances, clean counters, and spotless tile floor. Somehow momentarily forgetting the horror that brought her here, she thinks about her own cluttered kitchen, its floors and counters spotted with crumbs and sticky splotches.

Her in-laws will be there in less than an hour. She should clean—

Christ, what are you thinking? she demands of herself as the truth comes rushing back at her. *Rachel's dead.*

Tears well in her eyes. Unwilling to cry in front of the young cop, she fixes her gaze, knowing that if she blinks, the tears will spill over.

She looks down at the familiar table beside her with its vase of fresh flowers in the middle. The stargazer lilies that were tightly closed buds when she was last here are now open. The air here is pungent with their sweet scent.

There were lilies at her father's funeral. The perfume carries her back.

Daddy.

And Rachel.

Rachel loved fragrant flowers. . . .

Don't, Tasha warns herself, swallowing over the lump that still aches in her throat. *Don't make yourself cry.*

She forces her gaze away from the speckled pink blooms. It falls on a wooden puzzle lying beside the vase on the table. She idly notices that it's a colorful nursery rhyme picture, and the words printed around the border flit through her thoughts in a childish, singsong echo.

It's raining, it's pouring, the old man is snoring . . .

Okay.

Okay, she's going to be all right here. She isn't going to fall apart. Not in Rachel's kitchen, not in front of the young cop. She'll make it until she gets home. Then, she promises herself, she can go into the bathroom, lock the door, and sob her heart out.

Margaret feels along the back of the built-in bookshelf beside the master bedroom fireplace, her thoughts drifting back to that long-ago day here with Jane.

"You've got to see this, Margaret," her sister said, standing on tip-toes to reach the shelf above her head.

Jane was several inches shorter. It's no stretch for Margaret. Yet she doesn't know exactly what she's feeling for. She only knows that Jane reached up, and then, a few minutes later, there was a subtle clicking sound.

After making sure that she's truly alone in the room, Margaret swiftly removes the row of Jane's hardcover novels—romances, most of them—from the shelf. Now they're stacked haphazardly on the floor at her feet.

If Owen comes in and sees her—

Oh, what will I do?

She can't even think of it.

Just hurry, hurry, hurry . . .

Margaret's fingers graze a small bump, a barely raised knob of wood along the bottom of the shelf.

Can it be?

She presses it and is rewarded with some give . . . and then, pressing harder, with the same faint click she heard that day with Jane.

Sure enough, a section of the back wall of the shelf has fallen away like a small trapdoor. Behind it is a small niche.

"Henry DeGolier used to keep his tobacco in here," Jane told Margaret, laughing.

"Who's he?"

"The millionaire who built the house way back in the eighteen-hundreds. He had all kinds of quirks built in."

"How do you know?"

"The real estate agent showed me most of them the first time I came through, without Owen. He could care less about stuff like this, but don't you think it's fascinating?"

Margaret agreed that it was.

"Wait till I show you what's in the basement!" Jane said, closing the secret bookcase panel and leading Margaret from the room.

Now, holding her breath, Margaret feels her way past the back edge of the shelf, into the dark space beyond.

For a moment, she feels nothing but rough boards . . . *ugh,* and cobwebs.

Then her fingers close over something.

It can't be.

It was too easy.

And yet she knows without a doubt, even before she pulls it out and looks at it, what she's discovered.

Jane's missing journal.

Chapter Eleven

Karen dials Tasha's number after finishing her solitary lunch seated at the kitchen table. Taylor is still asleep in the swing. Normally, Karen welcomes the chance to eat without interruption from the baby. Today, however, she would welcome it.

"Hello?"

"Tasha, it's me," she says, carrying her plate to the sink.

"Oh, hi."

"You sound relieved."

"My in-laws are on their way over, and they always call from the car when they get close. I was hoping you weren't them. I need another half hour at least before they get here. The house is a disaster. And I want to order a couple of pizzas."

Karen is sympathetic, having weathered her own in-law visits—and having heard horror stories about Tasha's.

"So how are you dealing?" she asks. "I mean with the Rachel thing, not the in-laws."

"It's been hard. I had to go over to the house a little while ago."

"To Rachel's?" Karen leans against the counter. "Why?"

"Ben needed me to pick up some things for the kids. It was awful, Karen. I went upstairs, and . . . the door to her bedroom was closed, but I couldn't stop thinking about what had happened in there."

"Did you see Ben?"

"I spoke to him on the phone. Joel just left to drop off the stuff at his sister's house. I told him to tell Ben that we can take the kids for him again if he needs us. I don't know what else we can do to help."

"I know. I feel the same way." Karen clears her throat. "Tasha . . ."

"Hmm?"

"Are you scared?"

There's a pause.

"I'm trying not to be," Tasha says. "I want to think that what happened to Rachel happened for a reason."

"What could she possibly have done to deserve that?" Karen protests. "Did you hear what they said on the news? She was bludgeoned with a blunt object. They think it was one of her own barbells—you've seen them. She kept them by the bed. Whoever it was beat her head and face in so badly that she was unrecognizable."

"My God, Karen. Of course she didn't deserve that." Tasha's voice is tight. "I mean that whoever killed her didn't do it as a random thing. Because if it was random, then . . ."

"I know," Karen says when Tasha doesn't finish her

sentence. "If it wasn't random, then you or I could be next."

The phone rings. Fletch jumps, then rises from the couch and crosses the family room to answer it.

Silence, and then a click.

He frowns. Sharon's lover. It has to be. Fletch is no fool. This has happened before, when he's been home to answer the phone at a time when he normally wouldn't be here.

When he's not working or in Florida, he usually plays golf on Saturdays and then has drinks at the club.

Today he's done nothing but doze on the couch, waiting for some word about his nephew, or for his brother's return call. And when the phone finally rings, it's just a lousy hang-up.

Well, he realizes, maybe this is a twisted kind of justice. After all, he's made his share of hang-up calls.

"Uncle Fletch?"

He looks up to see Lily poking her head in from the kitchen, with Daisy right behind her.

"Hmm?"

"Was that someone calling about Jeremiah?" Daisy asks.

"No," he says simply. The twins have been nervous all day, drifting aimlessly around the house and holding whispered conferences. Yesterday Sharon sat them down and told them that their brother is missing. It turned out they already knew that the police suspect him in the Leiberman murder.

"Everyone at school is talking about it," Lily told Fletch last night. "Carrie Frost said her brother Peter thinks he might have seen Jeremiah in the woods near where he found that lady's baby the other day, too.''

"That's ridiculous," Fletch said, and the twins looked relieved. Then they wanted to know whether Fletch thought Jeremiah had anything to do with what happened to the lady down the street.

"Of course I don't think that," he said, and then he changed the subject.

"Uncle Fletch?" Lily asks again now. "When is Jeremiah's dad going to come home?"

"I don't know. I put in a call to him. I left word that there's an emergency. As soon as he gets the message, I'm sure he'll call us back and make plans to come."

"I guess."

Daisy says, "Remember when Mommy died? We couldn't reach him right away then, either."

"Your stepfather has an important job," Fletch tells them. "It isn't always easy to get in touch with him."

"I know." Daisy looks glum. "But I wish he would hurry and come back so he can help us find Jeremiah."

"Maybe your brother will turn up on his own," Fletch suggests.

"Maybe," Lily says, giving her sister's arm a squeeze. "Come on, let's go outside and jump rope."

I should offer to do something with them, Fletch thinks, watching them leave the kitchen. *I should take them out for ice cream, or down to that festival in town.*

He knows they had their hearts set on entering their giant pumpkin in the annual contest. They told him that Jeremiah had promised to help them get it into town.

Fletch offered to do it in his place, but the twins turned him down. Clearly their hearts aren't in it now that their brother has disappeared.

Fletch heads upstairs to find Sharon. He can't stand

it anymore. He's got to get out of the house for a little while.

He walks into the bedroom. Sharon is there, standing in the open closet doorway, wearing only a bra and panties. She cries out when he speaks her name behind her.

"What's wrong?" he asks, as she whirls around, wide-eyed.

"You scared me. My God, Fletch, don't go around sneaking up on people."

"Why are you so jumpy?"

"Maybe it's because a woman was murdered a few doors down and whoever did it hasn't been caught," she flings back at him. She grabs a sweater from the closet and pulls it over her head. "Or maybe," she adds slowly, shaking her hair free of the neckline, "it's because I'm worried that the killer might happen to live under this roof."

Jeremiah. She means Jeremiah, he assures himself, keeping his face carefully expressionless.

"I'm going out," he tells her. "Listen for the phone."

"When will you be back?"

"I don't know. Later."

He turns and walks away. He's halfway down the stairs before he realizes that she hasn't asked him who called earlier. Which means she probably already knows. So he was right. She must have been expecting a call from her lover.

That's fine, he tells her silently as he puts on his leather coat in the hallway at the foot of the steps. He's not jealous of the other man. When all of this is over, he and Sharon will go their separate ways at last. It's ridiculous to keep up the charade any longer.

After all, he knows all about her.

And he's beginning to wonder what, exactly, she knows about him.

Haven Meadows looks just as its name suggests, Paula thinks as she drives through the entrance gates. On either side of the lane are broad, grassy fields. The last time she was here, they were still dotted with wildflowers. Now the blooms have dried and faded with autumn.

The old rambling clapboard farmhouse at the end of the lane does indeed seem like a haven tucked among the ancient, brilliantly colored trees that seem to be standing guard over it. It was privately owned until the early seventies, when it was converted into an infirmary.

Paula parks in one of the half-dozen spaces to the left of the house, turning off the car engine. She takes a last drag on her cigarette, then unplugs her cell phone where it has been charging in the cigarette lighter socket. Mitch called earlier, finally. He said he had just gotten up, and of course she believed him. He always sleeps late on Saturdays.

Their conversation was brief. He assured her that he was fine and that he would see her tomorrow night when his father drops him off at home. Paula refrained from questioning Mitch about Frank pulling him out of school early. No need to drag her son into it. The battle is between her and Frank.

"Be careful, Mom," Mitch had said before hanging up.

"I'm always careful, Mitch."

"Well, have they caught the guy who killed that lady yet?"

"No," she said grimly. "They haven't. But don't worry about me, Mitch, okay? I'm safe."

Tucking the phone into her pocket now, Paula opens the door and steps out onto the gravel drive, acutely aware of the hush that is broken only by chirping birds. It's peaceful here.

When she was younger and he was always working, Pop used to say that he only wanted a little peace and quiet.

Well, now you've got it, Pop, she tells him silently as she mounts the steps and opens one of the double front doors. *Only I bet this wasn't what you had in mind.*

The place might look like a quaint home outside, but upon entering, a visitor becomes instantly aware of its clinical purpose. The front hall, which surely must once have had a carpeted or hardwood floor, is paved in white linoleum. The lighting overhead is bright and fluorescent. Several vinyl chairs and a low table stacked with well-thumbed magazines make up a small waiting area to the right of the door. Straight ahead, there's a long counter manned by a youngish woman in a nurse's uniform, and behind her are rows of file cabinets. The scent in the air is more musty and medicinal than it is homey.

Paula strides forward, offering a perfunctory smile at the nurse, who looks up expectantly. She must be new. Paula doesn't recognize her.

"I'm Paula Bailey," she says. "I'm here to see my father, Joe Bailey."

"Oh, hello, Mrs. Bailey. Your father will be pleased to have another visitor so soon."

Is she being sarcastic? If so, the attitude is uncalled-for. Paula gets here as often as she is able. She wonders if the nurse—who looks well rested, can't be more than twenty-two, isn't wearing a wedding ring, and has a figure that appears too perfect to have been subjected to childbirth—can possibly understand what it's like to be a single working parent.

"I get here when I can," she tells the nurse, who nods, wearing an understanding expression.

"If you'll just sign in here, Mrs. Bailey."

"It's *Ms.*," Paula corrects as she reaches for the clipboard the nurse slides across the counter.

She glances at the page. A line is drawn in ink horizontally across the middle of it, just below the signature of yesterday's last visitor. At least there's some satisfaction, somehow, in being the first visitor of the day, Paula thinks as she scrawls her name, address, telephone number, and the time on the first line below today's date.

She's about to hand it back to the nurse when something catches her eye.

Startled, she darts a gaze to the familiar name at the top of the page, under yesterday's date.

What the hell . . . ?

"We're going to win the prize with this pumpkin, don't you think, Mommy?" Hunter asks, patting the enormous orange vegetable. Joel has just unloaded it from the Expedition, with help from several male bystanders. Now it's lying amid several other pumpkin contest candidates in a sheltered corner of the shady green that runs through the center of town.

Tasha doesn't have the heart to tell Hunter that she's already spotted half a dozen pumpkins that are larger than theirs.

"I don't know, sweetie," she says, as they begin walking beneath a scarlet-and-gilt canopy of towering trees toward the cluster of concession stands set up nearby. "You have a good chance of getting the prize, but even if you don't, you should be proud. This is a huge pumpkin. Let's just wait and see."

"If you don't win, the judges won't know what they're talking about," Ruth, Joel's mother, pipes up. She's walking between Hunter and his sister, holding their small hands.

"Well, let's just tell the judges to pick ours," Victoria suggests.

"That's not a bad idea. Do you know who the judges are?" Irv, Joel's father, turns to Tasha, who's pushing Max in his stroller. "Maybe we can say hello to them. It's always good to make an impression."

"Um, I don't know who they are." Tasha tries to catch Joel's eye, but he looks distracted. He probably hasn't even been listening to the conversation. Clearly, his thoughts are miles away. He's been quiet ever since he got back from dropping off the stuff for Ben's kids at Ben's sister's house.

When Tasha asked him how they were, he said he hadn't gone in, just handed the bag over at the door to Ben's brother-in-law.

"Didn't you even ask to see Ben?" she asked.

He shook his head, saying he didn't want to intrude.

Is Joel thinking about that now? Or is it work that's on his mind? Or something else—something Tasha doesn't even want to think about.

He's been so quiet all afternoon. Even his mother commented on it, back at the house, when they were all gathered around the kitchen table eating the takeout pizza Tasha ordered.

"You're not yourself. Are you coming down with something, Joel?" Ruth asked, concerned.

Then again, she always thinks people are coming down with something, especially the kids. She goes around feeling their foreheads with the back of her hand and saying things to Tasha like, "She feels warm," or "I don't like his color; he's flushed."

In fact, just this afternoon before they left the house, Ruth announced, "Max has a fever." She was holding the baby as Tasha packed the diaper bag and Joel got the other kids into their coats.

"He doesn't have a fever," Tasha asserted after feeling the baby's head herself. Okay, maybe he was a little warm, but Ruth was overreacting.

Ignoring her, Ruth made Irv, and then Joel, feel the baby's head. She was insisting that they get the thermometer out and take his temperature when the doorbell rang. A reporter, naturally, wanting to interview the Bankses about the murder.

That threw Ruth offtrack, and mercifully she stopped talking about the baby's fever. Instead, she launched into a spiel about how Joel should put their house on the market and move because the neighborhood obviously isn't safe.

"In all our years in Brooklyn, there has never been a murder on the block, has there, Irv?" she keeps saying. Her husband, of course, agrees with her. He always does when Ruth puts him on the spot, but Tasha often wonders what he's thinking.

Every time her mother-in-law brought up the murder, Tasha tried to shush her. "The kids don't know," she told her in a whisper more than once. "Please, Ruth—we don't want to scare them."

"You can't hide this from them forever," her mother-in-law said disapprovingly. "They're going to find out somehow, if you don't tell them."

Unfortunately, Tasha knows she's right. When Hunter goes back to school on Monday he's bound to find out. But she isn't ready to tell him yet about Rachel. Maybe she and Joel can do it together, before Joel leaves for Chicago.

She doesn't want to think about that, though. She never likes to be alone in the house at night. How is she going to manage two nights alone—especially after what's happened?

Don't think about that now. You're supposed to be having fun.

Tasha sighs, shuffling her feet through the loose carpet of fallen leaves. She's been looking forward to this harvest festival for weeks. Now, with her in-laws tagging along and her best friend lying dead in the morgue, she only wants it to be over so that she can go back home—and barricade herself in the house.

The fear that took root at the first news of Jane Kendall's disappearance has been growing, poking at the back of her mind all day. Now, it threatens to burgeon into full-fledged panic—but only if she lets it.

You can't give in to it, Tasha. You can't let it take over.

She glances at her mother-in-law. Ruth, with her short, dark hair sprayed into place and her attractive face expertly made-up, is chattering away to the children, swinging their arms as they walk.

Irv, his silver hair hidden beneath a cotton brimmed hat he always wears on visits up here "to the country," is two steps behind his wife. His expression is bland, his gait unencumbered as he strolls along with his hands in the pockets of his neatly-pressed khakis.

Joel has shed that distracted appearance and is speaking intently to his father, no doubt about something dry, like the stock market or foreign affairs.

Isn't anybody else thinking about the murder? Isn't anybody else wondering who killed Rachel? And why?

And how can something so utterly horrifying have happened in a place like this?

Tasha looks around, beyond the infuriatingly oblivious members of her own family.

The crowd on the town green is thinner at this year's festival than it has been in the past. Is it because of the murder and disappearance?

Maybe it's the weather, Tasha tells herself, looking up at the overcast sky. The Weather Channel forecast predicts a big nor'easter moving up the coast into the area later tonight or tomorrow, as her mother-in-law keeps reminding her. Ruth is worried about driving home to Brooklyn in bad weather and has already informed Tasha and Joel that they'll be leaving before dark.

Which is absolutely fine with Tasha, of course.

Anyway, it hasn't started raining yet and isn't supposed to until much later. Last year it drizzled on and off during the festival, and still there was a big crowd. Tasha specifically remembers it. Enormously pregnant, she was seized by a fierce craving for fried bread dough with cherry pie filling smeared on top. She was forced to wait on a long line at the concession stand, and when she finally had the coveted treat in her hand, someone jostled her arm and she dropped it.

Today, there are no lines and no crowds to jostle her.

In fact, the few dozen people milling about the commons seem subdued. Most of them are teenagers or men who are volunteers from the local civic club that runs the festival. There aren't many families this year. There are a couple of reporters with camera crews, though, stopping passersby for man-on-the-street interviews.

Tasha passes a young mother standing by two toddlers in a double stroller and notices that she's clinging tightly to her husband's hand.

Another woman is seated on a nearby bench beneath the sweeping, dazzling foliage of a maple tree, bottle-feeding her baby. Her gaze meets Tasha's and she realizes that the woman's expression is wary, almost as if she's ready to bolt and run if she has to.

But the killer would never strike here in public, in broad daylight. He would wait until he could find his victim alone. . . .

If he even *is* going to strike again. There's no reason to think that he is.

But then, there's also no reason to think that he isn't.

And if he does . . .

Tasha glances at the young mother feeding the baby.

At the young mother holding her husband's hand.

At her own reflection in a puddle as she steps around it on the sidewalk.

If he does . . .

Who's going to be next?

It can't be.

Concealed in the trees at the edge of the woods, Jeremiah gazes in disbelief at the sign in the clearing before him.

HIGH RIDGE PARK.

All this time, he's been going in circles.

He's back in Townsend Heights.

Now what?

Where is he supposed to go from here? What is he supposed to do?

One thing is certain. Nothing could be worse than

spending another night alone in the woods. Not even jail.

He wants to go home. To his own bed. To his father . . .

But after all that's happened, that won't happen. Dad will never understand.

Torn, Jeremiah stares at the sign.

As he does, an idea formulates in his mind. A brilliant idea.

Maybe he doesn't have to go home just yet.

That is, not to Uncle Fletch's house.

Maybe he doesn't have to face whatever's waiting there until he's ready.

If he ever is.

There's another place. Somewhere he can be safe.

Somewhere nobody will think of looking . . .

Or will they?

Maybe eventually. Or maybe they already have searched and dismissed it.

He'll be taking a chance by going there, but what other option does he have? The woods. And night will be falling soon.

His mind made up, Jeremiah retreats from the clearing. He doesn't dare make his way through the park, or through the streets of Townsend Heights. But now that he knows where he is, he knows how to get where he's going through the woods. It's a long, roundabout path, but if he takes it he'll be able to skirt the park, the streets, and the neighborhoods until he gets to his destination. Maybe he'll even reach it before dark.

But before he goes, there's something he has to do.

Looking down at the bundle in his hands, he wishes he had a shovel.

Well, he'll just have to make do.

The important thing is that he bury it where nobody will ever find it.

Paula reaches the top of the steps outside her father's room just in time to see a white-uniformed nurse come through the doorway into the second-floor hall.

She hurries along the corridor toward the nurse. Some doors are closed, but most are open, and the occupants of the rooms call out to her as she passes. That has always given her the creeps: the pathetic moans and mutterings of her father's fellow residents. Sometimes she thinks his silence is preferable to that.

"Excuse me . . ." Paula comes to a halt beside the nurse, whom she's fairly certain she's never seen before. "Were you on duty in this room yesterday?"

The woman looks up at her without recognition, then shakes her head. "No, I'm only here on weekends."

Paula frowns. That's what the woman at the desk downstairs said, too.

"Would there be anyone here today who worked yesterday?" Paula asks the nurse, who has gone back to writing something in her chart.

She looks up from the folder. "Not unless somebody on the weekday staff called in sick and one of us was called to replace them."

"So there are two different staffs? Weekday and weekend?"

"Yes. We're part-time. They're full-time." She eyes Paula. "Are you here to visit somebody, or do you need to speak to a staff member?"

"Both," Paula tells her. She gestures at the doorway leading to the room the nurse just exited. "My father is in there."

"Mr. Bailey?" The woman shakes her head. "That poor man. He had a terrible night."

"Yes, I know. He hasn't been sleeping?"

"Actually, he is now. He's been so agitated. The doctor was here a little while ago and prescribed something to calm him."

"How long will it last?" Paula asks in dismay.

"He may not be alert while you're here," the nurse says apologetically. "But Mr. Bailey is usually noncommunicative as it is, so . . ." She trails off and shrugs, as if to say, *so your visit won't be much different if he's asleep.*

Paula moves past her into the room. It's small, with a single window above the lone guest chair. Having spent considerable time in that spot looking out, Paula knows that the view below is of the woods at the back of the house.

She looks around.

White.

Everything here is stark white, Paula notices, not for the first time. The walls are painted hospital white, their only decor Mitch's drawings that are taped here and there. The floor is covered in white linoleum. There's a white paper cup on the bedside table. Paula peers into it and isn't surprised to see two white capsules. More of his sleeping medication, probably.

The bed is made with white sheets and a white blanket.

And in it lies her father. Pale, sunken skin. Angular, withered features. More white—a shock of snowy hair against the pillow. His head is thrown back, mouth open, snoring slightly.

Paula stands over him, looking down for a long time.

"Pop?" she murmurs at last.

No response.

Well, she didn't expect one, did she? The nurse said

he was drugged. But somewhere in the back of her mind, she thought—hoped—that the sound of her voice might stir him.

"I'm here," she goes on. "They said you were calling my name, and I came as soon as I could."

Silence, except for the rhythmic, snorting breaths coming from his throat.

"I wish you'd wake up, Pop," she says, touching his hand. "It's me, Paula. Come on. Wake up, Pop."

Nothing.

"Please, Pop. I need to know. If I could only ask you . . ." She exhales heavily, realizing it's futile, but going on just in case there's some glimmer of a chance for a response. "After all these years, why the hell was Frank here yesterday? What did he say to you, Pop? What did he do to you?"

Bored with his electronic game, Mitch turns off the PlayStation and tosses the control onto the floor beside the television.

Now what?

He looks around his room, taking it all in. The entertainment center with the PlayStation, television, DVD player, and stereo. The queen-size four-poster bed with its nautical red-and-navy quilt. The big wooden armoire that matches the bureau and desk. The overstuffed red-upholstered chair. The closed double doors that lead to his walk-in closet and the opened single one that leads to his bathroom. The navy shades half-drawn over the oversize windows that overlook the pool out back. The built-in bookshelves lined with novels his stepmother thought he would like: the Harry Potter series, Animorphs, Goose Bumps. She keeps buying more, too. Hasn't she noticed that Mitch doesn't really like to read?

He can't help but compare Shawna to his mother. Shawna tries too hard. She doesn't know anything about kids. She doesn't give him much space. How many times has she poked her head into his room since lunchtime, checking up on him?

"I just wanted to make sure you were still here," she said the last time, and it was all Mitch could do to keep from saying, "What do you think I'm going to do, run away?"

He tells himself to be fair, that she probably means well. But how can she not know that you shouldn't smother a person?

His mother doesn't do that.

His father doesn't, either.

In fact, Dad isn't even here. He's been gone all day. When Mitch woke up and went downstairs, he found Shawna in the smoke-filled kitchen burning the French toast. After she stopped crying about having ruined his breakfast, she told him that his father had left for the day. Upset, Mitch went straight back to his room, where he's been ever since.

He ate the sandwich Shawna brought him for lunch, but he realizes now that he's hungry again. Well, there wasn't much besides lettuce between the two thin slices of whole-grain bread, and she probably used low-fat cheese and mayonnaise.

Shawna's a health nut.

Another difference between her and Mom.

Mitch has spent enough time with his stepmother to know that Shawna thinks people shouldn't eat meat, and that they should exercise every day, and that smoking is a disgusting habit. He agrees on that last one and has been trying to get his mother to quit ever since the school nurse handed out a little booklet about the dangers of cigarettes. Mitch doesn't want his mother to die of lung cancer.

But that's pretty much the only place he and Shawna agree—about cigarettes being unhealthy, that is.

Mitch doesn't like exercise, and he really likes to eat meat.

And right now, he's so starved he can no longer hide away in his room.

Reluctantly he gets to his feet and goes out into the hallway, where he pauses, listening.

With any luck, his stepmother is taking a nap, or maybe she even went out to do some errands or something. But he knows that's unlikely. She barely leaves him alone in his room for fifteen minutes at a time; she wouldn't leave him alone in the house.

He hears the low rumble of a masculine voice below. His heart leaps. Dad is home!

He's halfway down the stairs before he realizes the sound is coming from the television in the family room.

Oh.

"Mitch, is that you?" Shawna hurries out into the hall at the foot of the stairs.

Geez, she's like a security guard, Mitch thinks.

Aloud, he asks, "Do you know when my dad is coming home?"

"I don't," Shawna says. "Probably later tonight. He didn't really say."

"Well, where is he?"

"I don't know exactly," she tells him.

Something about that strikes him as odd. Did his father really not tell her where he was going? Maybe their marriage is in trouble, Mitch thinks. It would be cool if Dad split up with Shawna. Then Mitch would have him all to himself when he visits. Just like he has Mom all to himself at home. When she's not working.

Or does Shawna really know where Dad is, and she's trying to hide it from Mitch? But why the heck would she do that?

He looks into his stepmother's green eyes. There's all this gunk around them—brown eye shadow and dark pencil lines on her lids and black stuff on her eyelashes. She has pink, shiny stuff on her lips and darker pink stuff on her cheeks.

Mom doesn't wear all that makeup, and she's just as pretty as Shawna, he thinks defensively. Well, in a different way.

Shawna is the kind of woman you'd see in a movie, with her long, straight blond hair and her super-skinny body. She dresses like a teenager or a fashion model, in the latest styles, like short skirts and shirts that show her flat stomach, stuff like that. Her fingernails—toenails, too—are always polished. She wears jewelry every day, and not just her big, sparkly diamond wedding ring.

Mom just looks like a regular person—like a Mom.

"Do you want a snack?" Shawna asks.

How did she know that? He nods.

She looks all happy. "Let me fix it for you."

"I can get it." He starts for the big kitchen that runs the length of the back of the house.

"I'll help," she says, following him.

Mitch grits his teeth, wishing his dad would hurry up and come home.

Sitting stiffly on the edge of the bed in the third-floor guest room, Margaret closes the journal in her lap.

So.

Now she knows.

She isn't the only sister who has a secret.

Page after page of Jane's neat script have revealed something Margaret somehow never suspected—or dared to hope, in those long, lonely years when she so fervently coveted her sister's life. . . .

Her sister's husband.

No wonder Jane concealed this volume in the clandestine compartment behind the bookshelf, where Owen could never come across it and discover the truth about his perfect wife.

This will change everything.

Everything.

Margaret's heart beats faster at the very notion of what lies ahead. She presses her fingers to her trembling lips, lips that have waited a lifetime to touch Owen's. She had expected to wait longer . . . much longer.

Until the mourning is over.

Until Owen is ready to love again.

There's no telling how long that would take.

But now . . .

Now she holds the key that will unlock the door that slammed in her face the day Owen looked down from that diving board, so clearly oblivious to Margaret's existence, so utterly smitten with Jane.

Now at last, she, too, will have the perfect life—the life her sister and so many other women so foolishly take for granted.

But Margaret never will.

She rises and goes to the mirror, checking her reflection.

She'll change her clothes, she decides, appraising the

wool slacks, the silk blouse. Put on something more feminine. More romantic.

The trouble is, she doesn't have anything like that—
not in the austere clothing she brought with her, nor in
her closet and bureau back at home.

She could slip out to buy something, but that would
mean delaying the moment that is finally within her
grasp. And after a lifetime of longing, Margaret can wait
no longer.

She needs something feminine and pretty, and she
needs it *now* . . .

And she knows exactly where she can find it.

Her mind made up, she slips out into the hall and
down the stairway to the second floor. Owen is downstairs,
presumably in his study. Her mother put the baby down
to sleep more than an hour ago and then said she was
going to take a sleeping pill and go to bed. Both their
doors are closed.

Margaret stands for a long time in the corridor anyway,
listening. Just to make sure nobody is stirring.

Then, for the second time today, she gingerly turns
the knob and enters the master bedroom suite.

Sooner or later, they're going to find out.

It isn't the first time the thought has drifted through
Fletch Gallagher's mind as he sits moodily at the bar,
sipping the single-malt scotch that Jimmy pours so gener-
ously.

Uncertain at this point whether "they" are the Townsend Heights police, the swarming press, Sharon, or all
of the above, he stares at his reflection in the mirror
above the bar.

Is this what it comes down to, then?

On a barstool, alone, drunk . . . desperate to escape the inevitable?

Unwilling to meet his own gaze in the mirror, he glances away . . . directly into the seductive eyes of a woman seated on a stool down the way.

She's attractive. Definitely interested. And—he notes the diamond-covered band on the fourth finger of her left hand—*married.*

Yes, she meets every one of his usual requirements.

But not tonight, he thinks regretfully as he breaks the eye contact, pushes away his empty glass, and reaches into his pocket for his wallet.

Alone in her living room, Karen tries to focus on the paperback bestseller she bought months ago. Naively she packed it in her bag to take to the hospital, thinking . . . what? That she was going to lounge around and read during labor? Or—even more laughable—*afterward?*

She picked it up once or twice in the early days after Taylor's birth, usually when she was still struggling to nurse the baby and thought it might help if she relaxed, or when she finally climbed into bed at night. But something always happened after a page or two. Either Taylor started fussing or spit up, or Karen fell asleep.

She doubts she'll sleep tonight.

At least, not until Tom is safely home.

He called a short time ago to say he's still with the client and that he'll be stuck there for at least a few more hours.

Now, as Karen rereads a paragraph for the fifth or sixth time, she notices the wind gusting in the trees outside, creaking the branches and rustling the drying leaves.

There's going to be a storm. A big one. A nor'easter.

She saw the weather forecast earlier—several times, actually, before shutting off the news channel she's watched all day.

Now, reluctant to hear any more about Rachel or Jane Kendall, she wants only to escape into the pages of her book.

As she's starting the same paragraph a seventh time, she hears a car door slamming outside. Tom?

The sound came from out front, not in the driveway, but sometimes he parks at the curb.

She gets up, goes to the window that faces the street, and parts the curtain. As she looks out, her hope dissolves instantly.

It's not Tom.

A dented two-door Honda sits in front of her house.

In the streetlight's glow, she watches a woman walk away from it, toward the house next door. Karen vaguely recognizes her. Paula something, a reporter for the local newspaper. She's seen her around town before, notebook and camera in hand.

Unlike the swarm of press that has roamed the street for well over twenty-four hours now, randomly ringing the residents' doorbells, seeking comment on the Leiberman case, this woman seems to have specifically targeted the Gallagher house.

Why?

Seized by a sudden impulse to stop her, to tell her what she saw Jeremiah doing yesterday in the yard, Karen forces herself to hold back.

"Whatever you do, try not to get involved," was Tom's parting advice before leaving this morning, after Karen once again mentioned her nagging urge to tell someone about it.

But she had been thinking she would tell the police, if anyone. Certainly not the press.

With only a shred of uncertainty, she lets the curtain fall back into place and restlessly returns to the couch and her book.

With her in-laws long gone and the kids finally tucked into bed, Tasha walks into the living room wearing a pair of newly laundered flannel pajamas, the fresh smell of detergent and fabric softener wafting around her as she sinks into the cushions of the couch at last.

Joel is asleep in the recliner, the remote control in his hand, a Yankees playoff game blasting on the television.

For a few minutes, Tasha watches it absently, her mind elsewhere.

Gradually, the overwhelming tension of the day seeps out of her. Maybe too easily, she thinks, unable to focus any longer on the horror of Rachel's murder or the fear that the elusive killer who struck so close to home will strike again—even closer.

She has been consumed by all of that for hours. Days. Now all she wants is to let go, if only for a moment's reprieve from reality.

Maybe there's something else on television. The game won't hold her attention.

She doesn't want the news, either. She knows, having flipped on the television in the bedroom earlier, that coverage of the Townsend Heights disappearance and murder dominates not only the Westchester County station but also those in New York City—and even the national networks.

Well, maybe she can find something on HBO or Cinemax. There's no news on those cable networks.

She gets up to take the remote away from Joel.

He stirs and his grasp tightens as she tries to remove it from his hand.

"What are you doing?" he sputters.

"Changing the channel. Can I please have the remote?"

"I'm watching this."

"No, you're not. You're sleeping."

He forces himself to look alert, gazing at the screen. "I'm watching this," he repeats.

Tasha sighs and returns to the couch, knowing he'll be asleep again in a matter of seconds.

How often has this ritual played itself out over the course of their marriage?

Was there really a time when she found it vaguely amusing?

Yes.

But tonight, it's only irritating.

Why?

Because she desperately needs some kind of pleasant, mindless diversion so that she can lose herself, forget what's happening around her . . .

And yes, because she's angry at Joel.

Angry because he's been so distant lately . . .

And angry because he's leaving.

Tomorrow.

With a murderer on the loose in Townsend Heights.

She gazes blankly at the television as the ball game suddenly vanishes, replaced by the network logo and the staccato musical beat they always play when a special bulletin is imminent.

Naturally Joel doesn't notice; he's already asleep.

Tasha sits up straight on the couch, riveted to the anchorwoman who appears on the screen.

"Good evening. For several days, the nation's attention has been glued to the idyllic village of Townsend Heights, New York, a wealthy suburb of New York City where one woman inexplicably vanished and another was brutally murdered. . . ."

"Joel!" Tasha glances at him. "Joel, wake up!"

"Wha . . . ? I'm awake. I'm watching the game," he says automatically, then blinks at the screen.

"To bring you a shocking new development, we now go live to our reporter Mike Matthews, who is standing by in Townsend Heights. . . ."

Tasha's heart beats a painful rhythm in her chest as she stares in trepidation at the reporter.

Margaret slowly descends the stairs to the first floor, clutching the banister tightly to keep from pitching forward in the uncomfortable shoes that are so pretty.

Owen is there somewhere. She heard the telephone ring a short time ago, just once. That means someone snatched it up downstairs. Mother and Schuyler are sound asleep. Margaret boldly looked in on both of them moments ago, just to be absolutely sure there would be no interruptions.

Mother lay in bed, breathing evenly, aided by her prescription tranquilizers.

Schuyler was snugly tucked into her crib, eyes closed, her thumb sweetly in her mouth as she gently sucked on it in slumber.

Margaret will be alone with Owen.

Her well-brushed dark hair hangs almost to her waist, its weight swaying behind her as she moves.

Beneath Jane's flowing robe, she wears Jane's nightgown. The fabric hugs her more snugly than it must fit her sister, accentuating curves Margaret didn't realize she possessed, revealing a provocative length of bare leg, making her feel daringly seductive.

The peignoir set is white silk. Margaret chose it over the red (too blatant) and the black (too slutty).

White is virginal.

Brides wear white.

And now, walking slowly down the steps toward Owen somewhere below, the robe trailing behind her like a train, Margaret feels like a bride.

Her size-eleven feet are jammed into narrow size-eight slippers that look more like dancing shoes to Margaret but strike her as more appropriate than bare feet—or any of the cloddish shoes in her closet. Jane's slippers . . .

A cloud of perfume wafts around her as she moves, an expensive floral scent. Jane's perfume.

Clasped in both hands, like a bouquet, is Jane's journal.

Only the pearls at her throat are her own.

You're my beautiful girl, Margaret.

Do you really think so, Daddy?

If only Daddy were alive. He could walk her down the aisle.

She reaches the first floor and turns toward Owen's study, seeing the shaft of light beneath the door.

For a moment, she is poised there in the hall, wanting to savor the giddy anticipation.

Should she knock?

No.

Not this time.

Never again.

Taking a deep breath, Margaret reaches out and pushes the double doors open. Both doors, so that he'll see her framed there, like a bride in the back of a church.

Owen is seated at the desk.

He looks up.

His face is streaming with tears.

He looks ravaged.

Bewildered, Margaret watches as the raw anguish in his expression gives way to astonishment as he gapes at her.

"Margaret," he says after a moment, so obviously stunned. "What are you . . . ?"

"Owen . . ." She moves forward, holding out the journal, needing to show him, to tell him the truth about her sister. About herself.

"They found her," he says in a strangled tone, watching her, incredulity and bewilderment blatant in his red-rimmed eyes.

So caught off-guard is she by the state in which she has found him that it takes a moment for her to register his words.

Then her jaw drops in dismay as she realizes what he's saying.

Jane.

They've found Jane.

Chapter Twelve

Clutching a cigarette in one hand and the steering wheel in the other, Paula guides her Honda expertly along Townsend Avenue toward the town hall at twice the speed limit.

The business district is normally quiet at this hour on a Saturday night. The few eating establishments are cafés that cater to a lunch and breakfast crowd. The only bar is the Station House Inn, and it doesn't attract large crowds even on weekends. Besides that, all that's typically open on Townsend Avenue on weekend evenings are the deli and the newsstand, both directly across from the Metro North station.

But tonight, as she noticed earlier when she drove through town on her way to Fletch Gallagher's house, nearly every storefront along the entire three-block stretch is brightly lit. Every parking spot is filled within blocks of the downtown radius, mostly by news vans and cars emblazoned with press logos. The cafés have stayed open; the small gourmet groceries, too. Even the pricey shops and boutiques have OPEN signs in their windows, the owners clearly hoping to capitalize on the flood of media people who have invaded the town.

But they're currently deserted, Paula notes as, in passing, she glances into one brightly lit business after another. The doors are temporarily closed and locked, the proprietors having hurried over to the big, windowless meeting room in the basement of the town hall.

Well, of course. A press conference is about to begin, if it hasn't already. It's sure to be jammed.

Paula was sitting on a couch with Fletch Gallagher's sobbing wife when the call came over her cell phone. Her first thought, upon hearing the news about Jane Kendall, had been *They've found her now, of all times?*

Hanging up, she told Sharon Gallagher that she had to leave. And she apologized for the bombshell she had dropped in the course of what she had promised the poor woman would be a simple interview. As it turned out, she wasn't the only one with an eye-opener up her sleeve. The conversation yielded a revelation that was utterly unexpected. Paula still doesn't know quite what to do with it. She needs time alone to process it.

But not now.

Not when the Townsend Heights police are about to expand on this bombshell of their own.

She looks desperately for a parking spot, knowing it's futile even as she zooms around the block. Returning to the town hall, her foot on the brake, she looks around, certain that no vacant spot will have materialized in the past thirty seconds. Why would it? Nobody is leaving until the event is over. Even the blue-designated spots reserved for the disabled are occupied by brazen drivers, most with out-of-state plates, who are clearly willing to pay tickets in exchange for attending this historic press conference.

Paula can't afford a parking ticket.

No, but she happens to live here in town—and she's on a first-name basis with the Townsend Heights cops. They like her. They help her out when they can, just as she helps them.

After a moment's deliberation, she steps on the gas and pulls the Honda into place in the diagonally striped Fire Lane zone in front of the town hall.

She steps out beneath a sign that reads

NO PARKING ANY TIME. TOW AWAY ZONE.

You do what you have to do, she tells herself grimly, looking around. Good. There's not a soul in sight. Nobody's watching.

Her heart pounding, she hurries away from the car, the tapping of her heels along the pavement echoing through what suddenly appears to have become a ghost town.

"I can't believe it, Joel," Tasha sniffles, wiping her eyes with a Kleenex from the box he's brought her after going to answer the ringing phone in the other room. "I can't believe she's dead, too. And what a horrible way to die."

"I know." He sits heavily beside her on the couch.

"Who was on the phone?"

"Some reporter," he tells her. "He wanted to reach Ben for a comment on Jane Kendall."

"Why did he call here?" Tasha asks in disbelief.

"Because the press doesn't know where Ben is staying, and they figure we probably do. We never should have listed our number. Anyway, I left the phone off the hook so we don't have to listen to it ring all night."

Tasha nods absently, her gaze fixed on the television screen again. The special bulletin has given way to live coverage of a press conference that's just beginning down at the town hall to officially announce what has just been reported: that Jane Kendall's body has been dredged from the bottom of the Hudson River.

"I knew they were diving and dragging the river," she tells Joel. "And after what happened with Rachel, I thought they'd probably—but it's still a shock."

"I know." Joel pats her arm. "It'll be all right, Tash."

"Not for Jane Kendall's baby. Not for her husband. And not for Ben and the kids, either."

"No." He exhales heavily. "But it'll be all right for us."

"How can you possibly say that so confidently? What if I'm next?"

"You won't be."

She shifts her gaze from the television back to his face. He looks *old*, she realizes with a start. Not senior-citizen old, but the lines around his dark eyes have deepened and his thick dark hair has a few strands of gray at the temples. And he's lost weight, too, she notes with a twinge of guilt. Well, she hasn't exactly been cooking for him the way she used to when they first married.

But it isn't all my fault, she reminds herself, a defensive streak replacing the guilt. *He's rarely home for dinner. He's rarely home at all. I can't help it if he doesn't feed himself when he's not here.*

Still, Joel is her husband. She loves him. She doesn't

want to see the job stress taking such a heavy physical toll on him.

And if it's not job stress . . . well, something is doing it.

"Are you hungry?" she asks him suddenly.

He blinks. "Am I *hungry?*"

She nods.

"Are you?"

"Yes," she says automatically. Even though it takes her a moment to realize it's true.

When was the last time she ate? She didn't touch the takeout pizza she served when Joel's parents were here. Nor did she take so much as a bite of the fried bread dough and candy apples they bought the kids from the concession stands at the harvest festival—consolation for losing the pumpkin contest to a couple of high school boys.

And back home, after making the three of them Kraft macaroni and cheese from a box for their dinner, Tasha didn't polish off their leftovers while clearing the dishes, the way she usually does.

Yes, she's hungry. Despite Jane Kendall. Despite Rachel. Despite her nagging, growing fear.

"We never ate dinner," Joel points out, as though he's just realized it.

"I'll be right back," she says, rising from the couch. Suddenly she doesn't care about watching the press conference. In fact, she'd rather not.

"Where are you going, Tash?"

"Into the kitchen to see what I can find for us to eat."

"Is there sandwich stuff?"

"No. I haven't been to the deli in days. The supermarket, either. But maybe I can defrost some hamburger or something."

"No, Tash." He stands, too. "Don't cook."

"Why not?"

"Because . . . you've been through hell." His tone catches her by surprise.

She turns to look at him. There's clearly concern in his eyes. Along with something else.

"We'll just order some takeout Chinese, and I'll go pick it up."

"But you don't like takeout Chinese," she tells him. Actually, he used to love it. But that was when they lived in the city. Up here in Westchester, he avoids it. He says the suburban takeout places aren't any good, which has always infuriated Tasha, because whenever he says it, she hears his mother's voice. Ruth thinks everything is better in the city. The Chinese food. The pizza. The delis. In her opinion, absolutely anything to be had north of the Bronx is inferior.

"But *you* like it," he says. "And you're always saying you miss it."

That's true. She doesn't order it without him. There's not even a menu in the house. She points that out to him.

"But they all serve the same stuff up here," Joel says, somehow without a trace of disdain. He's treading so carefully, so obviously trying to avoid the argument that has become so inevitible. "You don't even need a menu to order."

Well, he's right about that. "Okay, we can get the number for Panda Palace from the phone book," she tells him. "And we'll have them deliver so you don't have to go out. It's supposed to storm."

"No, I'll just go in, get a menu, and order it." He goes to the hall closet and takes out his brown leather jacket.

"But you just said we don't need a menu," she says, following him.

"I just said *you* don't need a menu. But maybe I can find something I might like if I look at one. Besides, then we don't have to wait for it to be delivered. They always take forever . . . even in the city," he adds.

Guilt, she realizes as he looks at her. That's what she sees mingling with the concern in his eyes. He's being so nice to her. Maybe he's finally realizing that he hasn't been here for her in so long.

"While I'm gone, Tash, why don't you go up and take a bubble bath or something?" he suggests.

When she gapes at him, he says, "You look so tired. Like you need to relax and forget about everything for a while. I'll tell you what. I'll swing by Blockbuster while I'm out and pick up a video, too."

"Which one?"

"Something light and funny that'll take your mind off of everything."

"It's a Saturday night," she reminds him, then hates herself for having to find the downside to his sweet efforts. He's being so nice. Still, she can't help pointing out, "Nothing good is ever left in Blockbuster on a Saturday night. The new releases are always gone."

"Well, since we haven't seen anything that's come out in months—"

"Years," she injects wryly.

"You're right. Years. I don't think it needs to be a new release. Right?"

Takeout Chinese and a video on a Saturday night. Just like old times. Before the kids. Before the job promotion. Before the murders.

"Let me see if I remember," Joel says, keys in hand,

poised by the door. "Hot-and-sour soup, chicken with broccoli, and an egg roll."

"Spring roll," she amends, surprised that he remembers. "But otherwise, you've got my favorite order down pat."

He smiles at her, then walks out into the night.

Maybe he finally gets what I've been trying to tell him, Tasha thinks as she walks wearily up the stairs to draw a bath. *Maybe things really will change from now on.*

"That was your father on the phone," Shawna tells Mitch, returning to the kitchen and replacing the cordless phone in its cradle.

Mitch is sitting at the table, reading a comic book and eating the enormous ice-cream sundae she made for him right before the phone rang. She answered it and took it into the next room. Mitch figured it was so he wouldn't hear whatever she was saying.

"When is he coming home?"

"He's still busy," Shawna tells him, screwing the top back onto the jar of hot fudge sauce and putting it into the fridge.

"With what?"

"I don't know, Mitch. You want any more ice cream before I put it away?" She holds up the carton.

He shakes his head.

She spoons some into her mouth with the scoop, then tosses the scoop into the sink and closes the carton. "Mmm. That's so good," she says, smacking her lips.

"Then why don't you just have some?"

"Too fattening."

Mitch rolls his eyes, disgusted. He's never seen her

take more than a little nibble of anything that tastes good. All she ever eats is salad.

"Want to play a game or something?" Shawna asks.

"Like what?" He's so bored—lonely, too—that even some dumb board game with her sounds tempting.

"Cards," she says, and adds, when he looks interested, "for money. Come on, I'll teach you how to gamble."

"Yeah?" He raises an eyebrow at her. Maybe she's not so bad after all.

Yes, she is, he reminds himself as loyalty toward his mother sweeps through him. But that doesn't mean he can't play cards with her. Anything to kill some time until Dad comes home from wherever he is.

Karen hangs up the cordless phone again, frustrated. Tasha's line has been busy for almost an hour. Does she know what's happened—that they've found Jane Kendall's body?

Karen wouldn't know herself if she hadn't finally thrown aside the romance novel and turned on the television just in time to see the special bulletin.

The news shouldn't have startled her the way it did. Hasn't she known all along that Jane was most likely dead?

The police haven't ruled out a connection to the Leiberman murder.

Nor have they ruled out suicide.

But you never thought from the beginning that Jane killed herself, Karen remembers. It just wouldn't make sense, despite her family history.

Karen had seen Jane with her daughter, week after week, at Gymboree and Starbucks. No mother who so clearly loved her child would ever willingly leave her.

Somebody pushed Jane off that cliff.

Just as somebody slaughtered Rachel in her bed.

Again, she punches out Tasha's number on the phone.

Still busy.

Damn.

She needs to tell Tasha about Jeremiah. Tasha can help her decide whether his actions warrant Karen's calling the police. Her instincts are screaming at her to do it—especially now.

The only thing stopping her is that Tom doesn't want her to get involved.

But Tom isn't here.

Tasha will know what I should do, Karen thinks, punching out her friend's number once again.

Fletch Gallagher comes home to find his wife's Lexus SUV gone and the house deserted. The outside lights are on. And more inside lights than usual, too. Why is the lamp on in the seldom-used living room?

He turns it off, then retreats back to the hallway, stopping to turn up the heat. The house is chilly, and it's freezing outside.

There's music blasting upstairs. Loud, teenage music with a throbbing beat. One of the kids must have left the stereo on again. Or else . . .

"Jeremiah?" Fletch calls, taking the steps two at a time.

The music is definitely coming from his nephew's room.

Fletch strides down the hall and knocks on the door.

The music turns off abruptly on the other side.

"Who is it?" a voice calls.

A female voice.

Fletch opens the door to find Lily and Daisy sprawled

on their brother's bed. Lily has the stereo remote control in her hand, and Daisy is clutching a bunch of CDs.

"Hi, Uncle Fletch." Lily gives a little wave.

"We just wanted to see how our CDs sounded on Jeremiah's stereo," Daisy tells him.

"We only want to hear one more," Lily says. "You don't mind, do you?"

"Where's your aunt?"

"She went someplace."

"And left you here alone?" Fletch frowns. That's not like Sharon. "Where did she go?"

"I don't know," Lily tells him. "She just stuck her head in and told us she had to go out for a little while and she'd be back later."

Out.

Resentment swoops through Fletch as he stands there, still gripping the doorknob. He called Sharon less than an hour ago to see if there had been any word of his nephew or a call from his brother. Nothing yet. She told him she would be waiting by the phone, just as she had been all day, and then, sounding irritated, she asked him where he was.

"At the gym."

"Well, when will you be home?"

"Soon," he promised, before hanging up.

Well, she didn't wait for him. Apparently, his wife had suddenly found something more interesting to do on a Saturday night. Something more important—to her—than waiting for information about her missing nephew, or a call from his father overseas.

And Fletch has a good idea what that something is.

"Has anybody called?" he asks his nieces.

They shake their heads.

"How long have you had the stereo on full volume?"

They look at each other.

"A while," Lily says, indicating the stack of CDs in her sister's hand. "We've played all of those."

They wouldn't have heard the phone if it rang. Nor would they have overheard any call Sharon might have placed before leaving.

Well, it doesn't matter.

Fletch doesn't need evidence to have his suspicions confirmed. He can do that himself.

"I'm going out for a little while, too," he tells his nieces abruptly. "Do me a favor. Keep the stereo volume down so that you can hear the phone if it rings."

"In case it's Jeremiah?" Daisy asks.

He nods. "Or your stepfather. Aidan's got to get the message and get back to me sooner or later. If he does, don't tell him Jeremiah's missing. I'll do that. Just tell him to stay where he is so I can call him when I get back."

"Where are you going, Uncle Fletch?"

"To find your aunt," he says grimly.

Back upstairs in her room, Margaret breathlessly strips off Jane's clothing, blindly tossing the gown, the robe, the shoes into a heap on the floor beside the bed.

She eyes the long, high-collared plain blue flannel nightgown hanging on the hook beside the door. She's worn nightgowns like that all her life. Now it looks like she always will.

Standing naked but for the string of pearls still clasped around her neck, she closes her eyes, shutting out the nightgown, attempting to shut out what just happened with Owen in his study.

But she can't.

The horrible scene replays against the screen of her eyelids.

Owen staring at her in shocked silence as she blurted the truth—the whole truth. About Jane. About herself. About her feelings for him.

Her eyes still squeezed closed so tightly they ache, Margaret half-turns, grasps for something—the bedpost—needing support as the cruel irony rams into her all over again.

Despite Jane's death—even more painful, despite Jane's bitter betrayal—Margaret will never have the man she loves.

He made it clear that even in death, Jane lays claim to what will be denied Margaret for the rest of her life.

At which point did Owen start to sob? At which point did he vomit into the wastebasket beside his desk? At which point did his grief and disbelief turn to wrath? At which point did he order her to get out?

Mercifully, it's a blur now.

Dazed, Margaret opens her eyes.

She finds herself facing the window across from the bed. The window that looks down on the front yard and Harding Place beyond, where the press and curious onlookers are still encamped. The numbers have dwindled a bit these past few days as the Leiberman murder took center stage, only to explode with tonight's development. Cameras trained on the house, floodlights, police officers, the private security firm Owen hired to keep everyone back, beyond the barricades . . .

Margaret stares down upon the garish circus from her window, feeling momentarily like a doomed tower prisoner.

But it dawns on her, as it has before, that she isn't imprisoned in this house. Not really.

She swiftly begins to dress again, pulling on the stiff denim jeans again, and heavy socks, and a dark turtleneck over the strand of pearls. She needs the pearls. Daddy's pearls. They'll give her the strength to do what has to come next.

Fully clothed, wearing shoes and a warm coat, she kneels beside the bed and slides out the suitcase she has stowed beneath it. She unpacked the contents into the bureau and closet when she arrived earlier in the week— all but two items.

She unlocks the suitcase and removes those items now, carefully stashing them in the deep pockets of her hooded down parka.

Then she takes a flashlight from the drawer of the night table.

She's ready.

Taking one last look around the room, Margaret tells herself that she has no choice. It has to be this way. She failed miserably in her final effort to avoid the inevitable, forever sealing her fate in those moments in Owen's study.

As she descends through the silent house, she becomes acutely aware of certain sounds. The massive grandfather clock ticking in the foyer. The hum of the oversize refrigerator in the kitchen. The distant hubbub of the crowd at the gate. And her own accelerated respiration that seems to grow more audible with every intake of breath.

She closes the basement door behind her, then, training the flashlight beam on the steep stairway, continues her journey into the depths of the old house.

It's cold down here. Damp. Cobwebs brush against her face as she makes her way through one cavernous room after another. The wine cellar. The root cellar. The coal bin.

At last reaching the back wall of the stone foundation that was dug well over a century ago, Margaret opens the rough-hewn door to a moldering storage closet. Her beam illuminates a few rusted old tools that hang on the walls. Otherwise, the closet is empty.

Not quite. Margaret shudders, hearing a sudden scurrying somewhere at her feet as she steps inside.

Holding the flashlight steady with one hand, training it on the back wall of the closet, she reaches out, feeling for the concealed latch Jane showed her that day so long ago.

One tug, and the back wall of the closet transforms into a door.

A door that leads to an underground tunnel that will take her away from the house and into the woods, far beyond the glare of the lights and cameras.

Margaret steps over the threshold and pulls the door safely shut after her, one hand clutching the flashlight, the other feeling in her pocket to make sure they're still there.

The photograph.

And the butcher knife.

Wrapped in her flannel bathrobe, Tasha scuffs downstairs in her big fuzzy slippers, wondering where Joel can possibly be.

He left over an hour ago to pick up the food and the video.

In the front hall, she peers out into the night. The wind is gusting and it's raining now. Just a light rain that patters against the windows, but Tasha knows that a nor'easter is predicted at some point this weekend.

Maybe Joel won't be able to go to Chicago tomorrow, she thinks hopefully.

Or maybe she should just come right out and ask him not to go.

Before his sudden shift in mood earlier tonight, she wouldn't have dared. But the way he treated her earlier, before he left . . . well, he might have realized how much she needs him. He might be willing to tell his boss that he can't make the trip.

Tasha decides to ask him about it when he gets home.

Where is he?

How long can it possibly take to get Chinese food and a video? Okay, he did have to order the food and wait for it to be prepared. And he did have to browse in the video store. Plus, the strip with Panda Palace and Blockbuster is a few miles from here, outside of town.

Even considering all of those things, he should be back by now.

What if something has happened? Like a fender bender?

Then he would have called, she tells herself.

Worried, Tasha paces into the kitchen.

Her gaze falls on the telephone receiver lying face-up on the counter, and a wave of relief washes over her.

Of course. Joel said he was taking the phone off the hook because of reporters. If he tried to call her to say he would be delayed, he wouldn't get through.

Tasha hangs up the phone, hoping he'll call—or better yet, walk in the door—soon.

You should have known better than to come here, Sharon. You should have trusted your senses. But your curiosity got the best of you, didn't it.

Look at her, picking her way through the marshy ground overgrown with grass, looking over her shoulder every few seconds, almost as though she suspects she's being watched. But she doesn't think to look ahead of her, over toward the shed. Not that she would see anything if she did. A perfect hiding place, here in the shadows behind the overgrown lilacs alongside the shed.

Ah, Sharon.

Even glimpsed from a distance, through the murky darkness and driving rain, she's beautiful, with that stunning figure and that blond hair of hers.

Does she sense that these are her last moments of life? Does she realize she's about to draw her last breath? Does she know now that she's no better, no different, than the others?

A few more steps, and she'll be in position.

One . . .

Two . . .

Three . . .

She gasps, looking up. "My God," she says in the split second before she realizes. "You just scared the hell out of me. What are you doing here?"

And then she knows, in an instant, her surprised expression giving way to horror and then a twisted mask of agony as her hair is yanked back and the blade swiftly slices her throat.

At last Jeremiah arrives at his destination, shivering, soaked from the rain that, thankfully, didn't begin falling until a short time ago. As he picks his way through the last few yards of mist-draped woods over finally familiar terrain toward the clearing just ahead, he can think only of food. And sleep.

He hasn't eaten all day today, either. He couldn't bring himself to even consider ingesting anything he could possibly find in the forest. Certainly not raw game, or worms, or grubs. He sipped water from a cold, clear stream. It had a faintly metallic flavor, but his throat was so parched it didn't matter.

Now maybe he can find something to eat in the remains of the vegetable garden he and the twins planted last spring. The deer have probably taken any tomatoes and beans that survived the light frosts they've had until now, but you never know. And there are pumpkins, not all of them the size of the enormous prize one that he was supposed to help his sisters lug to the harvest festival. Maybe he can cut into some of the smaller sugar pumpkins using his father's axe, as long as it's still in the shed.

Shivering, Jeremiah remembers that there used to be a couple of old blankets in the shed, too. They used them for a long-ago day at the Jersey Shore, and Melissa refused to allow them back into the house to be washed, saying she didn't want her washing machine full of sand. Jeremiah's dad stashed them on a shelf with citronella candles and potting soil and rose spray, and they were still there the last time Jeremiah looked.

In fact, everything beyond the charred ruins of the house—the shed, the garden, the girls' wooden swing set—is just as it was left the night of the fire. Jeremiah knows his father intends to sell the property when he comes back home from the Middle East.

And then what? He's pretty sure his father doesn't intend for him and his stepsisters to live with Uncle Fletch and Aunt Sharon forever.

But now, with everything that's happened, Jeremiah has no idea what his future holds. For all he knows, he could spend the rest of his life in prison for murder.

Swallowing hard, his throat sore from two days hiking in the cold, damp air, he steps into the overgrown yard. The rain is coming down harder now, and the ground is marshy beneath his feet.

He'll check out the vegetable garden first, then the shed.

Then, coming into view of the garden, he stops short. No . . .

It can't be.

Needing to believe that the scene before him is distorted by the rain and mist, Jeremiah takes a step forward. Then another.

Then a scream escapes him as he finally understands that the gruesome sight is no illusion.

Paula hurries toward Officer Brian Mulvaney as he stands in front of her car parked in the fire lane in front of the town hall. His ticket pad is in his hand and he's shaking his head.

"Brian, I'm so sorry," she calls to him.

He looks up in surprise, spotting her amid the swarm of people coming from the press conference. "Paula, hi."

"That's my car," she says apologetically, jingling the keys. "I couldn't find a spot for the press conference— every spot in front of my apartment two blocks away is taken, and even the commuter parking lot is full."

"I know. I'm headed over there next," he tells her, gesturing around them at the throng of chattering reporters. "I can't believe these out-of-town idiots don't even give a second glance at the signs that say you need a permit to park in that lot or you get towed."

"They don't care. They just want their story. And so

do I, I guess," she admits, knowing she's guilty as charged. And she can't exactly come right out and ask him not to ticket her. But with any luck . . .

He grins and tears up the ticket he was writing. "Yeah, but you're local, Paula," he says. "The least I can do is cut you a break. I was just about to have you towed away. I've just about had it with this town being overrun by outsiders, and it doesn't look like that's going to change any time soon."

"Thanks, Brian. You don't know how grateful I am. This is the second favor you've done for me today."

His grin fades. His voice low, he tells her, "Yeah, but don't tell a soul about the other one. I mean, I don't want this getting out, either. But cops rip up tickets all the time. The other thing—letting you check out the murder scene—they won't understand."

"Don't worry, Brian. I promised I wouldn't tell anyone about that, and it was really helpful for my story. You know, to set the tone," she lies.

Soon enough, Paula—not the local cops, not the seasoned detectives, not the big-city investigative reporters—will blow open the Leiberman and Kendall cases by revealing the shocking clues everyone else has missed. Then Brian Mulvaney will realize that he—and everyone else in town—underestimated Paula's journalistic skills.

"I really appreciate what you did for me, Brian," she says. "I know how busy you are with everything that's going on."

"Well, if the coroner's office can rule out suicide in Jane Kendall's death, you'll have an even bigger story than you originally thought." He shakes his head. "Two murdered women in Townsend Heights."

Three, Paula corrects him silently. *You've forgotten Melissa Gallagher. But I haven't. . . .*

* * *

Tasha, on the couch, awakens with a start, hearing footsteps in the kitchen. Her heart racing, she calls out, "Joel?"

What if it's not? Her mind whirls. Her gaze falls on the fireplace tools across the room. Can she make it there and arm herself with a poker before she's attacked?

"It's me," he calls.

"Thank God." Relieved, she rubs her eyes and gets to her feet, glancing at the clock. She sat down only five minutes ago to wait for him, but apparently she drifted off. She's so exhausted, all she really wants is to go upstairs and crawl into bed, but she can smell the savory aroma of the Chinese food. She'll have to eat. After all, Joel got it just for her.

Making her way into the kitchen, she finds her husband hanging his dripping raincoat on one of the hooks beside the door.

"What happened to you?" she asks.

"It's a monsoon out there, that's what happened." He takes off his soggy shoes and puts them on the mat, then strips off his socks, too.

"I mean, why did it take you so long?" She peers into the shopping bag filled with boxy white takeout cartons. "I was worried."

"I tried to call you, but the phone was off the hook, remember?"

"I know, I just figured that out a few minutes ago, actually. So what happened?"

"The Panda Palace was jammed. Not just people eating there and coming in to pick up takeout, but their phone was ringing off the hook for deliveries because of the weather. So by the time I placed our order, then waited for it, then went to the video store . . ."

"Well, I really appreciate it," she tells him, grabbing napkins from a drawer and carrying them and the bag to the living room. "What movie did you rent?"

"That Steve Martin thing from last year."

She knows which movie he means. She already saw it one night on cable when he was working late. But she doesn't have the heart to tell him that after all he went through to get it, so she says, "Sounds great."

"I'm going upstairs to change into dry clothes. I'll be back in a few minutes."

She's just set the food down in the living room when the phone rings. Tasha sighs. It must be a reporter. As she goes to answer it she tells herself she'll let the machine get the next one, or just take it off the hook again now that Joel is home.

"Tasha? It's me."

"Karen, hi. I thought you were going to be another reporter."

"They're still calling?"

"There was a lull, but they've started again. You're lucky you're unlisted."

"Well, you know Tom. Mr. Privacy." Karen's tone is subdued. "Did you hear about Jane?"

"Yes. It's horrible."

"I know. I keep picturing that sweet little girl without a mommy."

"Me, too. I guess I almost expected that this was how it would turn out, but somehow it's still a shock."

"I know. And I've got to tell you about something strange that happened. Tasha. Do you know Fletch Gallagher's nephew?"

Fletch Gallagher. As always, the mere mention of his name makes her uneasy.

"I know who he is," she tells Karen. "He babysat for Rachel's kids the night she—"

"Exactly."

Karen goes on to tell Tasha what she saw: Jeremiah Gallagher lurking around the shed in his backyard, then disappearing into the woods with some kind of bundle. She says she hasn't seen him since.

"Tom thinks I'm being paranoid or nosy or both, but I can't help thinking maybe he had something to do with Rachel's death."

Tasha considers that. She barely knows Jeremiah, but from what she can tell, he's something of a loner. Which doesn't mean he's capable of murder, but you never know. Besides . . .

"What about Jane?" she reminds Karen. "If she was killed, too, do you think he had something to do with that? Because I don't know if he had any connection to her."

"I don't know what to think," Karen tells her. "All I know is that he was behaving suspiciously, and two women are dead. Tom doesn't think I should get involved. What do you think I should do?"

"I'm honestly not sure," Tasha says as Joel comes into the room wearing sweat pants and a thermal pullover. He gives her a questioning look. "Wait, let me see what Joel thinks."

"About what?" he asks. "Who's on the phone?"

"Karen." She briefly explains the situation to him. "Should Karen call the police?"

"Definitely," Joel says without hesitation. "It sounds like they already consider the kid a suspect. This could be important information."

"Joel says to call the police," Tasha tells Karen.

"I heard him." Karen sighs.

"Are you going to do it?"

"I think I'll sleep on it," she decides, and adds, *"If* I manage to get any sleep. Tom will be out late tonight, and I'm jittery."

"I know what you mean. If you need anything, Joel and I are home, okay?"

Tasha hangs up. Her husband hands her a pair of chopsticks and a carton.

"Did you get a whole quart of this?" she asks, surprised by the size.

"I figured you can have the leftovers while I'm away." He grabs another container and opens the flap.

Tasha slides the chopsticks from their paper sleeve, considering his words. She chooses hers carefully. "So you're still going away tomorrow, then?"

He looks at her in surprise. "Why wouldn't I be?"

"Because of what's going on here, Joel."

She forces herself to keep her manner calm, almost casual. She doesn't have the energy for an argument. Besides, she doesn't want to put Joel on the defensive, knowing that will make him even less likely to change his travel plans—if there's any chance of that at all. Judging by his expression, there's not.

"Look," he says after a beat. "I'd stay here if I could, Tasha. But my job is on the line—"

"Joel, our *lives* could be on the line. Mine and the kids'." So much for staying calm.

"If you're afraid—"

"I have good reason to be afraid! Two of my friends have been murdered—"

"You should go stay with my parents."

"No," she says flatly. "How can I do that? Hunter has school—"

"He missed Friday. He can miss again. It's kindergarten, Tasha. He'll recover."

"And I can't stand the thought of listening to your mother tell me how we were fools to ever move up here, and how dangerous it is, and—"

"She won't say that, Tasha."

"Where have you been, Joel?" she asks, frustrated. "She already did say it. All day today." But Joel, as usual, had been miles away, spaced out, thinking about whatever it is that lately consumes his thoughts, his time.

"Just tune her out, the way I do," Joel advises, his mild tone rankling.

He acts as though it's so simple.

Maybe it is, some reasonable part of Tasha points out, but it's overwhelmed by the part of her that is fed up, and frightened, and hurt. She wants Joel to say, "To hell with the job, I'm staying here to protect you."

But he won't.

She tosses the chopsticks onto the table and stands.

"Where are you going?"

"To bed," she flings over her shoulder as she walks toward the stairs.

"What about your food?"

"I'm not hungry. I'll have plenty of leftovers for tomorrow. While you're *gone.*"

The tears don't start until she's upstairs, lying alone in their queen-size bed, listening to the wind and rain lashing against the house. She tells herself that Joel will come up to apologize.

But she realizes, as she drifts off to sleep later, that he isn't going to come up at all.

* * *

The phone is ringing when Fletch walks into the house. He hurries across the kitchen to answer it, conscious that he's tracking mud across the floor, and not giving a damn.

"Hello?"

"Fletch?"

His brother's voice catches him off guard. He'd been expecting David, or the detectives looking for Jeremiah, or even the kid himself.

"What the hell is going on there?" Aidan asks, his voice crackling across the wires. The distance or the storm: Fletch isn't sure which is responsible. "I got an urgent message to call you."

"Why did it take you so long?"

"I can't say," Aidan tells him. "I was just out of reach for a few days."

Fletch realizes his brother is involved in military operations that are top secret. This has happened before. It took him a few days to get through to Aidan when Melissa died, too. Still, it strikes him as irresponsible, now that his brother is a single parent, for Aidan to be so far away, and so out of touch.

Well, it's not his business to judge. Or is it, since he's the one burdened with Aidan's kids while he's overseas?

Fletch quickly explains the situation. His brother is silent for a long time.

Then he asks, "Have the police come looking for Jeremiah again yet?"

"My lawyer seems to feel it's just a matter of time. They don't know he's missing. But when they find out, it definitely won't look good."

"No, it won't," Aidan agrees. "Listen, Fletch, I'll be home as soon as I can."

"How long?"

"I have no idea. But if Jeremiah shows up in the meantime, tell him to hang in there. I'll be on my way."

Yeah, Fletch silently tells his brother, hanging up. *You'll come back. But how long will you stay? Just long enough to get things straightened out—whatever that takes. And then you'll be gone again, playing soldier overseas when your kids need a hero here at home.*

Well, who is he to judge? He's no hero himself.

And who's to blame? Not him. Not Aidan.

One person is responsible for what Fletch and Aidan have become, and that's their father. If it weren't for him, they might have had normal lives. Lived happily ever after.

Instead . . .

Sighing heavily, Fletch goes up the steps, certain his nieces are sound asleep in their room, and that he'll have the bed to himself in his.

On nights like this, Eric Stamitos always wishes he had any other job—anything at all. Even working the grill on the overnight shift at his father's Queens diner, which he did for a few years after high school. Then he met Elena, got married, moved out of the city, and found it necessary to work a couple of jobs to support them. His mother had never worked, not even in the diner. His father was proud of that. Eric doesn't want Elena to work, either.

That's why he took the job driving the tow truck on weekends for the service station where he's a mechanic during the week. It's not bad, most of the time. Only in winter, when he's called out in raging blizzards to tow fancy cars out of ditches because their hotshot owners don't know enough not to speed when it's icy. Or on raw nights like this, when the rain is coming down in sheets and the town is overrun with oblivious parking violators who either don't believe the signs or don't give a shit whether their cars are towed.

With a sigh, Eric props his lit cigarette in the ashtray and pulls up in front of the final car he has to tow from the commuter parking lot. Unlike most of the others, this one has a local plate. It's a beauty, too—a new Lexus SUV. Not only doesn't it have the required permit sticker in the rear window, but the driver left it in a handicap spot. Nice.

After pulling the tow truck into position, Eric jumps out to attach the chains to the Lexus. As he does, he notices that the door on the driver's side is unlocked.

You don't see that very often, even around here.

Well, that makes his job a little easier. He opens the door and climbs inside to shift it into neutral. The interior smells faintly of perfume. And it's clean. Not even a speck of mud on the mats or a stray wrapper or spare change in the console.

But he's sitting on something.

He pulls the flat wooden rectangle from beneath his bottom and glances at it.

That's odd.

The car is so spotless, he would have sworn the owner didn't have kids. But he's holding a puzzle.

An illustration of a nursery rhyme Eric's mother had taught him long ago.

The one that begins, "Peter, Peter, pumpkin eater . . ."

Stashing the wooden puzzle under the seat, Eric shifts the SUV into neutral, then climbs out to resume his job.

* * *

She was supposed to be the last.

Sharon.

But that was before, when it was all in a planning stage. And anyone knows that plans are subject to change.

Once the plans were under way, circumstances presented unexpected complications. Well, no matter. It will be even better this way. As it turns out, the pieces will fall perfectly into place with the addition of the last one.

Tasha.

Does she suspect what's coming?

Does she sense that peril is closing in on her even now, as she lies in her bed in the wee hours of this stormy Sunday morning?

Or is she peacefully asleep, unaware that before the day ahead has drawn to a close, her cozy little world will be shaken to its very core?

Sleep well, Tasha. This may be the last time you ever will . . .

Sunday, October 14

Chapter Thirteen

Tasha awakens on Sunday to the sound of the rain overhead.

Lulled by it, she rolls lazily onto her side and snuggles beneath the quilt, her gaze falling on the digital clock on the bedside table. It's a few minutes past twelve.

Twelve . . .

Noon?

How can she have slept so late?

She bolts out of bed, noticing as she does that hers is the only side that's been disturbed. Last night rushes back at her. Joel must have slept on the couch.

But what about the kids? They have to be up by now. Why didn't they wake her? Why doesn't she hear them?

She hurries into the hallway. Their bedroom doors are open, the shades pulled up to let in what dreary light there is.

"Hunter? Victoria? Max?" She checks one room after

another, her voice unnaturally hollow to her ears. The second floor is deserted

So is the rest of the house. She can feel it, hear it, sense it, even before she descends the stairway to find no evidence of her family in the hall, the living room, the bathroom, the family room. Everything is unnaturally quiet. Unnaturally tidy.

In the kitchen, she finds a row of empty hooks beside the back door.

They've gone out? The kids . . . and Joel?

Her heart is pounding even as she tells herself not to panic. Of course the kids are safe. Of course they're with their dad.

It's just that this never happens.

She never sleeps this late.

And Joel never leaves the house with all the kids. He usually complains about bringing even one of them along if he has to run an errand. In fact, she can't recall him ever taking two of them out at a time without her, let alone three.

So . . .

Where did they go?

And why is she so apprehensive?

Joel would never let anything happen to the kids, she reminds herself. He's their daddy. It's his duty to protect them.

All of them. Tasha, too.

Again, the nagging question troubles her.

If that's true—if Joel is her protector—then why is he leaving town when somebody out there is clearly preying on young stay-at-home mothers exactly like her?

* * *

Fletch hangs up the telephone slowly, having just been notified that his wife's Lexus has been towed after being illegally parked in the town commuter parking lot.

"Was that Aidan, Uncle Fletch?" Lily asks.

He looks up to see her standing in the doorway of the master bedroom. Daisy is right behind her. They're both in pajamas, their hair disheveled from sleep. If Sharon were here, they'd be washed and dressed, their beds neatly made.

"No, it wasn't Aidan," he says slowly, distracted by his thoughts. "But he called last night after I got home."

"We tried to listen for the phone," Daisy tells him apologetically. "But we got really tired."

"We figured we'd hear it ringing even if we were in bed, but we must've fallen asleep," Lily says.

"It's okay. I heard it."

"Well, what did Aidan say when you told him about Jeremiah running away?" Daisy asks.

"He's coming home."

"When?" Lily wants to know.

Fletch shrugs, looking from one twin to the other. "As soon as he can get away. I'm sure it won't be long."

The sisters look at each other.

Then Daisy asks, "Where's Aunt Sharon?"

"I don't know," Fletch tells her, trying not to betray his uneasiness.

"Didn't she come home last night?"

"I'm not sure."

"Do you think she ran away too?" Lily asks.

"I doubt that," Fletch tells her. "Why don't you two get dressed now? I have to go take a shower."

They leave the room.

He closes the door behind them. After a moment, he locks it.

Then he reaches for the phone again.

The visitors' waiting area at Haven Meadows is always busy on Sunday afternoons.

Today, when Paula walks in, she finds the rows of vinyl chairs occupied by an assortment of visitors: gray-haired spouses sitting in thoughtful silence; middle-aged children clutching bouquets of flowers or white bakery boxes tied with string; small, antsy grandchildren, perhaps great grandchildren, chasing each other up and down the rows as their elders shush them.

With any luck, Paula won't have to linger here. Some days she does. Others, like yesterday, she doesn't.

The nurse behind the counter is the same young blonde she met yesterday. She smiles when she recognizes Paula.

"Mr. Bailey's daughter, right?"

"That's right."

The woman pushes the clipboard across the counter toward her. "If you'll sign in, I can call upstairs and see if you have to wait, or if you can go right up."

Paula accepts the clipboard and takes a pen from the cup on the counter. She pretends to scan the list for a place to sign.

"At the bottom of the page," the nurse points out helpfully.

"Thanks," Paula mutters, taking her time putting the pen to paper. There's no sign of Frank's name. But today's entries began on the previous page. Or he could have come back yesterday, after her. Does she dare flip the page to see if his name is there?

The nurse is busy on the phone.

Paula lifts the page and sneaks a peek at the row of names below yesterday's date: she sees her own. No Frank.

Not unless he used a different name. She wouldn't put that past him. She wouldn't put anything past him.

"Okay, you can go right up," the nurse tells her. "Your father is asleep, but they said he'll probably wake up soon."

"Did they give him more medication?" Paula asks as a group of elderly women walk in the door behind her, dressed as though they've come straight from church.

"You'll have to check with the nurse upstairs," the woman says, turning her attention to the newcomers.

Paula climbs to the second floor, wrinkling her nose at the smell that hovers in the air. Cooked cabbage, antiseptic, and age—the house and its residents.

Well, she won't stay long.

She finds her father lying in the same position as yesterday, his breathing soft and rhythmic. The hallway is deserted for a change. Still, she closes the door. That's allowed, for privacy's sake, during visits.

"Hi, Pop," she says, sitting carefully at the edge of the bed. "It's me, Paula. I'm back. I wanted to see how you were doing."

No reply.

She peers at his face, at skin that resembles an old road map: a yellowed network of lines and wrinkles. He's so old. So helpless.

"I know Frank was here, Pop," Paula says softly. "I was wondering why. If you can hear me, Pop, I wish you'd open your eyes. I wish you'd tell me."

Silence.

She stares at him, remembering.

Not just the recent times, when he lived with her and Mitch in the tiny Townsend Heights apartment . . .

But the old times, too.

When she was a little girl, wanting nothing more than to spend time with him. Just the two of them. She remembers how he would put her on his shoulders and carry her around their small apartment in the Bronx, bouncing her and pretending he was going to drop her. But her mother always cut that game short, yelling that it was dangerous, that Paula was going to fall or bump her head on the low ceiling. She resented her mother for that. She resented her mother for a lot of things.

But that was so long ago. . . .

It's all so unimportant now.

Now there are other worries. Other problems.

Biting her lip, Paula reaches for her father's hand.

"Pop?" she says again, squeezing it. "Pop? Can you hear me?"

Tightly clutching an umbrella over her head as the wind threatens to whip it from her grasp, Karen hurries up the wet concrete steps of the Townsend Heights police station. Funny how you can live in town for several years and drive by the familiar small red-brick building every single day without ever wondering what it looks like inside.

Now, as she collapses the dripping umbrella and wipes her feet on the rubber mat just inside the double glass doors, she finds herself in a medium-size room. There are several doors and interior windows leading to separate areas.

She takes in the drinking fountain, the American flag, the wilted potted plant too far from the lone high window to absorb any light. The few rigid plastic chairs in a waiting area beside the door. The high desk a few yards in front of her. And the uniformed police officer seated behind it.

"Can I help you?" he asks, watching her as she lingers beside the door.

Here goes, she thinks, walking toward him, wondering if she'll regret her decision. When she told Tom her intention this morning, he wasn't thrilled. But he didn't protest when she asked him to stay with Taylor while she came down to talk to the police. She figured it should be done in person rather than over the phone. That way, they could see for themselves that she's not a crank or a meddling-old-lady type.

Or so she hopes.

She clears her throat and addresses the desk sergeant, who is clean-shaven and baby-faced. He can't be more than twenty-five years old, Karen realizes. She shouldn't be intimidated by someone his age, even if he is a cop.

"I'd like to talk to someone about the Leiberman murder," she says at last.

He raises his eyebrows and she wonders what he was expecting. Clearly not this. He probably thought she was coming in to complain about a parking ticket or a neighbor's dog.

"What about the Leiberman murder?"

"I live on Orchard Lane. I have information that might be helpful to the investigation."

"Just a second," the sergeant says. He picks up a phone and punches a number, barking into it, "Where's Summers?"

He listens for a minute.

Then he says, "Well, then, tell Ed to get up here. I've

got someone who knows something about the Leiberman case.''

''I *might* know something,'' Karen amends.

He ignores that, hanging up the phone.

''Take a seat,'' he tells her. ''Someone will be right out to talk to you.''

Before she's taken two steps, a door opens and a short, stocky, balding man hurries toward her. He's wearing an ill-fitting sport shirt and a pair of slacks that could stand to be ironed.

''I'm Detective Matteo,'' he says. ''We can talk back there.''

Karen allows herself to be escorted into a small, windowless office behind one of the doors—not the one the detective came through. Once they're inside, he closes the door behind them and offers her the chair beside the paper-cluttered desk, then sits behind the desk. He breathes heavily through his nose, probably because he's so overweight, she thinks.

Before beginning a conversation, he takes down information about her: name, age, address—just the basics, really, but she's uncomfortable. Tom wouldn't like this. Well, it's too late to back out now.

''Now, Ms. Wu, you say you have knowledge about the Leiberman murder?''

''I'm not sure.'' She pauses. ''It's just that I saw something that didn't seem quite right.''

''Why don't you tell me about it?''

She does. To her relief, he doesn't scoff or tell her that she's wasting his time. He listens carefully, and he takes notes.

Then he tells her something that catches her completely off-guard.

It seems that not more than an hour ago, Fletch Gallagher filed two missing persons reports: one on his nephew, the other on his wife.

The green Ford Expedition, with Joel and the kids in it, pulls into the driveway shortly after one o'clock. Tasha is pacing the living room, one eye on the television screen, the other on the driveway outside the window.

The TV is tuned to the Weather Channel, partly because she's concerned about the storm, and partly because the others are mainly showing football or coverage of the deaths in Townsend Heights.

Tasha meets them at the door.

"Mommy, we got Happy Meals!" Victoria squeals as they burst into the house. She waves around a colored plastic gadget of some sort. "See my prize?"

"Look at mine," Hunter says, holding up something similar. He reports, "Victoria didn't eat any of her Chicken McNuggets, and Daddy let her have the prize anyway. I told him you only give it to her if she finishes all her food."

"That's okay." Tasha kisses him on the head, and Victoria, too, and holds out her arms to take a clamoring Max from Joel, who doesn't look at her.

"How come you wanted to sleep so late, Mommy?" Victoria asks.

"Daddy already told us," Hunter says, rolling his eyes. "She keeps asking that, Mom."

"What did Daddy say?" Tasha asks, pulling Max's arms out of his rain-dampened fleece jacket.

"That you were really tired and you needed to catch up on your sleep," Hunter tells her.

Joel, hanging his own coat on a hook, says to Hunter, "Come over here, buddy." He helps his son out of his coat, hangs it up, then says, "Take off your shoes. The floor is clean."

Tasha looks down, about to protest. But he's right. The floor *is* clean. Did he clean it? He obviously straightened up around the house, but she hadn't noticed that the crumbs and sticky patches have disappeared from the linoleum.

"I didn't know where you all were," she says to all of them, but mostly to Joel.

"We went out for a drive, and then we had lunch. Right, guys?"

"It was fun, Mommy," Victoria says. "Even though Max kept crying for you."

"Did he?" Tasha kisses his round, fuzzy head.

"He was fine. Wasn't he, guys?" Joel says. "He even had some french fries."

"French fries?" Tasha hasn't yet given him french fries, afraid he'll choke. She bites her tongue, reluctant to challenge Joel's judgment in front of the kids.

"I have to go up and pack," he says, turning to her. "I'm leaving for the airport in an hour."

"Okay."

She shrugs. So some things have changed. Others have not.

"What about the weather?" she calls after him as he goes toward the stairs. "It's nasty out." And according to the Weather Channel, the worst of the storm is yet to come, expected to grow in intensity later today and tomorrow.

"I called the airport earlier. Some flights are delayed, but most of them are still going. I've got to go, Tasha."

"I know."

"Daddy says he'll bring me back a really big present from Chicago," Victoria announces.

"He didn't say really big," Hunter contradicts. "And he's bringing something for all of us."

"Even for Mommy, Daddy?"

Tasha watches Joel look at Victoria, then raise his gaze to her. "Even for Mommy," he agrees. Then he turns away and heads for the stairs.

Mitch watches his father dig into a steaming plate of ravioli across the small, square restaurant table. Shawna, on the side between them, picks at her small green salad—no dressing.

"Can you please pass the cheese, Mitch?" his father asks.

Mitch picks up the glass jar with the grater top, dumps some Parmesan on his spaghetti, and hands the container to his father. He twirls several long strands on his fork, holding the prongs against a spoon, like his father taught him.

"No, it's like this," his dad says, putting his own fork down and demonstrating with Mitch's. "Now, you try."

Mitch does, clumsily. He manages to get most of it into his mouth in one bite, though, sucking the rest in so that his mouth is smeared with sauce.

Shawna laughs and hands him a napkin.

"Do you like this place, Mitch?" his father asks.

"It's great." Dad is big on Italian restaurants. It was his idea to come here for lunch. Mitch had figured they would probably just stay home because the weather is so lousy.

That's probably why the place isn't very crowded. It's small, located not far off the Long Island Expressway exit—the kind of place where there are mints by the cash register and napkin dispensers on the dozen or so tables, and you can hear pots clattering in the kitchen every time the waitress comes through the doors.

Which she does now, to ask if everything is all right.

Mitch's father orders another Coke for himself and, without asking, one for Mitch, too. Shawna says she doesn't need another glass of white wine. Mitch notices that she's barely touched the one she has.

Still, he's not as irked by her today as he usually is. Maybe because they had a good time playing cards last night, and Mitch won more than ten bucks.

"Mitch," his father says, when his plate is almost empty, "I want to talk to you about something."

"About what?" Mitch looks from his father to Shawna, who's suddenly interested in her wine after all.

"About you coming to live with us for good."

Stunned, Mitch just looks at him.

"Would you like that, Mitch?"

"You mean ... I'd move in with you and Shawna instead of living with my mom?"

"Exactly."

He puts his fork and spoon down, his stomach suddenly churning. "Did something happen to her?" he asks in dread.

"No," his father says quickly. "Nothing happened to her, Mitch. We just think it would be better for everyone if you came to live here."

"Mom would never let me do that," Mitch tells him.

His father looks at Shawna.

Mitch can't tell what they're thinking.

"I spent the day yesterday with my lawyer, Mitch. Arranging it so that you can come live with me because your mother can't—"

Shawna interrupts, giving his father another look Mitch

doesn't understand. "You like it here with us, don't you, Mitch?"

She reaches out to touch his arm.

He shakes her off and pushes his chair back from the table. "Don't touch me," he says, fighting back tears. "You're not my mom. You'll never be my mom."

When the doorbell rings, Fletch looks at Detective Summers, who is seated across the dining room table from him.

"They'll get it," he tells Fletch, who knows that "they" refers to the two uniformed officers who accompanied the detective to the house a short time ago.

Fletch leans back in his chair, his arms folded, and glances at David, who is seated beside him. The lawyer shrugs and rubs his beard.

Moments later, Fletch hears a familiar voice in the hall. Then, to his astonishment, his brother is in the room.

"Aidan!" he exclaims, rising and hurrying toward the familiar uniformed figure. "I didn't expect you to get here so soon."

"I came as fast as I could."

To his horror, he feels himself start to sag in Aidan's embrace. But he regains control quickly, hopefully before the detective—or David—has noticed his weakness. He doesn't want them to see, to wonder, any more than they've already seen and wondered.

He introduces Aidan to the others, then tells him that the girls are safely at a schoolmate's house. He hasn't told them of Sharon's disappearance.

"There's been no word from Jeremiah?" Aidan asks, sinking into a chair and rubbing his eyes. There are dark circles beneath them, Fletch notices, as though he hasn't slept.

"Nothing yet," Fletch tells him. "But there's something else...."

"What?" Aidan looks from Fletch to the detective. "What's wrong?"

"Your sister-in-law is also missing," Detective Summers says grimly.

"Sharon's missing?" Aidan's jaw drops. "Since when?"

"She hasn't been seen since last night, and her car was found abandoned in the commuter parking lot. They're going over it for prints now."

Aidan touches Fletch's arm. "I'm sorry."

Fletch shrugs. "I know it's not likely, because of her car being found ... and because of what's happened here in town. But I keep thinking that maybe she went off by herself. I was just telling Detective Summers that Sharon has certain ... *friends* ... I've never met. Some of them are men."

"In other words, she was having an affair," the detective bluntly tells Aidan.

"Or affairs," Fletch agrees.

Aidan looks shocked—or perhaps just pretends to, for the detective's benefit. *"Sharon?"*

"You're surprised, then, Mr. Gallagher?" the detective asks.

Aidan mumbles something, sinking into a chair beside Fletch. He looks at his brother. "You okay, Fletch?"

How is he supposed to answer that question? He decides not to, shifting his attention back to the detective.

Summers takes a sip from the takeout paper cup of coffee he brought with him when he arrived. It has to be lukewarm, or even cold, by now. Fletch idly wonders if he should offer to make a fresh pot in the kitchen.

But he doesn't even know how. That's something Sharon has always done, if they have company. She has always been responsible for getting beverages, putting things out on plates, asking people if they need anything.

As it hits Fletch that she's not here to do that today, he waits for it to hit him—some kind of heartache or sense of loss.

But there's nothing.

He's only numb.

He looks up to find the detective watching him intently and quickly shifts his gaze away, hoping the older man can't read his mind.

"Joel!" Tasha calls to him from the doorstep as he prepares to get into his car and drive off to the airport. "You forgot to leave me your itinerary!"

He glances up, rushed. "I don't have one this time."

He doesn't have one this time? Tasha is momentarily caught off guard. When he leaves town on business, his agency's travel department always gives him a printout listing all the pertinent information: his flight numbers and times, the rental car confirmation, the reservation information and phone number of the hotel where he's staying. His ritual is to put it under one of the magnets on the refrigerator door so that Tasha will know the details if she needs to locate him in an emergency. Plus, there's something reassuring about knowing his flight number so that she can call the airline's toll-free telephone number or check on the Internet to see that he's landed safely. Joel is supposed to call her whenever he reaches his destination, but sometimes he forgets. And she always worries when he flies.

This time, however, as he's been preparing to leave

home, her worries have nothing to do with air safety issues. After he packed, there was barely time for hasty good-byes to her and the kids in the foyer before he dashed out the door with his briefcase and overnight bag.

Now Tasha watches helplessly as Joel climbs into his car on the driveway. "I'll call you when I land and give you the hotel number," he calls to her. "It's the Park Hyatt."

"What about the flight?" She raises her voice to be heard above the rain.

"I don't know the number off the top of my head, Tash." Now he looks faintly annoyed.

"Well, what airline?"

"United. From La Guardia."

"To O'Hare? When do you take off and land?"

"I take off in about an hour and a half, and I have to check my bag, Tash"—he looks at his watch—"and I've got to go *now!* Good-bye!" With that, he slams his car door shut.

She watches him back out of the driveway, headlights on, wipers waving.

"Mommy?"

She looks down to see Hunter beside her on the door-step.

"You're all wet," he observes, and she realizes he's right. The wind-driven rain has dampened the front of her jeans and sweatshirt.

"Come on, sweetie, let's go back inside," she tells him.

"I wish Daddy didn't have to go away on an airplane."

So do I, she thinks, closing the door and making sure the lock and deadbolt are both solidly turned.

Aloud, she tells her son, "Don't worry, Hunter, he'll be back before you know it."

"When?"

"Tomorrow night."

"Before my bedtime?"

"I don't know." Why didn't he leave an itinerary this time? Does he really not have one?

Well, of course he really doesn't. Why would he lie about that?

You don't trust him, Tasha acknowledges grimly.

"What are we going to do while Daddy's gone?" Hunter asks.

"Why don't we play Fishin' Around?" she asks.

"That's for babies," Hunter complains.

"But Victoria can play, too," Tasha points out, although she's certain it won't be a selling point for Hunter. She manages to convince him and promises that she'll take them all out for dinner later, too.

Anything to take their minds—and her own—off the fact that Joel is gone and they're alone.

The news of Sharon Gallagher's disappearance reaches Paula via her cell phone when she's driving back to town from the nursing home. The first thing she does is join the crowd of reporters that have migrated to the opposite end of Orchard Lane like ants on a sidewalk moving on to a fresher, tastier dropped crumb than the last.

A press conference has yet to be announced, so there isn't much to do but stand in the rain, stare at the house, and wait. Every so often a police officer or detective arrives or leaves. One of the recent arrivals, a young rookie Paula vaguely recognizes, shows up with a cardboard tray loaded with takeout coffees from the deli in town. A few of the reporters tease him as he passes, and his ears go red below his cap, poor kid. Paula tries to catch his eye, to show him that she isn't one of them, but he keeps his gaze on his shoes until he has disappeared into the house.

George DeFand is there. Paula manages to avoid him until she feels somebody tapping her on the shoulder about an hour into the stakeout.

"You need a bigger umbrella," is his greeting.

Naturally, he has a big, expensive one with a tentlike spread and a hooked wooden handle. Seething, she clutches hers, with its straight plastic handle and one broken spoke, and asks, "Why? I'm perfectly dry."

He shrugs. "So how's it going? Get any leads? After all, you're a local. You have the inside track, don't you?"

"You don't really think I'm going to scoop you, do you, George?" She keeps her tone light, but her expression should show him she's deadly serious.

"Looks like we've got a serial killer on our hands," he comments. "Three victims."

Four, she mentally amends, wondering how long it'll be before somebody else looks more closely at Melissa Gallagher's death. Considering these bloodhounds, not long. She has to work fast, or she'll lose her edge.

"If you'll excuse me, George, I've got to go make a phone call."

"Don't you have a cell phone?"

"I do, but the battery's dead."

"Here, use mine." He produces the high-tech flip model she saw the other day and holds it out to her.

"No, thanks. I've got to make this call in private," she tells him.

She uses a pay phone in front of the pizza place a few blocks away. She hadn't intended to make this call until a little later, but any excuse to escape that smug bastard George DeFand.

The Bankses' phone beeps busy.

She lingers for a while under her dripping umbrella, trying again, and then again.

Still no luck.

Finally she decides there's only one thing to do. Show up on Tasha Banks's doorstep and hope for the best.

Eloise Danforth Knowles has visited her late husband Norbett's grave every day, rain or shine, since he passed away six months ago after a lengthy battle with colon cancer.

On days like this, with the chilly, wind-driven rain that's been falling incessantly and is predicted to grow worse, Eloise wishes that her husband were entombed in the mausoleum, rather than out in the open. That way, she could spend more time talking to him, telling him the latest developments with the children, grandchildren, and great-grandchildren.

As she carefully parks her big black Lincoln Town Car on the deserted gravel cemetery lane, she promises herself she'll only stay a few minutes. The roads are wet and it gets dark earlier and earlier every day. She doesn't want to be caught out on the highway in this storm.

She ties her rain bonnet snugly beneath her chin, then takes the red rose from the seat beside her. She brings Norbett a rose every day, snipping them each morning from the plants he had so loved and nurtured in the vast greenhouse on their Bedford estate.

As she makes her way across the marshy grass, clutching her black umbrella above her head, she's glad she changed from the pumps that she wore to church earlier. Now her feet are cozily encased in fur-lined boots.

She passes the series of monuments emblazoned with

familiar surnames, telling herself that if she doesn't have word before the end of this week about the stone she ordered for Norbett, she'll call and inquire again. He deserves something more than the temporary metal plaque that marks his grave. Something as grand as this stone belonging to the Bancroft family. Or the next, belonging to the Armstrong—

Eloise stops short.

As she stares at the Armstrong grave, she hears a shrill, high-pitched scream that goes on and on . . .

Until she realizes it's coming from her own throat.

Spinning around in terror, Eloise Knowles moves faster than she ever has in all her eighty-five years, blindly fleeing the grotesque sight.

"What do you know about Toyfactory.com, Fletch?" Detective Summers asks him, coming back into the family room after leaving to take a private call on his cell phone.

"I've never heard of it," Fletch tells him, sitting up straighter on the couch and glancing at Aidan, who shrugs.

"It's one of those on-line catalogue companies," the detective tells him. "They do phone orders, too. They sell toys. You know, dolls, games, puzzles."

"My kids are too old for that stuff," Fletch tells him.

"We thought so," the detective says. "Which is why it seems odd that you placed an order with them a few weeks ago over the telephone."

"A few weeks ago? Me?" Fletch clears his throat, glancing at Aidan, and then back at Summers. "I don't think so, Detective."

"You ordered a couple of wooden jigsaw puzzles. The

kind that are made for small kids. Preschool age kids. Know what I mean?"

"I know the kind of puzzles you mean, but I didn't order any. What—"

"Three puzzles were charged to your credit card number. They were delivered by UPS to the address of your cabin upstate, outside of Liberty."

"I haven't been up there in ages," Fletch protests. "They can't say I signed for any packages at the cabin—"

"I didn't say that you signed for them. Apparently UPS doesn't bother with signatures up there—if no one answers, they leave packages on porches."

"Maybe so, but I never ordered any puzzles and I don't understand why—"

"Why are you asking him about this?" Aidan cuts in. "What do puzzles have to do with anything?"

"One was found in your sister-in-law's car, Mr. Gallagher," the cop tells Aidan. "I won't get specific about it. However, I will add that a similar puzzle was found on Rachel Leiberman's kitchen table. Let's just say that in retrospect, it sheds a certain light on the nature of her death. But it seemed insignificant until one of the officers dusting the Lexus for prints came across the puzzle and thought it seemed out of place. Especially when another officer recalled a similar puzzle at the Leiberman house."

Fletch swallows hard. "Then what you're saying is that you think Jeremiah—"

"Jeremiah . . . or you yourself, Mr. Gallagher," Detective Summers tells him flatly.

Chapter Fourteen

Mitch is zipping his canvas overnight bag when his father knocks on his bedroom door.

"I see you're all packed," he says.

Mitch nods, uncomfortable. He hasn't seen him since their silent drive home from the restaurant, having retreated immediately to his room, closing the door behind him. He almost expected his father, or even Shawna, to knock before this, but they left him alone.

Which is what he thought he wanted. But he found himself wishing his father would check on him, if only so that he could apologize for the way he behaved. Now that he's had some time to think about it, he figures they were only trying to make him happy. Maybe they thought he would like to live here with them.

It's not as if he hasn't considered what that would be like.

But he can't just abandon his mother. Can't they see that?

"Listen, Mitch, the weather is awful. I just checked the forecast and we're supposed to get the brunt of the storm in the next few hours, maybe all night."

Mitch shrugs. He knows it's lousy outside. He's spent the last few hours staring at the swaying trees and driving rain beyond his window.

"I'm not going to be able to drive you back to Townsend Heights tonight."

Startled, he looks up at his father. "I'm sorry, Mitch, it's just too risky. The roads might flood. That happens sometimes out here."

"So I have to stay another night?"

His father nods. He looks kind of awkward, like he's expecting Mitch to throw a tantrum or something.

Determined to show him that he's not just some kid with a rotten temper, Mitch says only, "Did you call my mom to tell her?"

"I tried. I left her a message. She wasn't home."

"She has a cell phone."

"It isn't turned on."

"It's always turned on."

"Well, then maybe the battery's dead," his father tells him. "Don't worry, Mitch. Your mom will understand about the weather. Trust me, she wouldn't want me taking chances with you on the road. She'd want you to stay here tonight, safe and sound."

Mitch nods, resigned, yet thinking, *What about my mom? Who's going to keep her safe and sound?*

Seated in their living room, the shades drawn in a futile attempt to block out the commotion surrounding the house next door, Karen and Tom are glued to the television. Taylor is snuggled on her father's lap, contentedly sucking on a pacifier, oblivious to the drama unfolding on the screen before them.

Seeking distraction, they were watching a football game—Buffalo at Cincinnati—when the network broke in with a special bulletin.

Now, her heart pounding, Karen listens in disbelief to the news that the body of Jane Kendall's sister, Margaret Armstrong, has been discovered in a cemetery on the outskirts of Townsend Heights.

"The victim died of a stab wound through the heart, one that was almost certainly self-inflicted," the rain-soaked reporter at the scene announces. "In her hands, along with the large kitchen knife that caused the fatal wound, Margaret Armstrong clutched a photo of her brother-in-law, Owen Kendall, the husband of Jane Kendall, whose body was discovered in the Hudson River just yesterday. According to police, Mr. Kendall reported that his wife's sister had indicated last night that she was interested in a romantic relationship with him and showed little emotion when she was informed of her sister's death. It is unclear how she managed to leave the house last night without being seen by the members of the press that have surrounded it for several days. Now back to you, Peter."

Karen looks at Tom. "So Jane's sister killed her because she was in love with her husband? Is that what they're saying?"

"It seems so," he says quietly, bouncing Taylor a little, his eyes solemn behind his glasses.

Now the anchorman is echoing Karen's question, saying that while police have not confirmed that Margaret Armstrong was responsible for her sister's death, they strongly suspect that she was.

"Until now, the death of Jane Kendall has been linked, if not officially, to a murder that rocked the small village of Townsend Heights just days ago, and perhaps to the disappearance of a third person. Police have yet to name a suspect in the slaying of Rachel Leiberman, the wife of a popular local pediatrician and the mother of their two small children."

Karen looks at Tom. "It's going to come out sooner or later," she tells him. "When they say it's Jeremiah, are they going to announce that I was the one who saw him prowling around the yard?"

"I don't know," Tom says grimly. "Probably not. Hopefully not."

"I'm sorry, Tom. I should have listened to you. I shouldn't have told them."

"Yes, you should have," he says, catching her by surprise. "Look, Karen, if the kid is guilty, he'll be put in jail, where he belongs."

She nods. What if he's not guilty? She's wondered that, on and off, ever since she went to the police station this afternoon, where the detective was clearly intrigued by her information.

Still . . . what if she has caused them to suspect an innocent boy?

Then his innocence will come out when they investigate him, she assures herself. And she almost believes it.

The newscaster is saying, "Meanwhile, police have announced no leads in the case of Leiberman's neighbor Sharon Gallagher, also a stay-at-home mother and the wife of a well-known former Cleveland Indians pitcher, New York Mets sportscaster Fletch Gallagher. Today, the people of Townsend Heights find themselves wondering if perhaps the fates of these three women—women who seemed to have everything—may be unrelated after all. This has been a special bulletin. We'll bring you further coverage from Townsend Heights on our regular news broadcast."

Moments later, the game is back on.

Feeling restless, Karen gets up to try Tasha again. Her phone has been beeping out a busy signal all afternoon. Karen is tempted to take a walk down the street to see her friend, but she can't. Not with the throng of reporters lying in wait in front of the house next door.

There's nothing to do but pace. And worry.

And wait for something else to happen.

Tasha opens the door to find Paula Bailey on her doorstep, clutching a flat white box. She's wearing a bright yellow rain slicker and carrying an umbrella that seems to be doing little to keep her or the box dry.

"So you do open the door for reporters bearing pizza?" Paula jokes, grinning when she sees Tasha.

"I saw you coming up the walk," Tasha admits.

What she doesn't say is that she's been sitting in the window, staring at the street, for the past half hour at least. After four rounds of Fishin' Around, she occupied the kids in the family room with a video so she could come in here to think. About Joel. And look out the window. And ignore the members of the press who occasionally walk up and ring the doorbell. For some reason, there have been at least a dozen of them this afternoon. Probably because Jane Kendall's body has been found. Still, you'd think they would focus their efforts on the Kendalls' Harding Place neighbors instead of here. Yet Orchard Place is as crowded with the press as it had been the morning after Rachel's death—perhaps more so.

"I tried calling, but your line's been busy," Paula tells her. "So I took a chance."

"Come in," Tasha says, holding the door open.

Okay, showing up with a pizza is a bold move, and she isn't necessarily in the mood to talk to a reporter. But she did tell Paula Bailey that maybe they could get together Sunday or Monday.

Besides, she's lonely. And frightened. And she needs to take her mind off wondering about Joel. Right now, anything's better than being alone in the house with the kids.

She takes Paula's coat and hangs it on the knob of the hall closet, saying apologetically, "There are never enough hangers."

"I know how it is," Paula says with an easy laugh. "Besides, my slicker's too soaked for a closet. I've been out in this weather all day."

"Poor you."

"Yeah, poor me. Did your husband get off all right?"

Tasha nods, impressed that Paula remembered. But then that's her job, remembering details. She's a reporter.

"So . . . I brought pizza. Half cheese, half pepperoni. I wasn't sure how your kids like it."

"Oh . . . they like it with cheese."

She's promised to take them out for dinner, though. And they just had pizza yesterday, when Joel's parents were here. Then again, the kids love it so much they probably won't care about having it again. And the weather is so bad, this is better than going out.

"Well, I like pepperoni," Paula says.

"Me, too," Tasha tells her, adding, as though she's just remembered, "And I haven't eaten all day, actually. So I'll probably make a pig of myself."

She leads Paula into the family room first, where the kids are so engrossed in *Mulan* that they barely glance up when she introduces them to Paula. Except Max, who instantly stretches his arms up when he sees Tasha.

She picks him up and carries him to the kitchen, where Paula sets the pizza box on the counter.

"Do you mind waiting to eat till the video ends?" Tasha asks. "They won't budge until then."

"That's fine. I wanted to talk to you anyway."

Figures. Well, Tasha knows Paula isn't here just because she's looking for a new friend. She already admitted she's investigating Rachel's death. "Would you like some tea?"

"Sure."

"Herbal or regular?" Balancing Max on her hip, Tasha turns on the stove burner and reaches for the red tea kettle.

"Regular. I need the caffeine—I can tell it's going to be a long night now that Sharon Gallagher's missing, too."

Startled, Tasha drops the tea kettle. It clatters onto the stove.

Max begins to cry. "It's okay, Maxie, shh, it's okay," she says. "He doesn't like loud noises," she tells Paula as she tries to calm him.

Her heart is racing. Sharon Gallagher has disappeared? Fletch's wife?

She's afraid. Terribly afraid. Suddenly she wants Joel home so badly it's all she can do not to cry.

As soon as Paula leaves, she decides, she'll call him at his hotel and beg him to come home.

It's time.

Jeremiah can't put it off any longer. He's been barricaded in the shed for hours, all night and all day. At first he was in shock, huddled on the floor, rocking back and forth as he hugged his knees against his chest. But then, as the initial daze wore off and reality set in, he mostly just struggled to come up with some other alternative. Anything else.

Now night is falling again, bringing with it renewed force in the wind that howls around the shed, and in the rain that beats on its leaky, thin roof.

And Jeremiah knows what he has to do.

Unless he acts, they'll find him here. Maybe not tonight, but soon. And when that happens, he'll have no hope.

Not once they've seen the pumpkin.

His sisters' giant prize pumpkin, the one they were going to enter in the harvest festival.

The one that has been carved open, jack-o-lantern style, with the corpse of his Aunt Sharon stuffed inside.

Paula watches Tasha carefully, about to deliver news that will either startle her or bring a knowing look to her eyes. Anxious to see her reaction, Paula forces herself to sip her steaming tea first.

Then she clears her throat and leans closer to Tasha, across the table, not wanting the kids to overhear. Not that they're likely to. They're as caught up in their video as Mitch always is when he's watching television. *They don't call it the electronic babysitter for nothing,* she thinks wryly.

"Just between the two of us, Tasha," Paula says, "I think I've zeroed in on the person Rachel was with the night she was murdered."

"Who was it?"

"You really don't know?"

Tasha shakes her head.

"It was her lover." Paula hesitates, trying to read Tasha's expression. She can't. Tasha is suddenly looking down, stirring sugar into her tea and keeping Max's busy hands from knocking over her steaming cup.

"Did you know she was having an affair, Tasha?"

"I had heard, but not until after she . . . died. And I didn't know whether I believed it. Who was it?"

Paula takes a deep breath. "It doesn't mean that this person is necessarily responsible for her death, Tasha. You understand that, don't you?"

"But it means that he could be?"

Paula nods. "I think he might be. And if you have any knowledge at all about Rachel's relationship with him—"

"I told you, I didn't even know she was having an affair."

"But when you knew who it was, you might think of something. Some detail that could help the investigation."

"So who was he?" Tasha asks impatiently, finally looking up.

Paula sees trepidation mingling with curiosity in her troubled eyes. No, she really doesn't know.

But she suspects.

It's only two blocks from the shed behind the ruins of the house on North Street to the Townsend Heights police station, next door to the town hall.

Somehow, with his hood up and his head bent, Jeremiah walks those blocks undetected. It only takes a few minutes, but he braces himself the entire way for somebody to stop him. To arrest him.

Nobody does.

If anybody happens to glance at him through the window of a passing car, or from one of the houses or businesses along the route, they apparently don't recognize him.

At last—or perhaps too soon—he's mounting the wide stone steps of the police station.

Forcing himself to open the glass doors, to march directly up to the startled-looking cop seated behind the desk.

"My n-name is J-Jeremiah G-Gallagher," he tells him, the stutter worse than it's ever been before. "I kn-now you m-must be l-looking f-for m-me. I'm h-here to t-turn m-myself in."

As soon as they're finished eating the pizza, Paula leaves, conscious that Tasha wants to be alone. She barely spoke as the five of them sat around the kitchen table, and she ate only one of the two pieces Paula had put on her plate, despite her earlier proclamation about making a pig of herself. The kids polished off theirs, even little

Max, who nibbled at the cheese and then sucked on a crust.

"Do you think he'll choke?" Tasha asked, seeming worried.

"Nah," Paula reassured her with the experience of a longtime mom. "It probably feels good on his teeth."

That was one of the few times they spoke directly to each other since the conversation about Rachel. Ever since Paula revealed that Fletch Gallagher was Rachel's mystery lover, Tasha was subdued. After that, Paula mostly talked to the kids—the kind of mindless chatter that keeps them entertained.

Now, as Paula steers her Honda away from the Banks home, up the winding lane that's crowded with press vehicles on both sides, she decides to stop again at the Gallaghers' to see if there are any new developments. She double-parks at the curb and hurries toward the crowd, spotting Brian Mulvaney in his blue uniform nearby.

"How's it going, Brian? Any news on Sharon Gallagher—or anything else?"

"Haven't you heard?"

"Heard what?"

"Big news, Paula. The kid just turned himself in—Gallagher's nephew."

She gapes at him, her pulse racing. "Jeremiah? He admitted to the murders?"

"Not yet, but I'm sure he'll admit to the Leiberman one. Haven't you heard about Jane Kendall's sister yet, either?"

Jane Kendall's sister.

An image pops into Paula's head. She remembers the gaunt, homely woman she saw scurrying toward the Kendall mansion that first day after Jane's disappearance. "What about her?" she asks Brian Mulvaney.

"She was in love with the husband."

"Jane's husband?" Paula's thoughts are scrambled as she tries to keep up with the flurry of new details.

"Right. Owen Kendall. Last night after Jane's body was found she made a move on him. When he wouldn't go for it, she went to the cemetery and killed herself on her father's grave. Looks like she murdered her sister to get her out of the way. The Kendall case isn't related to the Leiberman one after all."

"It doesn't look like it, does it, then?" Paula agrees, even as she silently tells Brian Mulvaney, *Don't be so sure about that. Don't be so sure about anything.*

Fletch is staring miserably at his reflection in the rain-spattered bay window when the telephone rings behind him.

With his body facing the room, head twisted toward the window, he doesn't even bother to turn around at the sound.

It's been ringing all afternoon. One of the police officers answers it every time.

Now, as a stormy twilight descends outside, he notices that the lights have come on in the house around him. That's why he can see his reflection.

He looks like his father.

The unavoidable truth is right there in front of him. He looks just like the bastard who ruined his mother's life and then Fletch's. Aidan's, too, although his brother would never admit it. Aidan likes to pretend that everything is fine. Even after losing first one wife, and then another. Even now, with his son missing and suspected of murder—along with his brother.

And what the hell is Fletch supposed to do about that? There's nothing he can do. This time there's no escape. When they start digging into his past, they're going to find out—

"Fletch?"

He sees someone come up behind him in the window as he registers the voice. It's Detective Summers.

Fletch doesn't reply.

"I'm afraid I have some bad news for you, Fletch."

This is it.

They know.

Fletch braces himself, his hands clutching the edges of the window seat beside his thighs.

"Sharon has been found, Fletch. I'm sorry. She's dead."

After tucking the kids into bed, Tasha goes to the phone in the kitchen and tries Joel's cell phone again. She's been calling it every so often, with no response. Not this time, either. Not surprising. She knows he uses it mainly for outgoing calls and rarely keeps it turned on. She doubts he even checks his voice mail for that phone, so she doesn't bother leaving a message.

Instead, she dials information.

"The Hyatt Hotel, Chicago, Illinois," she says succinctly into the receiver when an automated voice asks for the listing.

Moments later, a female voice comes on the line. "Which Hyatt Hotel, ma'am? There are several in Chicago."

Of course there are. Tasha pauses. What did Joel say?

She thinks back to this afternoon, when he tossed the name over his shoulder. Belatedly, she realizes that it was something more specific than just the *Hyatt,* but she has no idea what it was.

Reluctantly she takes down the numbers for all of the Hyatt hotels in metropolitan Chicago. It isn't a short list.

Does she really need to call all of them looking for Joel?

No, she realizes. She doesn't. It's a long shot, but she can try to reach his secretary at home. She'll probably know where he's staying. After all, Joel says she has a photographic memory.

As always, Tasha feels a stab of jealousy at the thought of Stacey McCall being privy to every detail of her husband's professional life when she herself is in the dark about most of them. But this time, she reminds herself, she should be glad the secretary keeps such close track of his schedule.

She dials information to get the phone number, figuring it'll probably be unlisted—or, with any luck, she'll be given a list of S. McCalls to try. If that happens, she'll have to weigh the list against the list of Hyatts, and decide which will be less time-consuming.

To her surprise, though, there's only one S. McCall on Sutton Place. Better yet, she recognizes the voice that answers.

"Stacey, hi. This is Joel's wife."

A pause, as though it takes a moment for that to register, and then an incredulous-sounding, "Tasha?"

"I'm so sorry to call you at home on a Sunday night." She paces nervously across the kitchen floor. "Joel left on his business trip this afternoon and I can't seem to find the phone number of his hotel. I was wondering if you knew which Hyatt he's at."

"Business trip?" Stacey echoes.

Tasha frowns. So Miss Photographic Memory isn't as brilliant as Joel thought.

"He's not on a business trip, Tasha."

"Yes, he is. He just left this afternoon." Even as the slightly smug words spill out of Tasha's mouth, she realizes, with a sudden, sick feeling, what's coming.

"All I know is that he's off tomorrow," Stacey tells her. "He told me he was taking a personal day. It's been on his calendar for two weeks now."

"Are . . . are you sure?" It's all Tasha can do to force her voice from her throat.

"Positive."

"I guess . . . I guess I forgot," she says in a futile, feeble attempt to appear in control. To appear as anything other than what she is: a wife whose husband has lied to her.

It's no comfort that he's obviously not with Stacey McCall . . . or is he? Is she covering for him? Is he there, in her apartment with her? Are they now, after Tasha has hung up, making fun of how blind she is not to have guessed?

You can't think that way, she tells herself, wrapping her arms around herself, trying to calm the swarm of butterflies in her gut. *You don't really believe that Joel would lie to you, do you? Even though Stacey said . . .*

There has to be some explanation for this.

There *has* to.

He said he was going to be at the Hyatt in Chicago, and she's going to prove that he is.

She sits at the kitchen table to place the first call.

By the third, she's standing.

By the fifth, she's pacing.

After the last, she tosses the receiver on the table, the pizza she has eaten churning in her stomach.

Outside, the storm rages.

Inside, the house is silent except for her own quickened breathing.

She hears the dial tone, then a clearly audible announcement in a robotic masculine voice. *If you'd like to make a call please hang up and try again. If you need help, hang up and dial your operator.* Then a loud, fast-paced beeping.

Tasha ignores it.

It'll stop soon.

The phone can be off the hook all night, for all she cares.

She knows that the one person who matters won't be calling her.

There is no Joel Banks registered at any of the Hyatt Hotels in Chicago.

Jeremiah's father rushes into the interrogation room just as he's telling the detectives, once again, that he didn't kill his aunt. That he didn't kill anybody.

"Dad!" he cries out, looking up to see the familiar figure, arms outstretched.

His father strides over and embraces him tightly. "It's going to be all right, Jeremiah," he says, his voice sounding choked up, the way it was before Melissa's funeral.

"Dad, I didn't kill Rachel. And I didn't kill Aunt Sharon. I swear it."

His father pats his head, then sits beside him. Jeremiah sees a big smudge of dirt along the front of his dark uniform and realizes it's from him. He's filthy.

"I've called a lawyer," Aidan tells the three stern-looking detectives. "Jeremiah won't answer any more questions until he gets here."

"But I want to talk to them, Dad," Jeremiah protests. "I want to tell them everything, because I'm innocent. I swear I am."

"If you're innocent, Jeremiah," one of the detectives says, leaning across the table, "then why did somebody see you sneaking around the shed behind your Uncle Fletch's house? What was in the bundle you took out of the shed, Jeremiah? And why did you carry it into the woods with you when you left?"

A soft knock on Mitch's door awakens him. Confused, he looks around the darkened room, locating the glowing digital clock on his shelf. It's past ten. He's been asleep for more than an hour. Why would somebody be knocking on his door?

"Come in," he calls, his voice croaking a little the way it does when he's been sleeping. He rubs his eyes and props himself on his elbows as the door opens and a shaft of light from the hall spills into the room.

Shawna is in the doorway.

"Mitch, I have something to tell you," she says, crossing the room.

Something about her tone makes his stomach instantly queasy.

"What is it?" he asks, swallowing hard.

"There's no easy way to say this, Mitch. I wish I didn't have to be the one to tell you."

Mitch braces himself for whatever is to come, his hands clutching the edges of the nautical quilt, trembling.

Please, don't let it be Mom. Please, don't let it be Mom.

* * *

"All right," Jeremiah finally says, his voice breaking as he looks at the detectives, at the lawyer, at his father. "All right, I'll tell you. But only because then you'll know the whole truth. And I didn't kill those women. I swear I didn't."

"But you're hiding something, Jeremiah," one of the detectives tells him. "You've admitted to that. It's time to tell us what it is. What was in that bundle you carried off into the woods? And where is it now?"

Jeremiah looks down at his hands, clenched tightly before him on the wooden table. His fingers are filthy, caked with dirt and scratches and smears of dried blood, the nails blackened with grime.

"Jeremiah," one of the detectives prods.

He takes a deep breath.

Then, haltingly, he begins to talk. He stares at his hands as the words pour from him, as he spills his darkest secret, not wanting to meet his father's gaze—or the bitter disappointment and shame he knows he'll find in it.

"I'm worried about Tasha," Karen tells Tom as he turns off the television set across from their bed, plunging the room into dark silence.

"Why are you worried?"

"Her phone has been busy all day. I just tried it again when I went down to get a bottle for Taylor, and it still is."

"You said she probably took it off the hook again because of the reporters. We can relate to that."

He's right. Their phone number might be unlisted,

but there's nothing to stop the reporters from ringing their bell. They've done it all day and night—even once or twice after Tom and Karen turned off all the lights and came upstairs to watch television in their bedroom with Taylor tucked cozily between them.

Now the baby is in her crib down the hall. But tonight, for the first time, Karen has left her door wide open, and theirs, too. That way, she can lie awake and listen for any unusual sound that might disturb the quiet household.

"I'm sure Tasha's fine," Tom tells her.

"Joel's away. She's alone with the kids. Maybe one of us should go down and check on her."

Tom is silent for a minute. "You're not going out alone in this weather, Karen."

She listens to the pouring rain, to the wind creaking the tree branches high above their house.

"You want me to go?" he finally asks reluctantly.

She considers it. Then she would be alone in the house with the baby.

And Tom would be alone out in the stormy darkness.

"No," she says decisively. "Not now. But first thing in the morning, one of us will go over there."

"Okay. Good night." He rolls over.

She murmurs a reply.

Long after Tom's breathing has grown rhythmic, Karen lies awake, unable to get past a growing feeling of uneasiness as she listens to the howling storm.

Alone in the house after the last detective has left, Fletch goes into his den. He pulls out the leather chair behind his desk and sinks heavily into it.

The phone calls to Randi and Derek were the hardest.

He promised to fly down and get Randi in the morning and bring her home from college, and in the meantime he has made sure that her friends and the RA are going to stay with her all night. She was hysterical after he told her.

Derek took the news surprisingly well, or else he was stoned when Fletch finally tracked him down at one of his buddies' homes. Maybe so. In any case, he said he would be home tomorrow. He didn't even ask how Fletch is holding up.

Neither Randi nor Derek seemed surprised to hear that Jeremiah has been arrested for their mother's murder.

Not that the kid has admitted anything to the police. At least, not murder. Not to ordering those puzzles using Fletch's credit card, either.

What he has admitted to, however, is being a pervert.

No surprise there.

Look at his grandfather.

Fletch hasn't spoken to Aidan since he went down to the station after Jeremiah turned himself in. He doesn't blame his brother. He wouldn't want to face anyone with that kind of story, either. It was Detective Summers who told Fletch about his nephew.

Fletch wonders if Sharon ever suspected the kid of sneaking into her lingerie drawers, of stealing her panties, her bras—of trying them on, even.

Apparently, he did the same thing at Rachel's house the night he babysat.

Sure enough, his prints showed up all over her room.

And after the detectives badgered him long enough, the kid reportedly directed them to the spot in the woods where he had buried the bundle containing not just Sharon's and Rachel's undergarments, but Melissa's, too.

Jeremiah broke down and admitted to keeping the stuff stashed in the woodshed behind the house, saying that he figured nobody would find it there. That nobody would stumble across him prancing around in women's underwear.

Fucking fairy.

Fletch slams his hand down on the desk, shaking his head in disgust.

He should be grateful that he knows.

There isn't enough evidence to convict Jeremiah of murder—not yet—but there's more than enough for the police to hold him for a while.

And there's more than enough evidence for them to shift their investigation away from Fletch, thank God. They've finally left him alone, the new widower, to grieve in peace.

By now, they have begun checking out his alibis. Making sure that he really was where he said he was yesterday, at the Station House Inn—which Jimmy backed up—and then at the gym. Apparently, he had hidden his intoxication well, or else Michael, his trainer, didn't mention it to the police. If he had, that bastard Summers would definitely have brought it up.

Fueled by liquor and pent-up fury, Fletch had had a hell of a workout.

Liquor.

He could use a stiff drink right now. But not a workout. Just a drink—or two—and then bed.

He spins in his chair, reaching into a low cupboard behind the desk. As he takes out a bottle of single-malt scotch, an unexpected sound pierces the silence.

The telephone is ringing.

* * *

Tasha awakens to a loud pounding.

Startled, she sits up in bed, trying to gather her thoughts.

Did she take Tylenol PM again before bed? She must have. The last thing she remembers is watching the news. The television is still on, she notes vaguely, seeing the bluish glow in the room.

Her head feels fuzzy, and she's having trouble waking up. . . .

That pounding sound again.

What is it?

Facts come tumbling back at her.

Joel is gone. . . .

She's alone in the house with the kids. . . .

There's a storm. . . .

Rachel.

Jane.

Sharon.

The ten o'clock newscast . . .

"Sharon Gallagher's body has been found at an undisclosed location . . ."

More pounding.

Dazed, she realizes somebody's knocking on the door. It's directly below her window.

That means the side door facing the driveway, not the front door.

She gets out of bed.

Goes into the hall.

Something nags at her subconscious as she hurries down the steps. . . .

Something she should be noticing.

Remembering.

Filled with inexplicable apprehension, she can't grasp whatever it is; her mind is too fuzzy, her head still too heavy with sleep.

This must be Joel knocking, she tells herself in the kitchen, trying to calm her fears as she reaches for the doorknob. Nobody ever uses the side entrance but the two of them. You can't even see it from the street. Surely one of those reporters wouldn't be so brazen as to prowl around the house and knock on the side door at this hour. . . .

Which hour?

Glancing at the illuminated dial of the clock on the stove, she sees that it's past one in the morning.

The dead of night, she thinks, not liking the phrase even as it settles into her muddled brain.

Well, of course it must be Joel. That's why he wasn't at any of the hotels.

An entire scenario flits into her mind. Stacey got it wrong about the personal day. Maybe the perfect secretary isn't so perfect. Maybe Joel flew to Chicago, then realized he couldn't stay. He was too worried about her. He tried to call, but the phone was off the hook. So he flew back home. Along the way, he lost his keys.

Yeah, right, she tells herself, poised in front of the door. She can see a silhouette outlined against the frosted glass, and it's not tall enough to be Joel's.

She flicks the light switch beside the door to illuminate the step, but nothing happens. It must have burned out again, she thinks vaguely.

"Who is it?" she calls, her hand poised on the doorknob.

"It's me. Paula Bailey," a familiar voice calls back.

Relieved—and perplexed—Tasha opens the door.

As she does, she realizes that the deadbolt hasn't been locked. Only the one on the knob, the one that, if it's turned, locks automatically when you close the door.

But didn't she check the deadbolt several times before going to bed?

Well, didn't she?

She tries to think clearly, but it's impossible. Her mind is still foggy.

Paula stands on the step, bundled into a dark-colored parka that glistens with rain. "I'm so sorry to wake you," she tells Tasha. "I tried calling, but your phone is still . . ."

Still what? Oh. "I know. Off the hook." She yawns. Her brain just isn't working. It's that damned Tylenol PM. When did she take it? She has no recollection. How long before it wears off?

"Can I come in?" Paula is asking. "Tasha, I've just found out something you're not going to believe."

Mitch bunches his soggy pillow beneath his head, sniffling and listening to the storm.

His father is out in this.

And so is his mother.

Shawna told him that Dad had gone to try and find her to tell her the news.

About Grandpa.

The nursing home has tried calling her at home a couple of times and has left messages. She hasn't returned their calls. She hasn't answered her cell phone, either, Shawna said.

Somehow, the nursing home figured out that they

should call Dad's house to say that Grandpa died quietly today in his sleep.

Mom is going to be so upset when she finds out.

There's no way Mitch can leave her alone after this.

No way he could ever come to live with Dad and Shawna . . .

Not that he wants to, he reminds himself hastily.

Tasha hands Paula a towel from the downstairs bathroom and watches her rub it over her face and hair. She's soaked and shivering.

"Are you all right?" Tasha asks.

"I'll be fine. I just need to warm up for a minute," Paula tells her. "Do you . . . look, you can say no if you want, and I'll understand, but can I please smoke a cigarette?"

The first thought in Tasha's mind is that it would bother Joel to see somebody smoking in their house. He hates cigarettes.

"Go ahead," she says, finding a coffee mug in the sink for Paula to use as an ashtray.

"Thanks. It's a disgusting habit, I know, but I haven't managed to quit yet."

Tasha watches Paula light a cigarette and take a deep drag.

Then, stifling another huge yawn, she asks, "What is it that you found out?" She's still so sleepy . . .

But bed is the farthest thing from her mind, especially after Paula's next words.

"It's about Fletch Gallagher, Tasha."

"What about him?" she asks nervously, struggling to keep her voice level.

Does Paula know?

About her and Fletch?

Tasha's mind whirls back to that day more than two years ago. It was August. One of those blazing hot days when there isn't a breath of wind or a cloud in the sky, and the heat shimmers off the pavement.

Tasha was outside, washing the car, wearing shorts and a bikini top.

Joel was at work. Hunter was in preschool, Victoria napping in her crib.

He strolled down the street with a dog on a leash. She recognized the black Lab, but not the man. Usually Sharon Gallagher, whom Tasha knew well enough only to say a casual hello, walked that Lab.

This, she learned when he stopped to introduce himself, was Sharon Gallagher's husband. She had heard all about him, of course. Fletch Gallagher was the star baseball player turned sportscaster.

It was all she could do to keep her eyes focused on his face as he chatted with her, mentioning that he was glad there was no Mets game today because he really needed a day off.

He was shirtless, wearing only a pair of faded denim cutoffs, his tanned chest, washboard stomach muscles, and bulging biceps like something out of a male pinup calendar.

The next thing she knew, she was inviting him in for lemonade. Or maybe he invited himself.

And soon after that, she found herself in his arms in the kitchen, with him kissing her. She doesn't know how it happened. It certainly hadn't been her intention when she let him into her house. Somehow, they were talking one minute, and then he just leaned closer, and his lips were on hers before she could protest.

Okay, so it wasn't one-sided.

She had responded instinctively.

She definitely kissed him back, and Joel and the kids were the farthest thing from her mind.

He was just so damned sexy. He made her feel incredibly desirable.

And it had been so long since Joel kissed her like that. There had been the first baby, and then the house, and then the second baby, and his job, and her exhaustion. . . .

She still remembers the erotic heat of Fletch Gallagher's lips on hers, the smell of the coconut sunscreen she had applied earlier wafting up as her bare, damp skin slid against his.

It didn't lasted long.

Just as she realized what they were doing . . .

Just as alarm bells went off in her head and she commanded herself that she had to stop, remembering who she was, that she was married, they both were . . .

His wife arrived.

Sharon Gallagher had come looking for her husband. Seeing the dog tied to the lamppost in front of the Banks home, she had knocked at the screen door. The inner door—the one with no window, the one that would have blocked Sharon Gallagher's view of the interior of the house—was wide open that day because of the heat.

Tasha and Fletch were in the part of the kitchen directly across from the front door.

Sharon Gallagher had seen everything.

Tasha will never forget the expression on her face.

She didn't look particularly shocked, or even disturbed. She simply said, "There you are, Fletch."

Then she turned and walked away.

"It's okay, I'll call you," Fletch whispered to Tasha before hurrying after his wife.

To her utter amazement, he did. He called her the next day. And the next. It took him a while to get the hint that she had absolutely no intention of getting involved with him. And then he was gone when the Mets left town again, and by the time he came back, she had learned to avoid him.

Tasha will never forget those first tense days after the kiss, when, shaken by her own indiscretion, she lived in utter fear that Joel would find out. That Sharon Gallagher would tell him, or would tell somebody else, and that sooner or later it would get back to Joel.

But it never had.

As far as Tasha knows, nobody besides her and Fletch and Sharon is aware of what happened that steamy August day in this very kitchen. For whatever reason, Sharon Gallagher apparently kept what she had seen to herself.

And now she's dead.

Now only Tasha and Fletch know.

Unless Fletch told somebody else . . .

Rachel.

Fletch could have told Rachel. They were together. They were lovers.

But if Rachel had known about Fletch and Tasha, she never let on. She kept quiet about it. Which wasn't Rachel's style . . .

"Tasha," Paula Bailey is saying.

Tasha shifts her attention to Paula, idly watching a wisp of cigarette smoke floating around her head.

"Tasha, Fletch Gallagher had an affair with Jane Kendall, too. It wasn't just Rachel."

"It wasn't just Rachel?" Tasha echoes.

Jane Kendall. Perfect, pretty Jane. She had been involved with another man? With someone like Fletch? But how . . . ?

But Tasha knows how. She's been there. Left behind by a busy working husband, lonely in her suburban house day after day, vulnerable to a man like Fletch Gallagher, a man who was so clearly looking for trouble . . .

"But . . ." The truth sinks in. "Jane Kendall is dead, too."

"I know. And so is Melissa Gallagher. His brother's wife. The one who died in that fire."

"Are you saying he was involved with her, too? That the fire was no accident?"

"That's what I'm—what's that?" Paula asks, breaking off in mid-sentence.

Tasha follows her gaze.

She's pointing at something on the tall counter that separates the kitchen from the family room area.

The countertops are so neat, Tasha vaguely notes. Joel tidied everything before he left this morning.

There's nothing on the counter Paula's pointing to except the canisters and the paper towel holder and . . .

And . . .

What's that?

Slowly Tasha crosses the room toward the flat, rectangular object in front of the row of cannisters.

Her heart is pounding.

She sees what it is.

A puzzle. A big cardboard one, assembled on the counter.

A puzzle isn't unusual. The kids have so many puzzles. . . .

Except that the counter is high above their heads.

And it wasn't here when she went up to bed.

She distinctly remembers cleaning the kitchen, throwing the pizza box in the garbage, wiping everything down, turning off the light.

Okay.

So maybe one of the kids . . .

The kids.

Tasha's heart beats faster.

Again, she tries to grasp the nagging thought that darted into her mind earlier, and then out again. Struggling to capture it, she stares at a puzzle she's never seen before. A nursery rhyme puzzle.

Little Bo Peep has lost her sheep . . .

The familiar rhyme is lost in the roar that fills Tasha's head as she snags the elusive thought at last.

This morning she came downstairs to find that Joel had taken the children, and she knew it before she finished searching.

She knew it instinctively then, on the stairway, as she knows it now.

The house is empty.

The children are gone.

Chapter Fifteen

"How much farther?" Tasha asks from the seat beside Paula, well over an hour later.

"Not much, I don't think," Paula tells her, checking the speedometer. She's going over sixty. The speed limit on this mountainous stretch of highway is fifty-five, and the rain is coming down in torrents. She doesn't want to risk an accident. She's not used to driving this big a vehicle—a truck, really—but here they are in Tasha's Ford Expedition. She told Tasha the Honda would never make it where they are going.

"Do you think the cops are there by now?" Tasha asks for the millionth time.

"I told you, I called the local police on my cell phone and explained the situation while you were throwing your clothes on upstairs." The wet road reflects the glaring headlights of the car behind her, blinding her in the mirror. She flips it up, keeping her gaze on the windshield, looking for the sign.

"What did you say, exactly?"

"That your children weren't in their beds," Paula says patiently, focused on the slick, deserted road snaking ahead. She craves a cigarette, but she doesn't dare light one. Not here. She needs both hands on the wheel. The wind keeps slamming into the SUV, as though in an effort to push it off the road.

"What else?" Tasha asks, with a mother's intense need to know everything, every detail.

"I said that I thought Fletch Gallagher had taken them, and that I was pretty sure where he had them."

"I just don't understand why he would take my kids," Tasha says tearfully.

"He's desperate, Tasha. He's about to be arrested for three murders."

"So he's using them as hostages?" Tasha sobs. Outside, lightning flashes. "But why my kids? It doesn't make sense. . . ."

When she trails off and falls silent, Paula darts a glance at her. Tasha's face is turned away. She's gazing out the window.

"Two of the women Fletch murdered were his lovers, Tasha," she says quietly, over the distant rumble of thunder. "Three, if you count Melissa. The police seem to have overlooked her, but I haven't."

"Have you told them?"

"No." She exhales. "It's just a guess. But I'm sure I'm right. And the last woman he killed was his wife—presumably because Sharon found out what he'd done."

Tasha says nothing.

Finally, Paula comes right out with it. "Think about

it. What reason could he possibly have for wanting to hurt *you*, Tasha?"

For a time, the steady, rapid beating of the windshield wipers is the only sound inside the car.

Then, taking a deep breath, Tasha turns away from the window and finally admits what Paula has already known, ever since she sat beside Sharon Gallagher on the couch little more than twenty-four hours ago.

"There was something between me and Fletch, once, Paula."

"What happened?" Paula asks, feigning surprise. "Did you have an affair?"

Tasha's answer catches her off guard.

"No. Not an affair."

Trying to hide her surprise, Paula asks, "Then what happened?"

"We kissed. Just once. Nothing more than that. It came out of nowhere. I'd never even met him before, and I'd never done anything like that . . . Maybe it was because I was stuck in the house with a new baby, and Joel was starting to get busier at work, and I didn't feel very attractive because of the weight I'd gained with pregnancy . . . whatever it was, Paula, it happened only once. I wouldn't let it happen again."

"But he wanted it to?"

"He tried calling me a few times. Then I guess he moved on. To Jane. Or Rachel. Or someone else."

Or someone else.

Paula clenches the steering wheel tightly as she guides the Expedition around a sharp curve.

"What about that puzzle?" Tasha asks suddenly. "You said something about it back when we were home, but I was too far gone to even hear you."

"I've been investigating, Tasha. There were similar

puzzles linked to every murder. All nursery rhymes. One was in Sharon's car. A nursery rhyme. Peter, Peter, Pumpkin Eater . . .''

"Had a wife and couldn't keep her," Tasha murmurs, quoting the rhyme her mother taught her when she was a child.

"Sharon had a lover, too, Tasha. Did you know that?"

She shakes her head. Of course she didn't know that. But nothing could surprise her at this point.

"Not many people knew, but I'm guessing Fletch did," Paula says. " 'Had a wife and couldn't keep her.' Do you know the rest of the rhyme?"

" 'So he put her in a pumpkin shell, and there he kept her very well.' "

"Sharon Gallagher's body was found stuffed into a pumpkin that was growing in the garden behind the ruins of Aidan Gallagher's house that burned down."

"But . . . How do you know that? I saw the news last night, and they didn't say where—"

"I'm a reporter. I have sources. That's my job. A puzzle was found in Jane Kendall's carriage, too. That one was Humpty Dumpty. 'Humpty Dumpty sat on a wall . . .' "

"Humpty Dumpty had a great fall . . .' " Tasha says in a faraway tone. "My God. He's sick. So her sister didn't kill her after all."

"But the cops haven't figured that out yet. They've overlooked the puzzle. They probably thought it was one of her daughter's toys. They don't realize infants her age are too young for that kind of puzzle."

"How could they have missed that?"

"It's the kind of thing a mother notices, Tasha."

"But I missed it, too. Paula, I saw a puzzle on Rachel's table. I thought nothing of it at the time, but now I wonder why I didn't. Her house was always so clean. Not a toy out of place. Why would that puzzle have been on the table? Now I understand what it means. 'It's raining, it's pouring, the old man is snoring.' " Her voice trails off in a shuddering sigh.

" 'He went to bed and he bumped his head and he couldn't get up in the morning.' " Paula finishes it for her, quietly. "And then I saw the puzzle on your counter. And I knew right away that he'd taken the kids. 'Little Bo Peep has lost her sheep and doesn't know where to find them. Leave them alone and they'll come home—' "

"But we know they won't," Tasha cuts in, her voice wavering. "Not if we leave them alone. I hope to God the cops are there ahead of us. My babies . . ."

She breaks into another sob. She's not hysterical anymore, as she was in the kitchen back home, but she's been crying since they sped away from Orchard Lane. More than once she has said she wishes she could call her husband, but that she doesn't know where to reach him. That she doesn't have the phone number of the hotel in Chicago.

Now she says, "I can't believe I didn't think of it before now. We can use your cell phone, Paula. To find out from the cops whether they called the FBI, like you said. This is a kidnapping."

"I know, Tasha. I know. Stay calm, okay? I already thought of calling, but I left my phone on your kitchen table after I called the police. I just wasn't thinking straight. All I wanted to do was get on the road so that we can get to the kids on time. . . ."

Her words hang in the air between them, along with those she leaves unspoken.

We can get to the kids on time . . .
Before Fletch Gallagher harms them.

"Thank God you knew about his cabin," Tasha says shakily. "But what if they're not there?"

"They will be, Tasha," Paula assures her. "I've been looking into every angle of Fletch Gallagher's life. It makes perfect sense. That cabin is his getaway. Hardly anybody knows about it."

"Why do you?"

The question isn't suspicious. Tasha sounds more curious than anything else.

Still, it catches Paula off guard.

Should she tell Tasha the whole truth? Here? Now? Is there any way she can possibly avoid it?

"You were involved with Fletch Gallagher, too, weren't you, Paula," Tasha says softly.

Paula's breath catches audibly in her throat.

But that—and the rhythm of the windshield wipers—isn't the only sound in the car.

Paula's ears pick up a faint rustling sound.

And it's coming from inside the Expedition.

Fletch glances in the rear-view mirror.

Bright headlights are bearing down on the Mercedes. It's a Mack truck, roaring along the dark, rainy mountain highway as though it's high noon on a dry straightaway.

"Back off, you asshole," he growls at the driver behind him, accelerating.

The truck keeps coming, obviously wanting to pass him. They're always so cocky, truckers. Think they rule the road. Well, not this one.

Pissed, Fletch presses the gas pedal. He can outrun a freaking semi. He knows this road better than any trucker.

He's been coming up here to the Catskills for years

now. Day and night, in rain, in snow and ice. The route is familiar.

He just didn't expect to be driving it tonight. All he wanted was a glass of scotch and a warm bed all to himself.

Then the phone rang.

And now, here he is.

Careering into the mountains in a storm.

Hating that he's doing it, yet knowing only that he has no choice. She was right, of course. It's the only way to save himself.

Paula's slight gasp tells Tasha she's guessed correctly. Paula, too, has been involved with Fletch Gallagher. Christ, is there a woman in Townsend Heights he hasn't put the moves on?

I'll kill him, Tasha thinks, clenching her fists in her lap. And as pure rage courses through her tense body, she knows she's capable of it. He's taken her babies. If he's hurt her babies . . .

She hears herself cry out, sobbing, as a new wave of despair sweeps over her. Agony. This is agony. She has to save her children. If only they're not too late . . .

"Can you drive any faster?" she asks, glancing at Paula.

"I'm trying," Paula says, her expression suddenly anxious. "I'm going as fast as I—there it is! That's the turnoff!"

She hits the brakes.

The Expedition skids on the slick highway.

For a moment, Tasha is panicked, certain that Paula has lost control.

As they career sideways, headed for a massive tree, all Tasha can think is that she's going to die before she can get to her children.

No.

That can't happen.

They need her.

She isn't going to die, damn it. Not now. Not before she helps them.

Then she feels the vehicle turning, realizes Paula has regained the steering.

"Sorry," Paula tells her, looking shaken. She shifts into reverse, backs up a few feet, then turns up a narrow road leading away from the highway. "It's not far now. Hang in there. We're going to make it."

Tasha nods, not sure whether Paula is reassuring Tasha or herself.

The road is steep and winds through trees, climbing all the way.

Another turnoff.

Another steep road. This one isn't paved.

"How do you know you're going in the right direction?" Tasha asks.

"I've been here before," Paula says simply.

Finally they turn into a curving tree-lined dirt lane that Tasha belatedly realizes is a driveway. There's a cabin up ahead, around the last bend, perched at the very top of the incline, surrounded by a fringe of trees that hint at a steep drop-off just beyond.

The lights are on inside.

And Fletch Gallagher's silver Mercedes is parked at the door.

Inside the cabin, seeing the arc of approaching head-lights through the window, Fletch stiffens. He lifts his glass to his lips again, sipping the amber liquid he poured moments before.

He needs it.

To calm him.

To prepare him.

Because now, in addition to facing his screwed-up past—his own mistakes and his father's sins—he has to face *her*.

Still seated in a big leather chair by the massive stone fireplace, he raises the glass to his lips again and drains the scotch.

It burns all the way down.

Then, fortified for what lies ahead, he stands and walks to the door.

"Where are they?" Tasha screams, leaping from the car while it's still moving, hurtling out the moment she sees Fletch Gallagher framed in the doorway of the cabin, his silhouette outlined in the light behind him.

She rushes toward him, through the rain, vaguely conscious that there are no other cars in the driveway, that the police—or the FBI—haven't made it here before them.

No matter.

She'll handle this herself.

She'll do whatever she has to do.

In a flash of lightning, she can see his face.

He looks . . .

Baffled.

Did he think she wouldn't find him here? That she wouldn't track him down? That she wouldn't confront him, risk her life to save her precious children?

Then, almost simultaneously with the lightning's illumination comes the deafening boom of thunder.

No . . .

Not thunder.

It was different.

Just one loud report.

A gunshot.

Karen awakens with a gasp to a ringing telephone. In the first instant, before she opens her eyes, she assumes it must be morning. Then she sees that the room is pitch black, and that the glowing bedside clock says that it's almost three A.M. That's when she becomes nauseated with apprehension.

"Oh, God," she says as Tom sits up beside her, feeling blindly for his glasses on the table.

Karen reaches past him and snatches up the phone.

"Karen? It's Joel Banks."

"Joel!" And in that moment, she knows.

Something horrible has happened to Tasha.

She's dead, like the others. Jane. Rachel. Sharon.

And I knew it was coming, Karen realizes. Her friend has been on her mind all day. Why didn't she insist on going over to check? Why didn't she send Tom down there tonight, even if it was raining?

"Karen, I'm sorry to call in the middle of the night, but do you know where Tasha and the kids are? I just got home and they're not here. I thought they might have gone to my parents' after all, but I called and they're not there. Please say they're with you, Karen."

He's distraught. "Oh, Joel, they're not here."

"Oh, God. Where are they?" he asks.

Beside her, Tom is asking her what's wrong.

She whispers to him that Tasha and the children are missing as Joel goes on, "I should never have left. I had such a sick feeling about this. All day. On the way to the

irport. And then, when the flight was delayed . . . I
should have left then. I knew it after I boarded. And
while we were sitting on the runway for hours, I kept
worrying . . . . But by then it was too late. I was on my
way to Chicago."

Karen's mind is reeling. Confused, she asks, "Chicago?
But I thought you just said you were—"

"I am home, now. When I landed I turned around
and came right back on the next flight. It was delayed,
too, because of the weather. I kept trying to call her, but
the phone was busy—"

"She had it off the hook, because of the reporters."

"I figured. I've got to call the police. Unless—do you
have any idea where she could have gone, Karen?"

"No, but Joel—"

"Tell him they've made an arrest," Tom urges, beside
her.

He's right. She almost forgot that herself. "Joel, they've
got someone in custody for the Leiberman and Gallagher
murders—"

"Gallagher?"

"You don't know? Sharon Gallagher. She vanished last
night, and they found her body today. Her nephew did
it."

"The one who's staying with them?"

"Jeremiah. I saw him acting strangely, Joel. I talked to
the police about him. Believe me, he did it."

"Jane Kendall, too?"

She tells him quickly about Margaret Armstrong. About
the police theory that she killed her sister because she
was in love with Jane's husband. That it was simply a
coincidence in terms of timing.

"So you see, Joel, you don't have to worry," she tells
him, though she doesn't believe that herself. Her percep-

tion of Tasha in danger was too palpable for her to put herself at ease.

Still, she tells him, "There's no killer roaming the streets. Tasha and the kids are probably safe."

The word *probably* hovers between them.

"Then why aren't they here? Their beds have been slept in. All of them. Tasha always makes the beds in the morning, Karen. They're all rumpled. It looks like they fled in the middle of the night. Where are they?"

"I don't know," she says, breaking down in tears at last.

The first bullet slams into Fletch's arm.

Staggering backward, he looks down in astonishment at the red stain that quickly spreads on the sleeve of the thick gray cotton jersey he's wearing. The pain hits a split second after the shock does. He gasps as much at the intensity of it as he does at the realization that he's been shot.

"What the hell . . . ?" Dazed, dizzy from the searing ache in his arm, he looks out into the night, but all he can see is blinding headlights and the figure of a woman. She was rushing toward him, but now she's motionless, arms hanging limply at her sides, no sign of a gun in her hands.

Who is she? He can't see her face.

And who the hell shot him?

Bewildered, his good arm clutching the wounded one, he backs away from the doorway. He has to close the door. Lock it. Call for help . . .

That's when he hears the second shot fired.

Agony explodes inside him.

As Fletch Gallagher writhes on the floor, one word

whirls through his consciousness before everything goes black.

Why?

Panting, arms outstretched before her, Paula tightly clutches the gun—the one that belonged to Pop, one of his few possessions she kept after giving almost everything else away. That was shortly after the terrible fall that landed him in a nursing home with permanent brain damage.

"It could have killed him," the emergency room physician told her that day when she burst in, looking for Pop.

It was Mrs. Ambrosini who called the police. Apparently, she wasn't too deaf to hear an old man's screams as he fell headfirst down the steep flight of steps and landed with a thud not far from her door.

The police tried to track Paula down at the newspaper, and Tim reached her on her cell phone. She'll never forget her boss's somber words. *Paula, I'm afraid your father's had a terrible accident. He's in bad shape. You'd better get to the hospital as soon as you can . . .*

"My God, what have you done?! My God, my God . . ."

The shrieks are coming from Tasha, standing a few feet away, in the beam of the headlights.

Paula, balanced with one foot on the running board of the Expedition and the other on the dirt driveway, forces her attention back to the present. The SUV's engine is running, the driver's side door open beside her serving as a shield, she realizes, had Fletch Gallagher been prepared for her and shot back at her in defense.

But of course, he wasn't prepared.

She caught him off-guard.

Just as he had caught her off-guard the day he so callously told her it was over between them.

Tasha cries out, "My kids," and takes off, running for the cabin.

Paula watches her step hurriedly over Fletch's crumpled form in the doorway and disappear inside.

She climbs back into the driver's seat and cocks her head, listening.

Not a sound from the back now. Maybe it was her imagination. She's been so damned uptight . . .

But it won't be much longer now.

She turns the Expedition, then backs it carefully, yard by yard, then foot by foot, inch by inch, until it's aligned with the drop-off at the end of the drive just beyond the cabin.

The car still in reverse, her foot on the brake, she rolls down the window just in time to hear Tasha's anguished scream from inside the house, "They're not here! Paula! They're not here!"

Hastily dressed, her hair uncombed and her face unwashed, Karen dashes out through the rain to the curb the moment Joel pulls up in front of the house.

As she climbs into the car beside him, she gives him a quick hug. "It'll be okay," she tells him with a confidence she doesn't feel.

"Thank you for coming with me," he says simply.

She nods, fastening her seatbelt.

"If anything happened to them . . . I'll never forgive myself for leaving."

"You couldn't have known, Joel."

"But I felt it. I kept telling myself to ignore my gut feeling, because I needed to go."

"Pressing business?"

"Not exactly." He's silent.

She waits. Then, when he says nothing, she comes right out and asks. She's thinking of what Tasha said the other night. About how she was growing suspicious of Joel. Were her fears founded?

"It was an interview, Karen," he says heavily. "I had been interviewing for a job with a smaller agency. I thought that would make Tasha happy."

"You didn't tell her what you were doing?" she asks, relieved that at least Joel Banks is faithful to his wife. Her instincts hadn't been wrong.

He shakes his head. "You have to know what it's been like, Karen. With her. At home. We're both stressed. Her, because of the kids. Me, because of work. The pressure is unbelievable. The clients are demanding. I know she's pissed off that I'm never home. She doesn't understand that I took the promotion for us. So that we'd be able to afford this lifestyle. So that she wouldn't have to work. When I went after this new job, I figured I wouldn't tell her."

"Why not?"

"Jobs like these are rare. More money, less hours, less stress. I figured there wasn't much chance I'd get it. And if Tasha knew I was willing to switch, she'd be on me constantly to find something else. She doesn't know how hard it is to find an opportunity like this one."

"And now you let the opportunity slip by because you flew home."

He nods. "I had already gotten the green light from the agency people. They want to hire me. But before they can, I was supposed to meet with the CEO and product managers at their biggest client first thing in the morning. If everyone there liked me, the job would have been mine."

"And now it won't be."

"I don't even care, Karen. As long as Tasha and the kids are all right. Nothing else matters."

They ride in silence the rest of the way to the Townsend Heights police station.

On the verge of the hysteria that already consumed her once tonight—when she realized her children were truly gone—Tasha storms through the small, obviously empty cabin, back to the door and Fletch Gallagher.

It barely registers now that Paula shot him with no apparent confrontation. She'll find out why later.

What matters now is that he tell her what he's done with her children.

She looks down at him. He's bleeding from his upper arm and his side. His eyes are closed. She can see his chest rising and falling, can hear his labored gasps. He's still alive. But for how long?

She crouches beside him. "I need to know, you bastard. Where are they?"

No response.

"You took my children!" She hears her voice rising in panic, fights to keep it at bay. Not yet. She can't lose it yet. Not until she knows for sure. "Where are they?"

His eyes open halfway. He opens his mouth to speak. All that comes out is a guttural rasp of air before his lids flutter closed again.

What do I do? What do I do? Stay calm.

Tasha races frantically back outside into the rain.

Paula is still behind the wheel of the Expedition. She'll know what to do. Maybe there's a barn, or a shed . . . .

Yet even as the idea crosses Tasha's mind, she realizes it's a futile one. She can plainly see that there is no other structure in this small clearing. The cabin sits at the very edge of a cliff, surrounded by only a few pine trees.

Tasha runs over to the driver's side of the SUV. The window is rolled down. Paula looks at her, wearing a strange expression.

She must be in shock, Tasha realizes. She shot a man. Probably killed him. She glances down at the gun in Paula's hand. She hadn't even realized Paula was carrying it with her.

"Take it," Paula says, thrusting it toward her.

Only when her hand closes automatically around the weapon does Tasha realize that Paula is wearing gloves.

As Tasha holds the gun, trembling, Paula nods at her.

"Good," she says. "I won't need it anymore. He's dead, isn't he?"

"I . . . I don't know." Tasha's voice is quavering. Poor thing. She's been through so much.

Well, it'll be over soon. For everyone.

It's been such a long, hard road. Such a struggle. From the days in the Bronx to New Rochelle to her marriage to Frank to being a single mother to dealing with Pop . . .

"Why did you shoot him, Paula?"

"Why?" she echoes, attempting to focus on Tasha's plaintive question.

. . . to Fletch Gallagher coming along and making her fall in love with him. She'll never forget that first night she met him, at Jimmy's, where she had stopped for a glass of wine after a particularly grueling day. Just one glass. She isn't a drinker. She can't afford to be. Wine doesn't come cheaply at the Station House Inn.

When the bartender placed a second glass in front of her, she thought it was a mistake. And much as she wanted it, she couldn't keep it. She had a dollar left in her wallet, and her credit cards were maxed out. As she opened her mouth to tell him to take the glass back, he said the words that changed her life. "Compliments of the gentleman over there."

The gentleman over there, of course, was Fletch Gallagher. Paula knew who he was. She had even seen him around town.

But she and Fletch traveled in different circles.

She doesn't remember everything about that night they first met. Maybe it was the wine. Or maybe she doesn't want to remember. Because it was all a lie. Everything that night, and everything that came after.

He told her that he would take care of her.

Or did he?

Maybe it was just what she wanted so badly to hear. Maybe she twisted his words, desperately needing to believe that he was her Prince Charming, that he would rescue her and Mitch from their miserable little life.

Now she knows that she doesn't need to be rescued. She's taken matters into her own hands. She'll rescue herself.

But she believed, back then, that *he* would do it.

She believed him when he said he was planning to leave his wife just as soon as their children were out of the house. He said, *Sharon and I have an understanding.*

Turns out that part was true.

Well, anyway, the point is, he never left his wife.

Not for Paula.

Not for anyone else, either.

Her Prince Charming failed her. He moved on to a princess.

Jane Kendall . . .

And from Jane to Melissa . . .

From Melissa to Rachel . . .

Somewhere in there, to Tasha, too. That bit of news caught Paula off guard.

Just as Margaret Armstrong's suicide was pure coincidence, she showed up that day on the Bankses' doorstep that day purely by chance. She intended only to interview Tasha about Rachel's murder, so that she could quote her in the article. Cover all her bases.

She's done it all along.

Made a big show of investigating. Taking notes. Intending to interview every possible witness so that if there is ever a shadow of suspicion, they will vouch for her. All of them, from Minerva to Tasha to Brian Mulvaney.

Lest anyone later suspect that she hasn't been doing her job all along.

Lest anyone guess that Fletch Gallagher isn't the serial killer after all.

Paula looks at Tasha.

"You have everything, don't you?" she asks. "Just like they did."

Tasha is silent. Then the bewilderment drains from her expression, replaced by knowing dread.

"Well, now it's my turn to have everything," Paula tells her.

Her mind whirls back over her life. It's about time she got a break. She's always taken care of everybody else. Frank. Mitch. Pop . . .

Again, she thinks of that day. The day everything changed. The day Pop fell down the stairs.

What did Tim say?

"Paula, I'm afraid your father's had a terrible accident. He's

in bad shape. You'd better get to the hospital as soon as you can . . ."

She smiles, remembering. She made it there within minutes of his call.

Because when her cell phone rang, she was standing inside her own apartment a few blocks from the hospital. The apartment they all assumed, as they hovered at the foot of the stairs outside the door, was empty. No one guessed: not Mrs. Ambrosini, or the police, or the paramedics . . .

They presumed Pop had been home alone and was going out for a walk when it happened. That he had stepped out of the apartment and locked the door behind him before tripping at the top of the stairs and plunging forward, head over heels.

They never guessed, and couldn't know, that it was bolted from the inside, where Paula retreated after giving her father the mighty shove that was supposed to end his life.

And she came so close . . .

Serious brain damage. The doctors told her that it was unlikely he would ever communicate again. Nor would he ever come home again. Thank God. He was out of her hair.

It wasn't perfect. It wasn't the way she had intended. But it was good enough. Locked away in the nursing home, the old man spent his final years in silence. . . .

Until just the other day.

Until Frank Ferrante showed up to turn things upside down at a time when everything Paula had ever wanted was finally within her grasp.

What did Frank say to her father? Whatever it was had been enough to bring words to the old man's lips for the first time in years. No, one word. Her name.

But what if more were to follow?

She couldn't take that chance.

That was why she went back to Haven Meadows today. Why she held the pillow over his withered old face.

Just as she had done to her baby sister so many years ago.

The baby sister who had stolen Mom and Pop away from Paula. But not for long. Paula saw to that. It was so easy to get rid of her, once Paula figured out how. She simply imitated something she had seen on television, on one of those scary movies Mom liked to watch late at night when Pop was working.

Paula never thought they knew what she had done. Not until years later, when Pop was living with her. She saw him looking at her sometimes—as if he knew. About the baby. That her death hadn't been an accident.

Once she realized that he knew, she couldn't take the risk that he might tell. He probably wouldn't, after all these years, but what if he did? What if he slipped?

She wonders if Frank figured it out, too. If that was what he said to Pop the other day when he visited, leaving him agitated and calling Paula's name. The nurses thought he was beckoning her. That showed what they knew.

She knows Pop felt her hands on his back just before he fell down the stairs. She heard his horrified gasp.

Today, she feared that he would open his eyes in the split second before she pressed the pillow over his face. But he didn't.

It was quick, just like before. Pop didn't even struggle. He was too out of it because of the sleeping pills they had given him earlier.

Maybe they would think he had awakened at some point and swallowed the two additional pills that were left in the cup on his bedside table, too. Surely they would never suspect that Paula had slipped them into her purse before she left his room—the last part of her plan falling smoothly into place.

As she passed the nurse in the hallway, the woman smiled and asked, "How's your dad?"

Paula smiled back. "He's sleeping so soundly I didn't want to disturb him."

"That's probably a good idea. Have a nice afternoon."

"Oh, I will."

And she did.

Shopping.

Searching for another puzzle. The one that would complete her scenario. She still couldn't quite believe that she had found exactly what she was looking for: Little Bo Peep.

It wasn't wooden like the others. But it would do.

Have they discovered Pop's body yet? she wonders.

Probably by now, even if they thought he was merely sleeping the first few times they peeked into his room.

They wouldn't have been able to reach her with the news. She made sure she was out of touch, letting the battery run down on her cell phone earlier.

She can't afford to be interrupted. Not today. Not until this is over and she goes home to check her messages.

It really has worked out well, she marvels.

Now, in addition to admiration for solving the murders and courageously rescuing Tasha's children, she'll be showered with sympathy over the death of her father. That should be worth even more publicity. That should get her noticed nationally. Internationally.

Anxious to get on with it—to meet her future at last— she tells Tasha, "I'm going to explain what we're going to do next. Listen carefully."

As she talks, she sees Tasha's eyes widen and her jaw drop in petrified disbelief.

Sobbing, his whole body tense and shaking, Jeremiah looks from Joel Banks to Karen Wu to his father to his lawyer to the detectives. All of them are staring at him. Waiting.

Waiting for something he just can't give.

"I don't know what happened to your wife and kids," he tells Joel Banks. "I swear. I *swear*. And anyway . . . I've been here with the police all night."

"You say your wife and children disappeared sometime today?" someone asks the husband, who nods. "But you don't know when?"

Joel Banks shakes his head slowly, looking intently at Jeremiah as he asks the detectives, "What time did you take him into custody tonight?"

"It wasn't tonight, it was this afternoon," Jeremiah's dad corrects, squeezing Jeremiah's hand.

Silence.

Jeremiah can hear his own heart racing.

"Then it couldn't have been him," Joel says urgently, as though the light has just dawned.

"It *wasn't* me!" Jeremiah shouts. "I keep telling everyone—"

One of the detectives cuts him off as another asks, "How do you know it couldn't have been him, Mr. Banks?"

"Because they were home until some time tonight. Their beds had been slept in. The beds were made when I left."

"Are you sure?"

"I'm positive. Tasha always makes the beds. She has a thing about it."

"Maybe they went to bed early," another detective suggests.

Jeremiah wants to lunge at him. His father's grasp tightens reassuringly on his fingers. He forces himself to sit still, to remain silent.

Joel Banks is shaking his head. "In the afternoon? All of them? They would never do that. It was someone else. Somebody came into the house and abducted them tonight."

"You say there were no signs of a struggle."

"No. Nothing unusual. Just the puzzle . . ." Joel Banks says, his voice tight with emotion.

"A puzzle just like the ones that were ordered on Fletch Gallagher's credit card." Detective Summers looks at the others. "He might have ordered them after all. Maybe it wasn't the kid."

"It wasn't!" Jeremiah bursts out, unable to contain himself.

This time, nobody shushes him.

"Do you have any idea where your brother would go, Mr. Gallagher?" a detective asks Jeremiah's father.

Dad nods slowly, saying exactly the words that pop into Jeremiah's mind.

"The cabin."

"I don't believe you," Tasha says, her mind racing wildly.

Paula Bailey is insane.

And there hadn't been a clue . . .

Or had there?

"You don't believe me?" Paula echoes. "Then see for ourself, Tasha. Take a look in the back."

Trembling violently, Tasha forces herself to walk to he back of the Expedition. She peers through the rain-pattered tinted window. She glimpses a blanket draped n back. A quilt. She vaguely recognizes that it's the one that's usually folded at the foot of Hunter's bed.

Beneath the blanket are three distinct human bumps, one small enough to be Max, the others just the size of Victoria and Hunter.

"Are they . . . are they alive?" she asks, turning to Paula, terror clouding her mind.

"Of course they are."

"They're not moving."

"That's because they did such a wonderful job eating their pizza."

The pizza.

Tasha's thoughts are a maelstrom of details.

Paula's visit.

The big white box in her hands.

Paula serving the slices, her own last, laughingly saying she wanted the one with the most pepperoni.

She took that piece on purpose. She put something on the others. Something to make them sleep. No wonder Tasha managed to drift off despite her anxiety earlier. No wonder she felt so groggy that she assumed she had taken Tylenol PM and forgotten.

Tasha realizes that while she slept soundly in her bed, this deranged woman crept back into the house and carried her children outside, one by one. Then she hid them in the back of the Expedition and staged her own late-night visit.

"But how did you get in?" she asks, still trying to make sense of it. Any of it.

''You didn't even notice that your key ring was missing, did you, Tasha? I figured you wouldn't. You were so distracted after I told you about Fletch and Rachel. You're so much like him, you know. He never noticed his credit card was missing, either, when I slipped it out of his wallet one night when we were together. I figured he wouldn't miss it. He had so many. I figured I could use it for emergencies. . . .''

''Fletch . . . you're doing this because of Fletch?'' Tasha asks, struggling to keep her wits about her.

The wind-driven rain is coming down in sheets around them, thunder booming, lightning flashing. Above them, the tree limbs sway to an alarming pitch.

''The first time, I did it because of Fletch,'' Paula says matter-of-factly. ''After that, I realized he didn't matter. After that, I came up with the plan.''

''The first time?''

''Melissa.''

''Melissa . . .'' It takes a moment for Tasha to place her.

Melissa. Fletch's sister-in-law.

''I followed him over there that night and saw them together through the window. After he left, I went in and confronted her. Then I killed her. I certainly didn't plan it,'' she says, as though that excuses what she did. ''And when I realized she was dead—and that my finger-prints would be everywhere—I panicked. So I set the fire.''

''How?''

''Oh, it was easy. They had a gas stove. She was boiling a big pot of water for pasta. I made it look as though she had left it, and the flame from the burner had ignited an apron she'd left on the counter next to the stove. The fire spread from there. Nobody ever suspected that it was anything more than a tragic accident. And I wrote her obituary myself."

Mute with horror, Tasha hears the pride in her voice. She's sick. Sick enough to go through with the grisly plan she has described.

"Okay, it's time," Paula says, snapping out of her reverie as if on cue.

"Tell me first," Tasha says, desperately trying to buy a few more minutes, seconds, anything at all. "Tell me about the plan. Tell me what you did to Jane, and Rachel, and Sharon."

"Why should I? Stop stalling, Tasha. Go ahead and do it."

No! No! She can't get away with this . . .

Keep her talking. That's it. Keep her talking.

"Tell me again," she babbles. "What do you want me to do?"

"Walk away from me. Toward Fletch. Then put the gun in your mouth and pull the trigger. It shouldn't take long."

I can kill her, Tasha thinks, reeling, staring down at the gun in her violently shaking hand.

"You won't shoot me," Paula says, as though she's read her mind. "If you shoot me, my foot will come off the brake, and the car will go right back over the cliff with your kids in it. In case you didn't notice, Tasha, there's a slight downward slope here, and the tires are at the edge. It's in reverse. It'll roll back right away. You won't have time to jump in and stop it."

Tasha noticed when she pointed that out the first time. She's right.

If Tasha shoots Paula, her kids will die.

"Start walking, Tasha," Paula directs impatiently. "We don't have all night."

"If I do this, what's going to happen to my kids?"

"I've already told you. They'll be fine. I'll bring them to the police. I'll tell the police that Fletch had kidnapped them and driven them up here. That you and I followed. That Fletch told you the kids were dead and you killed him in a rage, then turned the gun on yourself. It will be clear why, won't it, Tasha?"

"Why?" she asks, her voice faint.

"Because you're a mother. And any mother knows life wouldn't be worth living if her children were dead. Jane knew that, Tasha. She made the same choice you're going to make."

Jane.

What had she done to Jane?

Forced her to jump off the cliff by threatening to harm her daughter?

"I'll tell the police that Fletch lied to you about the kids, for whatever reason. That I discovered them safe in the trunk of his car. I'll be their hero, Tasha. They won't remember any of this. They're too far gone because of course, *Fletch* drugged them." She chuckles. "All they'll know is that I was the one who delivered them safely to their father."

Joel.

What will Joel believe, Tasha? Will he ever suspect the truth?

"And then I'll write the exclusive story. The one that's going to get me the recognition I deserve, Tasha. The money, too. And the respect. Nobody will dare try to take my son away from me then," she mutters.

Help me, Joel, Tasha begs silently. *Wherever you are. I need you. Please.*

"Start walking," Paula barks. "Or I'll take my foot off

the brake and jump out and do it myself. I don't have to save the kids. That doesn't have to be part of it."

Her fingers clutching the cold metal gun, Tasha forces her rubbery legs to take a step. And then another, acutely aware that Joel can't help her now.

Nobody can help her now.

Nobody even knows where they are.

It's all over.

It was Uncle Fletch. Not me.

They have to know that at last . . . don't they?

Jeremiah listens, dazed, as the detectives ask his father about the cabin. Where it is.

Then they want to know if there's anything in his uncle's past they should know about. Anything that could cause him to suddenly go off the deep end.

Jeremiah's father shakes his head. "I can't imagine that my brother would be capable of any of this, any more than I believed my son was involved."

"What could have set him off? Does he have any psychological problems you're aware of?"

His father hesitates before answering.

Then he says, "I can only think of one thing that might be relevant."

And he begins to speak, telling the detectives something Jeremiah never knew. At least, not the whole story.

Dad had told him that his grandfather had left his grandmother when Dad and Uncle Fletch were young.

What Aidan had never revealed until now was the reason he left.

Not for another woman, as Jeremiah had always guessed.

For another man.

"Your brother was traumatized when he discovered that your father was a homosexual?"

"Absolutely," Aidan says, nodding. "It devastated both of us. We swore we would never tell a soul, and I never have. As far as I know, he didn't either."

"How did he react to what happened? At the time, I mean."

"Fletch was always a real macho type. You know. Sports. Girls. But after finding out about Dad, he became obsessed. He was on every team. Went out with every cheerleader. That sort of thing."

"Trying to prove his masculinity," Detective Summers speculates.

Jeremiah's father nods. "I guess we both were. I joined the military. My brother threw himself into athletics. Won scholarships. Dated beautiful women, and married one, too. But that didn't stop him. He's always had women."

"Was Tasha Banks one of them?"

Jeremiah hears a gasp.

He turns to see that Joel Banks has turned pale. "Not Tasha," her husband insists. "She wouldn't cheat."

"Ms. Wu?" the detective asks. "Do you know whether your friend was involved with Mr. Gallagher?"

Karen is hesitant, but then she shakes her head. "I don't think so. Joel's right. Tasha wouldn't cheat."

"And my brother couldn't kill anyone," Aidan bursts out suddenly. "I don't know why I'm going along with this."

"Your brother was a public figure. He had an image to protect. What if somebody had stumbled across the secret about your father?"

Jeremiah's dad shakes his head. "Fletch has his share of issues. But I know he didn't kill those women."

Looking doubtful, Detective Summers asks flatly, "Then who did?"

Tasha counts her steps methodically.

One . . .

Two . . .

Three . . .

Four . . .

"Okay, that's far enough," Paula's voice calls behind her, above the swishing sound of the rain in the trees.

"No," Tasha whispers. "Please, God . . ."

This can't be happening.

"Put the gun in your mouth," Paula instructs.

Too paralyzed with fright to move, Tasha tries desperately to think of an escape. Of any way to escape the fate Paula Bailey has planned.

"I can take my foot off the brake any time," Paula reminds her pointedly.

Tasha raises her hand to her quavering lips. Puts the barrel between her chattering teeth.

"Good. Now pull the trigger."

I can't do this.

God help me.

I can't do this.

"Do it!" Paula's voice is shrill. Harsh.

Tasha fumbles, trying to find the trigger.

She has to do this.

She has to.

It's the only way to save her children.

* * *

"How long would it take for the police to get to your brother's cabin from the nearest town?" Detective Summers asks.

"At least ten minutes—in good weather, if they know exactly where they're going," Jeremiah's father replies reluctantly. "Longer on a night light this, especially if they don't know the cabin's exact location. And they probably won't. It isn't easy to find."

"Ten minutes?" Joel Banks echoes. "Please call them. Get someone over there as soon as you can."

Paula squeezes her eyes closed, poised, waiting for the sound of the gunshot. She doesn't want to actually see the back of Tasha's head blown off. She can't stomach blood and gore.

Jane's death was easy.

Tasha's will be violent, but at least it will be at her own hand, not Paula's.

Melissa's death—that was relatively easy, too. It happened so impulsively, Paula didn't even realize what she was doing until she was holding the woman's head in the pot of scalding water on the stove, keeping her under until she stopped struggling.

But Rachel . . .

And Sharon . . .

She planned those. Was fully aware that she would have to beat Rachel over the head with the barbell until she was certain she was dead. She couldn't risk mere brain damage this time.

And Sharon . . .

It was brilliant, really, the way Paula lured her to the remains of the house on North Street. Risky, too. It depended on Fletch not coming home to find her there.

On Sharon's nieces staying upstairs with the stereo playing the whole time she was there.

But it worked. Luck was with her despite the unexpected ringing of her cell phone.

When she got the call from Tim telling her Jane Kendall had been found and a press conference was about to start, she was in the midst of telling Sharon she was convinced her husband had killed Rachel Leiberman and Melissa Gallagher. She was about to bring her over to the North Street property on the pretext of proving to her that Fletch had done it.

Before leaving, she had hurriedly told Sharon that the evidence was in the shed, refusing to elaborate.

She could see in the woman's eyes that it was going to work. That she wasn't going to wait for Paula to show her.

That she was going to head over to the shed the moment Paula left.

Which was even better.

Now Paula had an alibi.

She drove into town and left the car conspicuously parked in the fire lane in front of the town hall. Everyone who saw it would assume she had been in the press conference, and Paula figured it would be so crowded that no one would realize she wasn't there. No one would ever suspect that under cover of darkness, she had quickly walked the two and a half blocks to North Street. That she had crept up behind Sharon Gallagher and slit her throat so swiftly, so savagely that she couldn't make a sound.

The whole thing took ten or fifteen minutes, from carving the pumpkin to lugging Sharon's dead weight the few feet over to it and hoisting her inside, to washing surprisingly little blood from her own hands at the outside tap near the garden.

Then she hurried back downtown and joined the crowd exiting the press conference, just in time to see Brian Mulvaney—

What was that sound?

Not a gunshot.

Too late, she whirls around.

Somebody's here.

Yanking the door open.

Diving toward the floor.

Shoving the emergency brake.

"No!" she screeches, raising her foot, the one that has kept the brake depressed and the SUV balanced precariously on the edge of the cliff.

The vehicle remains perched there now as the emergency brake clicks loudly into place.

Strong arms toss Paula from the driver's seat. She feels herself hurtling through the air. Pain shatters her body as she lands in the mud.

She looks up, shocked, sputtering, to see the face of the man she loathes staring down at her.

The face of her ex-husband.

Stunned by the sudden outcry and commotion behind her, Tasha lowers the gun and whirls in one swift, instinctive movement.

Paula is on the ground.

A burly, dark-haired stranger stands over her.

"Bring me the gun," he calls to Tasha. "Hurry."

She feels herself going into motion, rushing toward him, thrusting the weapon into his large hand.

He immediately aims it at Paula, sprawled on the rain-soaked drive at his feet.

"It's over," he tells her bitterly. "I heard the whole thing. Every word of it."

"But how . . . ?"

"My car is parked down there." Tasha sees him jerk his head toward the drive. "Around the bend. I kept my lights off and stayed back after we left the main road. Then I got out and hiked up here."

"You were hiding? Listening to me?" Paula stares up at him, hatred glittering in her eyes. "But how did you know . . . how did you get here?"

"I was in Townsend Heights looking for you. I checked everywhere, including Orchard Lane. I've been following the story in the news. I knew that was where two of those women lived. I figured you'd be there, sniffing for your story. And I was right. At least, I thought that was why you were there when I saw your car parked down at the end of the street. So I parked, and I waited for you."

"You saw her carrying my kids out of my house?" Tasha asks breathlessly.

He doesn't look at her. His eyes, like the gun, are trained on Paula.

"No," he says. "I must have gotten there after she'd done that. But I saw the two of you come out together. When you drove away, I followed you. Figured you'd notice the headlights behind you on the highway the whole way, but somehow you didn't." He smirks at Paula. "I guess you didn't think to check. Maybe you figured you were too smart for anyone to be on your trail."

Paula only gapes at him, her body coiled in fury.

"I thought you were up to something, Paula, but I never guessed it was this—"

He breaks off, shaking his head, glancing at Tasha for the first time.

"Are you okay?" he asks her.

She nods, unable to speak.

"She said before that your kids are in the back there," her rescuer tells her, motioning toward the back of the SUV with his head, his gaze on Paula again. "You'd better go make sure they really are okay."

She hurriedly opens the door and climbs inside, leaning over the back seat. Her fingers grasp the edge of the quilt.

Holding her breath, her eyes closed in silent prayer, she pulls it away.

Then she opens her eyes, gazing down on her three children snuggled together.

Three *sleeping* children, their mouths open, chests plainly rising and falling in slumber.

"Thank you, God," Tasha whispers raggedly as she swiftly climbs over the seat, gathering her babies into her arms.

They wake slowly, in a stupor, looking up at her, dazed.

Victoria is the first to speak.

Just one word, uttered in confused recognition and relief.

The sweetest word in all the world.

"Mommy."

Epilogue

"What's it like in San Diego?" Lily asks, bouncing in the back seat.

"Hot," Jeremiah answers, watching his father disappear inside the real estate office on Townsend Avenue. He has to drop off some papers now that the North Street property sale is final.

Seated in the passenger's seat, Jeremiah turns so that he can see his sisters in the back. Lily's hair has grown past her shoulders. Daisy cut hers to the same length the other day. They look alike again.

But that's the only thing that's the same as it used to be.

"All the time?" Daisy wants to know.

"Pretty much," Jeremiah says. Like he knows. He's never been there. But he's read a lot about it. After all, he wants to know everything he can about his new home.

His therapist, Dr. Stein, has told him that's a good

sign—the fact that he's looking forward to the future. And why wouldn't he be? Dad is back to stay. He promised he'll never leave Jeremiah and his sisters again. They're going to live in California, and they're going to have a fresh start someplace where nobody will stare at Jeremiah as he walks down the halls.

Dr. Stein has even referred him to a therapist in San Diego. One who specializes in fetishes, as Dr. Stein does. Jeremiah is glad he'll have somebody to talk to out there. It'll help. But he has a feeling things will be much better anyway, just as soon as Townsend Heights—and everything that happened here—is behind him.

"Are there palm trees?" Lily asks.

"Yup. And lots of swimming pools. And beaches," Jeremiah tells her and Daisy.

"We can go to the beach any time, right?"

"Any time."

"It'll be good to see the sun again," Lily says after a long pause.

Jeremiah follows her gaze, looking out the window.

A light snow is falling on Townsend Avenue.

It looks pretty, with the old-fashioned lampposts wrapped in green garlands, and the businesses along the street decked out in wreaths and bows. The trees are draped in twinkling white lights, and there's a fake Santa ringing a bell beneath a decorated Christmas tree in front of the Metro North station at the far end.

"Yeah," Jeremiah says, staring out the window. "It'll be good to see the sun again."

"Can I please have the tape?" Mitch asks.

"Sure." Shawna passes him the roll, smiling at him. She looks ridiculous, Mitch thinks, with her blond hair sticking out from beneath that red-and-white Santa hat. But she doesn't seem to care.

She hums a Christmas carol as she reaches for another roll of wrapping paper.

"Deck the halls with boughs of holly . . ."

Mitch lays the sheet of candy-cane-printed paper face down on his half of the table and centers the tissue-wrapped rectangle on it. Inside the protective layers is a framed pastel landscape he drew himself, in art class. His new art teacher here on Long Island loves him. Things are different here. Maybe it's because he's got the good pair of sneakers at last—the kind all the other kids wear. Three pairs, actually. Shawna says he should have extras.

So. No more cheap sneakers.

No more Miss Bright.

No more Robbie Sussman.

Mitch toys with the package, making sure it's centered.

He has carefully removed the glass from the frame before inserting the drawing.

It's for Mom.

She's not allowed to have any kind of glass in prison.

"Need the scissors?" Shawna asks.

"Nope." He quickly folds the paper around it, fastening it with tape.

"I was thinking that we could make some Christmas cookies later," Shawna suggests after a few minutes.

Mitch shrugs. "I don't know. Maybe."

Shawna just sings softly, "Fa la la la la la la la la," busily wrapping a gift of her own. She buys a lot of presents for different people, Mitch has noticed. She has tons of friends. Everyone likes her.

Even Mitch.

Now.

But that doesn't mean everything is okay.

It doesn't mean he isn't still thinking about his mother.

Dad said she's sick. That she always has been. When they were married, he knew that she had problems. He made her go see a psychiatrist a few times. That was how he found out what was wrong with her.

Something called narcissistic personality disorder.

Mitch doesn't know what that means. Dad says it's why she did all those bad things. He said if she had let the psychiatrist help her back when they were married, she might have gotten well. But she stopped going to see him. And she kicked Dad out when he tried to make her.

Dad said he never even knew Mitch existed until she came asking for money for Mitch last spring. Mom never told him she was pregnant when she threw him out. "If I had known, Mitch, I never would have left her without looking back."

Mitch believes him.

Mom always said Dad was the one who left. That he didn't care about her or Mitch and he just walked out. But Mitch knows now that she was lying.

It took him a long time to believe that, and the other horrible things Mom has done. He still doesn't want any of it to be true. But he figures it probably is. That's why she's in jail. That's why she's never coming out.

Dad says he didn't think she was healthy enough to take care of Mitch. He and Shawna wanted Mitch to live with him from the minute they found out about him. So Dad started digging around, trying to find information that would help them to win custody.

Dad went to Haven Meadows just the other day to talk to Grandpa about her. That's how the nursing home had known to call Dad's house when Grandpa died—they got his phone number from the sign-in sheet.

Dad won't tell Mitch what he talked about with Grandpa—or if Grandpa talked back. He only said he wanted to ask Grandpa about something that had happened a long, long time ago. When Mom was a little girl.

Mitch hears a car door slam outside.

He looks up and finds Shawna smiling at him.

"There's your dad, home from work," she says.

He smiles back. He can't help it. She looks so goofy in that hat.

And Dad is home.

Moments later, his father comes into the kitchen, stamping the snow from his boots. He hugs Shawna and kisses her on the cheek.

Then he turns toward Mitch, opening his arms wide and grinning.

As Mitch settles into his father's warm, familiar embrace, he changes his mind.

Maybe everything is going to be all right after all.

"Do you have the tickets?" Tasha asks Joel as he slides into the front seat of the Expedition.

"Right here." He pats his jacket pocket.

She smiles at him and settles back in the passenger seat as he turns on the wipers. The blades move in a steady rhythm, sweeping away the fat, wet snowflakes as they land.

If Tasha lets it, the sound will carry her back . . .

Back to a rainy night when she sat in this very seat, with Paula driving. . . .

No.

She won't let it.

She won't go back.

"Ready?" Joel asks, glancing at her.

She grins. "Ready."

"We're ready too, Daddy," Victoria pipes up from the back, strapped into her car seat between her brothers.

Joel pulls out of the driveway.

Past the Leibermans' old house, where the new owners' minivan sits in the driveway. Tasha hasn't met them yet, but she watched the moving van being unloaded last weekend. A crib. A high chair. A toddler bed.

"Maybe they have kids who can be our friends, Mommy," Hunter said, beside her.

"Maybe they do," she told him, fighting back tears. For Rachel. For Ben and Mara and Noah, left behind.

She saw Ben last week when she brought Max in for his checkup. He said they were muddling along, but that Hanukkah was hard. He and the kids are still trying to settle into their new town house in Bedford, not far from his sister's place.

The wipers make a swishing noise as Joel steers up Orchard Lane.

Past Karen and Tom's, with the big wreath on the door and the tree sparkling in the picture window.

Past the Gallaghers', with its newly installed wheelchair ramp. Tasha heard the other day that Fletch Gallagher is home from the rehab hospital now. Karen said she went over with a home-cooked meal for him one night. She said the doctors still aren't sure whether he'll be able to walk eventually, and that Fletch was subdued. He didn't want to talk about what happened.

Nobody does.

Joel turns the corner and follows the network of tree-lined streets through town. House after house is decorated for the holidays; most in elegant white lights, with menorahs or Christmas trees—or both—in the windows.

Joel is whistling, she realizes. She smiles when she recognizes the tune.

It's "Home for the Holidays."

"Are you trying to tell me something, Joel?"

The new, relaxed Joel grins, looking at her. "Nope. That song just happened to pop into my head. You know I want to go to Centerbook. I'm looking forward to it."

"Are you sure Santa will be able to find us there?" Victoria asks worriedly from the back seat.

"He will. I wrote him a letter, remember?" Hunter says. "I told him we'll be at Grandma's."

Tasha smiles. She helped him mail the letter at the post office the day after Thanksgiving.

The following Monday, Joel started the new job—the one he had been interviewing for in October. A plum senior position at a smaller agency. It will mean more pay. A smaller workload. Shorter hours. All the things he thought would be impossible to find.

All the things that would make a tremendous difference in their world. In their marriage.

Joel told Tasha about it later—much later, long after they had fallen into each other's arms at the Townsend Heights police station as dawn broke that stormy Monday morning. He said there was no way he would get the job now. He assumed he had blown his chances when he left Chicago that night without waiting for his Monday-morning interview with the agency's important Midwestern client.

In light of what had happened, the agency persuaded the CEO to reschedule the interview.

And he landed the job.

Even after he told them he would need a week off for Christmas to be with his family.

"Oh, look!" Hunter exclaims as they round the corner.

"It's so pretty!" Victoria says in a hushed voice.

Townsend Avenue is lovely at dusk in the gently falling snow, with red-velvet bows and garlands of greens draped everywhere, and white Christmas lights twinkling.

Tasha will miss it while they're in Ohio for the next two weeks.

After all, this is home.

No, she thinks, glancing at Joel, and then back at the children.

Home is wherever they are. . . .

And that's where I always want to be.

ABOUT THE AUTHOR

Wendy Corsi Staub is the author of over fifty novels
for both adults and young adults under her own name,
as well as the pseudonyms Wendy Morgan and Wendy
Brody. She is currently working on her next suspense
novel, which will be published by Pinnacle Books in 2002.
Wendy lives with her family in New York. She loves to
hear from her readers and you may write to her c/o
Pinnacle Books. Please include a self-addressed stamped
envelope if you wish a response.

BOOK YOUR PLACE ON OUR WEBSITE AND MAKE THE READING CONNECTION!

We've created a customized website just for our very special readers, where you can get the inside scoop on everything that's going on with Zebra, Pinnacle and Kensington books.

When you come online, you'll have the exciting opportunity to:

- View covers of upcoming books
- Read sample chapters
- Learn about our future publishing schedule (listed by publication month *and author*)
- Find out when your favorite authors will be visiting a city near you
- Search for and order backlist books from our online catalog
- Check out author bios and background information
- Send e-mail to your favorite authors
- Meet the Kensington staff online
- Join us in weekly chats with authors, readers and other guests
- Get writing guidelines
- AND MUCH MORE!

**Visit our website at
http://www.pinnaclebooks.com**